The Faber Book of
Contemporary Stories
about Childhood

Lorrie Moore was born in 1957 in Glens Falls, New York. She attended
St Lawrence University and Cornell University. Her work has appeared
frequently in the *New Yorker* and *Best American Short Stories*, and she
has received fellowships from the Rockefeller Foundation, the National
Endowment for the Arts, the Guggenheim Foundation and the American
Academy of Arts and Letters. She is currently teaching English at the
University of Wisconsin in Madison. She is the author of two collections
of short stories, *Self-Help* and *Like Life*, and two novels, *Anagrams* and
Who Will Run the Frog Hospital?

The Faber Book of
Contemporary Stories
about Childhood

edited by Lorrie Moore

faber and faber
LONDON · BOSTON

First published in Great Britain in 1997
by Faber and Faber Limited
3 Queen Square London WC1N 3AU
This paperback edition first published in 1998

Phototypeset by Intype London Ltd
Printed and bound in Great Britain by
Mackays of Chatham PLC, Chatham, Kent

A CIP record for this book is
available from the British Library

ISBN 0-571-19201-7

2 4 6 8 10 9 7 5 3 1

Contents

Contents

Acknowledgements

'Lies' from *The Hottest Night of the Century* by GLENDA ADAMS (Angus & Robertson Publishers, 1979). Copyright © Glenda Adams, 1979. Reprinted by permission of the author.

'Betty' from *Dancing Girls* by MARGARET ATWOOD. Copyright © O.W. Toad Ltd, 1977, 1982. Reprinted by permission of Simon & Schuster, Inc.

'Gorilla, My Love' from *Gorilla, My Love* by TONI CADE BAMBARA. Copyright © Toni Cade Bambara, 1971. Reprinted by permission of The Women's Press.

'Gryphon' from *Through the Safety Net* by CHARLES BAXTER. Copyright © Charles Baxter, 1985. Reprinted by permission of the author.

'Flat Creek Road' by JOHN BENNETT. Reprinted by permission of the author. Copyright © John Bennett, 1986.

'Daley's Girls' by CATHERINE BRADY. Copyright © Catherine Brady, 1985. Reprinted by permission of the author.

'My Lucy Friend Who Smells Like Corn' and 'Barbie-Q' from *Woman Hollering Creek* by SANDRA CISNEROS. Reprinted by permission of Bloomsbury Publishing plc.

'Undertow' from *All There Is* by JENNIFER CORNELL. Copyright © Jennifer Cornell, 1995. Reprinted by permission of Brandon Book Publishers.

'The Point' by CHARLES D'AMBROISO, JR. Copyright © Charles D'Ambrosio Jr., 1991. Reprinted by permission of the author.

'I Know Some Things' by D. J. DURNAM. Copyright D.J. Durnam, 1987. Reprinted by permission of the author.

'Saint Marie' by LOUISE ERDRICH. Reprinted by permission of the author. Copyright © Louise Erdrich.

'Signs and Wonders' by MAX GARLAND. Copyright © Max Garland, 1991. Reprinted by permission of Melanie Jackson Agency.

'Victory Over Japan' by ELLEN GILCHRIST. Reprinted by permission of the author and Don Congdon Associates, Inc.

'Sex and Death to the Age 14' from *Sex and Death to the Age 14* by SPALDING GRAY. Copyright © Spalding Gray, 1986. Reprinted by permission of Vintage Books, a division of Random House, Inc.

'Kolla' from *Reef* by ROMESH GUNESEKERA. Reprinted by permission of Penguin Books Ltd.

'Tinsel Bright' by KIRSTY GUNN. Reprinted by permission of the author. Copyright © Kirsty Gunn, 1996.

'Gwen' by JAMAICA KINCAID. Copyright © Jamaica Kincaid, 1984. First published in the *New Yorker*. Reprinted by permission of Wylie, Aitken & Stone, Inc.

'My Mother's Clothes: The School of Beauty and Shame' by RICHARD MCCANN. Copyright © Richard McCann. Reprinted by permission of A.M. Heath & Company Ltd.

'The Ponoes' from *The Piano Tuner* by PETER MEINKE. Copyright © Peter Meinke, 1986. Reprinted by permission of the author.

'Murderers' from *I Would Have Saved Them If I Could* by LEONARD MICHAELS. Reprinted by permission of the author. Copyright © Leonard Michaels.

'Hiding' from *Monkeys* by SUSAN MINOT. Copyright © Susan Minot, 1986. Reprinted by permission of Georges Borchardt, Inc for the author.

Introduction

The word *know* is no stranger to narratives of childhood. In fact, it often seems to appear there recurrently, even in the titles, as if the subject of *knowing* or *not knowing* were the unshakable center of any childhood story. Sherwood Anderson's 'I Want to Know Why' or Henry James's *What Maisie Knew* come immediately to mind. When writers of fiction have made the effort to explore the mottled landscape of a child's secrets and understanding, they have often created stories of ferocious poignancy, stories whose narrators are no less reliable for their various struggles toward and through basic truths – sometimes even basic facts. To the James of *What Maisie Knew* a young female protagonist was 'no end' of sensibility; a child in the world was like a drummer boy in war. The novelist Fernanda Eberstadt has written that children are 'amnesiacs behind enemy lines ... Being a child is largely a flux of bold and furtive guesswork, fixed ideas continually dislodged by scrambling and tentative revision ... All our energy and cunning go into getting our bearings without letting on that we are ignorant and lost.'

As the most recently arrived to earthly life, children can seem in lingering possession of some heavenly lidless eye. Their appetite for observation is omnivorous and unsentimental, and their innocence, a kind of preternatural genius spent in the senses, spent in the hungry acquisition of *knowing*, is of natural interest to writers fashioning a record of human experience. 'I wanted proximity to darkness, strangeness,' says the narrator of Leonard Michaels's 'Murderers'. The wonderful stories included in this anthology are all first-person narratives, told either by a child or by the adult who once was that child. This narrative strategy preserves not only the child's role as both actor and witness, but that character's voice as well – in some cases the language of the evolving consciousness, the makeshift intelligence, the wily, rhetorical manipulations and inventions of someone not yet part of the grown-up world. The reader of these stories then enters the fantastic society of a child, with its blithely resourceful, spirited, and not entirely uninformed improvisations. Consider Sandra Cisneros's jazz hymn to girlhood pals, 'My Lucy Friend Who Smells Like Corn' ('Have you ever eated dog food? I have'), or Glenda Adams's 'Lies', Catherine Petroski's 'Beautiful My Mane in the Wind', or D. J. Durnam's 'I Know Some Things', in which the narrators' antennae – all raised to detect any hint of betrayal at home – are wildly idiosyncratic.

In other stories here the narrative employs the multi-layered voice of someone looking back, hindsight being the province and privilege of former children only. In Margaret Atwood's 'Betty' or Stephanie Vaughn's 'Dog Heaven' a vanished landscape and social milieu are reconstructed via a memory now skilled at selection, juxtaposition and irony. Experiences in these stories have been allowed, over time, to rise to the surface and be named, become myth. 'The life of a child,' wrote Katherine Anne Porter, 'which is in itself a mystery, . . . [is] legendary to that same child grown up.'

Almost all of these narratives are about moral occasions – moments in childhood when something becomes known, something else is tested, some fact steps fiercely forward, some circumstance is discerned or milestone encountered, perhaps only to be thoroughly understood years later. Nonetheless, the young child improvises a response. The grown child revises. In Atwood's 'Betty' forms of niceness and of mental cruelty are witnessed by a child who later learns to re-read them. An illusion has been snapped, the world has been revealed, and from then on life proceeds a little differently. The stories included here, then, are less about a Romantic notion of childhood as unconscious intercourse with beauty than they are about childhood as a state of formidable awareness – raw, secretive, tallying, assertive, forgiving or unforgiving. These children are often the camera and conscience of the adult world. They are citizens. They nab hypocrisies, delineate cruelties. The swindle of children by the grown-up world is protested both mournfully and with humor. Consider Hazel, the narrator of Toni Cade Bambara's 'Gorilla, My Love', bemoaning the 'trickified business' of her elders. 'And don't even say they sorry,' she laments at the end. Or consider the heart-stopping declaration of the narrator of Catherine Brady's 'Daley's Girls': 'I hate Dad.' More serious, even criminal, abuse of children is examined in stories by Louise Erdrich and Romesh Gunesekera – a reminder of those children forced to make their way alone through the daily menace of adult violence.

Although there are within these narratives sustained gazes at sibling bonds, it is parents, in both their mystery and plainness, that are most often examined here; parents are, after all, the drama most daily and powerfully present for children. A child's parents are both the impasse and gate to the world and to the heart. The parents perform well as protectors, gatekeepers, navigators and guides – or else they don't. In John Bennet's 'Flat Creek Road', the narrator's love for his stubborn, pridefully inept mother – his helpless animal attachment – aligns him with her, indulges her, softening a retrospectively critical eye. In Charles d'Ambrosio's 'The Point', Marly Swick's 'Heart' or Sheila Schwartz's 'Out-of-the-Body Travel' the nature of a parent's emotional collapse is intuited by children whose instinctive knowledge of psychological cause-and-effect smartens and burdens them, accelerates their entry into grown-up worlds and matters. 'I had developed a priestly sense of my position,' confides the young narrator of 'The Point', who regularly escorts home the drunken party guests at his house. In the similarly bruised sense of home that pervades Richard Yates's brilliant, 'Oh, Joseph, I'm So Tired', the vain stupidities of a boy's mother, though they taint the atmosphere, still cannot undo the stubborn magic of childhood, which, Yates's story seems to say, wants always to insist on itself, assert itself, even foolishly. Imagination and memory bring a sleepy provisional peace. Knowledge is the story; its rough and specific acquisition is the plot. Says Yates's narrator, 'Our mother was ours; we were hers; and we lived with that knowledge . . .'

Probably it is, indeed, mothers who figure most prominently for the narrators in this book. The fathers within these pages, though powerful figures, are often distant, iconic, romanticized; sometimes, as in Ellen Gilchrist's 'Victory Over Japan', they are simply formidable absences. They are also, by and large, reflective of their culture and time; they are likely to be in possession of their own, differentiated stories. The mothers, on the other hand, have commingled theirs with their children's and so we see the mothers' stories up close. In one interesting exception, Ben Okri's 'A Bizarre Courtship', the narrator, caught between his feuding parents, remarks, 'I chose to go after Dad – for with his mad passion lay the greater magnetic adventure.'

But over and over again it is the mothers in these stories who tend to loom most vividly, immediately, even grotesquely. 'It was just us,' says Linda Svendsen's narrator of life with her mother. 'Sometimes the hook of her nose scared me . . . I put her soft voice in mine . . . Her garter biting into my cheek would make a mark gone by morning.' The portraits drawn are rarely loveless; mostly they are bittersweet but clear-eyed. Consider Jamaica Kincaid's 'Gwen', in which the narrator effects a transfer of daughterly devotion to a girlfriend at school. A similar atmosphere of transition and shifting alliances pervades the suburban world of Richard McCann's 'My Mother's Clothes: The School of Beauty and Shame', in which the young protagonist begins to experience his own homosexuality in a maternal climate that offers both enticements and cruel forbiddance ('Our Mother of the Mixed Messages, Our Mother of Sudden Attentiveness'). Or there is the proud and overweening mother of Amy Tan's 'Rules of the Game', who can't bear not to have a part in her daughter's brilliant venture out into the world. In Edna O'Brien's 'My Mother's Mother' the mother as literary subject has already taken hold of the young narrator's mind. 'I thought how much I needed to be without her so that I could think of her, dwell on her . . . I resolved that for certain I would grow up and one day go away. It was a sweet thought, and it was packed with punishment.'

Also included among these selections, however, are stories in which the central adult figure is not a parent: uncles, cousins, teachers here serve as emissaries from some outside world, holding out to the child a rendition of adult life different from that of their parents. There is the evangelical Uncle Kelvin in Max Garland's 'Signs and Wonders', who offers a life-long spiritual lesson in the guise of a fishing trip. Or there is Miss Ferenczi in Charles Baxter's 'Gryphon', the eccentric substitute teacher, who, as the very figure of oddity and imagination, easily disrupts the institutional monotony of a child's life in school; when the regular teacher returned, notes Tommy, the narrator, he would 'test us on our knowledge'. There is Romesh Gunesekera's Mister Salgado, who the narrator watches 'unendingly, all the time', and learns 'to become what I am'. There are the turkey gutters in Alice Munro's 'The Turkey Season', with whom the fourteen-year-old protagonist has taken her first part-time job. 'I would still like to know things,' she says. What she learns then, however, she learns – like the children in the Baxter, Garland, and Gunesekera stories – through a passionate but passive presence among these strange new grown-ups.

In addition to 'The Turkey Season', two other stories in this volume center primarily on adolescents: Spalding Gray's famous 'Sex and Death to the Age 14' and Sheila Schwartz's 'Out-of-the-Body Travel', wherein a fifteen-year-old girl briefly enters the urban counter-culture of 1968 America. The stories are irresistible for their vocal brilliance, but are also included as a reminder of the range of childhood experience. They show older children encountering the sexual world of adults yet experiencing that world as children do: with a mix of bewilderment, quiet alarm, quick if partial understanding. Quite powerfully we see in these children's fumbling journeys the shapes and themes of whole lives.

Margaret Atwood, Alice Munro and Linda Svendsen are Canadian; Glenda Adams was born in Australia, Ben Okri in Nigeria, Romesh Gunesekera in Sri Lanka. Edna O'Brien and Jennifer Cornell are Irish. Jamaica Kincaid grew up in the Caribbean. All of their stories reflect the universality of certain childhood experiences while retaining the detail and texture particular to a childhood in Ontario or Sydney or Antigua. Other stories in this anthology address settings and circumstances that have most affected the contemporary family: divorce, alcoholism, poverty, wars (World War II, the Soviet–American Cold War, Vietnam, Northern Ireland). In Amy Tan's 'Rules of the Game' and Catherine Brady's 'Daley's Girls' the heartbreaking complexity of immigrant experience (the price of assimilation, the hardships of the working class) is rendered with both the toughness and sympathy of a child's eye. In Sandra Cisneros's narratives slices of the materially disadvantaged Chicana experience are offered up with complicated exuberance.

In all the stories there is not only beautifully recollected detail, but need and urgency in the telling. 'Our father,' begins Susan Minot's 'Hiding', as if it were a prayer, and what follows is a kind of choral, first-person-plural appeal. Peter Meinke's 'The Ponoes' opens with the hallucinations of a childhood insomnia, then recounts an epsiode of neighborhood bullies that mirrors the events of the Second World War; the world's terrors are a child's writ large. Stephanie Vaughn's narrator in 'Dog Heaven' is haunted by the memory of a dead pet: 'Every so often that dead dog dreams me up again,' she says. Each of these stories – poised on the lip of dream, or nightmare, or prayer – is part of a public record of what we are, were, saw, know. Each illumines the contours of childhood pain and understanding: knowledge of one's childhood becoming knowledge of the world. Each documents the author's wrestling something down through the fashioning of a tale. 'Behind every story that begins "When I was a child",' wrote the novelist Gail Godwin, 'there exists another story in which adults are fighting for their lives.'

An anthology is nothing if not an act of enthusiasm and admiration. The stories here are written by some of the best contemporary writers we have, both well-known and less so. They offer a set of symbolic truths, a group portrait of childhood that is both historical and emotional, dark and comic, and, I think, startling in its implications, intimacy and sweep.

Lorrie Moore, 1996

for Richard Yates and Toni Cade Bambara

Glenda Adams
Lies

Sometimes I tell lies, and sometimes I only tell stories, but never with intent to harm. I only want to please people and make them happy.

Father

My father was the first man in his family to sit at a desk from Monday to Friday and use his head to support his wife and child. On Sundays he sat at the head of the table and carved roast beef.

One Sunday Uncle Roger came. He was a sailor and had just got out of the Navy. He said he never wanted to see another ship as long as he lived, not even a rowing boat on a pond. He said he wanted a steady job in an office, like my father's, where he sat at a desk from nine to five. He wanted to meet girls after work and take them to the movies. He wanted to sleep safe and sound in a soft bed that didn't rock. He told us all this through his Yorkshire pudding.

My father said he'd help Uncle Roger find an office job, because he was his brother, but he'd have to start at the bottom and work his way up. My father said Uncle Roger would have to learn to eat without making a noise and not talk with his mouth full. He also said that Uncle Roger could stay with us while he looked for a job, and at the same time he could learn some table manners and learn not to say ain't and jeez.

'Ettie will teach you,' my father said and turned to my mother. 'Won't you, Ettie?'

'Oh, Joe, when will I have the time?' my mother said and blushed. She took the plates to the kitchen.

While she was in the kitchen my father said to Uncle Roger, in a low voice, 'And if it's a girl you want, to take out to the movies, etcetera, there's always Maxine next door.'

I

'She's not a girl,' I said. 'She's a woman at least, and a mother.'

'She's a lady,' my father said, and winked at Uncle Roger. 'Maxine's definitely a lady. I give you my personal assurances.'

Uncle Roger shrugged. 'And what would I do with a woman with a ten-year-old kid?' And then Uncle Roger and my father burst out laughing.

'Joanne is not *just* a kid,' I said. 'She's my best friend. And I call Maxine Auntie Maxine.'

My mother came back with the rice pudding, and we talked about clearing out the back room for Uncle Roger to stay in, while he looked for a job and learned manners.

Auntie Maxine

After lunch Auntie Maxine came and sat with my mother and my father and Uncle Roger under the willow at the back of the house. It was about ninety in the shade.

Uncle Roger wore old work pants and a singlet, and sweated. My father wore a white shirt, a grey tie and the pants of his navy blue suit, as if he were waiting for an emergency call at the office.

My mother wore a cotton dress, rather than a housedress, since it was Sunday. Auntie Maxine wore a black sweater without sleeves and electric-blue pedal-pushers. She flopped into a chair and stretched her legs before her and complained about the heat.

My father said to her, 'Tell Roger, Maxine, how he can't go about dressed in a singlet if he wants to be a gentleman and get a good job and marry a lady and settle down.'

Auntie Maxine looked at Uncle Roger's chest and his arms and his trousers and said, 'Oh, I don't know. It's a hot day, and it's Sunday, day of rest, and we're sitting out the back where no one can see.' She leant over and gave Uncle Roger a punch on the arm and laughed.

Uncle Roger laughed.

But my mother got up and asked who would prefer tea with milk and who without. And she went inside.

Then Auntie Maxine said, 'And even gentlemen wear singlets, and at times even less than that.' She laughed again and tapped her finger on my father's knee.

Joanne

Joanne and I stood in the sun and made shadows. Since my name was Josephine, after my father, Joseph, and hers was Joanne, and since she was only eight months younger than I, we pretended we were sisters and sometimes twins.

We stood in the sun and made our shadows move together.

'Look at Joanne and me,' I called to my father. 'We're twins.'

'What nonsense, what a story,' my father said.

'The sun's gone to your head,' said Auntie Maxine. 'Come into the shade.'

Mother

My mother taught Uncle Roger manners. He told her stories about sailors, and she corrected his grammar. Sometimes when I came home from school I stayed quietly in the kitchen and listened.

They sat on the back veranda next to each other on the old couch that was waiting to be thrown out. A lot of the time they were laughing, including my mother, who usually only smiled.

'This here bloke,' said Uncle Roger.

'There was a man,' my mother corrected.

'There was a man, he had two old ladies. The blonde hung out in Singapore and the brunette lived in Hong Kong,' said Uncle Roger.

'There was a man who had two wives. One had blonde hair and resided in Singapore. The other had brown hair and resided in Hong Kong,' my mother said and giggled.

When she saw me she jumped up and told me to come and tell Uncle Roger what I'd learned in school, especially grammar. 'And none of your stories,' she said to me. And to Uncle Roger she said, 'And don't you tell her any of your stories either.'

While my mother prepared dinner Uncle Roger and I sat on the couch and talked. He put his arm around me and called me his sweetheart. Once he taught me Indian wrestling.

Then one afternoon when I came home I heard Uncle Roger's loud laugh coming from Auntie Maxine's back veranda. And I found my mother alone on our back veranda stringing beans. She called me to her and made me sit beside her.

'Now I want you to tell me the truth,' she said. 'Has Uncle Roger ever taken liberties with you?'

I looked closely at her face to find what answer she was looking for. 'What do you mean?'

'Has he ever hugged you, or come into your room while you were in bed, or anything like that?'

And I understood what she was asking. 'Oh, sure, lots of times. He's always hugging and kissing me.'

She put the newspaper with the beans on the floor beside her feet and took me on her knee and hugged me and kissed me.

'He'll have to go,' she said.

'But I like Uncle Roger. I don't want him to go.'

My mother stopped hugging me and held me from her, at arm's length.

'I was kidding,' I said. 'I don't like him. And I want him to go away.'

And my mother hugged me again.

Later I heard her tell my father that Uncle Roger would have to go. 'He's hugging and pawing her,' she said. 'He's lascivious.'

'Who's he pawing? Maxine?' my father answered.

'Your daughter,' my mother said, softly, but she was angrier than I had ever heard her.

Finally my father said, 'Oh, all right, I'll tell him in the morning.'

Uncle Roger

I decided to make my mother and father both happy and get rid of Uncle Roger for them. I got out of bed and crept to Uncle Roger's room. He stayed at Auntie Maxine's for dinner and had just come in. He was sitting on his bed.

'Hi, sweetheart,' he said to me.

'Hi,' I said. 'You know, Uncle Roger, we're going to be needing this room.'

He frowned. 'What do you mean?' He stopped taking off his shoes and looked up at me.

'Well, I'm going to have a little baby brother in the not too distant future, and he's going to need this room.'

Uncle Roger sat up straight. 'What do you mean?' he said. And he put his hands on my shoulders and looked at me closely.

I shrugged. 'Oh, you know how it is. It's just one of those things. It's hush-hush. My mother doesn't want anyone to know.'

And the next morning when we woke up Uncle Roger had gone with his suitcase. He had left a note saying thank you for all the hospitality but he had decided to be a sailor after all.

Terence

My father told me I was to get a little baby brother called Terence. My mother would come home with him in a few days, he said. 'Aren't you glad you're getting a brother?'

'No,' I said. 'I already have Joanne, who's my sister.'

'I warned you about telling stories,' my father said. He looked as if he might hit me, but instead he turned and walked away from me.

'And that little baby brother isn't really my brother at all,' I called after him.

He turned back to me. 'What do you mean?' and he stooped down so that his head was next to mine. I looked into his eyes and searched for what I meant.

'Well,' I said, 'he's not really my brother because he's Uncle Roger's little baby. He belongs to Uncle Roger.'

Me

At school the teacher told us to write the story of our family. Or, if we preferred, we could write about what we did last summer. I chose to write the story of my family, and this is what I wrote:

'I have a father, mother, an Uncle Roger and an Auntie Maxine. And there is also Joanne and a baby called Terence, who are both related to me in one way or another. At first I lived with my mother and my father. Joanne lived next door with her mother, Auntie Maxine. Then Uncle Roger came. And later Terence came. And everything changed. Now, I live with my father and Auntie Maxine and Joanne. And Terence lives with my mother and Uncle Roger a long way away, in Vancouver.'

The teacher called me to him. He drummed his fingers on the desk.

'Now I asked for the true story of your family, biography, not a fairy tale.' He bent down close to me and looked into my face. 'This isn't the real story of your family, is it? You made it up, didn't you?'

I looked for a moment into his eyes, and then I answered, 'Yes, I made it all up. I thought you meant us to.'

He sat back in his chair and let out his breath and smiled. 'I'll overlook it this once,' he said, and he patted my cheek. 'But next time when I say I want the truth, then you must write the truth, and no more stories like this one, all right?'

Margaret Atwood
Betty

When I was seven we moved again, to a tiny wooden cottage on the Saint Marys River, upstream from Sault Sainte Marie. We were only renting the cottage for the summer, but for the time being it was our house, since we had no other. It was dim and mousy-smelling and very cramped, stuffed with all the things from the place before that were not in storage. My sister and I preferred to spend most of our time outside it.

There was a short beach, behind which the cottages, with their contrasting trim – green against white, maroon against robin's-egg blue, brown against yellow – were lined up like little shoeboxes, each with its matching outhouse at an unsanitary distance behind. But we were forbidden to swim in the water, because of the strong current. There were stories of children who had been swept away, down toward the rapids and the locks and the Algoma Steel fires of the Soo which we could sometimes see from our bedroom window on over-cast nights, glowing dull red against the clouds. We were allowed to wade though, no further than the knee, and we would stand in the water, strands of loose weed tangling against our ankles, and wave at the lake freighters as they slid past, so close we could see not only the flags and seagulls at their sterns but the hands of the sailors and the ovals of their faces as they waved back to us. Then the waves would come, washing over our thighs up to the waists of our bloom-ered and skirted seersucker bathing suits, and we would scream with delight.

Our mother, who was usually on the shore, reading or talking to someone but not quite watching us, would sometimes mistake the screams for drowning. Or she would say later, 'You've been in over your knees,' but my sister would explain that it was only the boat waves. My mother would look at me to see if this was the truth. Unlike my sister, I was a clumsy liar.

The freighters were huge, cumbersome, with rust staining the holes for their anchor chains and enormous chimneys from which the smoke spurted in grey burps. When they blew their horns, as they always did when approaching the locks, the windows in our cottage rattled. For us, they were magical. Sometimes things would drop or be thrown from them, and we would watch these floating objects eagerly, running along the beach to be there when they landed, wading out to fish them in. Usually these treasures turned out to be only empty cardboard boxes or punctured oil cans, oozing dark brown grease and good for nothing. Several times we got orange crates, which we used as cupboards or stools in our hideouts.

We liked the cottage partly because we had places to make these hideouts. There had never been room before, since we had always lived in cities. Just before this it was Ottawa, the ground floor of an old three-tiered red-brick apartment building. On the floor above us lived a newly married couple, the wife English and Protestant, the husband French and Catholic. He was in the Air Force, and was away a lot, but when he came back on leave he used to beat up his wife. It was always about eleven o'clock at night. She would flee downstairs to my mother for protection, and they would sit in the kitchen with cups of tea. The wife would cry, though quietly, so as not to wake us – my mother insisted on that, being a believer in twelve hours of sleep for children – display her bruised eye or cheek, and whisper about his drinking. After an hour or so there would be a discreet knock on the door, and the airman, in full uniform, would ask my mother politely if he could have his wife back upstairs where she belonged. It was a religious dispute, he would say. Besides, he'd given her fifteen dollars to spend on food and she had served him fried Kam. After being away a month, a man expected a good roast, pork or beef, didn't my mother agree? 'I kept my mouth shut and my eyes open,' my mother would say. He never seemed that drunk to her, but with the polite kind you couldn't tell what they would do.

I wasn't supposed to know about any of this. I was considered either too young or too good; but my sister, who was four years older, was given hints, which she passed along to me with whatever she thought fit to add. I saw the wife a number of times, going up or down the stairs outside our door, and once she did have a black eye. I never saw the man, but by the time we left Ottawa I was convinced he was a murderer.

This might have explained my father's warning when my mother told him she had met the young couple who lived in the right-hand cottage. 'Don't get too involved,' he said. 'I don't want her running over here at all hours of the night.' He had little patience with my mother's talents as a sympathetic listener, even when she teased him by saying, 'But I listen to *you*, dear.' She attracted people he called 'sponges'.

He didn't seem to have anything to worry about. This couple was very different from the other one. Fred and Betty insisted on being called Fred and Betty, right away. My sister and I, who had been drilled to call people Mr and Mrs, had to call them Fred and Betty also, and we could go over to their house whenever we wanted to. 'I don't want you to take that at face value,' our mother said. Times were hard but our mother had been properly brought up, and we were going to be, too. Nevertheless, at first we went to Fred and Betty's as often as we could.

Their cottage was exactly the same size as ours, but since there was less furniture in it it seemed bigger. Ours had Ten-Test walls between the rooms, painted lime green, with lighter squares on the paint where other people had once hung pictures. Betty had replaced her walls with real plywood and painted the inside bright yellow, and she'd made yellow-and-white curtains for the kitchen, a print of chickens coming out of eggshells. She'd sewed herself a matching apron from the leftover material. They owned their cottage rather than renting it; as my mother said, you didn't mind doing the work then. Betty called the tiny kitchen a kitchenette. There was a round ironwork table tucked into one corner, with two scrolled ironwork chairs, painted white, one for Betty and one for Fred. Betty called this corner the breakfast nook.

There was more to do at Fred and Betty's than at our house. They had a bird made of hollow coloured glass that perched on the edge of a tumbler of water, teetering back and forth until it would finally dip its head into the water and take a drink. They had a front-door knocker in the shape of a woodpecker: you pulled a string, and the woodpecker pecked at the door. They also had a whistle in the shape of a bird that you could fill with water and blow into and it would warble, 'like a canary', Betty said. And they took the Saturday col-oured funnies. Our parents didn't, and they didn't like us reading trash, as they called it. But Fred and Betty were so friendly and kind to us, what, as my mother said, could they do?

Beyond all these attractions there was Fred. We both fell in love with Fred. My sister would climb into his lap and announce that he was her boyfriend and she was going to marry him when she grew up. She would then make him read the funnies to her and tease him by trying to take the pipe out of his mouth or by tying his shoelaces together. I felt the same way, but I knew it was no good saying so. My sister had staked her claim: when she said she was going to do a thing she usually did it. And she hated my being what she called a copycat. So I would sit in the breakfast nook on one of the scrolled ironwork chairs while Betty made coffee, watching my sister and Fred on the living-room couch.

There was something about Fred that attracted people. My mother, who was not a flirtatious woman – she went in for wisdom, instead – was livelier when he was around. Even my father liked him, and would sometimes have a beer with him when he got back from the city. They would sit on the porch of Fred's cottage in Betty's yellow wicker chairs, swatting at the sand flies and discussing baseball scores. They seldom mentioned their jobs. I'm not sure what Fred did, but it was in an office. My father was 'in wallpaper', my mother said, but I was never very clear about what that meant. It was more exciting when they talked about the war. My father's bad back had kept him out of it, much to his disgust, but Fred had been in the Navy. He never said too much about it, though my father was always prompting him; but we knew from Betty that they were engaged just before Fred left and married right after he came back. Betty had written letters to him every single night and mailed them once a week. She did not say how often Fred had written to her. My father didn't like many people, but he said that Fred wasn't a fool.

Fred didn't seem to make any efforts to be nice to people. I don't think he was even especially handsome. The difficulty is that though I can remember Betty down to the last hair and freckle, I can't remember what Fred looked like. He had dark hair and a pipe, and he used to sing to us if we pestered him enough. 'Sioux City Sue,' he would sing, 'your hair is red, your eyes are blue, I'd swap my horse and dog for you . . .' Or he would sing 'Beautiful Brown Eyes' to my sister, whose eyes were brown as compared with my own watery blue. This hurt my feelings, as the song contained the line, 'I'll never love blue eyes again.' It seemed so final, a whole lifetime of being unloved by Fred. Once I cried, which was made worse by the fact that I couldn't explain to anyone what was wrong; and I had to undergo the humiliation of Fred's jocular concern and my sister's scorn, and the worse humiliation of being comforted by Betty in the kitchenette. It was a humiliation because it was obvious even to me that Betty didn't grasp things very well. 'Don't pay any attention to *him*,' she said, having guessed that my tears had something to do with Fred. But that was the one piece of advice I couldn't take.

Fred, like a cat, wouldn't go two steps out of his way for you really, as my mother said later. So it was unfair that everyone was in love with Fred, but no one, despite her kindness, was in love with Betty. It was Betty who always greeted us at the door, asked us in, and talked to us while Fred slouched on the couch reading the paper. She fed us cookies and milk shakes and let us lick out the bowls when she was baking. Betty was such a nice person; everyone said so, but no one would have called Fred exactly that. Fred, for instance, did not laugh much, and he only smiled when he was making rude remarks, mostly to my sister. 'Stuffing your face again?' he would say. 'Hey, baggy-pants.' Whereas Betty never said things like that, and she was always either smiling or laughing.

She laughed a lot when Fred called her Betty Grable, which he did at least once a day. I couldn't see why she laughed. It was supposed to be a compliment, I thought. Betty Grable was a famous movie star; there was a picture of her thumbtacked to the wall in Fred and Betty's outhouse. Both my sister and I preferred Fred and Betty's outhouse to our own. Theirs had curtains on the window, unlike ours, and it had a little wooden box and a matching wooden scoop for the lye. We only had a cardboard box and an old trowel.

Betty didn't really look like Betty Grable, who was blonde and not as plump as our Betty. Still, they were both beautiful, I thought. I didn't realize until much later that the remark was cruel; for Betty Grable was renowned for her legs, whereas our Betty had legs that started at her waist and continued downwards without a curve or a pause until they reached her feet. At the time they seemed like ordinary legs. Sitting in the kitchenette, I saw a lot of Betty's legs, for she wore halter tops and shorts, with her yellow apron over them. Somehow Betty could never get her legs to tan, despite the hours she spent crocheting in her wicker chair, the top part of her in the shade of the porch but her legs sticking out into the sun.

My father said that Betty had no sense of humour. I couldn't understand this at all. If you told her a joke she would always laugh, even if you got it mixed up, and she told jokes of her own, too. She would print the word 'BED', making the E smaller and thicker than the B and the D. 'What's this?' she would say. 'It's the little dark E in BED.' I didn't get this joke the first time she told it and she had to explain it to me. 'Little darkie,' she said, her slightly protruding teeth shining with good humour. We had never been to the United States, even though we could see it across the river, a strip of green trees that faded west into the blue of Lake Superior, and the only black people I had seen were the characters in the comics. There was Li'l 8-Ball, and the Africans in Tarzan, and Lothar in Mandrake the Magician, who wore a lion skin. I couldn't see what any of them had to do with the word 'bed'.

My father also said that Betty had no sex appeal. This didn't seem to bother my mother in the least. 'She's a very nice girl,' she would answer complacently, or, 'She has very nice colouring.' My mother and Betty were soon collaborating on a scheme for making the preserving easier. Most people still had Victory gardens, though the war was over, and the months of July and August were supposed to be spent putting up as many jars of fruit and vegetables as you could. My mother's garden was half-hearted, like most of her housekeeping efforts. It was a small patch beside the outhouse where squash vines rambled over a thicket of overgrown tomato plants and a few uneven lines of dwarfed carrots and beets. My mother's talent, we had heard her say, was for people. Betty and Fred didn't have a garden at all. Fred wouldn't have worked in it, and when I think of Betty now I realize that a garden would have been too uncontained for her. But she had Fred buy dozens of six-quart baskets of strawberries, peaches, beans, tomatoes and Concord grapes, on his trips into the city; and she persuaded my mother to give up on her own garden and join her in her mammoth canning sessions.

My mother's wood stove was unbearably hot for such an operation, and Betty's little electric range was too small; so Betty got 'the boys', as she called Fred and my father, to set up the derelict wood stove that until then had been rusting behind Betty's outhouse. They put it in our backyard, and my mother and Betty would sit at our kitchen table, which had been carried outside, peeling, slicing and talking, Betty with her round pincushion cheeks flushed redder than usual by the heat and my mother with an old bandanna wrapped around her head, making her look like a gypsy. Behind them the canning kettles bubbled and steamed, and on one side of the table the growing ranks of Crown jars, inverted on layers of newspapers, cooled and sometimes leaked or cracked. My sister and I hung around the edges, not wanting to be obvious enough to be put to work, but coveting the empty six-quart baskets. We could use them in our hideout, we felt; we were never sure what for, but they fitted neatly into the orange crates.

I learned a lot about Fred during Betty's canning sessions: how he liked his eggs, what size socks he took (Betty was a knitter), how well he was doing at the office, what he refused to eat for dinner. Fred was a picky eater, Betty said joyfully. Betty had almost nothing else to talk about, and even my mother, veteran of many confidences, began to talk less and smoke more than usual when Betty was around. It was easier to listen to disasters than to Betty's inexhaustible and trivial cheer. I began to think that I might not want to be married to Fred after all. He unrolled from Betty's mouth like a long ribbon of soggy newspaper printed from end to end with nothing but the weather. Neither my sister nor I was interested in sock sizes, and Betty's random, unexciting details diminished Fred in our eyes. We began to spend less of our playtime at Fred and Betty's and more in our hideout, which was in a patch of scrubby oak on a vacant lot along the shore. There we played complicated games of Mandrake the Magician and his faithful servant Lothar, with our dolls as easily hypnotized villains. My sister was always Mandrake. When we tired of this, we would put on our bathing suits and go wading along the shore, watching for freighters and throwing acorns into the river to see how quickly they would be carried away by the current.

It was on one of these wading expeditions that we met Nan. She lived ten lots down, in a white cottage with red trim. Unlike many of the other cottages, Nan's had a real dock, built out into the river and anchored around the posts with piles of rocks. She was sitting on this dock when we first saw her, chewing gum and flipping through a stack of airplane cards from Wings cigarettes. Everyone knew that only boys collected these. Her hair and her face were light brown, and she had a sleek plump sheen, like caramel pudding.

'What're you doing with *those?*' were my sister's first words. Nan only smiled.

That same afternoon Nan was allowed into our hideout, and after a cursory game of Mandrake, during which I was demoted to the lowly position of Narda, the two of them sat on our orange crates and exchanged what seemed to me to be languid and pointless comments.

'You ever go to the store?' Nan asked. We never did. Nan smiled some more. She was twelve; my sister was only eleven and three-quarters.

'There's cute boys at the store,' Nan said. She was wearing a peasant blouse with a frill and an elastic top that she could slide down over her shoulders if she wanted to. She stuck her airplane cards into her shorts pocket and we went to ask my mother if we could walk to the store. After that, my sister and Nan went there almost every afternoon.

The store was a mile and a half from our cottage, a hot walk along the shore past the fronts of other cottages where fat mothers basked in the sun and other, possibly hostile children paddled in the water; past rowboats hauled up on the sand, along cement breakwaters, through patches of beach grass that cut your ankles if you ran through it and beach peas that were hard and bitter-tasting. In some places we could smell the outhouses. Just before the store, there was an open space with poison ivy, which we had to wade around.

The store had no name. It was just 'the store', the only store for the cottagers since it was the only one they could walk to. I was allowed to go with my sister and Nan, or rather, my mother insisted that I go. Although I hadn't said anything to her about it, she could sense my misery. It wasn't so much my sister's desertion that hurt, but her blithe unconsciousness of it. She was quite willing to play with me when Nan wasn't around.

Sometimes, when the sight of my sister and Nan conspiring twenty paces ahead of me made me too unhappy, I would double back and go to Fred and Betty's. There I would sit facing backwards on one of Betty's kitchen chairs, my two hands rigid in the air, holding a skein of sky-blue wool while Betty wound it into balls. Or, under Betty's direction, I crocheted sweaty, uneven little pink and yellow dolls' dresses for the dolls my sister was, suddenly, too old to play with.

On better days I would make it as far as the store. It was not beautiful or even clean, but we were so used to wartime drabness and grime that we didn't notice. It was a two-story building of unpainted wood which had weathered gray. Parts of it were patched with tar paper, and it had coloured metal signs nailed around the front screen door and windows: Coca-Cola, 7-Up, Salada Tea. Inside, it had the sugary, mournful smell of old general stores, a mixture of the cones for the ice-cream cones, the packages of Oreo cookies, the open boxes of jawbreakers and licorice whips that lined the counter, and that other smell, musky and sharp, part dry-rot and part sweat. The bottles of pop were kept in a metal cooler with a heavy lid, filled with cold water and chunks of ice melted to the smoothness of the sand-scoured pieces of glass we sometimes found on the beach.

The owner of the store and his wife lived on the second floor, but we almost never saw them. The store was run by their two daughters, who took turns behind the counter. They were both dark and they both wore shorts and polka-dot halter tops, but one was friendly and the other one, the thinner, younger one, was not. She would take our pennies and ring them into the cash register without saying a word, staring over our heads out the front window with its dangling raisin-covered fly-papers as if she was completely detached from the activity her hands were performing. She didn't dislike us; she just didn't see us. She wore her hair long and done in a sort of roll at the front, and her lipstick was purplish.

The first time we went to the store we found out why Nan collected airplane cards. There were two boys there, sitting on the gray, splintery front steps, their arms crossed over their knees. I had been told by my sister that the right thing to do with boys was to ignore them; otherwise they would pester you. But these boys knew Nan, and they spoke to her, not with the usual taunts, but with respect.

'You got anything new?' one of them said.

Nan smiled, brushed back her hair and wiggled her shoulders a little inside her peasant blouse. Then she slid her airplane cards slowly out of her shorts pocket and began riffling through them.

'You got any?' the other boy said to my sister. For once she was humbled. After that, she got my mother to switch brands and built up her own pack. I saw her in front of the mirror about a week later, practising that tantalizing slide, the cards coming out of her pocket like a magician's snake.

When I went to the store I always had to bring back a loaf of wax-papered bread for my mother, and sometimes a package of 'Jiffy' Pie Crust, if they had any. My sister never had to: she had already discovered the advantages of being unreliable. As payment, and, I'm sure, as compensation for my unhappiness, my mother gave me a penny a trip, and when I had saved five of these pennies I bought my first Popsicle. Our mother had always refused to buy them for us, although she permitted ice-cream cones. She said there was something in Popsicles that was bad for you, and as I sat on the front steps of the store, licking down to the wooden stick, I kept looking for this thing.

I visualized it as a sort of core, like the white fingernail-shaped part in a kernel of corn, but I couldn't find anything.

My sister and Nan were sitting beside me on the front steps. There were no boys at the store that day, so they had nothing else to do. It was even hotter than usual, and airless; there was a shimmer over the river, and the freighters wavered as they passed through it. My Popsicle was melting almost before I could eat it. I had given my sister half of it, which she had taken without the gratitude I had hoped for. She was sharing it with Nan.

Fred came around the corner of the building and headed towards the front door. This was no surprise, as we had seen him at the store several times before.

'Hi, beautiful,' he said to my sister. We moved our rumps along the step to let him in the door.

After quite a long time he came out, carrying a loaf of bread. He asked us if we wanted a lift with him in his car: he was just coming back from the city, he said. Of course we said yes. There was nothing unusual about any of this, except that the daughter, the thinner, purple one, stepped outside the door and stood on the steps as we were driving off. She folded her arms across her chest in that slump-shouldered pose of women idling in doorways. She wasn't smiling. I thought she had come out to watch the Canada Steamship Lines freighter that was going past, but then I saw that she was staring at Fred. She looked as if she wanted to kill him.

Fred didn't seem to notice. He sang all the way home. 'Katy, oh beautiful Katy,' he sang, winking at my sister, whom he sometimes called Katy since her name was Catherine. He had the windows open, and dust from the rutted gravel road poured over us, whitening our eyebrows and turning Fred's hair gray. At every jolt my sister and Nan screamed gleefully, and after a while I forgot my feelings of exclusion and screamed too.

It seemed as if we had lived in the cottage for a long time, though it was only one summer. By August I could hardly remember the apartment in Ottawa and the man who used to beat up his wife. That had happened in a remote life; and, despite the sunshine, the water, the open space, a happier one. Before, our frequent moves and the insecurities of new schools had forced my sister to value me: I was four years younger, but I was loyal and always there. Now those years were a canyon between us, an empty stretch like a beach along which

I could see her disappearing ahead of me. I longed to be just like her, but I could no longer tell what she was like.

In the third week of August the leaves started to turn, not all at once, just a single red one here and there, like a warning. That meant it would soon be time for school and another move. We didn't even know where we would be moving to this time, and when Nan asked us what school we went to, we were evasive.

'I've been to eight different schools,' my sister said proudly. Because I was so much younger, I had only been to two. Nan, who had been to the same one all her life, slipped the edge of her peasant blouse over her shoulders and down to her elbows to show us that her breasts were growing. The rings around the nipples had softened and started to puff out; otherwise she was as flat as my sister.

'So what,' said my sister, rolling up her jersey. This was a competition I couldn't be part of. It was about change, and increasingly, change frightened me. I walked back along the beach to Betty's house, where my latest piece of grubby crocheting was waiting for me and where everything was always the same.

I knocked on the screen door and opened it. I meant to say, 'Can I come in?' the way we always did, but I didn't say it. Betty was sitting by herself at the iron table of the breakfast nook. She had on her shorts and a striped sailor top, navy blue and white with a little anchor pin, and the apron with the yellow chickens coming out of their eggs. For once she wasn't doing anything, and there was no cup of coffee in front of her. Her face was white and uncomprehending, as if someone had just hit her for no reason.

She saw me, but she didn't smile or ask me in. 'What am I going to do?' she said.

I looked around the kitchen. Everything was in its place: the percolator gleamed from the stove, the glass bird was teetering slowly down, there were no broken dishes, no water on the floor. What had happened?

'Are you sick?' I said.

'There's nothing I can do,' Betty said.

She looked so strange that I was frightened. I ran out of the kitchen and across the hillocky grass to get to my mother, who always knew what should be done.

'There's something wrong with Betty,' I said.

My mother was mixing something in a bowl. She rubbed her hands together to get the dough off, then wiped them on her apron. She didn't look surprised or ask me what it was. 'You stay here,' she said. She picked up her package of cigarettes and went out the door.

That evening we had to go to bed early because my mother wanted to talk to my father. We listened, of course; it was easy through the Ten-Test walls.

'I saw it coming,' my mother said. 'A mile away.'

'Who is it?' my father said.

'She doesn't know,' said my mother. 'Some girl from town.'

'Betty's a fool,' my father said. 'She always was.' Later, when husbands and wives leaving each other became more common, he often said this, but no matter which one had left it was always the woman he called the fool. His highest compliment to my mother was that she was no fool.

'That may be,' said my mother. 'But you'd never want to meet a nicer girl. He was her whole life.'

My sister and I whispered together. My sister's theory was that Fred had run away from Betty with another woman. I couldn't believe this: I had never heard of such a thing happening. I was so upset I couldn't sleep, and for a long time after that I was anxious whenever my father was away overnight, as he frequently was. What if he never came back?

We didn't see Betty after that. We knew she was in her cottage, because every day my mother carried over samples of her tough and lumpy baking, almost as if someone had died. But we were given strict orders to stay away, and not to go peering in the windows as our mother must have known we longed to do. 'She's having a nervous breakdown,' our mother said, which for me called up an image of Betty lying disjointed on the floor like a car at the garage.

We didn't even see her on the day we got into my father's second-hand Studebaker, the back seat packed to the window-tops with only a little oblong space for me to crouch in, and drove out to the main highway to begin the six-hundred-mile journey south to Toronto. My father had changed jobs again; he was now in building materials, and he was sure, since the country was having a boom, that this was finally the right change. We spent September and part of October in a motel while my father looked for a house. I had my eighth birthday and my sister turned twelve. Then there was another new school, and I almost forgot about Betty.

But a month after I had turned twelve myself, Betty was suddenly there one night for dinner. We had people for dinner a lot more than we used to, and sometimes the dinners were so important that my sister and I ate first. My sister didn't care, as she had boyfriends by that time. I was still in public school and had to wear lisle stockings instead of the seamed nylons my sister was permitted. Also, I had braces. My sister had had braces at that age too, but she had somehow managed to make them seem rakish and daring, so that I had longed for mouthful of flashing silver teeth like hers. But she no longer had them, and my own mouth in its shackles felt clumsy and muffled.

'You remember Betty,' my mother said.

'Elizabeth,' Betty said.

'Oh yes, of course,' said my mother.

Betty had changed a lot. Before, she had been a little plump; now she was buxom. Her cheeks were as round and florid as two tomatoes, and I thought she was using too much rouge until I saw that the red was caused by masses of tiny veins under her skin. She was wearing a long black pleated skirt, a white short-sleeved angora sweater with a string of black beads, and open-toed black velvet pumps with high heels. She smelled strongly of Lily of the Valley. She had a job, my mother told my father later, a very good job. She was an executive secretary, and now called herself Miss instead of Mrs.

'She's doing very well,' my mother said, 'considering what happened. She's pulled herself together.'

'I hope you don't start inviting her to dinner all the time,' said my father, who still found Betty irritating in spite of her new look. She laughed more than ever now, and crossed her legs frequently.

'I feel I'm the only real friend she has,' said my mother. She didn't say Betty was the only real friend she had, though when my father said 'your friend' everyone knew who he meant. My mother had a lot of friends, and her talent for wise listening was now a business asset for my father.

'She says she'll never marry again,' said my mother.

'She's a fool,' my father said.

'If I ever saw anyone cut out for marriage, it was her,' said my mother. This remark increased my anxiety about my own future. If all Betty's accomplishments had not been enough for Fred, what hope was there for me? I did not have my sister's natural flair, but I had thought there would be some tricks I could learn, dutifully, painstakingly. We were taking Home Economics at school and the teacher kept saying that the way to a man's heart was through his stomach. I knew this wasn't true – my mother was still a slapdash cook, and when she gave the best dinners she had a woman in to help – but I laboured over my blancmange and Harvard beets as if I believed it.

My mother started inviting Betty to dinner with men who were not married. Betty smiled and laughed and several of the men seemed interested, but nothing came of it.

'After the way she was hurt, I'm not surprised,' my mother said. I was now old enough to be told things, and besides, my sister was never around. 'I heard it was a secretary at his company he ran off with. They even got married, after the divorce.' There was something else about Betty, she told me, although I must never mention it as Betty found it very distressing. Fred's brother, who was a dentist, had killed his wife because he got involved – my mother said 'involved' richly, as if it was a kind of dessert – with his dental technician. He had put his wife into the car and run a tube in from the exhaust pipe, and then tried to pretend it was suicide. The police had found out though, and he was in jail.

This made Betty much more interesting in my eyes. It was in Fred's blood, then, this tendency towards involvement. In fact it could just as easily have been Betty herself who had been murdered. I now came to see Betty's laugh as the mask of a stricken and martyred woman. She was not just a wife who had been deserted. Even I could see that this was not a tragic position, it was a ridiculous and humiliating one. She was much more than that: she was a woman who had narrowly escaped death. That Betty herself saw it this way I soon had no doubt. There was something smug and even pious about the way she kept Mother's single men at a polite distance, something faintly nunlike. A lurid aura of sacrificial blood surrounded her. Betty had been there, she had passed through it, she had come out alive, and now she was dedicating herself to, well, to something else.

But it was hard for me to sustain this version of Betty for long. My mother soon ran out of single men and Betty, when she came to dinner, came alone. She talked as incessantly about the details sur-rounding the other women at her office as she had about Fred. We soon knew how they all took their coffee, which ones lived with their mothers, where they had their hair done, and what their apartments looked like. Betty herself had a darling apartment on Avenue Road, and she had re-done it all herself and even made the slipcovers. Betty was as devoted to her boss as she had once been to Fred. She did all his Christmas shopping, and each year we heard what he had given to his employees, what to his wife and children, and what each item had cost. Betty seemed, in a way, quite happy.

We saw a lot of Betty around Christmas; my mother said she felt sorry for her because she had no family. Betty was in the habit of giving us Christmas presents that made it obvious she thought we were younger than we were. She favoured Parcheesi sets and angora mittens a size too small. I lost interest in her. Even her unending cheerfulness came to seem like a perversion, or a defect almost like idiocy. I was fifteen now and in the throes of adolescent depression. My sister was away at Queen's; sometimes she gave me clothes she no longer wanted. She was not exactly beautiful – both her eyes and her mouth were too large – but everyone called her vivacious. They called me nice. My braces had come off, but it didn't seem to make any difference. What right had Betty to be cheerful? When she came to dinner, I excused myself early and went to my room.

One afternoon, in the spring of Grade Eleven, I came home from school to find my mother sitting at the dining-room table. She was crying, which was so rare that my immediate fear was that something had happened to my father. I didn't think he had left her; that particular anxiety was past. But perhaps he had been killed in a car crash.

'Mum, what is it?' I said.

'Bring me a glass of water,' she said. She drank some of it and pushed back her hair. 'I'm all right now,' she said. 'I just had a call from Betty. It was very upsetting; she said horrible things to me.'

'Why?' I said. 'What did you do?'

'She accused me of . . . horrible things.' My mother swabbed at her eyes. 'She was screaming. I've never heard Betty scream in my life before. After all that time I spent with her. She said she never wanted to speak to me again. Where would she get such an idea?'

'What idea?' I said. I was just as mystified as my mother was. My mother was a bad cook, but she was a good woman. I could not imagine her doing anything that would make anyone want to scream at her.

My mother held back slightly. 'Things about Fred,' she said. 'She must be crazy. I hadn't seen her for a couple of months, and then suddenly, just like that.'

'There must be something wrong with her,' my father said at dinner that night. Of course he was right. Betty had an undetected brain tumour, which was discovered when her strange behaviour was noticed at the office. She died in the hospital two months later, but my mother didn't hear about it till afterwards. She was contrite; she felt she should have visited her friend in the hospital, despite the abusive phone call.

'I ought to have known it was something like that,' she said. 'Personality change, that's one of the clues.' In the course of her listening, my mother had picked up a great deal of information about terminal illnesses.

But for me, this explanation wasn't good enough. For years after that, Betty followed me around, waiting for me to finish her off in some way more satisfactory to both of us. When I first heard about her death I felt doomed. This, then, was the punishment for being devoted and obliging, this was what happened to girls such as (I felt) myself. When I opened the high-school yearbook and my own face, in pageboy haircut and tentative, appeasing smile, stared back at me, it was Betty's eyes I superimposed on mine. She had been kind to me when I was a child, and with the callousness of children toward those who are kind but not enchanting, I had preferred Fred. In my future I saw myself being abandoned by a succession of Freds who were running down the beach after a crowd of vivacious girls, all of whom looked remarkably like my sister. As for Betty's final screams of hatred and rage, they were screams of protest against the unfairness of life. That anger, I knew, was my own, the dark side of that terrible and deforming niceness that had marked Betty like the aftermath of some crippling disease.

People change, though, especially after they are dead. As I passed beyond the age of melodrama I came to see that if I did not want to be Betty, I would have to be someone else. Furthermore, I was already quite different from Betty. In a way, she had absolved me from making the demanded choices by having made them so thoroughly herself. People stopped calling me a nice girl and started calling me a clever one, and after a while I enjoyed this. Betty herself, baking oatmeal cookies in the ephemeral sunlight of fifteen years before, slid back into three dimensions. She was an ordinary woman who had died too young of an incurable disease. Was that it, was that all?

From time to time I would like to have Betty back, if only for an hour's conversation. I would like her to forgive me for my rejection of her angora mittens, for my secret betrayals of her, for my adolescent contempt. I would like to show her this story I have told about her and ask her if any of it is true. But I can think of nothing I want to ask her that I could phrase in a way that she would care to understand. She would only laugh in her accepting, uncomprehending way and offer me something, a chocolate brownie, a ball of wool.

Fred, on the other hand, no longer intrigues me. The Freds of this world make themselves explicit by what they do and choose. It is the Bettys who are mysterious.

Toni Cade Bambara
Gorilla, My Love

That was the year Hunca Bubba changed his name. Not a change up,
but a change back, since Jefferson Winston Vale was the name in the
first place. Which was news to me cause he'd been my Hunca Bubba
my whole lifetime, since I couldn't manage Uncle to save my life. So
far as I was concerned it was a change completely to somethin sound-
in very geographical weatherlike to me, like somethin you'd find in a
almanac. Or somethin you'd run across when you sittin in the navigator seat with a wet thumb on the map crinkly in your lap, watchin
the roads and signs so when Granddaddy Vale say 'Which way,
Scout?' you got sense enough to say take the next exit or take a left or
whatever it is. Not that Scout's my name. Just the name Granddaddy
call whoever sittin in the navigator seat. Which is usually me cause I
don't feature sittin in the back with the pecans. Now, you figure
pecans all right to be sittin with. If you thinks so, that's your business.
But they dusty sometime and make you cough. And they got a way of
slidin around and dippin down sudden, like maybe a rat in the
buckets. So if you scary like me, you sleep with the lights on and
blame it on Baby Jason and, so as not to waste good electric, you
study the maps. And that's how come I'm in the navigator seat most
times and get to be called Scout.

So Hunca Bubba in the back with the pecans and Baby Jason, and
he in love. And we got to hear all this stuff about this woman he in
love with and all. Which really ain't enough to keep the mind alive,
though Baby Jason got no better sense than to give his undivided
attention and keep grabbin at the photograph which is just a picture
of some skinny woman in a countrified dress with her hand shot up to
her face like she shame fore cameras. But there's a movie house in the

background which I ax about. Cause I am a movie freak from way back, even though it do get me in trouble sometime.

Like when me and Big Brood and Baby Jason was on our own last Easter and couldn't go to the Dorset cause we'd seen all the Three Stooges they was. And the RKO Hamilton was closed readying up for the Easter Pageant that night. And the West End, the Regun and the Sunset was too far, less we had grownups with us which we didn't. So we walk up Amsterdam Avenue to the Washington and *Gorilla, My Love* playin, they say, which suit me just fine, though the 'my love' part kinda drag Big Brood some. As for Baby Jason, shoot, like Granddaddy say, he'd follow me into the fiery furnace if I say come on. So we go in and get three bags of Havmore potato chips which not only are the best potato chips but the best bags for blowin up and bustin real loud so the matron come trottin down the aisle with her chunky self, flashin that flashlight dead in your eye so you can give her some lip, and if she answer back and you already finish seein the show anyway, why then you just turn the place out. Which I love to do, no lie. With Baby Jason kickin at the seat in front, egging me on, and Big Brood mumblin bout what fiercesome things we goin do. Which means me. Like when the big boys come up on us talkin bout Lemme a nickel. It's me that hide the money. Or when the bad boys in the park take Big Brood's Spaudeen way from him. It's me that jump on they back and fight awhile. And it's me that turns out the show if the matron get too salty.

So the movie come on and right away it's this churchy music and clearly not about no gorilla. Bout Jesus. And I am ready to kill, not cause I got anything gainst Jesus. Just that when you fixed to watch a gorilla picture you don't wanna get messed around with Sunday School stuff. So I am mad. Besides, we see this raggedy old brown film *King of Kings* every year and enough's enough. Grownups figure they can treat you just anyhow. Which burns me up. There I am, my feet up and my Havmore potato chips really salty and crispy and two jawbreakers in my lap and the money safe in my shoe from the big boys, and here comes this Jesus stuff. So we all go wild. Yellin, booin, stompin and carryin on. Really to wake the man in the booth up there who musta went to sleep and put on the wrong reels. But no, cause he holler down to shut up and then he turn the sound up so we really gotta holler like crazy to even hear ourselves good. And the matron ropes off the children section and flashes her light all over the place and we yell some more and some kids slip under the rope and run up and down the aisle just to show it take more than some dusty ole velvet rope to tie us down. And I'm flingin the kid in front of me's popcorn. And Baby Jason kickin seats. And it's really somethin. Then here come the big and bad matron, the one they let out in case of emergency. And she totin that flashlight like she gonna use it on somebody. This here the colored matron Brandy and her friends call Thunderbuns. She do not play. She do not smile. So we shut up and watch the simple ass picture.

Which is not so simple as it is stupid. Cause I realize that just about anybody in my family is better than this god they always talkin about. My daddy wouldn't stand for nobody treatin any of us that way. My mama specially. And I can just see it now, Big Brood up there on the cross talkin bout Forgive them Daddy cause they don't know what they doin. And my Mama say Get on down from there you big fool, whatcha think this is, playtime? And my Daddy yellin to Granddaddy to get him a ladder cause Big Brood actin the fool, his mother side of the family showin up. And my mama and her sister Daisy jumpin on them Romans beatin them with they pocketbooks. And Hunca Bubba tellin them folks on they knees they better get out the way and go get some help or they goin to get trampled on. And Granddaddy Vale sayin Leave the boy alone, if that's what he wants to do with his life we ain't got nothin to say about it. Then Aunt Daisy givin him a taste of that pocketbook, fussin bout what a damn fool old man Granddaddy is. Then everybody jumpin in his chest like the time Uncle Clayton went in the Army and come back with only one leg and Granddaddy say somethin stupid about that's life. And by this time Big Brood off the cross and in the park playin handball or skully or somethin. And the family in the kitchen throwin dishes at each other, screamin bout if you hadn't done this I wouldn't had to do that. And me in the parlor trying to do my arithmetic yellin Shut if off.

Which is what I was yellin all by myself which make me a sittin target for Thunderbuns. But when I yell We want our money back, that gets everybody in chorus. And the movie windin up with this heavenly cloud music and the smart-ass up there in his hole in the wall turns up the sound again to drown us out. Then there comes Bugs Bunny which we already seen so we know we been had. No gorilla my nuthin. And Big Brood say Awwww sheeet, we goin to see the manager and get our money back. And I know from this we business. So I brush the potato chips out of my hair which is where Baby Jason like to put em, and I march myself up the aisle to deal with the manager who is a crook in the first place for lying out there sayin *Gorilla, My Love* playin. And I never did like the man cause he oily and pasty at the same time like the bad guy in the serial, the one that got a hideout behind a push-button bookcase and play 'Moonlight Sonata' with gloves on. I knock on the door and I am furious. And I am alone, too. Cause Big Brood suddenly got to go so bad even though my mama told us bout goin in them nasty bathrooms. And I hear him sigh like he disgusted when he get to the door and see only a little kid there. And now I'm really furious cause I get so tired grownups messin over kids just cause they little and can't take em to court. What is it, he say to me like I lost my mittens or wet on myself or am somebody's retarded child. When in reality I am the smartest kid P.S. 186 ever had in its whole lifetime and you can ax anybody. Even them teachers that don't like me cause I won't sing them Southern songs or back off when they tell me my questions are out of order. And cause my Mama come up there in a minute when them teachers start playin the dozens behind colored folks. She stalk in with her hat pulled down bad and that Persian lamb coat draped back over one hip on account of she got her fist planted there so she can talk that talk which gets us all hypnotized, and teacher be comin undone cause she know this could be her job and her behind cause Mama got pull with the Board and bad by her own self anyhow.

So I kick the door open wider and just walk right by him and sit down and tell the man about himself and that I want my money back and that goes for Baby Jason and Big Brood too. And he still trying to shuffle me out the door even though I'm sittin which shows him for the fool he is. Just like them teachers do fore they realize Mama like a stone on that spot and ain't backin up. So he ain't gettin up off the money. So I was forced to leave, takin the matches from under his ashtray, and set a fire under the candy stand, which closed the raggedy ole Washington down for a week. My Daddy had the suspect it was me cause Big Brood got a big mouth. But I explained right quick what the whole thing was about and I figured it was even-steven. Cause if you say Gorilla, My Love, you suppose to mean it. Just like when you say you goin to give me a party on my birthday, you gotta mean it. And if you say me and Baby Jason can go South pecan haulin with Granddaddy Vale, you better not be comin up with no stuff about the weather look uncertain or did you mop the bathroom or any other trickified business. I mean even gangsters in the movies say My word is my bond. So don't nobody get away with nothing far as I'm concerned. So Daddy put his belt back on. Cause that's the way I was raised. Like my Mama say in one of them situations when I won't back down, Okay Badbird, you right. Your point is well-taken. Not that Badbird my name, just what she say when she tired arguin and know I'm right. And Aunt Jo, who is the hardest head in the family and worse even than Aunt Daisy, she say, You absolutely right Miss Muffin, which also ain't my real name but the name she gave me one time when I got some medicine shot in my behind and wouldn't get up off her pillows for nothin. And even Granddaddy Vale – who got no memory to speak of, so sometime you can just plain lie to him, if you want to be like that – he say, Well if that's what I said, then that's it. But this name business was different they said. It wasn't like Hunca Bubba had gone back on his word or anything. Just that he was thinkin about gettin married and was usin his real name now. Which ain't the way I saw it at all.

So there I am in the navigator seat. And I turn to him and just plain ole ax him. I mean I come right on out with it. No sense goin all around that barn the old folks talk about. And like my mama say, Hazel – which is my real name and what she remembers to call me when she bein serious – when you got somethin on your mind, speak up and let the chips fall where they may. And if anybody don't like it, tell em to come see your mama. And Daddy look up from the paper and say, You hear your mama good, Hazel. And tell em to come see me first. Like that. That's how I was raised.

So I turn clear round in the navigator seat and say, 'Look here, Hunca Bubba or Jefferson Windsong Vale or whatever your name is, you gonna marry this girl?'

'Sure am,' he say, all grins.

And I say, 'Member that time you was baby-sittin me when we lived at four-o-nine and there was this big snow and Mama and Daddy got held up in the country so you had to stay for two days?'

And he say, 'Sure do.'

'Well. You remember how you told me I was the cutest thing that ever walked the earth?'

'Oh, you were real cute when you were little,' he say, which is suppose to be funny. I am not laughin.

'Well. You remember what you said?'

And Grandaddy Vale squintin over the wheel and axin Which way, Scout. But Scout is busy and don't care if we all get lost for days.

'Watcha mean, Peaches?'

'My name is Hazel. And what I mean is you said you were going to marry *me* when I grew up. You were going to wait. That's what I mean, my dear Uncle Jefferson.' And he don't say nuthin. Just look at me real strange like he never saw me before in life. Like he lost in some weird town in the middle of night and lookin for directions and there's no one to ask. Like it was me that messed up the maps and turned the road posts round. 'Well, you said it, didn't you?' And Baby Jason lookin back and forth like we playin ping-pong. Only I ain't playin. I'm hurtin and I can hear that I am screamin. And Grandaddy Vale mumblin how we never gonna get to where we goin if I don't turn around and take my navigator job serious.

'Well, for cryin out loud, Hazel, you just a little girl. And I was just teasin.'

' "And I was just teasin," ' I say back just how he said it so he can hear what a terrible thing it is. Then I don't say nuthin. And he don't say nuthin. And Baby Jason don't say nuthin nohow. Then Granddaddy Vales speak up. 'Look here, Precious, it was Hunca Bubba what told you them things. This here, Jefferson Winston Vale.' And Hunca Bubba say, 'That's right. That was somebody else. I'm a new somebody.'

'You a lyin dawg,' I say, when I meant to say treacherous dog, but just couldn't get hold of the word. It slipped away from me. And I'm crying and crumplin down in the seat and just don't care. And Granddaddy say to hush and steps on the gas. And I'm losin my bearins and don't even know where to look on the map cause I can't see for cryin. And Baby Jason cryin too. Cause he is my blood brother and understands that we must stick together or be forever lost, what with grownups playing change-up and turnin you round every which way so bad. And don't even say they sorry.

Charles Baxter
Gryphon

On Wednesday afternoon, between the geography lesson on ancient Egypt's hand-operated irrigation system and an art project that involved drawing a model city next to a mountain, our fourth-grade teacher, Mr Hibler, developed a cough. This cough began with a series of muffled throat clearings and progressed to propulsive noises contained within Mr Hibler's closed mouth. 'Listen to him,' Carol Peterson whispered to me. 'He's gonna blow up.' Mr Hibler's laughter – dazed and infrequent – sounded a bit like his cough, but as we worked on our model cities we would look up, thinking he was enjoying a joke, and see Mr Hibler's face turning red, his cheeks puffed out. This was not laughter. Twice he bent over, and his loose tie, like a plumb line, hung down straight from his neck as he exploded himself into a Kleenex. He would excuse himself, then go on coughing. 'I'll bet you a dime,' Carol Peterson whispered, 'we get a substitute tomorrow.'

Carol sat at the desk in front of mine and was a bad person – when she thought no one was looking she would blow her nose on notebook paper, then crumble it up and throw it into the wastebasket – but at times of crisis she spoke the truth. I knew I'd lose the dime.

'No deal,' I said.

When Mr Hibler stood us up in formation at the door just prior to the final bell, he was almost incapable of speech. 'I'm sorry, boys and girls,' he said. 'I seem to be coming down with something.'

'I hope you feel better tomorrow, Mr Hibler,' Bobby Kryzanowicz, the faultless brown-noser said, and I heard Carol Peterson's evil giggle. Then Mr Hibler opened the door and we walked out to the buses, a clique of us starting noisily to hawk and cough as soon as we thought we were a few feet beyond Mr Hibler's earshot.

Five Oaks being a rural community, and in Michigan, the supply of substitute teachers was limited to the town's unemployed community college graduates, a pool of about four mothers. These ladies fluttered, provided easeful class days, and nervously covered material we had mastered weeks earlier. Therefore it was a surprise when a woman we had never seen came into the class the next day, carrying a purple purse, a checkerboard lunchbox and a few books. She put the books on one side of Mr Hibler's desk and the lunchbox on the other, next to the Voice of Music phonograph. Three of us in the back of the room were playing with Heever, the chameleon that lived in the terrarium and on one of the plastic drapes, when she walked in.

She clapped her hands at us. 'Little boys,' she said, 'why are you bent over together like that?' She didn't wait for us to answer. 'Are you tormenting an animal? Put it back. Please sit down at your desks. I want no cabals this time of the day.' We just stared at her. 'Boys,' she repeated, 'I asked you to sit down.'

I put the chameleon in his terrarium and felt my way to my desk, never taking my eyes off the woman. With white and green chalk, she had started to draw a tree on the left side of the blackboard. She didn't look usual. Furthermore, her tree was outsized, disproportionate, for some reason.

'This room needs a tree,' she said, with one line drawing the suggestion of a leaf. 'A large, leafy, shady, deciduous . . . oak.'

Her fine, light hair had been done up in what I would learn years later was called a chignon, and she wore gold-rimmed glasses whose lenses seemed to have the faintest blue tint. Harold Knardahl, who sat across from me, whispered 'Mars', and I nodded slowly, savoring the imminent weirdness of the day. The substitute drew another branch with an extravagant arm gesture, then turned around and said, 'Good morning. I don't believe I said good morning to all you yet.'

Facing us, she was no special age – an adult is an adult – but her face had two prominent lines, descending vertically from the sides of her mouth to her chin. I knew where I had seen those lines before: *Pinocchio*. They were marionette lines. 'You may stare at me,' she said to us, as a few more kids from the last bus came into the room, their eyes fixed on her, 'for a few more seconds, until the bell rings. Then I will permit no more staring. Looking I will permit. Staring, no. It is impolite to stare, and a sign of bad breeding. You cannot make a social effort while staring.'

Harold Knardahl did not glance at me, or nudge, but I heard him whisper 'Mars' again, trying to get more mileage out of his single joke with the kids who had just come in.

When everyone was seated, the substitute teacher finished her tree, put down her chalk fastidiously on the phonograph, brushed her hands, and faced us. 'Good morning,' she said. 'I am Miss Ferenczi, your teacher for the day. I am fairly new to your community, and I don't believe any of you know me. I will therefore start by telling you a story about myself.'

While we settled back, she launched into her tale. She said her grandfather had been a Hungarian prince; her mother had been born in some place called Flanders, had been a pianist, and had played concerts for people Miss Ferenczi referred to as 'crowned heads'. She gave us a knowing look. 'Grieg,' she said, 'the Norwegian master, wrote a concerto for piano that was,' she paused, 'my mother's triumph at her debut concert in London.' Her eyes searched the ceiling. Our eyes followed. Nothing up there but ceiling tile. 'For reasons that I shall not go into, my family's fortunes took us to Detroit, then north to dreadful Saginaw, and now here I am in Five Oaks, as your substitute teacher, for today, Thursday, October the eleventh. I believe it will be a good day: all the forecasts coincide. We shall start with your reading lesson. Take out your reading book. I believe it is called *Broad Horizons*, or something along those lines.'

Jeannie Vermeesch raised her hand. Miss Ferenczi nodded at her. 'Mr Hibler always starts the day with the Pledge of Allegiance,' Jeannie whined.

'Oh, does he? In that case,' Miss Ferenczi said, 'you must know it *very* well by now, and we certainly need not spend our time on it. No, no allegiance pledging on the premises today, by my reckoning. Not with so much sunlight coming into the room. A pledge does not suit my mood.' She glanced at her watch. 'Time *is* flying. Take out *Broad Horizons*.'

She disappointed us by giving us an ordinary lesson, complete with vocabulary word drills, comprehension questions and recitation. She didn't seem to care for the material, however. She sighed every few minutes and rubbed her glasses with a frilly perfumed handkerchief that she withdrew, magician style, from her left sleeve.

After reading we moved on to arithmetic. It was my favorite time of the morning, when the lazy autumn sunlight dazzled its way through ribbons of clouds past the windows on the east side of the classroom, and crept across the linoleum floor. On the playground the first group of children, the kindergartners, were running on the quack grass just beyond the monkey bars. We were doing multiplication tables. Miss Ferenczi had made John Wazny stand up at his desk in the front row. He was supposed to go through the tables of six. From where I was sitting, I could smell the Vitalis soaked into John's plastered hair. He was doing fine until he came to six times eleven and six times twelve. 'Six times eleven,' he said, 'is sixty-eight. Six times twelve is . . .' He put his fingers to his head, quickly and secretly sniffed his fingertips, and said, 'seventy-two.' Then he sat down.

'Fine,' Miss Ferenczi said. 'Well now. That was very good.'

'Miss Ferenczi!' One of the Eddy twins was waving her hand desperately in the air. 'Miss Ferenczi! Miss Ferenczi!'

'Yes?'

'John said that six times eleven is sixty-eight and you said he was right!'

'*Did* I?' She gazed at the class with a jolly look breaking across her marionette's face. 'Did I say that? Well, what *is* six times eleven?'

'It's sixty-six!'

She nodded. 'Yes. So it is. But, and I know some people will not entirely agree with me, at some times it is sixty-eight.'

'When? When is it sixty-eight?'

We were all waiting.

'In higher mathematics, which you children do not yet understand, six times eleven can be considered to be sixty-eight.' She laughed through her nose. 'In higher mathematics numbers are . . . more fluid. The only thing a number does is contain a certain amount of something. Think of water. A cup is not the only way to measure a certain amount of water, is it?' We were staring, shaking our heads. 'You could use saucepans or thimbles. In either case, the water *would be the same.* Perhaps,' she started again, 'it would be better for you to think that six times eleven is sixty-eight only when I am in the room.'

'Why is it sixty-eight,' Mark Poole asked, 'when you're in the room?'

'Because it's more interesting that way,' she said, smiling very rapidly behind her blue-tinted glasses. 'Besides, I'm your substitute teacher, am I not?' We all nodded. 'Well, then, think of six times eleven equals sixty-eight as a substitute fact.'

'A substitute fact?'

'Yes.' Then she looked at us carefully. 'Do you think,' she asked, 'that anyone is going to be hurt by a substitute fact?'

We looked back at her.

'Will the plants on the windowsill be hurt?' We glanced at them. There were sensitive plants thriving in a green plastic tray, and several wilted ferns in small clay pots. 'Your dogs and cats, or your moms and dads?' She waited. 'So,' she concluded, 'what's the problem?'

'But it's wrong,' Janice Weber said, 'isn't it?'

'What's your name, young lady?'

'Janice Weber.'

'And you think it's wrong, Janice?'

'I was just asking.'

'Well, all right. You were just asking. I think we've spent enough time on this matter by now, don't you class? You are free to think what you like. When your teacher, Mr Hibler, returns, six times eleven will be sixty-six again, you can rest assured. And it will be that for the rest of your lives in Five Oaks. Too bad, eh?' She raised her eyebrows and glinted herself at us. 'But for now, it wasn't. So much for that. Let us go to your assigned problems for today, as painstakingly outlined, I see, in Mr Hibler's lesson plan. Take out a sheet of paper and write your names in the upper left-hand corner.'

For the next half hour we did the rest of our arithmetic problems. We handed them in and went on to spelling, my worst subject. Spelling always came before lunch. We were taking spelling dictation and looking at the clock. 'Thorough,' Miss Ferenczi said. 'Boundary.' She walked in the aisles between the desks, holding the spelling book open and looking down at our papers. 'Balcony.' I clutched my pencil. Somehow, the way she said those words, they seemed foreign, Hungarian, mis-voweled and mis-consonanted. I stared down at what I had spelled. *Balconie*. I turned my pencil upside down and erased my mistake. *Balconey*. That looked better, but still incorrect. I cursed the world of spelling and tried erasing it again and saw the paper beginning to wear away. *Balkony*. Suddenly I felt a hand on my shoulder.

'I don't like that word either,' Miss Ferenczi whispered, bent over, her mouth near my ear. 'It's ugly. My feeling is, if you don't like a word, you don't have to use it.' She straightened up, leaving behind a slight odor of Clorets.

At lunchtime we went out to get our trays of sloppy joes, peaches in heavy syrup, coconut cookies and milk, and brought them back to the classroom, where Miss Ferenczi was sitting at the desk, eating a brown sticky thing she had unwrapped from tightly rubber-banded wax paper. 'Miss Ferenczi,' I said, raising my hand. 'You don't have to eat with us. You can eat with the other teachers. There's a teacher's lounge,' I ended up, 'next to the principal's office.'

'No, thank you,' she said. 'I prefer it here.'

'We've got a room monitor,' I said. 'Mrs Eddy.' I pointed to where Mrs Eddy, Joyce and Judy's mother, sat silently at the back of the room, doing her knitting.

'That's fine,' Miss Ferenczi said. 'But I shall continue to eat here, with you children, I prefer it,' she repeated.

'How come?' Wayne Razmer asked without raising his hand.

'I talked with the other teachers before class this morning,' Miss Ferenczi said, biting into her brown food. 'There was a great rattling of the words for the fewness of ideas. I didn't care for their brand of hilarity. I don't like ditto machine jokes.'

'Oh,' Wayne said.

'What's that you're eating?' Maxine Sylvester asked, twitching her nose. 'Is it food?'

'It most certainly *is* food. It's a stuffed fig. I had to drive almost down to Detroit to get it. I also bought some smoked sturgeon. And this,' she said, lifting some green leaves out of her lunchbox, 'is raw spinach, cleaned this morning before I came out here to the Garfield-Murry school.'

'Why're you eating raw spinach?' Maxine asked.

'It's good for you,' Miss Ferenczi said. 'More stimulating than soda pop or smelling salts.' I bit into my sloppy joe and stared blankly out the window. An almost invisible moon was faintly silvered in the daytime autumn sky. 'As far as food is concerned,' Miss Ferenczi was saying, 'you have to shuffle the pack. Mix it up. Too many people eat . . . well, never mind.'

'Miss Ferenczi,' Carol Peterson said, 'what are we going to do this afternoon?'

'Well,' she said, looking down at Mr Hibler's lesson plan, 'I see that your teacher, Mr Hibler, has you scheduled for a unit on the Egyptians.' Carol groaned. 'Yessss,' Miss Ferenczi continued, 'that is what we will do: the Egyptians. A remarkable people. Almost as remarkable as the Americans. But not quite.' She lowered her head, did her quick smile, and went back to eating her spinach.

After noon recess we came back into the classroom and saw that Miss Ferenczi had drawn a pyramid on the blackboard, close to her oak tree. Some of us who had been playing baseball were messing around in the back of the room, dropping the bats and the gloves into the playground box, and I think that Ray Schontzeler had just slugged me when I heard Miss Ferenczi's high-pitched voice quavering with emotion. 'Boys,' she said, 'come to order right this minute and take your seats. I do not wish to waste a minute of class time. Take out your geography books.' We trudged to our desks and, still sweating, pulled out *Distant Lands and Their People*. 'Turn to page forty-two.' She waited for thirty seconds then looked over at Kelly Munger. 'Young man,' she said, 'why are you still fossicking in your desk?'

Kelly looked as if his foot had been stepped on. 'Why am I what?'

'Why are you . . . burrowing in your desk like that?'

'I'm lookin' for the book, Miss Ferenczi.'

Bobby Kryzanowicz, the faultless brown-noser who sat in the first row by choice, softly said, 'His name is Kelly Munger. He can't ever find his stuff. He always does that.'

'I don't care what his name is, especially after lunch.' Miss Ferenczi said. '*Where is your book?*'

'I just found it.' Kelly was peering into his desk and with both hands pulled at the book, shoveling along in front of it several pencils and crayons, which fell into his lap and then to the floor.

'I hate a mess,' Miss Ferenczi said. 'I hate a mess in a desk or a mind. It's . . . unsanitary. You wouldn't want your house at home to look like your desk at school, now, would you?' She didn't wait for an answer. 'I should think not. A house at home should be as neat as human hands can make it. What were we talking about? Egypt. Page forty-two. I note from Mr Hibler's lesson plan that you have been discussing the modes of Egyptian irrigation. Interesting, in my view, but not so interesting as what we are about to cover. The pyramids and Egyptian slave labor. A plus on one side, a minus on the other.' We had our books open to page forty-two, where there was a picture of a pyramid, but Miss Ferenczi wasn't looking at the book. Instead, she was staring at some object just outside the window.

'Pyramids,' Miss Ferenczi said, still looking past the window. 'I want you to think about the pyramids. And what was inside. The bodies of the pharaohs, of course, and their attendant treasures. Scrolls. Perhaps,' Miss Ferenczi said, with something gleeful but unsmiling in her face, 'these scrolls were novels for the pharaohs, helping them to pass the time in their long voyage through the centuries. But then, I am joking.' I was looking at the lines on Miss Ferenczi's face. 'Pyramids,' Miss Ferenczi went on, 'were the repositories of special cosmic powers. The nature of a pyramid is to guide cosmic energy forces into a concentrated point. The Egyptians knew that; we have generally forgotten it. Did you know,' she asked, walking to the side of the room so that she was standing by the coat closet, 'that George Washington had Egyptian blood, from his grandmother? Certain features of the Constitution of the United States are notable for their Egyptian ideas.'

Without glancing down at the book, she began to talk about the movement of souls in Egyptian religion. She said that when people die, their souls return to Earth in the form of carpenter ants or walnut trees, depending on how they behaved – 'well or ill' – in life. She said that the Egyptians believed that people act the way they do because of magnetism produced by tidal forces in the solar system, forces produced by the sun and by its 'planetary ally', Jupiter. Jupiter, she said, was a planet, as we had been told, but had 'certain properties of stars'. She was speaking very fast. She said that the Egyptians were great explorers and conquerors. She said that the greatest of all the conquerors, Genghis Khan, had had forty horses and forty young women killed on the site of his grave. We listened. No one tried to stop her. 'I myself have been in Egypt,' she said, 'and have witnessed much dust and many brutalities.' She said that an old man in Egypt who worked for a circus had personally shown her an animal in a cage, a monster, half bird and half lion. She said that this monster was called a gryphon and that she had heard about them but never seen them until she traveled to the outskirts of Cairo. She said that Egyptian astronomers had discovered the planet Saturn, but had not seen its rings. She said that the Egyptians were the first to discover that dogs, when they are ill, will not drink from rivers, but wait for rain, and hold their jaws open to catch it.

'She lies.'

We were on the school bus home. I was sitting next to Carl Whiteside, who had bad breath and a huge collection of marbles. We were arguing. Carl thought she was lying. I said she wasn't, probably.

'I didn't believe that stuff about the bird,' Carl said, 'and what she told us about the pyramids? I didn't believe that either. She didn't know what she was talking about.'

'Oh yeah?' I had liked her. She was strange. I thought I could nail him. 'If she was lying,' I said, 'what'd she say that was a lie?'

'Six times eleven isn't sixty-eight. It isn't ever. It's sixty-six, I know for a fact.'

'She said so. She admitted it. What else did she lie about?'

'I don't know,' he said. 'Stuff.'

'What stuff?'

'Well.' He swung his legs back and forth. 'You ever see an animal that was half lion and half bird?' He crossed his arms. 'It sounded real fakey to me.'

'It could happen,' I said. I had to improvise, to outrage him. 'I read in this newspaper my mom bought in the IGA about this scientist, this mad scientist in the Swiss Alps, and he's been putting genes and chromosomes and stuff together in test tubes, and he combined a human being and a hamster.' I waited, for effect. 'It's called a humster.'

'You never.' Carl was staring at me, his mouth open, his terrible bad breath making its way toward me. 'What newspaper was it?'

'The *National Enquirer*,' I said, 'that they sell next to the cash registers.' When I saw his look of recognition, I knew I had bested him. 'And this mad scientist,' I said, 'his name was, um, Dr Frankenbush.' I realized belatedly that this name was a mistake and waited for Carl to notice its resemblance to the name of the other famous mad master of permutations, but he only sat there.

'A man and a hamster?' He was staring at me, squinting, his mouth opening in distaste. 'Jeez. What'd it look like?'

When the bus reached my stop, I took off down our dirt road and ran up through the back yard, kicking the tire swing for good luck. I dropped my books on the back steps so I could hug and kiss our dog, Mr Selby. Then I hurried inside. I could smell Brussels sprouts cooking, my unfavorite vegetable. My mother was washing other vegetables in the kitchen sink, and my baby brother was hollering in his yellow playpen on the kitchen floor.

'Hi, Mom,' I said, hopping around the playpen to kiss her. 'Guess what?'

'I have no idea.'

'We had this substitute today, Miss Ferenczi, and I'd never seen her before, and she had all these stories and ideas and stuff.'

'Well. That's good.' My mother looked out the window behind the sink, her eyes on the pine woods west of our house. Her face and hairstyle always reminded other people of Betty Crocker, whose picture was framed inside a gigantic spoon on the side of the Bisquick box; to me, though, my mother's face just looked white. 'Listen, Tommy,' she said, 'go upstairs and pick your clothes off the bathroom floor, then go outside to the shed and put the shovel and ax away that your father left outside this morning.'

'She said that six times eleven was sometimes sixty-eight!' I said. 'And she said she once saw a monster that was half lion and half bird.' I waited. 'In Egypt, she said.'

'Did you hear me?' my mother asked, raising her arm to wipe her forehead with the back of her hand. 'You have chores to do.'

'I know,' I said. 'I was just telling you about the substitute.'

'It's very interesting,' my mother said, quickly glancing down at me, 'and we can talk about it later when your father gets home. But right now you have some work to do.'

'OK, Mom.' I took a cookie out of the jar on the counter and was about to go outside when I had a thought. I ran into the living-room, pulled out a dictionary next to the TV stand, and opened it to the Gs. *Gryphon*: 'variant of griffin'. *Griffin*: 'a fabulous beast with the head and wings of an eagle and the body of a lion'. Fabulous was right. I shouted with triumph and ran outside to put my father's tools back in their place.

Miss Ferenczi was back the next day, slightly altered. She had pulled her hair down and twisted it into pigtails, with red rubber bands holding them tight one inch from the ends. She was wearing a green blouse and pink scarf, making her difficult to look at for a full class day. This time there was no pretense of doing a reading lesson or moving on to arithmetic. As soon as the bell rang, she simply began to talk.

She talked for forty minutes straight. There seemed to be less connection between her ideas, but the ideas themselves were, as the dictionary would say, fabulous. She said she had heard of a huge jewel, in what she called the Antipodes, that was so brilliant that when the light shone into it at a certain angle it would blind whoever was looking at its center. She said that the biggest diamond in the world was cursed and had killed everyone who owned it, and that by a trick of fate it was called the Hope diamond. Diamonds are magic, she said, and this is why women wear them on their fingers, as a sign of the magic of womanhood. Men have strength, Miss Ferenczi said, but no true magic. That is why men fall in love with women but women do not fall in love with men: they just love being loved. George Washington had died because of a mistake he made about a diamond. Washington was not the first *true* President, but she did not say who was. In some places in the world, she said, men and women still live in trees and eat monkeys for breakfast. Their doctors are magicians. At the bottom of the sea are creatures thin as pancakes which have never been studied by scientists because when you take them up to the air, the fish explode.

There was not a sound in the classroom, except for Miss Ferenczi's voice, and Donna DeShano's coughing. No one even went to the bathroom.

Beethoven, she said, had not been deaf; it was a trick to make himself famous, and it worked. As she talked, Miss Ferenczi's pigtails swung back and forth. There are trees in the world, she said, that eat meat: their leaves are sticky and close up on bugs like hands. She lifted her hands and brought them together, palm to palm. Venus, which most people think is the next closest planet to the sun, is not always closer, and, besides, it is the planet of greatest mystery because of its thick cloud cover. 'I know what lies underneath those clouds,' Miss Ferenczi said, and waited. After the silence, she said, 'Angels. Angels live under those clouds.' She said that angels were not invisible to everyone and were in fact smarter than most people. They did not dress in robes as was often claimed but instead wore formal evening clothes, as if they were about to attend a concert. Often angels *do* attend concerts and sit in the aisles where, she said, most people pay no attention to them. She said the most terrible angel had the shape of the Sphinx. 'There is no running away from that one,' she said. She said that unquenchable fires burn just under the surface of the earth in Ohio, and that the baby Mozart fainted dead away in his cradle when he first heard the sound of a trumpet. She said that someone named Narzim al Harrardim was the greatest writer who ever lived. She said that planets control behavior, and anyone conceived during a solar eclipse would be born with webbed feet.

'I know you children like to hear these things,' she said, 'these secrets, and that is why I am telling you all this.' We nodded. It was better than doing comprehension questions for the readings in *Broad Horizons*.

'I will tell you one more story,' she said, 'and then we will have to do arithmetic.' She leaned over, and her voice grew soft. 'There is no death,' she said. 'You must never be afraid. Never. That which is, cannot die. It will change into different earthly and unearthly elements, but I know this as sure as I stand here in front of you, and I swear it: you must not be afraid. I have seen this truth with these eyes. I know it because in a dream God kissed me. Here.' And she pointed with her right index finger to the side of her head, below the mouth, where the vertical lines were carved into her skin.

Absent-mindedly we all did our arithmetic problems. At recess the class was out on the playground, but no one was playing. We were all standing in small groups, talking about Miss Ferenczi. We didn't know if she was crazy, or what. I looked out beyond the playground, at the rusted cars piled in a small heap behind a clump of sumac, and I wanted to see shapes there, approaching me.

On the way home, Carl sat next to me again. He didn't say much, and I didn't either. At last he turned to me. 'You know what she said about the leaves that close up on bugs?'
    'Huh?'
    'The leaves,' Carl insisted. 'The meat-eating plants. I know it's true. I saw it on television. The leaves have this icky glue that the plants have got smeared all over them and the insects can't get off 'cause they're stuck. I saw it.' He seemed demoralized. 'She's tellin' the truth.'
    'Yeah.'
    'You think she's seen all those angels?'
    I shrugged.
    'I don't think she has,' Carl informed me. 'I think she made that part up.'
    'There's a tree,' I suddenly said. I was looking out the window at the farms along County Road H. I knew every barn, every broken windmill, every fence, every anhydrous ammonia tank, by heart. 'There's a tree that's . . . that I've seen . . .'
    'Don't you try to do it,' Carl said. 'You'll just sound like a jerk.'

I kissed my mother. She was standing in front of the stove. 'How was your day?' she asked.
    'Fine.'
    'Did you have Miss Ferenczi again?'
    'Yeah.'
    'Well.'

'She was fine. Mom,' I asked, 'can I go go my room?'

'No,' she said, 'not until you've gone out to the vegetable garden and picked me a few tomatoes.' She glanced at the sky. 'I think it's going to rain. Skedaddle and do it now. Then you come back inside and watch your brother for a few minutes while I go upstairs. I need to clean up before dinner.' She looked down at me. 'You're looking a little pale, Tommy.' She touched the back of her hand to my forehead and I felt her diamond ring against my skin. 'Do you feel all right?'

'I'm fine,' I said, and went out to pick the tomatoes.

Coughing mutedly, Mr Hibler was back the next day, slipping lozenges into his mouth when his back was turned at forty-five-minute intervals and asking us how much of the prepared lesson plan Miss Ferenczi had followed. Edith Atwater took the responsibility for the class of explaining to Mr Hibler that the substitute hadn't always done exactly what he would have done, but we had worked hard even though she talked a lot. About what? he asked. All kinds of things, Edith said. I sort of forgot. To our relief, Mr Hibler seemed not at all interested in what Miss Ferenczi had said to fill the day. He probably thought it was woman's talk; unserious and not suited for school. It was enough that he had a pile of arithmetic problems from us to correct.

For the next month, the sumac turned a distracting red in the field, and the sun traveled toward the southern sky, so that its rays reached Mr Hibler's Hallowe'en display on the bulletin board in the back of the room, fading the scarecrow with a pumpkin head from orange to tan. Every three days I measured how much farther the sun had moved toward the southern horizon by making small marks with my black Crayola on the north wall, ant-sized marks only I knew were there, inching west.

And then in early December, four days after the first permanent snowfall, she appeared again in our classroom. The minute she came in the door, I felt my heart begin to pound. Once again, she was different: this time, her hair hung straight down and seemed hardly to have been combed. She hadn't brought her lunchbox with her, but she was carrying what seemed to be a small box. She greeted all of us and talked about the weather. Donna DeShano had to remind her to take her overcoat off.

When the bell to start the day finally rang, Miss Ferenczi looked out at all of us and said, 'Children, I have enjoyed your company in the past, and today I am going to reward you.' She held up the small box. 'Do you know what this is?' She waited. 'Of course you don't. It is a tarot pack.'

Edith Atwater raised her hand. 'What's a tarot pack, Miss Ferenczi?'

'It is used to tell fortunes,' she said. 'And this is what I shall do this morning. I shall tell your fortunes, as I have been taught to do.'

'What's fortune?' Bobby Kryzanowicz asked.

'The future, young man. I shall tell you what your future will be. I can't do your whole future, of course. I shall have to limit myself to the five-card system, the wands, cups, swords, pentacles, and the higher arcanes. Now who wants to be first?'

There was a long silence. Then Carol Peterson raised her hand.

'All right,' Miss Ferenczi said. She divided the pack into five smaller packs and walked back to Carol's desk, in front of mine. 'Pick one card from each of these packs,' she said. I saw that Carol had a four of cups, a six of swords, but I couldn't see the other cards. Miss Ferenczi studied the cards on Carol's desk for a minute. 'Not bad,' she said. 'I do not see much higher education. Probably an early marriage. Many children. There's something bleak and dreary here, but I can't tell what. Perhaps just the tasks of a housewife life. I think you'll do very well, for the most part.' She smiled at Carol, a smile with a certain lack of interest. 'Who wants to be next?'

Carl Whiteside raised his hand slowly.

'Yes,' Miss Ferenczi said, 'let's do a boy.' She walked over to where Carl sat. After he picked his five cards, she gazed at them for a long time. 'Travel,' she said. 'Much distant travel. You might go into the Army. Not too much romantic interest here. A late marriage, if at all. Squabbles. But the Sun is in your major arcana, here, yes, that's a very good card.' She giggled. 'Maybe a good life.'

Next I raised my hand, and she told me my future. She did the same with Bobby Kryzanowicz, Kelly Munger, Edith Atwater and Kim Foor. Then she came to Wayne Razmer. He picked his five cards, and I could see that the Death card was one of them.

'What's your name?' Miss Ferenczi asked.

'Wayne.'

'Well, Wayne,' she said, you will undergo a *great* metamorphosis, the greatest, before you become an adult. Your earthly element will leap away, into thin air, you sweet boy. This card, this nine of swords here, tells of suffering and desolation. And this ten of wands, well, that's certainly a heavy load.'

'What about this one?' Wayne pointed to the Death card.

'That one? That one means you will die soon, my dear.' She gathered up the cards. We were all looking at Wayne. 'But do not fear,' she said. 'It's not really death, so much as change.' She put the cards on Mr Hibler's desk. 'And now, let's do some arithmetic.'

At lunchtime Wayne went to Mr Faegre, the principal, and told him what Miss Ferenczi had done. During the noon recess, we saw Miss Ferenczi drive out of the parking lot in her green Rambler. I stood under the slide, listening to the other kids coasting down and landing in the little depressive bowl at the bottom. I was kicking stones and tugging at my hair right up to the moment when I saw Wayne come out to the playground. He smiled, the dead fool, and with the fingers of his right hand he was showing everyone how he had told on Miss Ferenczi.

I made my way toward Wayne, pushing myself past two girls from another class. He was watching me with his little pinhead eyes.

'You told,' I shouted at him. 'She was just kidding.'

'She shouldn't have,' he shouted back. 'We were supposed to be doing arithmetic.'

'She just scared you,' I said. 'You're a chicken. You're a chicken, Wayne. You are. Scared of a little card,' I singsonged.

Wayne fell at me, his two fists hammering down on my nose. I gave him a good one in the stomach and then I tried for his head. Aiming my fist, I saw that he was crying. I slugged him.

'She was right,' I yelled. 'She was always right! She told the truth!' Other kids were whooping. 'You were just scared, that's all!'

And then large hands pulled at us, and it was my turn to speak to Mr Faegre.

In the afternoon Miss Ferenczi was gone, and my nose was stuffed with cotton clotted with blood, and my lip had swelled, and our class had been combined with Mrs Mantei's sixth-grade class for a crowded afternoon science unit on insect life in ditches and swamps. I knew where Mrs Mantei lived: she had a new house trailer just down the road from us, at the Clearwater Park. She was no mystery. Somehow she and Mr Bodine, the other fourth-grade teacher, had managed to fit forty-five desks into the room. Kelly Munger asked if Miss Ferenczi had been arrested, and Mrs Mantei said no, of course not. All that afternoon, until the buses came to pick us up, we learned about field crickets and two-striped grasshoppers, water bugs, cicadas, mosquitoes, flies and moths. We learned about insects' hard outer shell, the exoskeleton, and the usual parts of the mouth, including the labrum, mandible, maxilla and glossa. We learned about compound eyes and the four-stage metamorphosis from egg to larva to pupa to adult. We learned something, but not much, about mating. Mrs Mantei drew, very skillfully, the internal anatomy of the grasshopper on the blackboard. We learned about the dance of the honeybee, directing other bees in the hive to pollen. We found out about which insects were pests to man, and which were not. On lined white pieces of paper we made lists of insects we might actually see, then a list of insects too small to be clearly visible, such as fleas; Mrs Mantei said that our assignment would be to memorize these lists for the next day, when Mr Hibler would certainly return and test us on our knowledge.

John Bennet
Flat Creek Road

It was a new house – only four years old. There was indoor plumbing – a fact of some note on Flat Creek Road – but it didn't work. Something to do with the pump, out in the well. The stones around the well had been taken down; there was just a round hole in the ground. My mother told me horrible things about that hole, and generally I stayed away from it. One day, while Mother was in the back of the house, I decided to go sneaky-peeping – to look where I wasn't supposed to look. The well was in the front yard, a few feet from the screen porch. I got down on my belly and inched across the dirt toward the hole. Even at five, I never felt completely certain of my footing, and crawling was a way of being sure I wouldn't fall now – pre-falling. I got closer and closer to the edge. Finally, very cautiously, I stretched my neck on the ground until just the top of my head and then my eyes were over the edge. The rest of my body was an anchor flat against the dirt. I looked down, saw the water, saw the bucket awash in it. That's all there was to that particular sneaky-peeping.

Because of the broken pump, my family needed the bucket to get the water into the house. To flush the toilet you had to pour a bucket of water into it, and somebody had to go outside and draw the water. I don't remember how we took baths. Hauling up the bucket wasn't easy. Mother did most of it. 'I work like a *horse*, Teddy,' she'd say to me. 'Oh, Lord.' Stuff like that. She seemed resigned to days of drawing water from a well. She had been the salutatorian at one of the largest high schools in Dallas. Class of '29. Her family, modestly respectable, had owned its own house. She played the lead and spoke French in the French Club play. Then she married a man who would turn out to be a drunk. There was more to him than that, but that was the gist of it. The Depression ruined all their plans. Then an uncle left her six unusable acres in East Texas, near Horace, and it was the only place they had to live. Three children and a worthless husband – not much to work with. But she was also to blame, because she didn't really seem to care. When *Gone with the Wind* was published, she told me later, she stayed up three nights in a row reading it straight through. She saw the movie, too. Scarlett said, 'As God is my witness, I'll never be hungry again.' But my mother, much as she admired that book – and she admired it more than any other – never said that, or anything like it. She'd say, 'Oh, *damn!*' or 'Pshaw!' and laugh at her own expense.

I don't know how they'd got the money to put up the new house. Some wartime windfall, I guess. My father, a construction worker, had finally begun getting jobs in various defense boomtowns – Galveston, Amarillo – and he'd be away for months at a time making fair money and sending part of it home. Before they built the house, they were living in a converted chicken house. I was born just before VJ Day, just before the new house. After the war, my father got a job doing construction work on Guam for the United States government, and was gone several years. He sent self-important letters saying his word was 'secret' and he couldn't talk about it. This amused my mother. 'You'd think he was building atom bombs over there.'

Sometimes he sent money, apparently, and sometimes he didn't. The chicken house they had moved out of reverted to chickens, and as I got older my mother collected the eggs every day and every third day would walk down Flat Creek Road to the highway with a bushel basket in her arms. She gave eggs to the A & P in exchange for groceries.

If money didn't arrive from my father, she'd say, 'People aren't much.' The same when neighbors didn't pick us up on Sunday morning to drive us to church. Or if my brother or sister let her down in some way.

Something was wrong with the way I talked. I would ask for a piece of cake, and my sister, who was fifteen, would say, 'Not take, *cake*! Say cake.'

I would say it, and my sister would tell my mother, 'He keeps saying "take" for "cake" and "turch" for "church".'

'He'll get it some of these days.'

My sister's boyfriends spent a lot of time at the house. The one I liked best was Roy. He was in his mid-twenties – a big guy who worked at the feed store in town – and he was very cheerful, always grinning in a pleasant way. He took me for a walk once. Just out into the back pasture, not far from the house. It was twilight. I guess my sister was still getting ready. He was smoking a cigarette. For some reason, I said, 'God damn it to hell.' It was probably something I'd heard my brother say. He was fourteen.

'Hold it, there,' Roy said. He became serious. 'Do you know what Hell is?'

I don't remember what I said.

'Well, you shouldn't use big words unless you know what they mean. And Hell is a big word.' He bent down and held his cigarette pointed toward me. 'Do you see the end of this cigarette?' he said. 'See how it's glowing fiery red? See how hot it is? Well, that's what Hell is like, only it's much, much bigger – bigger even than this pasture, or even the whole town of Horace. And God is up in the sky. Sometimes you can see his face in the clouds. He has a white beard. And someday you're going to die – everybody has to die – and if you're bad God will send you to Hell, where you'll burn in pain just the way the tip of this cigarette would burn you if I were to touch your stomach with it. And you won't just burn for a little while – you'll burn forever.'

Roy was ordinarily very happy-go-lucky. Other than being crazy about my sister and wanting her to marry him before she even graduated from high school, he never seemed to have much on his mind. He certainly wasn't religious. But he was serious now, and his seriousness impressed me. Today I wonder what was going on in his mind that he would talk that way to a child. Maybe somebody had once talked that way to him. Maybe he thought that by marrying my sister he would become my father, since my father was away. (This prospect thrilled me.) Maybe he was just killing time waiting for my sister.

Roy had another claim to fame. One morning I woke up and pulled open my clothes drawer in my mother's bureau and found it filled with kittens. Fiddlesticks, the mother, was with them. I yelled, 'Mama, come look!'

'Well, I'll be,' she said. 'You can keep 'em for a while.'

That afternoon, my sister took the kittens out of the bureau drawer and put them in a milk box on the screen porch. As they grew, they began to climb out of the box. Eventually, they climbed through a tear in the screen. I was always afraid one of them would fall into the well hole. My favorite was a nearly all-white kitten. My brother named her: Snow Cup. The upshot of all this is that one day when Roy came to pick up my sister and was backing his car around the side of the house one of his tires crushed Snow Cup. Because of that, my sister broke up with him. For a while, my mother would see his car going down Flat Creek Road – an out-of-the-way place for him – but he never stopped.

My mother had a thin face, but to me she seemed unusually beautiful. She was nearly forty then. She looked fifty or fifty-five. Later, relatives said she did all the aging in her life between thirty-five and forty. After that, she was so far ahead she didn't have to age anymore. She didn't seem to mind that her face was wrinkled. Her smile carried her through, I guess. When we went to church, and she was wearing her good dress, with shoulder pads, and her hair was carefully braided, she'd smile and laugh at the breakfast social after the service, but sometimes it wasn't her real smile. These socials were a big deal to her. Being with the ladies. There she didn't seem beautiful. She'd be edgy, and she'd snap at us.

One day, while I was standing on the screen porch looking at the trees down by the creek, I must have turned blue. I wasn't aware of it. My sister called for my mother to come quick.

'He looks pale,' my mother said. 'I can't see that he's blue.'

'Well, he *was* blue,' my sister said.

'Maybe he hasn't been eating. I'll get some hungry medicine at the store tomorrow.'

The next day, my mother opened a bottle of brown syrup and held out a teaspoonful for me to swallow. 'This don't taste good, but it's mighty good for you,' she said. 'It's a special medicine that'll make you hungry, so you'll have some appetite.' The medicine had a bad taste.

Flat Creek Road had a blacktop surface. In the summer you couldn't really walk on it, because the tar burned your bare feet. In other seasons, it was good and hard. Somebody from the church had dropped off an outgrown tricycle, and for a long time I rode it in the house and on the screen porch while my mother sat in the kitchen during the day. When she began to take the eggs to town, after I turned five, I suddenly had more opportunities. I would drag the tricycle across the sand – our driveway, which was fifty or sixty yards, consisted of two ruts in the sand – and set it on the edge of the road and climb on it and pedal back and forth. People driving by would stop and chew me out, and I'd promise to stay off the road, but I didn't have to keep those promises. Considering that it was a country road, cars came down it fairly fast, but they always slowed when they saw me. I got to where I could hear them way back before they came into sight.

One day, a neighbor visited and chatted with my mother awhile and said, 'I wouldn't let him play in the road if I was you.'

I was annoyed that she was telling my mother this.

Mother took my side. 'Well, he'll be starting first grade next year and catching the bus to school. He has to learn.'

She must have done a lot of chores – hauling water, tending chickens – but she didn't do them early in the morning. She had to sit and have her coffee and smoke cigarettes for a couple of hours before she was awake enough to start wondering what needed to be done. She was a nighttime farmer, and was more likely to be feeding the chickens when the sun was going down than when it was coming up. In my memory, she was always sitting in the kitchen smoking a cigarette and drinking coffee. There was an old upholstered chair there, my favorite chair of all we had – the pink fabric was torn, and the cotton stuffing could be pulled out and then pushed back in again. The chair sat right in the middle of the kitchen floor, where a table would ordinarily have been. She drank coffee all day long. Years later she told me, 'I was twenty-seven years old before I tasted my first cup of coffee. That was the first day of my life, really.'

Our house was surrounded by huge pastures that we didn't own. Some of them had been neglected and were grown over with brush. One of the neglected fields had been an orchard, and was filled with gnarled plum trees. Those trees were easy to climb, and I'd get right to the top. Once or twice, my foot got caught in a fork in the branches and I had to wait until somebody came to find me. I always had to watch out for bull nettles – a plant that was a delicacy, provided somebody older was around to cut it open for you. I was afraid of bull nettles, because every time I got near them I would fall on them and get stuck all over with needles. I also liked something called sour dock; it had a long, grooved stem that you could insert gradually into your mouth and chew on a bite at a time. It had a lot of flavor.

I began to go farther and farther from the house. The fields that weren't neglected were planted with corn or watermelons. The summer I turned five, I probably cracked open one green watermelon for every day of the summer until, in what must have been July, I found a red one. There was nothing illicit about this. There were so many watermelons in those fields that it didn't make any difference. The cornfields weren't very interesting in early summer, but they became wonderful in July. In the beginning, I had to bend over to hide in them, but by July the stalks were taller than I was, and I could walk around in the rows until I was almost dizzy, and finally emerge with no sense at all of what side of the field I was on or even where the house was.

Once when this happened, I was completely bewildered. I was so far away, so deep in the pastures, that I couldn't hear cars on the road. I needed to find the road in order to find our house. I set off in what I thought was the direction of the road. I came to a pasture I'd never seen before. A farm machine stood in the middle of it. As I bent over to step through the barbed-wire fence, I ripped my shirt. After I got clear of the fence, I could see that the farm machine was an old plow, with rusted red disks and a bicycle-type seat without upholstery – a plow meant to be dragged behind a horse, I think. It was overturned – the seat post and the hitch formed a sort of V in the air. I remember thinking, Nobody wants this plow. It could be mine. If I had a horse, I could plow with it.

I started walking again. I saw an animal on the ground – a dead fox. Ants were crawling all over its head and back. It had been dead a long time. It was just a bunch of fur, really. I thought, It looks like it's still a fox but it's not still a fox. Something strange began happening to me, and I had to stop. I sat down in the dirt. I had lost my breath. After a while, I felt better.

Now I knew where I was. I was at the lake – a lake that we passed every time we went down Flat Creek Road – but I was at the wrong end of it. The road was clear across on the other side. The lake had dozens of fingers; its shore was jagged and sometimes marshy. Getting around it took me nearly the whole afternoon. At one spot, three bamboo fishing poles were stuck in the mud at the edge of the water. The corks on their lines floated on the surface. But no one was around. In the shade of a willow was a shiny tin washtub. It was filled with water, and two fish were alive in it.

I make us sound poor, but there were niceties. We had a piano, for instance. I don't know if it was any good – it was an upright, in my sister's bedroom – but it was apparently in tune, because my sister used it for voice practice. She wanted to be an opera singer, and a woman in town who had had formal training gave her voice lessons in return for babysitting and housecleaning. At home, my sister would strike a note on the piano and sing up and down a scale.

There had once been a fancy dog in the household – a Sealyham terrier that my grandfather, a fire-truck salesman who served as judge at all the bigger Texas dog shows, had given the family years before. The dog's name was Blink, and everybody talked about it a lot, but it had run off before I was old enough to remember it.

My brother had rifles. One of them had a telescopic sight. During the summers, he worked for nearby farmers loading watermelons into trucks. When he was paid, he would go buy ammunition and stand out behind the house and shoot. He was handy with machinery.

My mother had two Hummel dolls: a boy playing a violin and a girl sitting against a truncated tree. They were on a small corner shelf in the living-room, out of my reach.

We had electricity. There was a radio in the living-room. But I also remember coal-oil lamps. Maybe there were times when the service was cut off. The smell of the oil was rich and filled the room. These lamps were always being tinkered with: the wicks needed constant attention. But the light was extraordinary. If the lamp was in a corner, the shadow of the glass made a statuesque pattern on the walls and ceiling. Other corners became dark and inviting.

Years later, in talking about this period, I asked my sister if she and my brother had realized that we were poor.

She answered, 'What do you think?'

One day, I decided to make poison. I went first to the dump. This was a large, lion-trap-size pit back beyond the chicken house. Every year, my brother would cover the hole over with dirt and dig another. As a hole became filled, its sides would erode, so that I could climb in and out. It contained mostly tin cans and broken glass, and it was blinding – reflecting an entire sky of sunshine. I was looking for a container of some kind. What I found was a huge, lidless mayonnaise jar – it must have been something meant for a diner or a school lunchroom. The neck was extremely wide. I picked the jar up and held it against my chest and climbed out of the pit. Then I looked back and saw some coffee grounds in a soggy paper bag. I went back for them and put them in the jar.

I set the jar down by the entrance to the chicken house and stepped in. This was scary. The chickens flew all around, flapping their wings and squawking. I never liked being around the chickens. I reached in amid the fluttering and grabbed two eggs for my jar.

I went into the house. 'Mama, can I have some baking soda?'

She was sitting in the chair. 'You making poison?'

'Yes.'

'There's no baking soda. It's all gone.'

I walked outside and began looking around. On the way to the creek was an old tractor shed that my brother used as a garage for his car. He had bought a shot two-seater Chevrolet for five dollars and persuaded a friend to tow it to our house. He worked on it all the time, visiting junk yards to look for parts. It had a rumble seat, which I liked to sit in, and an engine crank, which I couldn't turn. What caught my attention now was a red tin gas can. The can made a swishing noise when I tilted it. I tried to wiggle it and shake it, but it was too heavy. Pouring some of the gas – or kerosene, or coal oil, or whatever it was – into the mayonnaise jar wouldn't be easy. It must have occurred to me to put my thumb in the pouring spout of the can to get a better grip. In any case, that's what I did, and when I moved the can my thumb suddenly hurt. I tried to pull it out but couldn't, and blood seemed to be flowing upward, all over my hand.

The shed was some distance from the house. I don't know how long I shouted. Suddenly my mother was there. 'Don't pull on it!' she said. 'Let me try to get it out.' She took my hand in her fingers and pushed down on the skin at the base of my thumb and tried to work it out. The blood just got worse – the tin of the spout, which had appeared so rounded and smooth and safe, was simply curled under; the part you couldn't see was broken in jagged points. 'I can't get it,' she said. 'Hold on. Now, don't move it. Stand stock-still!'

She ran to the house and returned with some rags from under the sink and knotted them around my hand. She opened the main cap on the gas can and somehow held me and the can in such a way that the fuel spilled out on the ground. She picked me up and lifted me over her shoulder with one arm while she held the empty can with the other. She carried me out to the road and began walking toward the Tyler highway, nearly a mile away. You took the Tyler highway to get to Horace. It also led, in the opposite direction, to Tyler, but Tyler was so far away I'd never been there. She had to stop and put me down every little while. There were other houses along the road – neighbors, people we knew, including the woman who had mentioned my playing in the road – but my mother didn't stop at any of those houses. The lake shone blue.

Where Flat Creek Road met the highway that went to Horace, there was a big clay pit – a huge pit, as big as a farm, a place I'd always wanted to play in, with hard red earth and water-filled craters and mountainlike peaks and caves. An old steam shovel was parked in the pit, but you almost never saw anybody working there. On the other side of the road was Tilson's trailer park – another dreamy place for me, because the people there lived close together, in houses that could roll on wheels from town to town. Lots of children lived in the trailer park; I'd always noticed them whenever we went past on the way to church.

My mother set me down on the shoulder of the highway. 'We're going to Dr Hart's,' she said.

'Where's Dr Hart's, Mama?'

'On the Palestine highway.'

That highway, which led from Horace to the town of Palestine (pronounced Palesteen), was on the other side of Horace. We would have to walk all the way through town. (I doubt if I understood this. All I probably knew was that town was someplace most people drove to, not walked to.)

A car pulled over. It belonged to Roy, my sister's old boyfriend. 'Need some help?' he said. 'Goodness gracious! Cain't get it off? Let me drop you at the doctor's.' (As a result of this coincidence, my sister began going out with Roy again, and they went off to Oklahoma one weekend and secretly got married.)

My love for my mother was absolute. It had no qualifications; nothing was held back. I loved her for every aspect of her nature. She was mindless of discipline, so there were practically no hard feelings between us – almost none of the hard feelings that ordinarily occur between a parent and a young child. I loved her for everything: for the way she wore her clothes, the way she drew water from the well, the way she said, putting an old horse collar around her neck, 'If I'm going to *work* like a horse, I might as well *look* like one.' (Years later, someone told me that that was a line from a Ma and Pa Kettle movie; my mother had probably seen it at the Dixie, on the square in town.) I loved her for the way I could persuade her to let me do things; if I kept at something long enough, she'd always give in. The freedom she gave me was a bond of our love, not a cause for sadness. Little as I knew about other families and other lives, I was vaguely aware, even then, that this was something special between us. Other kids in other families had to mind, and had to be in the house at suppertime and had to go to bed at a certain hour every night, but I didn't have to do any of those things. It's true I carried in my head a picture of a large house in town. It was a three-story house, with stairs, and through the windows you could see that the lights were turned on in every room. And on the stairs – softly carpeted stairs – kids, lots of kids, my age and maybe just a little older, played games in their pajamas while their mother and father, in fancy dressing gowns, stood by and gave encouragement. That house was a house of play. But the image of that house was a vague image. I really didn't know enough about such houses to pine for them. I knew that my days were very long and very boring – at home alone with my mother, my brother and sister not due until the afternoon school bus, if they chose to come home. I wanted lots of things that I couldn't have; the world outside came to me in scraps, in pages from the Sears catalogue – people in dressing gowns, kids on swing sets. But whatever I lacked, and knew that I lacked, I loved my mother. I never had bad thoughts about her. At least, that's how it seemed then and how I remember it now. I never thought, Mother's wrong, or Mother should have done this, or Mother shouldn't have done that. I never thought, as most children apparently do from time to time, I hate my mother.

Dr Hart undid the rags and tried, gently, to work the thumb out. There was a large brown spot on the back of one of his hands. He spoke to his nurse: 'Joyce, let's let you run over to Tom's' – a service station – 'and ask him to give us some tin cutters or wire cutters. And a hacksaw.' Then he turned to my mother. 'How long has it been like this?'

'About an hour or so,' my mother said.

'How come it took so long to get him here?'

'Well, I had to walk most of the way.'

'Why didn't you call?'

'Phone's out.'

'You couldn't ask a neighbor?'

My mother's voice took on a defensive tone. 'I *carried* him here,' she said. When the nurse returned with the tools, the doctor took the hacksaw and began sawing through the spout on the gas can. After it was separated, he took the wire cutters and began cutting up from the base of the spout toward my thumb. It took him a long time. 'I only like' – lack – 'a few snips more,' he said.

He washed my hand off under a faucet – it burned, and I told him so – and put in some stitches. He must have given me a local anesthetic, because I don't remember the stitches hurting. In any case, he had a very reassuring voice and he kept telling me that there was only a little bit more and it would all be over. He promised me an ice-cream cone if I would just hold still.

When he was finished and the thumb was bandaged, he told my mother, 'I might as well look him over, while he's here. I know you don't have a chance to get in that often.'

'I don't really have any money, Dr Hart.'

'Don't worry about that.'

Once more he fixed his entire attention upon me. 'Open up your mouth, bub. Say *ahhh*. I guarantee that this won't hurt.' He meant the tongue depressor.

Then he said, abruptly and not to me, 'How long has he been like this?'

'About an hour,' my mother said again.

'I mean in here. Just look in here! Keep it open, boy – it's all right. Can't you *see*? His whole throat has filled with adenoids. Adenoids and tonsils. They've blown up like a balloon in there. No wonder he can't talk right. I've never seen anything like it. I'm surprised he can draw breath.'

'I don't know *how* it happened,' my sister said not long ago. She meant this whole period of impoverishment. She was driving me from the airport to the funeral home in Dallas where my mother's body was. Two years after my sister married Roy, she had left him and gone to the junior college in Horace and then to T.C.U., where she paid her tuition by working nights as a switchboard operator at the telephone company. She is now a professor of English literature. We weren't going to have a funeral. My brother, who lives in Oregon, couldn't come down.

'What can I say?' she went on. 'We should have known better, but we didn't, that's all. I was just a fifteen-year-old kid. I suspected things weren't right, but what did I know? It was Mother who should have known. But she didn't. She just tuned it all out. She didn't want to face up to it.'

'Come on, that was an incredibly hard life,' I said.

'She could have done something about it. She could have found a job in town. She could have divorced him and looked around for somebody else. Found a provider. My God, we were her kids.'

Dr Hart said, 'He's got to go to Tyler to have all this removed. He has to go right now.'

'All the way to Tyler?' my mother said. 'Well, I can't take him. I'll get Dad to come down from Dallas and drive him.' She meant my grandfather.

'No, he has to go right now, I'm afraid. I'll call Skip Cousins, over in the courthouse. He'll make the arrangements.'

'I don't want that,' my mother said. 'I don't want the Welfare mixed up in it.'

'You *must* agree to this.' He picked up the phone.

'Thank you and goodbye!' my mother said.

Outside, she began talking to me. 'Let's don't go by the square,' she said. 'Let's take a side street.' She said a lot of other things – things I didn't really get.

To walk from the Palestine highway, on one side of the square, to the Tyler highway, on the other, without crossing the square itself involved a circuitous route. I didn't mind, because as my mother kept talking I began to realize something: if I asked her questions, she would answer in great detail and with obvious sincerity.

I asked her who she loved more – me, my brother or my sister.

'Why, *you*! You're my *baby* boy. And, truly, I don't think much of them, either one.'

I asked her why she was mad at the doctor.

'He's a big shot. Tried to high-hat us. Wants them to take you to Tyler and cut your tonsils out. Put you in with the polio kids.'

I asked her if I would ever burn in Hell.

'Son, you might. But you shouldn't study it. If it's going to happen, it's going to happen.'

Later, on the highway, a sheriff's car pulled up. The sheriff walked over and stood talking to my mother. He wore a gun, but he was not unfriendly. In a few minutes, a gray jeep with a canvas top pulled up. It belonged to the county, and a man and a woman got out. The man was heavy-faced and wore a white straw hat and a double-breasted suit. The sheriff called him Skip. The woman, who was a little older, was an assistant of some kind. She was thin and had a tight, pinched face. They were the Welfare. Both were gloomy; both wore pained expressions. They began telling my mother why I had to go to Tyler. I hid, enfolded in her skirts. The more they said, the more I loved her.

Catherine Brady
Daley's Girls

My father came home from work on weeknights long after we had eaten our supper and gotten into our pajamas. The six of us watched from the living-room while he sat at the kitchen table to have his supper. My mother set down his dinner before him, steam rising from the plate she'd kept warm over a pot of boiling water. Loading his fork with his knife, he bent to his dinner, not looking up from the plate until he had pushed it away from him, empty.

Then we could approach him. It was a favorite game of ours to tackle my father and plead with him to show us his keys. If he was in a good mood, he would pull the heavy key ring from the pocket of his khaki work pants and fan out the keys in the palm of his huge thick hand. In would poke my finger or one of my sister's, tiny, pink, translucent. 'What's this one for?' 'This one?' Belching, he would say, 'the shop', the car dealership where he was foreman of the mechanic crew, or 'the boss's office', but most of them he would let us guess at, leaving us to imagine all the possible worlds we'd never seen but which he had access to.

Sometimes he would let one of us trace the new scars and scratches on his rough palms, across the sworled knuckles, the calloused joints. We would ask him where he got the scratches. 'In the shop,' he would say, that work world where he spent his day strange and omnipotent, its own answer, but we would ask again, and he would answer, 'Fell over a hen and a duck picked me.'

He was no more informative about the town in Ireland where he grew up, or his marriage to my mother in Belfast, or what brought them to America. I would ask my mother what my father did, since he would not tell us. 'Oh,' she would say vaguely, 'he runs the shop for Mr Knowles and on Saturdays he takes care of his lawn for him and does the Harpers' and Ashtons' lawns as well.' She'd think for a moment, as if it were as much a mystery to her as to us children. 'He works hard, Sally. I don't think they could run the shop without him.'

Her territory was limited to the house itself, a limit imposed by her six daughters. We were each born roughly a year and a half apart, and with Peggy, the baby, only three, we were a physical yoke of unrelenting need. My mother would not, she said, trust her babies to a stranger. Once a week my father took her grocery shopping, packing the six of us in the car, and on Sundays he took all of us to Mass. When there was a decision to make – whether to purchase a new car, to repair or replace the leaking washing machine – he made the decision and notified her. 'You know best, Joe,' she would say, not looking up from sewing a button back onto a shirt while one of us was still in it, snapping the thread with her teeth when she'd finished.

My father's work remained a potent mystery for most of my childhood, tantalizing, for that knowledge seemed to be the source of his enviable power over us. The only clues I had were the occasional visits to our house by the men who worked for him in the shop. They came when my parents had anything old to sell or give away – a worn-out sofa, the battered playpen, the washing machine that had rusted out. Like my father, these men wore khaki pants creased with grime, and the skin of their hands, too, was crosshatched with black grease, their knuckles swollen, raw. My father startled us by calling them, to their faces, Pollack, Dago, Hillbilly, but these men, who mumbled when they spoke to my mother, laughed loudly and roughly at the names he had for them.

The summer I turned nine, when my mother was pregnant with her seventh child, we were invited for the first time to the Fourth of July party the Knowleses gave every year for their family and the car salesmen. The picnic was held at their summer house on Wheeler Lake; they had six acres and a private beach, and my father did the yard work there, too. My mother showed my father the invitation when he got home from work. She pushed it toward him on the table and he looked at it over the spine of his laden fork. She waited, watching him. He went on eating, silent. 'Go on out, you,' my mother said to Sheila and me; we'd been standing behind my father's chair waiting for him to finish so we could scoop out the marrow from the bone of his steak.

We retreated around the corner into the living-room, a purely formal concession. Even over the blare of the TV, my sisters and I would listen; there was no way not to in that tiny, crowded house. We knew the lock-step progress of every quarrel they had. If she pressed him too hard the first time, she would have to ask a second and a third time. She would want things for us, underwear or school shoes or milk money, and she would go to him for the money and he would say no or not answer her. 'I'm pleading with you,' she would say. 'I haven't got a dime in my pocket.' No dime, no checkbook, and no driver's license in that newly slapped together suburb. He might say nothing, or offer, 'I haven't got it,' or 'They don't need it.' And then, finally, he might accuse her, 'Woman, you can't spend what you don't have.' She had no way of knowing what they did have; he kept a bank account in the city where he worked and locked the passbook in the glove compartment of the car.

My mother lowered her voice. 'D'you think we should go?'

'We were invited, weren't we?'

'Joe. You make it so difficult to talk.'

'Who's stopping you?'

'I thought they didn't invite the shop, Joe – '

'What do you go saying things like that for? The man invited you, didn't he?'

'I won't know a soul.'

'So?'

'I'm to sit by myself while you're working the whole time carting soda pop and I don't know what else.'

There was a silence punctuated only by the rasp of my father's fork and knife on the plate. Then my mother's voice again.

'I'll need a new dress if we're to go. And the girls should have sandals.'

'You don't need a new dress for a picnic, for Chrissake.'

'Oh, Joe. You don't listen.'

'What the hell's that got to do with it?' His chair scraped the floor, violence so tangible that Sheila and I pulled back from the doorway. By this time he was shouting. 'If I bought a new dress every time you asked for one, we'd be in the poorhouse. Don't forget you almost put us there, too.' After having the last word – and he, who talked so little, always put the finish to their arguments – he took his newspaper from the table and came into the living-room. We scrambled to keep clear of him as he stepped over the tangle of bodies sprawled out on the floor. Still he'd find a reason to stoop and swat one of us before settling into his armchair behind the paper.

Sheila whispered to me, screwing up her eyes. 'I hope we go. Maybe we'll get new shoes.'

'Why won't he let Mommy have a new dress?'

'You think you're so smart,' Sheila said, older sister wise, drawing out the syllables to emphasize that she was in on a secret I had no inkling of. 'He – hasn't – got – it.'

'But now she'll be crying.'

'Yeah, but Mom cries for everything.'

My father spent every Saturday of that June at the Knowleses' house on the lake. He had to rake the sand beach, mow the lawn, fix the gate hinge, patch the screen windows on the porch. The weekend before the party my father took Sheila and me with him, a privilege we'd been granted several times that summer, because we were the oldest. He also brought his fishing gear; he wanted to bring home some bluegill for supper. My father lifted Sheila and me over the chain-link fence that bordered the Knowleses' beach and set to work fitting new pins in the gate. Only when he had finished with the gate and stood fishing from the sun-bleached dock, lacing the line out over the water, a cigar in his mouth, could we swim.

Before we left, my father had to open the house for Mrs Knowles. He gave Sheila his dripping string of bluegills and struggled with the two bolts on the kitchen door. I'd never seen the interior of the house; I slipped in behind him without asking permission.

'Shake the sand off your shoes before you come in here,' he growled when he heard me. He went from room to room opening windows, the wood sticking and catching on the worn sashes.

The house, with all the shades drawn, smelled of dust and mildewed carpet. It seemed impossible to imagine anyone living in this fairy-tale house: pitchers and basins set out on oak washstands, antique phone, old Victrola, overstuffed chairs and sofa, and pale blue wallpaper with a pattern of velvet swirls.

My father struggled with the window in the living-room. 'This sash is snapped completely. Told the missus I'd fix it for her, too.' He gave one more tug and gave up.

He stood squarely in the middle of the living-room, his hands, black with the dust from the windows, planted on his hips. He surveyed the spindly-legged chairs, the decorative stone fireplace. 'She's got it fixed up real nice.'

I strained to catch every nuance of pleasure in his voice, frail, but there, a satisfaction I witnessed so rarely in him that I thought of it as something he kept from us. I was waiting for the moment when he turned back into the other father, tired, tyrant of our house. In this house I glimpsed a stranger who only slipped out furtively, recognized in him the satisfaction of a man at once within his rights – that fistful of keys – and sneaking, as I was, uneasy with the sense of touching and pleasuring in what wasn't ours.

As soon as he brought us home from the lake that afternoon, he began issuing orders, as he did every Saturday. He marshalled the six of us around the yard, raking, weeding the hedge, picking up scraps of paper that had blown onto the lawn, hosing down the cement front porch, plucking dandelions from the grass. When the yard work was done, we had to polish his Sunday shoes, as well as our own, and leave them in a row on the kitchen floor for inspection. After dinner there would be countless small tasks – shining pots and pans, handing him the nails while he did repairs around the house, sweeping his basement workshop.

We had to do all this in the misery that no job was ever done to his satisfaction – I suppose it was as much of a misery to him. For blowing the tufted dandelion seeds on the grass, for opening the freezer door and letting cold air escape, for streaking the polish on his shoes, for jumping the hedge, for arguing with each other, we were slapped, pinched, knocked off our feet by a blow on the shoulders. His blows always caught me by surprise, as if they were not intended for me alone. And he grew more and more short-tempered as the weekend dragged on, as if that awful quality in us that he must punish were unbearable for him at such close quarters.

Yet Sunday evenings, after dinner, he called us down to the basement and reached up into the exposed rafters, pulling down a package of Wrigley's spearmint gum, or, if we were lucky, Hershey bars. He unwrapped his gifts and divided them among us, feeding us from his hands, licking the chocolate from his fingers and saving the last piece for himself. If one of my sisters sulked because of a blow that still smarted, he'd urge candy on her, saying in his rough voice, 'What's got into you? Why're you so crabby?'

On the day of the picnic my mother washed our hair and then lined us up in the kitchen to singe the split ends of our wet hair with matches. With the sweet thick smell of sulphur and burning fur filling the kitchen, she told us all the things my father would not hear: 'Your father's a good man, but he's tightfisted with money. Y'see, he hadn't any when he was growing up. And once I got us into trouble when I was paying the bills. And I see that he's the right one to be doing it, but it's like I'm never to be forgiven for the one mistake, and that only being unable to squeeze blood from a turnip.'

This lilt, litany, song, was woven into all the functional intimacy motherhood required. She had that knowledge to lull us by, as well as her unerring intimate knowledge of our bodies – her fingers brisk but never rough, prying into small fists, ears, mouths, the corners of our eyes.

She ran the match up and down a strand of my hair, inching words past the bobby pins in her mouth. 'If it wasn't for me, you kids'd be in rags. Only I go down on my knees to him week after week or you'd be in last year's dresses with your knees showing. D'y'see? . . . He's an intelligent man, in his way. But he doesn't see that I can't go to the Knowleses' picnic looking so shabby. He's no pride.'

Before we left for the picnic, my father lined us up in the living-room, in order, each an inch or two taller than the next, in our matching pink summer dresses. My mother stood at the head of our line, in a pink dress that looked as if someone else had worn it out before handing it on to her, her pregnancy making her stand belly out, just as we did. While she made a hopeless effort to tuck our bathing suit straps under our sleeveless dresses, my father gave us strict instructions. 'Someone offers you a Coke, you say, "No, thank you." If I see one of you drinking up the soda, you'll get the back of my hand. And you're not to run where there's people sitting. And I don't want you going in and out of the house, or you'll sit next to me the rest of the evening.'

The gravel road that led to the house was choked with cars when we arrived, and the lawn was littered with chairs and people. Mrs Knowles came out of the crowd to greet us. She was old, but she didn't smell old. She smelled of perfumed cosmetics, a husky smell that I liked. Even her pleated dress gave off the powdery scent of perfume. 'Maureen,' she said, putting an arm around my mother, 'I'm so glad to see you here. I told Daley I'd never forgive him if he didn't bring you and the girls.' She smiled at us. 'Don't they look a picture, all in pink. And you look lovely in pink, too, Maureen. It suits your coloring.'

My mother blushed, and her hands, as if seeking comfort in habit, fluttered in search of a daughter.

'Now let's see how good I am at remembering your names,' Mrs Knowles said. But of course my mother had to tick them off for her as she went down the line, bending down and taking the hand of each child. When she came to me, I was tongue-tied, frightened by her clean husky smell, her voice that carried across the lawn. She looked up at my mother.

'Shy,' she said, laughing. 'And Daley told me she was a little chatterbox.'

Mrs Knowles turned and waved at the crowd until a thin old man appeared. He was a deflated version of the Mr Knowles I had imagined. He said hello to us and then he turned to my parents. 'Maureen. Joe.' He stood with his hands in his pockets, as if he were waiting for someone to speak. The grown-ups all smiled at us as if we were neutral territory.

'Well,' Mr Knowles said. 'I hope you girls are going to have a nice time today.'

'I second the motion,' Mrs Knowles said. 'There's an ice chest on the porch with soda pop for you children, and somewhere back there you'll find my granddaughter Jessica. She's been looking for someone to play with.'

We waited for my father's signal.

'Go on,' he said. 'You can play with Jessica but no soda.'

We took off, Mrs Knowles calling after us, 'Don't listen to your father. Drink all the soda you like.'

We found Jessica sitting on the ice chest, greedily drinking from a Coca Cola bottle. She was quite small, but I guessed her age at a year younger than mine.

'You can't have any,' she said when we approached. 'My grandpa said I get to say who can have soda.' She eyed us suspiciously. 'You're all awfully big,' she said, wavering between disapproval and envy.

We regarded her with approximately the same mixture of feelings. Her lank brown hair had been pulled up in two pigtails and tied with braided ribbons of red, yellow and blue. She wore a satiny fringed cowboy shirt, corduroys and patent leather shoes. I decided right away that she was spoiled; *we* weren't allowed to talk to anyone like that.

'How come you all look alike?' she said.

'We're triplets,' Sheila said. 'Two sets of triplets.'

Jessica's disapproval gave way to admiration. She hopped off the ice chest. 'I guess you can have some soda if you want it.'

'No, thank you,' came the chorus, all of us conscious of my father not thirty yards away.

'Then you can help me set up croquet,' she decided. Obediently we hammered the metal hoops into the lawn under her direction.

When my father wandered over to where we were playing, Jessica threw down her mallet and ran to meet him. 'Daley!' she shouted, stopping just short of arm's reach.

'Picklepuss,' my father said, 'you're no bigger than the last time I saw you. What's the matter with you, don't you know how to grow?'

She giggled into her cupped hands. '*You're* the picklepuss.'

My father reached out and ruffled her bangs. She shrieked and pulled at his arm.

Sheila insinuated herself between them. 'This is my Dad.'

I was more jealous of Jessica at that moment than I had ever been of any of my sisters. My father had never made up silly names for us, nor ruffled our hair, nor allowed us to tug on him like that. It was a jealousy so entire that I felt it for my sisters as well as myself.

To Sheila, my father said, 'You watching the younger ones?'

'Yeah.' If there had been a shorter answer, she'd have given it.

'See that you do. I'm going to help them set the tables up in the tent and I don't want any bad reports on you.' He disengaged Jessica, grinning at her with his tongue between his teeth, and left.

'Daley brings me lemon drops when he comes to my Grandma's,' Jessica said.

'So what,' I said. 'He gives us Hershey bars every day.'

She shrugged. 'Are we playing or not?' My sisters took their places. Curious, as if she had been waiting for the opportunity to ask a question that grown-ups wouldn't allow, she asked me, 'How come Daley doesn't wear a uniform?'

'What for?' I said. For eight years old, she was dumb.

'Like the Mexicans. When the Mexicans come to do my mother's lawn, they wear uniforms.'

I flushed, feeling that somehow she'd tricked me, only I didn't know how.

'My Grandpa says you can't trust them.' She giggled. 'Grandpa's a stupid bitch.'

I stalked off, nursing a grudge against my father that had had its start in his flirtation with Jessica and had been fired by her question, which made me feel foolish, as if she knew something I didn't. I walked around to the back of the house and stood looking in the kitchen window at the maids, all of them in white uniforms. The women's skin was shiny with sweat; I could feel the heat from the oven coming in waves from the window. Lenora, the Knowleses' live-in maid, saw me and waved a spoon in greeting. She knew me; sometimes, when the Knowleses were at the lake, my father took me along on Saturday when he mowed the lawn of their house in town. If it was a hot day, she gave us lemonade in ice-frosted glasses at the kitchen door.

Once when Lenora wasn't there, my father took me in to the kitchen to get a glass of water, filling glasses with ice and water from two spigots built into the refrigerator door. 'See that? That's convenience.' With the back of his hand, he brushed his glistening forehead. 'You been in here before?' he said.

I shook my head.

'I'll show you how the other half lives.'

We cautiously walked through the house. The living-room he showed me made me think of a museum; it had the same cavernous hush, the same collection of fragile things locked in gleaming display cabinets. He led me through the rest of the house, stopping in each doorway, swaying back on his heels, the glass held to his chest, looking in with a satisfaction that bordered on the proprietary. Empty, the Knowleses' house had seemed like a series of mirrors in which I might glimpse that other, more complete father. Now, looking in at the maids in the kitchen, I could discover no clues.

I found my mother sitting by herself under the shade of an oak tree. She was rubbing her hands one across the other, the fingers fanned out, looking down at them in her lap, the way she did at home whenever she was thinking.

'Your father's gone off and left me sitting here. I don't know a soul.'

'I don't like Jessica.' I told my mother what she had said about her grandfather.

'She's very bold.' My mother sighed. 'Did you see your father?'

'Daddy likes her. He lets her call him names. She's spoiled.'

'She is,' my mother said firmly. 'You six should steer clear of her. Mind you, she can't help herself. Her parents leave the poor thing off at the grandparents every weekend, they've no time for her.'

Later my mother took us down to the lake to swim. The water was crowded with children and adults, inflatable rafts, inner tubes. We'd always had the lake to ourselves when we came to the house. This time, we were hard put to find enough space to leave our towels and strip to our suits. Sheila and I found an inflatable raft on the beach and dragged it into the water, suffering Maryann to climb on with us.

Jessica paddled up to us, buoyed up by water wings. 'That's my raft,' she said.

'We got it first,' Sheila said.

'Get lost,' I said.

'It's mine. I want it. My Grandpa didn't say Daley's girls could have it.'

'Baby,' I sneered. 'You can't even swim without a float.'

We paddled the raft away from her, but she caught one end and held on. 'Give it to me.'

Her voice rose to a shriek. 'It's mine. I'll tell my Grandpa, he'll make you, he'll make you.' Her words crescendoed into gasping sobs.

'Girls. Girls.' My mother waved to us. 'Come out of the water.'

We relinquished the raft, but Jessica was still sobbing loudly when we reached shore. My mother's face was a bright red. She bent down to us, so her voice wouldn't carry. 'I told you not to go near her.'

'Mom, we didn't do anything,' Sheila said.

'Sh.' My mother took her by the arm. 'We're making a show of ourselves.' It was true; people had turned to watch our small procession.

I squirmed in between Maryann and my mother. 'Mom.'

She leaned down.

'It's not our fault.'

'I know.'

'It's not *fair*.'

'You, Peggy,' she called. 'Stay near the shore.'

She turned back to me. 'Lots of things aren't fair.' The bright sunlight revealed the sharp frown lines around her mouth. Those lines seemed to speak of a woman separate from the mother who fed, bathed, dressed and consoled us, a woman who might harbor wants and resentments that dwarfed my own.

'I'm going to tell Dad on Jessica,' Maryann announced.

'Shut up,' Sheila said.

'*You* shut up.'

'Girls,' my mother said.

Maryann had her chance when my father showed up carrying a thermos that he set up on a card table. He filled paper cups with lemonade, and we got in line for our cups, standing beside him until he poured the last cup for himself and downed it.

'Dad, Jessica took our raft,' Maryann said.

My father grinned. 'I'm glad. You must have done something on her.'

'We didn't.' I stamped my foot.

'Shut up, you guys,' Sheila said.

Maryann tugged at my father's thick forearm. 'Daddy, we had it first! Mommy made us give it to her.'

I said, 'Jessica thinks she gets to have her way just because she's Mr Knowles's granddaughter.'

He pinched me, hard. 'I'll wash your mouth out with soap if you say that again.'

His pinch left a red welt on my arm. I rubbed at it.

'I told you,' Sheila mouthed at me.

My father called out to Jessica. She had dragged the raft onto the beach and was sitting on it, plucking at her toenails. 'They're telling me you did something on them.'

She approached my father at a slow walk, dragging her toes in the sand. 'They're lying,' she said, letting her lower lip tremble. 'They wouldn't let me play on the raft and it's mine in the first place.'

'Boo hoo,' my father said. He made a face at her.

'Daley.' She put her hands on her hips. 'Tell them not to do it again. Or I'll tell Grandpa.'

My father's laughter came out suddenly, like expelled breath.

My mother appeared at his elbow, her arms heaped with our fluffy pink dresses.

'Look here, miss,' she said to Jessica. 'You're not to talk that way to grown-ups. Or I'll be telling your Grandpa a thing or two.'

Jessica's lower lip fell. She pursed her lips to answer back, then reconsidered. Shrugging her shoulders, she turned away.

My mother turned to my father. 'You shouldn't let her talk to you like that. It's not right.'

My father looked into the bottom of his paper cup. 'She's only a child,' he said. 'No harm done.'

My mother snorted. 'Come on, girls, we'll go up to the house and you can change your clothes.'

Arms full of pink, the six of us fanning out behind her, she led us down the path, head high. I looked back to catch a glimpse of my father, still standing by the thermos, the thin paper cup in his large hard hand, alone, as my mother had been alone all afternoon. For a minute I felt our superiority as females. *We* knew when we were being insulted. Hot on the heels of that came the shame I felt for him, standing there, arms akimbo, stoop-shouldered, his feet planted far apart, his pleasure nakedly written on his face, as it had been those few times I'd glimpsed it in houses that weren't his.

I turned and ran to catch up with my sisters.

When I reached Sheila, she looped an arm through mine. 'Maybe Mom will let us have a soda while he's not around.'

'I hate Dad,' I said.

Sandra Cisneros
My Lucy Friend Who Smells Like Corn

Lucy Anguiano, Texas girl who smells like corn, like Frito Bandito chips, like tortillas, something like that warm smell of *nixtamal* or bread the way her head smells when she's leaning close to you over a paper cut-out doll or on the porch when we are squatting over marbles trading this pretty crystal that leaves a blue star on your hand for that giant cat-eye with a grasshopper green spiral in the center like the juice of bugs on the windshield when you drive to the border, like the yellow blood of butterflies.

Have you ever eated dog food? I have. After crunching like ice, she opens her big mouth to prove it, only a pink tongue rolling around in there like a blind worm, and Janey looking in because she said Show me. But me I like that Lucy, corn smell hair and aqua flip-flops just like mine that we bought at the K mart for only 79 cents same time.

I'm going to sit in the sun, don't care if it's a million trillion degrees outside, so my skin can get so dark it's blue where it bends like Lucy's. Her whole family like that. Eyes like knife slits. Lucy and her sisters. Norma, Margarita, Ofelia, Herminia, Nancy, Olivia, Cheli, *y la* Amber Sue.

Screen door with no screen. *Bang!* Little black dog biting his fur. Fat couch on the porch. Some of the windows painted blue, some pink, because her daddy got tired that day or forgot. Mama in the kitchen feeding clothes into the wringer washer and clothes rolling out all stiff and twisted and flat like paper. Lucy got her arm stuck once and had to yell Maaa! and her mama had to put the machine in reverse and then her hand rolled back, the finger black and later, her nail fell off. *But did your arm get flat like the clothes? What happened to your arm? Did they have to pump it with air?* No, only the finger, and she didn't cry neither.

Lean across the porch rail and pin the pink sock of the baby Amber Sue on top of Cheli's flowered T-shirt, and the blue jeans of *la* Ofelia over the inside seam of Olivia's blouse, over the flannel nightgown of Margarita so it don't stretch out, and then you take the work shirts of their daddy and hang them upside down like this, and this way all the clothes don't get so wrinkled and take up less space and you don't waste pins. The girls all wear each other's clothes, except Olivia, who is stingy. There ain't no boys here. Only girls and one father who is never home hardly and one mother who says *Ay! I'm real tired* and so many sisters there's no time to count them.

I'm sitting in the sun even though it's the hottest part of the day, the part that makes the streets dizzy, when the heat makes a little hat on the top of your head and bakes the dust and weed grass and sweat up good, all steamy and smelling like sweet corn.

I want to rub heads and sleep in a bed with little sisters, some at the top and some at the feets. I think it would be fun to sleep with sisters you could yell at one at a time or all together, instead of alone on the fold-out chair in the living-room.

When I get home Abuelita will say *Didn't I tell you?* and I'll get it because I was supposed to wear this dress again tomorrow. But first I'm going to jump off an old pissy mattress in the Anguiano yard. I'm going to scratch your mosquito bites, Lucy, so they'll itch you, then put Mercurochrome smiley faces on them. We're going to trade shoes and wear them on our hands. We're going to walk over to Janey Ortiz's house and say *We're never ever going to be your friend again forever!* We're going to run home backwards and we're going to run home frontwards, look twice under the house where the rats hide and I'll stick one foot in there because you dared me, sky so blue and heaven inside those white clouds. I'm going to peel a scab from my knee and eat it, sneeze on the cat, give you three M&Ms I've been saving for you since yesterday, comb your hair with my fingers and braid it into teeny-tiny braids real pretty. We're going to wave to a lady we don't know on the bus. Hello! I'm going to somersault on the rail of the front porch even though my *chones* show. And cut paper dolls we draw ourselves, and color in their clothes with crayons, my arm around your neck.

And when we look at each other, our arms gummy from an orange Popsicle we split, we could be sisters, right? We could be, you and me waiting for our teeths to fall and money. You laughing something into my ear that tickles, and me going Ha Ha Ha Ha. Her and me, my Lucy friend who smells like corn.

Sandra Cisneros
Barbie-Q
for Licha

Yours is the one with mean eyes and a ponytail. Striped swimsuit, stilettos, sunglasses and gold hoop earrings. Mine is the one with bubble hair. Red swimsuit, stilettos, pearl earrings and a wire stand. But that's all we can afford, besides one extra outfit apiece. Yours, 'Red Flair', sophisticated A-line coatdress with a Jackie Kennedy pillbox hat, white gloves, handbag and heels included. Mine, 'Solo in the Spotlight', evening elegance in black glitter strapless gown with a puffy skirt at the bottom like a mermaid tail, formal-length gloves, pink chiffon scarf and mike included. From so much dressing and undressing, the black glitter wears off where her titties stick out. This and a dress invented from an old sock when we cut holes here and here and here, the cuff rolled over for the glamorous, fancy-free, off-the-shoulder look.

Every time the same story. Your Barbie is roommates with my Barbie, and my Barbie's boyfriend comes over and your Barbie steals him, OK? Kiss kiss kiss. Then the two Barbies fight. You dumbbell! He's mine. Oh no he's not, you stinky! Only Ken's invisible, right? Because we don't have money for a stupid-looking boy doll when we'd both rather ask for a new Barbie outfit next Christmas. We have to make do with your mean-eyed Barbie and my bubblehead Barbie and our one outfit apiece not including the sock dress.

Until next Sunday when we are walking through the flea market on Maxwell Street and *there*! Lying on the street next to some tool bits, and platform shoes with the heels all squashed, and a fluorescent green wicker wastebasket, and aluminum foil, and hub-caps, and a pink shag rug, and windshield wiper blades, and dusty mason jars, and a coffee can full of rusty nails. *There*! Where? Two Mattel boxes. One with the 'Career Gal' ensemble, snappy black-and-white business suit, three-quarter-length sleeve jacket with kick-pleat skirt, red sleeveless shell, gloves, pumps and matching hat included. The other, 'Sweet Dreams', dreamy pink-and-white plaid nightgown and matching robe, lace-trimmed slippers, hairbrush and hand mirror included. How much? Please, please, please, please, please, please, please, until they say okay.

On the outside you and me skipping and humming but inside we are doing loopity-loops and pirouetting. Until at the next vendor's stand, next to boxed pies, and bright orange toilet brushes, and rubber gloves, and wrench sets, and bouquets of feather flowers, and glass towel racks, and steel wool, and Alvin and the Chipmunks records, *there!* And *there!* And *there!* And *there!* and *there!* and *there!* and *there!* Bendable Legs Barbie with her new page-boy hairdo. Midge, Barbie's best friend. Ken, Barbie's boyfriend. Skipper, Barbie's little sister. Tutti and Todd, Barbie and Skipper's tiny twin sister and brother. Skipper's friends, Scooter and Ricky. Alan, Ken's buddy. And Francie, Barbie's MOD'ern cousin.

Everybody today selling toys, all of them damaged with water and smelling of smoke. Because a big toy warehouse on Halsted Street burned down yesterday – see there? – the smoke still rising and drifting across the Dan Ryan expressway. And now there is a big fire sale at Maxwell Street, today only.

So what if we didn't get our new Bendable Legs Barbie and Midge and Ken and Skipper and Tutti and Todd and Scooter and Ricky and Alan and Francie in nice clean boxes and had to buy them on Maxwell Street, all water-soaked and sooty. So what if our Barbies smell like smoke when you hold them up to your nose even after you wash and wash and wash them. And if the prettiest doll, Barbie's MOD'ern cousin Francie with real eyelashes, eyelash brush included, has a left foot that's melted a little – so? If you dress her in her new 'Prom Pinks' outfit, satin splendor with matching coat, gold belt, clutch and hair bow included, so long as you don't lift her dress, right? – who's to know.

Jennifer C. Cornell
Undertow

It was close to September and the date of the wedding when my father started bringing us to Castlerock. After breakfast we'd board the first train from Central Station that went south to Lambeg and Lisburn before turning north and arriving eventually beside the sea. We'd spend the rest of the day there on the rocks above the beach, hurling stones into the oncoming waves and fishing without bait until it was time to catch the last train from Derry home. The train leaned hard into the left shoulder just before the platform came into sight, and as we moved towards the exits to be ready when it stopped, I would watch the reflection of the streetlights on the far side of the Lagan wink on the spiral whenever a fish rose up for air.

What's that flashing? I'd asked my father the first time I'd seen it.

Fairy lights, he answered.

Bullshit, Ricky said, under his breath. He was five years my senior, thirteen and no longer a baby; rebellion came easily to him like a dog. We were fifty yards from the platform and the sign above him told him No, but still he'd thrown his weight against the window, pulled it down and thrust his head out into the wind. He would not take my father's hand as we stepped down from the train.

My mother was sitting at the kitchen table with John-O Noonan when we got home. John-O's fingers were yellow from nailtip to knuckle and his whole hand twitched with desire; there was no smoking allowed in my mother's house.

It's happened again, she told my father.

Has it indeed? What's it of this time?

I'm flat out of paint, she said, so you'll have to go get some. I won't have that damn thing on the side of my house.

After our tea we went out to look at it. This time they'd painted flags and emblems, and every letter of the words that went with them was outlined in black and at least two feet high. The last time they'd done a map of the country with a pair of armed soldiers on either side, and before that there'd been a bright yellow shield on a powder blue background, and a list of the names of the most recent dead. Each time my mother had covered it over by climbing a stepladder and chucking buckets of paint at the house.

When do they do it, that's what I'd like to know, John-O said. He lived in the house which terraced ours, where he spent his days minding his sister's children and keeping his eye on the Help Wanted columns, in case something came up that my father could do. He shook his head with slow admiration. How the hell do they do it when youse're here all the time?

I wish to God I could catch them at it, my mother said. I don't care who they are. That's the last bit of painting they'd ever do.

It's a real shame, my father said.

Don't start with me, Joe, my mother told him. I've no time for hoods. I'll get the paint myself if I have to.

First thing tomorrow, he answered. The shops'll be closed now, anyway.

The next day my father and I lay on till eleven. My mother was working at the kitchen table when I went downstairs to make us tea. She'd been working steadily since early that morning but the sound of machinery hadn't disturbed us, because each sequin and pearl was sewn on by hand. By this time the shell of the dress was nearly finished – the bodice and skirt, the two mutton sleeves, the veil, the head-dress, and the wide, four-foot train. She had still to complete the undergarments, and she'd promised to hem the girl's linens, embroider their edges, and inscribe the corners with the first letter of her name.

Your brother's gone out, my mother told me, so it's up to you to look after your father. Don't let him come home without that paint. I stood just behind her while the kettle boiled, skewering beads on her upright needle as soon as she'd fastened the previous one. Oh here, listen, she said, and reached under the fabric in search of her purse. The table was lost under cover of satin, a full bolt of chiffon lay unwrapped on the floor, and thick books of patterns sat on each chair, their insides fat with slips of paper, receipts, and newsprint torn into strips to mark a page. A spool of white thread, luv, she said, giving me money, say you want the kind for all types of fabric, and get me at least two hundred yards. I'd ask your daddy but you know he won't do it.

Because I don't think it's right, my father said from the threshold. Taking advantage of a foolish woman when you know rightly there won't be a wedding on the twenty-first. You can't have a wedding without a groom.

More's the pity, my mother said, and unnecessarily switched on her machine.

Well I won't be part of it, my father continued. I will not add to that girl's disappointment.

For God's sake, Joe, my mother said, it's none of my business what they want the clothes for. That girl placed an order same as anyone else.

A wedding gown's different, my father told her. Especially this.

I didn't ask to hear her life's story, Joe, my mother told him, and what she does with her money is her own affair. If she wants to waste it on fortune-tellers that's got nothing to do with me.

I think we are obligated to protect the innocent, my father said quietly.

Fair enough, my mother answered, but only if they're mine. That girl pays good money, in advance and on time. I've got this family to worry about, Joe.

We spoke no more about it, though my father refused to come in the shop with me when I went in to purchase thread. We bought two tins of paint, a tray and a roller, and were in the sitting-room stirring the tins when Ricky came home with a sackful of chestnuts.

How come they're called conkers? I asked my father.

Why d'you think? Ricky said. He took one whose green armoured shell had not yet broken and slapped it, palm open, against his head.

It began with a farmer, my father answered, who owned a good bit of land not far from Mullan Head. He was a man who didn't like to spend money, and it's not like he didn't have it to spend. Every night he sat in the dark so he wouldn't have to run the electric, and all the beasts on his farm had bad teeth and were spindly because he was too cheap to give them a decent feed. Now there was a tree on that land and the farmer didn't like it. Its shade kept him cold, he said, and it made his house dark. He blamed the tree for his own mean nature, and one day he decided, I'll cut the thing down. But the tree saw him coming with his rolled-up sleeves and his heavy boots and the toothy new saw in his hand. It got so frightened it shook and heaved, and a whole shower of chestnuts fell on the farmer, sticking and pricking him with their rubbery spines. He was so bruised and battered he spent six weeks in hospital, and as soon as he got out he picked up and left. Then a husband and wife with two little children, a boy and a wee girl about your age, came to live in the house. They put a swing on the tree and built a conservatory, and the house is so full of light now that they built a train past it, and if you're a good wee girly this evening and eat all your peas, I'll show you it tomorrow on the way to Castlerock.

Joe, my mother said from the other room. How old is your daughter?

So why don't all trees throw conkers all the time?

Cuz it's all bollocks, that's why, Ricky said. They fall cuz the stems rot, that's why it's easy to knock em down.

You know what your problem is, Ricky? my mother called to him.

Humankind has grown impatient, my father answered. The cold facts of science take less time to tell.

The side of our house stayed white for six days. On the morning of the seventh my mother noticed the additional shadow when she stepped outside to bring in the milk.

Joe, she called from the bottom of the stairs, c'mere till you see this.

From the room next to mine I heard my parents' bed creak as my father rolled onto his back and sighed.

Ah, Belle, he said, it's not even seven.

They've left a ladder, my mother said, and I'll tell you right now they're not getting it back.

Not very good, is it? John-O said an hour or so later. Still in his dressing gown and pyjamas, he'd seen our door lying open when he'd let the cat out, and had jumped the low fence that ran between us, calling our names as he hurried into the house. My mother, lugging a tarpaulin and paint thinner, had nearly run over him as she backed out the door.

Different artist, my father answered. This wee fella's got no sense of colour.

It's God awful, John-O said. I'm with you, missus – get rid of it. That bloody thing's hard on the eyes.

It's going today, my mother said firmly. I've a girl coming by for a fitting tomorrow, and this will not be the first thing she sees.

What time tomorrow? my father said suddenly.

For a moment my mother looked like she'd bitten her tongue. I know what you're thinking, Joe, she said, and it's not going to happen.

Go on, Belle. What time's she coming?

I should have known you'd pull something like this, my mother said bitterly. Why can't you stay out of it? It's got nothing to do with you.

Right! John-O said. See youse all later.

I just want to talk to her, Belle, that's all.

What for? What good'll it do? She's not getting a refund, you know, even if you do manage to make her change her mind.

C'mon now, folks, John-O said, don't do this outside.

It's not just about money, my father answered. It's her state of mind. What's going to happen to her two weeks from Friday? I'm not convinced she's going to survive.

Alright, Joe, my mother said. I give up. Stay in if you want to tomorrow; just get the hell out of my way today.

There now, John-O said cheerfully, that's better. Youse two had me worried there for a while.

We'd missed the first train to Derry, but we did catch the second. Ricky stayed behind to help my mother; intending to keep the ladder as evidence, she'd said no when he'd asked for it and offered to let him paint the wall instead. When we arrived in Castlerock we headed at once for our regular café, where we each ordered a fish and chip dinner and my father explained why fish had it so bad – because they bore grudges, resenting all those who'd stood on four feet at the birth of Jesus, and the dove for finding the olive branch, and all the rest of the animal kingdom for having a place set aside for them on the ark. It didn't matter that God had conferred on them wisdom, that He'd warned them about the flood in advance. And so they are regularly captured and eaten, they fall ill easily and are tormented by cats, and though they gasp with the effort of trying to buy freedom with the secrets the Almighty had shared, they can never produce the human words necessary, never can make themselves understood. And that, said my father, is apt punishment for arrogance – that they die ignominiously, out of their element, impressive only because of their size.

Then our dinners were ready and he went up to fetch them. He came back with two plates and a plastic lemon, which he set down on the table next to the salt. If Ricky'd been with us he'd have been embarrassed, and my father would have explained yet again how he met my mother. She'd been the new girl at the local chippy where he went occasionally for a take-away, and he'd asked her for a wedge of lemon, which naturally enough the shop didn't have. The dinner rush was at its most frantic when my mother put on her coat and took her umbrella and went down to a grocer two blocks away to buy my father a bagful of lemons with her own money, because there was something about his face she fancied. At this establishment, my father said as if I'd protested, my custom is valued. Did she really empty them out on top of you? I asked him. Right in my lap, he said. There must have been two or three dozen at least.

And then what happened?

Then? Then your mother was sacked and I was ejected. We never went near the place again.

After our dinner we walked to the beach. A buttress of rocks spilled into the sea, their surfaces pitted with shallow depressions, warm water puddles of algae and snails and keyhole limpets whose airtight seals resisted all efforts to prise their shells loose. A man hurled a stick and his dog sailed after and caught it each time in its open jaws, the wide arc of its body in motion continuing on into the water with the same compact force of those who ran barefoot from one rock to another to fling themselves off the final one, their knees to their chests and their arms wrapped around them, their hair and clothes still heavy with water from the previous jump. There's our friend, said my father, and I turned to see a horse approaching, its rider bouncing like a ball on a string as the horse's hooves pummelled the surf, leaving prints that the tide made more cavernous, brown sugar sand tumbling in on all sides. They'd been there every day since we first started coming. The man lived by himself in a one-room caravan staked to flat ground just beyond Castlerock, and he kept his horse on a small slab of pasture which belonged to no one and which he'd cleared himself. He's a nutter, Ricky had said when my father told us. Everyone says so. You must learn the difference between fraud and fiction, Ricky, my father said. It's true, Ricky'd said sullenly. There's even a petition to get him put out. The darkness of Mankind is truly untellable, my father said later, more to himself than to either of us. It shouldn't surprise me but it always does.

The man rode bareback and the horse wore no bridle, yet they pulled up beside us with the flourish expected when reins are drawn tight, hot breath expelled from the horse's nostrils, sand splashing over us with each sweep of its tail.

You're late today, the man said.

I know it, my father said. What about ye?

The man shrugged. Yerself?

We're alright, aren't we, luv? said my father. Do you still want a ride?

C'mon up, luv, the man said, and I reached for his hand. Up close the horse smelled like brass and worn leather; I filled my fists with its oily mane, my father put his hand on my ankle and I felt the knees of the man behind me press against the horse's ribs. We walked past the mouth of the tunnel, that long stretch of darkness from which trains hurtle out, startling their passengers with the sudden proximity of sand and seawater, of gulls suspended above black shards of rock. Then we turned and came back at a canter, my father too on the animal's strong back, past boys Ricky's age who were playing football, past new groups of people sitting on jackets drinking beer and soft drinks from oversized tins, up the very steps which led to the street. Look after yourself now, my father said. You worry too much, the other man told him, and urged the horse through the small crowd of children that had gathered around him and headed back the way we'd just come.

In Coleraine while we waited to transfer I stood at the edge of the platform to watch the incoming train, signalled by sirens and the lowering of booms, a mad dash of assorted pedestrians and small dogs on leads hurrying from one side of the road to the other before the train, with the same graceful movements of things buoyed by water, came round the corner and eased into the station.

Stand back now, my father said. Let them get off. But my eyes were not on the entrance but on the red diamond in the centre of the train's yellow face. We'd chosen a car that was practically empty, so once we were settled with our tickets ready, our crisps on the table, our feet outstretched towards the seat across from us, and our coats and umbrellas on the rack above our heads, I asked my father to tell me the story he'd promised the last time.

Oh yes, he said, I'd nearly forgotten. When the iron horse was first brought to Ireland, the other animals found it a bad-mannered beast. It was loud and filthy and single-minded, it stopped on no whim or for any diversion, just proceeded directly from A to B. To be so oblivious to the world around you was a dangerous condition, the other beasts said, for what if one of them happened to stop in its path? But once they realized that the train only ran on the tracks set down for it, and only at more or less predictable times, they began to enjoy its daily passage. They even grew rather possessive, and boasted about it when they'd had too much to drink. Our train can beat any birds flying, the beasts would say loudly, whenever birds were around to hear – which naturally the birds took as a challenge, and eventually they sent someone over to accept. But the two parties couldn't agree on the details of the contest, until finally the bird representative said How about this: you set the distance, and we'll set the course. The beasts were confident their man could travel over any terrain, so they said OK, but we're not crossing water – and then congratulated themselves for being so clever. About the same time as all this was happening a new model of train was introduced. This one was even faster, the beasts read in the advertisements they found in the newspapers that passengers tossed from the windows, along with their cigarette butts and their empty tins. When the birds found this out they flew into a panic, but agreed to play one hand of pontoon, the winner to decide which train would be run. Three times the dealer peeled cards from the deck; then the birds (with a hand adding up to fifteen) and the beasts (with a five, a two, and the queen of spades) decided to ask for just one more. Twenty! the birds said when they got theirs, and if they'd been playing poker they'd have been hard to beat, for what they had in front of them was a straight flush of hearts. The beasts sucked their teeth and said they were sorry but they didn't mean it, for their hidden card was the three of diamonds, and with the ace they'd been given they'd just made twenty-one.

Listen! my father said as our train passed another, and I heard in the jolt and clatter of the tracks the sound of a deck of iron cards being shuffled. What about the race? I asked. Did the train beat the birds? Well, no, my father said. Sure the beasts had forgotten that a train can't run if there aren't any tracks. The birds chose a course that never crossed water, but it also didn't pass through A or B. As soon as they discovered the situation, all the earth-moving beasts got stuck in right away, but no one could lift the rails from the stack in the depot, let alone move them to the ground they'd prepared. It was very frustrating, my father conceded, his arm growing heavy around my shoulders and his own gaze wandering to the scenery outside. I watched the outgoing tracks sprinting beside us, and imagined a pair of simultaneous tunnels, blind, flowered snouts and efficient fingers churning the soil up from below.

We reached our gate just as John-O was leaving, and it was clear from my mother's expression that she'd been trying to ease him out for some time. When John-O saw us his face brightened. My mother's brows drew together like curtains; she exhaled audibly and went back inside.

Talk sense to this woman, John-O pleaded, walking backwards in front of my father. She won't listen to me.

The dress was loosely assembled now. My father stooped to gather a fallen crinoline and struggled to drape it over the back of a chair, the garment appearing to defy gravity until my mother took it off him and dropped it back onto the floor.

I want to go to the council, get a sign put up.

A sign to say what?

Keep Off, that's what, my mother said irritably. I'm tired of wasting my time and money. It should be the council's problem, not mine.

Don't let her do it, John-O said to my father. She'll only annoy them. You're lucky they've let you paint the thing over. How many times has it been now? Three?

Four. If the council won't listen I'll go to the police.

You don't know who they are, John-O said. They could put you out first.

Is that right? Well just let them try.

It's not worth it, John-O said earnestly, even if it is just kids. Kids can be wee bastards, too, you know.

Where's Ricky? my father said after John-O went home.

Upstairs with Jason. Can't you hear that damn racket?

Go tell him to lower it, luv, my father said, and I had to twice before Ricky would. When I came down the second time my father, whose hands were cool even in summer, had placed his palms on the back of her neck, right where the spine makes its small mountain ridge, and was kneading her shoulders in generous handfuls, his own cheek resting on the top of her head.

I'm still going to do it, Joe, she said.

Ricky's friend left a short while later, and my father herded me upstairs to bed. I'm not tired, I told him, I slept on the train. Go on, luv, he said, lie down, close your eyes. Don't you worry. Everything's going to be OK. Here – tell me three things you saw today and I'll make you a story.

A tub in a field, I said. And a tree island. And a whole fence full of plastic bags.

Right, he said, here goes the first one. There once was a king whose greatest wish was for peace and quiet. Though his country had not been to war for many years, and though the land was fertile and the climate kind, still his people fought and bickered amongst themselves, and the king, as the arbiter of all disputes, found himself again and again called away from love or meditation to pass judgement on a trivial disagreement, or soothe the ego of some individual who felt insulted or slighted by somebody else. The king consulted with the greatest minds in study and politics, but no one could offer any good advice. Finally the king commissioned a wizard who said he'd cast a spell that'd do the trick – he'd send a fog so thick it'd cover the land like heavy cream, and when it cleared all those thinking evil thoughts about another would be revealed for what they were. The king agreed, and for nine days afterwards a fog was on them, thicker on the ninth day than it had been on the first. On the tenth day the sun was so brilliant that most folks just marvelled – until they heard the embarrassed cries of the evil thinkers, caught stark naked in their bathtubs out in their fields for all the world to see. For the wizard had set an additional spell, so that all the vicious and petty people would be taking a bath at just the same time. The tubs that exposed them have been there ever since, collecting rain for the livestock to drink. The land itself has changed hands so often, hardly a soul remembers why they're there now. Are you asleep yet?

Not yet, I said, but I already was.

Not so long ago the Hardest Working Couple in the World was living with their children in Island Magee. Though the mother and father had earned the title by working continuously for more than ten months, even so they barely had enough for the bills and the shopping, and though Christmas was coming they hadn't been able to buy any gifts. On Christmas Eve on the road home from work the woman met an old man with such heavy wrinkles he had to use a forked branch to keep his brows up. What can I do to please my children? the woman asked him, because she was desperate for someone to talk to. We've laboured long and hard, but we're no richer for it. We don't even have stockings to hang over the hearth. Take one empty sack for each in your family and tie them to the fence that keeps your cows in, the old man said, and tomorrow your children will thank you for it. The woman did what he'd told her, and the next morning every sack was full of chocolate and oranges, picture books and pens and mechanical toys. A month or so later it was one child's birthday, and again his parents had no money to spare. On the off chance of a second miracle the woman tied another sack to the fence – and sure enough the next morning it was so heavy it pulled the fence after it on its way to the ground. Why should we work, the woman wondered as she watched her son enjoying his presents, when all we want can be had for the asking? But the spirit that filled the bags was no eedjit; it knew what their game was when later that night the woman and her husband covered their fence with empty bags. The next morning all the sacks looked full from a distance, but up close it was clear they held only wind. The worst of it is the mother and father never learned their lesson: they kept leaving sacks on the fence for generations, and wasted so much time waiting for nothing they lost their title of Hard Working Couple to a rival team from Markethill. And that's why there's plastic bags on the fences, because people are greedy past the point of good sense.

My mother put down her scissors and looked at me. He told you this. I nodded.

What do you think of your father's stories?

I think he should sell them, John-O said. A letter requesting my father's attendance at an interview that afternoon had arrived the same morning, and John-O, who had spotted the post in the Job Finder listings, was waiting in our kitchen to see him off. He'd make a fortune, John-O continued. Youse could get out of Belfast, buy a big house with at least fifteen bedrooms, a huge garden and a two-car garage – you could buy a good car with that kind of money. That's what I'd do if I was him.

Well, said my mother, he left a part out of this one. Farmers put bags on their fences to frighten their cows, luv. It's to keep them away from the wire so they don't try to get into other people's fields.

You could even go somewhere exotic. John-O said. I hear the weather's brilliant in Florida. An annual rainfall of less than three inches and sunshine ten months out of every year.

Alright? said my father on his way past the kitchen. He'd come down the stairs at a run, his hand already reaching for the outside door.

Where's your tie? my mother demanded.

He patted his pocket. It's too warm, Belle. I'll put it on when I get there.

No, said my mother. Come over here. Stop fussing, Joe, she continued pre-emptively, it won't take a minute. Standing behind him she

85

tugged at his waistband, and the cuffs of his trousers snapped to attention. How's that? Too tight?

I could borrow a belt, my father suggested.

It's done now, my mother said, and ran her razor down the short seam at the back of the garment and plucked the torn stitches out with a pin. Hand me that thread, luv, she said, and I snapped off a strand and moistened its end, and she pushed it through the eye of the needle she held with the same hand that gripped the thin fabric of my father's summer suit. There, she said after a minute, tugging his sleeves and smoothing his shoulders, her fingers running over his lapels till he caught her wrists and drew her to him, placing a kiss on each open palm. Go on, get out of here, she said, you'll be late, but she stood at our gate and with me and John-O and even waved back to him as he waited for the bus.

Alright, everybody, she said as the bus pulled away, show's over, back to work. But the expected client was late for her fitting, and when John-O sent his niece over with cream buns later, my mother agreed she had made enough progress to stop and have one with a quick cup of tea. It was some time after that when the girl rang our bell.

C'mon in, my mother shouted from the kitchen where she'd taken a break from replacing a zipper to clean the grit out of Ricky's wounds. He'd been fighting again, though he wouldn't admit it. He'd told my mother he'd slipped on the ladder she'd told him expressly to stay away from, knowing the clout she was likely to give him would have been worse if he'd told her the truth. That's it there, my mother said before the girl could apologize, go ahead and try it on.

The girl took a step towards the dress and looked around her, at the no longer sterile roll of cotton and the bottle of alcohol on the kitchen counter, at Ricky's arm in my mother's firm grasp, at the teetering piles of new jeans and chinos purchased on sale from shops in the town, every one of them too long in the legs to be worn immediately and belonging to boys from our estate.

Where d'you want me?

Right here, my mother said. Ricky, go do something. He gave me a look as she released him, corked the bottle, and tossed the used swabs, but he needn't have bothered. I remembered the last time he'd gotten in trouble. He'd been one of a crowd of children who'd demolished a car that had been in an accident and was moved temporarily to the side of the road. The front left-hand corner had been shorn off on impact, but apart from that there'd been little damage, and those who'd come running when they heard the collision were saying it was too bad the driver was uninsured when a boy took a stick and smashed the taillights. Within half an hour all the windows were broken, the roof had caved in, and someone had started an ineffectual fire in the foam rubber stuffing they'd pulled out of the backseat. That afternoon Ricky and I went out with my father, who'd been in town when it happened, and found the owner of the car sitting on the kerb. Whose fault was it? my father asked him. It was his, the man said, but what does it matter? He's already got witnesses to say it was me. Later that night I'd informed on my brother, but my father said only, Yes, I know, and told me a story about Belfast Courthouse. A long time ago its four walls were formed out of living flora, a garden attended by Justice herself. But the crimes of Mankind had been so dazzling they had left Justice blind, and with no one to tend it the building itself had turned into stone, the grey marble leaves and flowers blackened by soot and ringing the pillars outside the court the only reminder of what Justice once was. So is Ricky not going to get beaten, then? I'd asked. No, he said, that's not the point. People don't often get what's coming to them, one way or the other. The important thing is to keep trying to make sure they do.

The dress opened and closed by button only. At least three dozen ran from the small of the back towards the high collar, each one fastened through a tight elastic loop. My mother lay a board across two tins of paint and tested it briefly; then the girl stepped onto it, the heavy folds of her skirts gathered high in both hands.

Are you redecorating? she asked.

All the time, my mother said. Lift up now; that's right.

I need to buy wallpaper myself, the girl said, holding her arms away from her sides. I was trying to get the house ready for Friday, but it's taking forever. I still have another two bedrooms to go, and I've done nothing else but that house all week.

How many bedrooms, altogether?

Five – well, four and a half, really. There's a wee room at the top that'd suit a child. It used to be part of the other back bedroom, but I put up a partition. We can always take it down again if we need the space. She dropped her arms on my mother's instruction and smiled. I retiled the bathroom, too, and lay new lino in the kitchen. I bought seeds to replant the garden, and a trellis for the side of the house, but I won't have the chance till after we've moved in.

If you don't mind me asking, my mother said, where are you getting the money for all this?

I won the pools, the girl said simply. I played the numbers Fortuna gave me, and I won about two thousand pounds. My mother was on her knees adjusting the hem so the lace trim of the underskirt would show more clearly; she glanced up at the girl but did not pause. She's been right about other things, too, the girl continued. She knew my sister miscarried the first time, and told her she was pregnant again before she knew herself. She can tell things about you just by holding your hand.

I don't think I'd like that, my mother said. Turn this way, please.

I know, the girl said, I thought I wouldn't, either. But it's OK, it's nothing like I expected. She's awful good. My girlfriend saved for two years to put a deposit on a trip to Corfu, and the first thing Fortuna says to her is You're going to travel. And she told my mum she was going to get better and it was six months before she took sick again.

I don't know, my mother said. Here, try the veil on. The pools thing's impressive, but the rest of it sounds pretty familiar.

You should go, the girl said generously. She knew wee things about me I never told anyone. I was ill myself last year and she knew about it. She even knew what was in my head at the time.

Upstairs Ricky kicked a football through the door of his room onto the landing and down the stairs into the hall. I saw the ball bounce on its way past the kitchen and then heard the sound of it striking wood. Go easy! my mother warned him when he came in, but he only grinned.

Da's back, he said.

My father seemed surprised when he saw us together, the girl on her platform, my mother on her knees, myself on a chair in charge of the pincushion, and Ricky with the football under his arm, spoiling his supper with the last cream bun.

This is my husband, my mother said through her teeth. The girl nodded quickly, flushed and self-conscious, but at that height even her awkwardness was elevated to grace. She wore the veil as it's worn after the vows, the thin film of gauze spilling over her shoulders like freshly brushed hair. My father stood beneath her, gazing up.

You look very beautiful, he said.

It's lovely, isn't it? the girl said eagerly.

It's alright, my mother said, but I knew she was pleased. I'd helped her select the low, smooth bodice, and approved the change to sleeves which began off the shoulder and tapered to a point just past the wrist. I'd been there when she'd added a bustle, and replaced a full skirt which just brushed the ground with one more narrow, with a heavy train. Think elegant, my mother had said as we looked through the patterns. What we don't want is to make the thing vulgar. Feminine, yes, but not delicate, necessarily. Handsome? I'd offered. That's it, she'd said. Whatever else happens, at least she'll look strong.

We won't be much longer, my mother told him. Why don't you go next door for a while? I'll send Ricky over when the supper's ready.

No need, my father said heartily, almost before John-O came into the room. John-O, this is the wee girl that's getting married.

Oh, aye? John-O said. Congratulations. What's your financé do, by the way?

Not now, my mother said sharply. We're not finished here.

Fortuna says he'll be a baker. She says he'll come home with flour in his pockets, and he'll leave white footprints on the carpet when he takes off his shoes. She says I'll never smell another woman on him, only bread from the oven and marzipan.

My father's mouth opened, but when no words were coming John-O stopped waiting and turned back to the girl.

Is he from round here, your boyfriend?

Oh no, she said, he's from the country. That's why I got a house near Bellevue. Fortuna said he'd like it, being close to Cave Hill.

An outdoorsy type, is he?

He'll like having a garden, the girl said, he can make anything grow. I was just going to get roses, put a few bushes at the front of the house, but Fortuna said I should invest in a fruit tree or something, since she didn't see us moving house for a while. Course, I'm useless with flowers, and I can't cook. That's why Fortuna thinks we'll make a good match.

Right, my mother said, that's us finished. Could youse all get out while she changes, please?

After they'd gone she brought out the linens, four sets of sheets and eight pillowcases so heavy that when she set them down on the kitchen table loose scraps of thread and less durable fabrics jumped up in protest, and the hair around all three of our faces was moved by the puff of air she'd displaced. Your shift and things aren't finished yet, she told the girl, but I'll have them all ready for Wednesday. You can come and collect them any time after noon.

Can't I have them delivered? It's just I still have so much to do.

If you want, my mother said. It's a bit risky. Personally I like to have a good look at a thing before I pay the bill. But it's up to you. If you want them sent over I need the balance off you now.

That's OK, the girl said, I brought money with me. The bills she counted onto the table were still crisp and in sequence like the sheaves that spill from unmarked envelopes or are stacked and banded in open briefcases and pushed across deserted warehouse floors, and I thought of a trick that John-O had taught me, a way to fold bank notes to make the face printed on them smile or frown. That only works with the real ones, my father had added. All the forged ones do is grin.

It really is lovely, the girl said as she pulled on her coat.

I think it suits you, my mother said, following her out. You'll look well on the day. Are you getting your hair done?

Aye, I am, I'm putting it up. I brought in that picture you gave me, the one you drew the first time I came here. The girl in the salon said she could do something that'd set off the dress. I hope it's OK – I nearly rang you up to get your opinion, but you'd have to have seen it, really, to know. Here, why don't you come? she suggested suddenly. I've booked a wee room for the reception after – there's one right beside where they do the service.

Sorry, my mother said, but I'm up to my eyes in work at the minute. Thanks all the same.

It'd only be for an hour. There's another couple booked in for one o'clock. Please come. And think about going to see Fortuna. It's only five pounds for a palm reading, ten if you want the crystal ball.

My father sighed as he closed the door after her. So what d'you think? John-O asked him. Is she crazy?

No more than most.

Will there not be a wedding, then?

You never know, luv, he said. She might find someone yet. It's easier now, certainly, than it used to be. A long time ago there were rules about who you could marry. If a man fell in love with a widow, for example, he couldn't marry her unless he was a widower himself.

That's true enough, John-O said before my mother could protest. I heard about that on *Celebrity Squares*.

One boy in particular, my father continued, fell in love with a girl who was already married. Many years went by and the young man grew old, but he stayed a bachelor, for he knew he'd be no good as a husband without her as his wife. He spent his time writing bad poetry and romantic letters which of course he never sent, for the woman herself was happily married, and whatever his feelings he'd never do anything that might cause her pain. He wished no harm on her husband, either. In fact, he was almost resigned to a life as Love's martyr then word reached him that his beloved had been widowed at last. After a period of respectful courtship he crossed his fingers and made his proposal; naturally he was over the moon when she said yes. To get round the rules he married a tree the following morning, chopped it down to be widowed around three o'clock, and that very evening joined his sweetheart in holy matrimony.

Married a tree, my mother repeated.

You see? Ricky said. If that girl's not crazy, what d'you call him?

It's all true, John-O protested. I remember the programme.

If there is a wedding, I asked my mother, are you going to go?

I am not, she said. She glanced at my father. And neither are you.

Maybe we ought to, he said. She shouldn't be alone.

She's got family. Her sister'll be there. She'll be alright.

Aye, she will, Ricky said. If she can't find a man she can marry a tree.

What's going to happen? I asked my father when he came in later to kiss me good-night. I don't know, luv, he said. Maybe she'll be lucky. Lots of people are.

I rolled towards the weight of him on the edge of my bed, and for a long time his fingers brushed the hair from my brow and temple, smoothing and shaping it over my ear. We did not speak. I kept my eyes closed when he finished, and he stood up without asking if I were asleep. I opened them only when his back was turned and saw my mother in the doorway, watching him come.

Well? she asked. How'd it go?

He took her hand from her pocket and turned it over.

You'll have a long life, he said, and two lovely children. But you'll live in a house that brings only trouble, and you'll marry a man who'll be good for nothing and make your life seem longer still.

Did it not go well, then.

Not very.

Why, what happened?

He tilted her palm for a further reading but she put her other hand on his shoulder, and he stopped and frowned and looked at her arm.

Tell me, she said.

What's there to tell? I'm thirty-eight years old; I've not worked in six years. How good could it go?

But you got an interview.

Yes, he said. There is that.

There'll be other jobs, she said, and though I could not see her face with the hall light behind her I imagined the way it had summoned its power the first morning she'd discovered they'd painted our wall.

We went to Portrush on the day of the wedding. My father asked John-O to come along with us, but he'd promised to take his nephew and niece to the zoo. There was a polar bear there that they wanted to see, which took two steps backwards for every twelve it walked front, and an elephant seal that spent most of its time under the water and only pretended to enjoy human company. Why does he do that? I'd asked my father. We'd been lucky; we were far from the Plexiglas when we saw the beast spew, the small group who'd gathered to laugh or admire stumbling backwards in confusion, holding their soaked shirts and blouses away from their skin. He's proud, my father explained, and he values his privacy. This is his way of pointing back.

It was strange not to transfer when we got to Coleraine. On good days the cast-iron bridge that vaulted the tracks was warm to the touch as I held onto the rail, the pigeons so bold on the ledge just beneath us that they barely noticed when we passed, their heads subsiding between their shoulders, the dreary stains and splotches of their city colours made as beautiful in the sunlight as the faint iridescence around their necks. But this time we stayed seated and watched other passengers collect their belongings and empty out of the small wooden doors which let the breeze in. A few people came on but walked through to Smoking, then the doors were snapped shut along the length of the carriage. I heard someone whistle, and the train pulled away.

The forecast had been hopeful, so we'd brought food for a picnic. In a concrete shelter which faced the sea my mother announced the contents of the sandwiches she'd made and distributed them to us with a packet of crisps and carton of orange, and for a while there was only the sound of crunch and swallow, and the spluttering sighs of liquid reversing through straws.

A gull stalked the wall that bordered the walkway, harassing a dog in the shade underneath. We threw scraps and the gull descended, riding the air with wings outstretched as if it were lowered by invisible strings, and soon more arrived, each one as possessive of the air space in front of us as if it had the right of being there first. In the interest of fairness I threw a crust to the dog. It raised its chin to watch the bread land but apart from that it didn't move. No, my father agreed when I showed him, they aren't very intelligent. The Sixth Day of Creation was a busy one for God; the dogs had to wait for several hours while He was fashioning the other beasts, and by that time all the best attributes had been given out. Loyalty and patience and an affectionate nature seemed more attractive to them than intelligence at the time. Not such a poor choice, my mother said. No, my father responded. I don't think they regret it.

Here, Da, Ricky said, wait'll you see. He called the dog by some generic name, and the animal rose from its haunches and came over, smiling and nodding and wagging its tail.

Sit, Ricky said, and the dog sat down indifferently like a man whose thoughts are somewhere else. Give us your paw, he said, and the animal did so with bored amusement, as if it were humouring a tiresome friend. Hand me a hammer, Ricky said with the same inflection, and the dog withdrew its right arm and lifted its left. See? Ricky said. You can tell'm anything. It's all got to do with your tone of voice. What do you want me to make him do?

Have him roll over, my mother said.

Fly round, Ricky said, addressing the dog, go on, fly round. The dog stretched lazily, its rump raised and waving till its chest touched the ground. That's it; now – throw bowlers! Ricky commanded, but the dog looked at him sceptically, its eyebrows raised. Throw bowlers, he said again, like an invitation, and the dog lay its ear on the tarmac and rolled onto its back. For some time preoccupied with its own hips and shoulders, it finally rose and shook itself violently, spattering us with flecks of saliva, fragments of glass, sand and lawn clippings and other footpath garbage. When it had finished it calmly accepted the crisps Ricky fed it and offered its ears to my father's caress.

The dog followed briefly when we headed for Waterworld, but soon was distracted by the sight of something at the far end of the beach. Let him go, son, my mother said when Ricky called after him, then slipped her arm through his as if she found walking difficult and she needed his help. They don't allow dogs where we're going, anyway.

The complex featured a selection of swimming pools and three water slides, twisting tunnels of bright coloured plastic which plunged thirty feet into the water, jiggling like innards each time they were used, and a hidden machine which produced six-foot waves. The smell of chlorine was sharp close to the pools, and even the foyer was warm and damp. In the changing rooms at the back of the building wet swimsuits and towels slapped to the ground beside the benches and outside the stalls with the finality of things attracted by magnets, and steam rose from the threshold of water through which all new arrivals were required to pass. For a while I just stood by the railing and watched others pop from the slides with all the surprise of people whose chairs have been pulled out from under them. A siren erupted every half hour, and those on the lip of the pool with their feet in the water twisted round on their palms and slipped over the side. Then the machine was switched on and the contents of the pool sloshed over its edges, slapping the steps at the opposite end where the concrete floor hurried up at an anxious angle, and the water was so shallow it was still almost white. Because Ricky dared me I climbed the scaffolding which led to the slides. Someone behind me gave me a push, and I was carried down on a thin sheet of water, my hips riding furiously up the sides of the tube. All I could see was the white mouth of the exit swinging far in front, at the centre of a world which was otherwise yellow, backlit and uniform and almost translucent, and I thought of small, pallid insects and what they might see traversing the contours of delicate blossoms, following the easy confluence of grooves.

When we got home my mother of course was the first to spot it, and she saw it as soon as we stepped from the bus. At the bottom men and women with various weapons stood with bowed heads against the ruins of battle while others fired a volley into the folds of a banner strung up with barbed wire and printed all over with shields and crests. Above all this a golden youth towered, her gaze flung backwards over her shoulder, her right arm raised and beckoning to the dark silhouettes of the marchers who followed her – Opportunity! Culture! their placards promised, Houses! Jobs! Education for All!

Charles D'Ambrosio, Jr
The Point

I had been lying awake after my nightmare, a nightmare in which Father and I bought helium balloons at a circus. I tied mine around my finger and Father tied his around a stringbean and lost it. After that, I lay in the dark, tossing and turning, sleepless from all the sand in my sheets and all the uproar out in the living-room. Then the door opened, and for a moment the blade of bright light blinded me. The party was still going full blast, and now with the door ajar and my eyes adjusting I glimpsed the silver smoke swirling in the light and all the people suspended in it, hovering around as if they were angels in Heaven – some kind of Heaven where the host serves highballs and the men smoke cigars and the women all smell like rotting fruit. Everything was hysterical out there – the men laughing, the ice clinking, the women shrieking. A woman crossed over and sat on the edge of my bed, bending over me. It was Mother. She was backlit, a vague, looming silhouette, but I could smell lily of the valley and something else – lemon rind from the bitter twist she always chewed when she reached the watery bottom of her vodka-and-tonic. When Father was alive, she rarely drank, but after he shot himself you could say she really let herself go.

'Dearest?' she said.

'Hi, Mom,' I said.

'Your old mother's bombed, dearest – flat-out bombed.'

'That's OK,' I said. She liked to confess these things to me, although it was always obvious how tanked she was, and I never cared. I considered myself a pro at this business. 'It's a party,' I said, casually. 'Live it up.'

'Oh, God,' she laughed. 'I don't know how I got this way.'

'What do you want, Mom?'

'Yes, dear,' she said. 'There was something I wanted.'

She looked out the window – at the sail-white moon beyond the black branches of the apple tree – and then she looked into my eyes. 'What was it I wanted?' Her eyes were moist, and mapped with red veins. 'I came here for a reason,' she said, 'but I've forgotten it now.'

'Maybe if you go back you'll remember,' I suggested.

Just then, Mrs Gurney leaned through the doorway. 'Well?' she said, slumping down on the floor. Mrs Gurney had bright-silver hair and a dark tan – the sort of tan that women around here get when their marriages start busting up. I could see the gaudy gold chains looped around Mrs Gurney's dark-brown neck winking in the half-light before they plunged from sight into the darker gulf between her breasts.

'That's it,' Mother said. 'Mrs Gurney. She's worse off than me. She's really blitzo. Blotto? Blitzed?'

'Hand me my jams,' I said.

I slipped my swim trunks on underneath the covers.

For years, I'd been escorting these old inebriates over the sandy playfield and along the winding boardwalks and up the salt-whitened steps of their homes, brewing coffee, fixing a little toast or heating leftovers, searching the medicine cabinets for aspirin and Vitamin B, setting a glass of water on the nightstand, or the coffee table if they'd collapsed on the couch – and even, once, tucking some old fart snugly into bed between purple silk sheets. I'd guide these drunks home and hear stories about the alma mater, Theta Xi, Boeing stock splits, Cadillacs, divorce, Nembutal, infidelity, and often the people I helped home gave me three or four bucks for listening to all their sad business. I suppose it was better than a paper route. Father, who'd been a medic in Vietnam, made it my job when I was ten, and at thirteen I considered myself a hard-core veteran, treating every trip like a mission.

'OK, Mrs Gurney,' I said. 'Upsy-daisy.'

She held her hand out, and I grabbed it, leaned back, and hoisted her to her feet. She stood there a minute, listing this way, that way, like a sailor who hadn't been to port in a while.

Mother kissed her wetly on the lips and then said to me, 'Hurry home.'

'I'm toasted,' Mrs Gurney explained. 'Just toasted.'

'Let's go out the back way,' I said. It would only take longer if we had to navigate our way through the party, offering excuses and making those ridiculous promises adults always make to one another when the party's over. 'Hey, we'll do it again,' they assure each other, as if that needed to be said. And I'd noticed how, with the summer ending, and Labor Day approaching, all the adults would acquire a sort of desperate, clinging manner, as if this were all going to end forever, and the good times would never be seen again. Of course I now realize that the end was just an excuse to party like maniacs. The softball tournament, the salmon derby, the cocktails, the clambakes, the barbecues would all happen again. They always had and they always would.

Anyway, out the back door and down the steps.

Once, I'd made a big mistake with a retired account executive, a friend of Father's. Fred was already falling-down drunk, so it didn't help at all that he had two more drinks on the way out the door, apologizing for his condition, which no one noticed, and boisterously offering bad stock tips. I finally got Fred going and dragged him partway home in a wagon, dumping his fat ass in front of his house – close enough, I figured – wedged in against some driftwood so the tide wouldn't wash him out to sea. He didn't get taken out to sea, but the sea did come to him, as the tide rose, and when he woke he was lassoed in green kelp. Fortunately, he'd forgotten the whole thing – how he'd got where he was, where he'd been before that – but it scared me, that a more or less right-hearted attempt on my part might end in such an ugly mess.

By now, though, I'd worked this job so long I knew all the tricks.

The moon was full and immaculately white in a blue-black sky. The wind funnelled down Saratoga Passage, blowing hard, blowing south, and Mrs Gurney and I were struggling against it, tacking back and forth across the playfield. Mrs Gurney strangled her arm around my neck and we wobbled along. Bits of sand shot in our eyes and blinded us.

'Keep your head down, Mrs Gurney! I'll guide you!'

She plopped herself down in the sand, nesting there as if she were going to lay an egg. She unbuckled her sandals and tossed them behind her. I ran back and fetched them from the sand. Her skirt fluttered in the wind and flew up in her face. Her silver hair, which was usually shellacked with spray and coiffed to resemble a crash helmet, cracked and blew apart, splintering like a clutch of straw.

'Why'd I drink so damned much?' she screamed. 'I'm toasted –

really, Kurt, I'm totally toasted. I shouldn't have drunk so damn much.'

'Well, you did, Mrs Gurney,' I said, bending toward her. 'That's not the problem now. The problem now is how to get you home.'

'Why, God damn it!'

'Trust me, Mrs Gurney. Home is where you want to be.'

One tip about these drunks: my opinion is that it pays in the long run to stick as close as possible to the task at hand. We're just going home, you assure them, and tomorrow it will all be different. I've found if you stray too far from the simple goal of getting home and going to sleep you let yourself in for a lot of unnecessary hell. You start hearing about their whole miserable existence, and suddenly it's the most important thing in the world to fix it all up, right then. Certain things in life can't be repaired, as in Father's situation, and that's always sad, but I believe there's nothing in life that can be remedied under the influence of half a dozen planter's punches.

Now, not everyone on the Point was a crazed rumhound, but the ones that weren't, the people who accurately assessed their capacities and balanced their intake accordingly, the people who never got lost, who never passed out in flower beds or, adrift in the maze of narrow boardwalks, gave up the search for home altogether and walked into any old house that was nearby – they, the people who never did these things and knew what they were about, never needed my help. They also weren't too friendly with my mother and didn't participate in her weekly bashes. The Point was kind of divided that way – between the upright, seaworthy residents and the easily overturned friends of my mother's.

Mrs Gurney lived about a half mile up the beach in a bungalow with a lot of Gothic additions. The scuttlebutt on Mrs Gurney was that while she wasn't divorced, her husband didn't love her. This kind of knowledge was part of my job, something I didn't relish but accepted as an occupational hazard. I knew all the gossip, the rumors, the rising and falling fortunes of my mother's friends. After a summer, I'd have the dirt on everyone, whether I wanted it or not. But I had developed a priestly sense of my position, and whatever anyone told me in a plastered, blathering confessional fit was as safe and privileged as if it had been spoken in a private audience with the Pope. Still, I hoped Mrs Gurney would stick to the immediate goal and not start talking about how sad and lonely she was, or how cruel her husband was, or what was going to become of us all, etc.

The wind rattled the swings back and forth, chains creaking, and whipped the ragged flag, which flew at half-mast. Earlier that summer, Mr Crutchfield, the insurance lawyer, had fallen overboard and drowned while hauling in his crab trap. He always smeared his bait box with Mentholatum, which is illegal, and the crabs went crazy for it, and I imagined that in his greed, catching over the limit, he couldn't haul the trap up but wouldn't let go, either, and the weight pulled him into the sea, and he had a heart attack and drowned. The current floated him all the way to Everett before he was found, white and bloated as soggy bread.

Mrs Gurney was squatting on the ground, lifting fistfuls of sand and letting them course through her fingers, the grains falling away as through an hourglass.

'Mrs Gurney? We're not making much progress.'

She rose to her feet, gripping my pant leg, my shirt, my sleeve, then my neck. We started walking again. The sand was deep and loose, and with every step we sank down through the soft layers until a solid purchase was gained in the hard-packed sand below, and we could push off in baby steps. The night was sharp, and alive with shadows – everything, even the tiny tufted weeds that sprouted through the sand, had a shadow – and this deepened the world, made it seem thicker, with layers, and more layers, and then a darkness into which I couldn't see.

'You know,' Mrs Gurney said, 'the thing about these parties is the thing about drinking is – you know, getting so damnably blasted is . . .' She stopped, and tried to mash her wild hair back down into place, and, no longer holding on to anything other than her head, fell back on her ass into the sand.

I waited for her to finish her sentence, then gave up, knowing it was gone forever. Her lipstick, I noticed, was smeared clownishly around her mouth, fixing her lips into a frown, or maybe a smirk. She smelled different from my mother – like pepper, I thought, and bananas. She was taller than me, and a little plump, with a nose shaped exactly like her head, like a miniature replica of it right in the middle of her face.

We finally got off the playfield and onto the boardwalk that fronted the seawall. A wooden wagon leaned over in the sand. I tipped it upright.

'Here you go, Mrs Gurney,' I said, pointing to the wagon. 'Hop aboard.'

'I'm OK,' she protested. 'I'm fine. Fine and dandy.'

'You're not fine, Mrs Gurney.'

The caretaker built these wagons out of old hatches from P.T. boats. They were heavy, monstrous, and made to last. Once you got them rolling, they cruised.

Mrs Gurney got in, not without a good deal of operatics, and when I finally got her to shut up and sit down I started pulling. I'd never taken her home before, but on a scale of one to ten, ten being the most obstreperous, I was rating her about a six at this point.

She stretched out like Cleopatra floating down the Nile in her barge. 'Stop the world,' she sang, 'I want to get off.'

I vaguely recalled that as a song from my parents' generation. It reminded me of my father, who shot himself in the head one morning – did I already say this? He was sitting in the grass parking lot above the Point. Officially, his death was ruled an accident, a 'death by misadventure', and everyone believed that he had in fact been cleaning his gun, but Mother told me otherwise, one night. Mother had a batch of lame excuses she tried on me, but it only made me sad to see her groping for an answer and falling way short. I wished she'd come up with something, just for herself. Father used to say that everyone up here was *dinky dow*, which is Vietnamese patois for 'crazy'. At times, after Father died, I thought Mother was going a little *dinky dow* herself.

I leaned forward, my head bent against the wind. Off to starboard, the sea was black, with a line of moonlit white waves continually crashing on the shore. Far off, I could see the dark headlands of Hat Island, the island itself rising from the water like a breaching whale, and then, beyond, the soft, blue, irresolute lights of Everett, on the distant mainland.

I stopped for a breather, and Mrs Gurney was gone. She was sitting on the boardwalk, a few houses back.

'Look at all these houses,' Mrs Gurney said, swinging her arms around.

'Let's go, Mrs Gurney.'

'Another fucking great summer at the Point.'

The wind seemed to be refreshing Mrs Gurney, but that was a hard one to call. Often, drunks seemed on the verge of sobering up, and then, just as soon as they got themselves nicely balanced, they plunged off the other side, into depression.

'Poor Crutchfield,' Mrs Gurney said. We stood in front of Mr Crutchfield's house. An upstairs light – in the bedroom, I knew – was

on, although the lower stories were dark and empty. 'And Lucy –
God, such grief. They loved each other, Kurt.' Mrs Gurney frowned.
'They loved each other. And now?'

Actually, the Crutchfields hadn't loved each other – information I
alone was privy to. Lucy's grief, I was sure, had to do with the fact
that her husband died in a state of absolute misery, and now she
would never be able to change things. In Lucy's mind, he would be
forever screwing around, and she would be forever waiting for him to
cut it out and come home. After he died, she spread the myth of their
reconciliation, and everyone believed it, but I knew it to be a lie. Mr
Crutchfield's sense of failure over the marriage was enormous. He
blamed himself, as perhaps he should have. But I remember, one night
earlier in the summer, telling him it was OK, that if he was unhappy
with Lucy, it was fine to fuck around. He said, You think so? I said,
Sure, go for it.

Of course, you might ask, what did I know? At thirteen, I'd never
even smooched with a girl, but I had nothing to lose by encouraging
him. He was drunk, he was miserable, and I had a job, and that job
was to get him home and try to prevent him from dwelling too much
on himself.

It was that night, the night I took Mr Crutchfield home, as I walked
back to our house, that I developed the theory of the black hole, and
it helped me immeasurably in conducting this business of steering
drunks around the Point. The idea was this – that at a certain age, a
black hole emerged in the middle of your life, and everything got
sucked into it, and you knew, forever afterward, that it was there, this
dense negative space, and yet you went on, you struggled, you made
your money, you had some babies, you got wasted, and you pretended it wasn't there and never looked directly at it, if you could
manage the trick. I imagined that this black hole existed somewhere
just behind you and also somewhere just in front of you, so that you
were always leaving it behind and entering it at the same time. I
hadn't worked out the spatial thing too carefully, but that's what
I imagined. Sometimes the hole was only a pinprick in the mind, often
it was vast, frequently it fluctuated, beating like a heart, but it was
always there, and when you got drunk, thinking to escape, you only
noticed it more. Anyway, when I discovered this, much like an astron-
omer gazing out at the universe, I thought I had the key – and it
became a policy with me never to let one of my drunks think too

much and fall backward or forward into the black hole. We're going home, I would say to them – we're just going home.

I wondered how old Mrs Gurney was, and guessed thirty-seven. I imagined her black hole was about the size of a sewer cap.

Mrs Gurney sat down on the hull of an overturned life raft. She reached up under her skirt and pulled her nylons off, rolling them down her legs, tossing the little black doughnuts into the wind. I fetched them, too, and stuffed them into the straps of her sandals.

'Much better,' she said.

'We're not far now, Mrs Gurney. We'll have you home in no time.'

She managed to stand up on her own. She floated past me, heading toward the sea. A tangle of ghostly gray driftwood – old tree stumps, logs loosed from booms, planks – barred the way, being too treacherous for her to climb in such a drunken state, I thought, but Mrs Gurney just kept going, her hair exploding in the wind, her skirt billowing like a sail, her arms wavering like a trapeze artist's high up on the wire.

'Mrs Gurney?' I called.

'I want – ' she started, but the wind tore her words away. Then she sat down on a log, and when I got there, she was holding her head in her hands and vomiting between her legs. Vomit, and the spectacle of adults vomiting, was one of the unpleasant aspects of this job. I hated to see these people in such an abject position. Still, after three years, I knew in which closets the mops and sponges and cleansers were kept in quite a few houses on the Point.

I patted Mrs Gurney's shoulder, and said, 'That's OK, that's OK, just go right ahead. You'll feel much better when it's all out.'

She choked and spat, and a trail of silver hung from her lip down to the sand. 'Oh, damn it all, Kurt. Just damn it all to hell.' She raised her head. 'Look at me, just look at me, will you?'

She looked a little wretched, but all right. I'd seen worse.

'Have a cigarette, Mrs Gurney,' I said. 'Calm down.'

I didn't smoke, myself – thinking it was a disgusting habit – but I'd observed from past experience that a cigarette must taste good to a person who has just thrown up. A cigarette or two seemed to calm people right down, giving them something simple to concentrate on.

Mrs Gurney handed me her cigarettes. I shook one from the pack and stuck it in my mouth. I struck half a dozen matches before I got one going, cupping the flame against the wind in the style of old war movies. I puffed the smoke. I passed Mrs Gurney the cigarette, and she dragged on it, abstracted, gazing off. I waited, and let her smoke in peace.

'I feel god-awful,' Mrs Gurney groaned.

'It'll go away, Mrs Gurney. You're drunk. We just have to get you home.'

'Look at my skirt,' she said.

True, she'd messed it up a little, barfing on herself, but it was nothing a little soap and water couldn't fix. I told her that.

'How old am I, Kurt?' she retorted.

I pretended to think it over, then aimed low.

'Twenty-nine? Good God!' Mrs Gurney stared out across the water, at the deep, black shadow of Hat Island, and I looked, too, and it was remarkable, the way that darkness carved itself out of the darkness all around. But I could marvel over this when I was off duty.

'I'm thirty-eight, Kurt,' she screamed. 'Thirty-eight, thirty-eight, thirty-eight!'

I was losing her. She was heading for ten on a scale of ten.

'On a dark night, bumping around,' she said, 'you can't tell the difference between thirty-eight and forty. Fifty! Sixty!' She pitched her cigarette in a high, looping arc that exploded against a log in a spray of gold sparks. 'Where am I going, God damn it?'

'You're going home, Mrs Gurney. Hang tough.'

'I want to die.'

A few boats rocked in the wind, and a seal moaned out on the diving raft, the cries carrying away from us, south, downwind. A red warning beacon flashed out on the sandbar. Mrs Gurney clambered over the driftwood and weaved across the wet sand toward the sea. She stood by the shoreline, and for a moment I thought she might hurl herself into the breach, but she didn't. She stood on the shore's edge, the white waves swirling at her feet, and dropped her skirt around her ankles. She was wearing a silky white slip underneath, the sheen like a bike reflector in the moonlight. She waded out into the water and squatted down, scrubbing her skirt. Then she walked out of the water and stretched herself on the sand.

'Mrs Gurney?'

'I've got the fucking spins.'

Her eyes were closed. I suggested that she open them. 'It makes a difference,' I said. 'And sit up, Mrs Gurney. That makes a difference, too.'

'You've had the spins?' Mrs Gurney asked. 'Don't tell me you sneak into your mother's liquor cabinet, Kurt Pittman. Don't tell me that. Please, just please spare me that. Jesus Christ, I couldn't take it. Really, I couldn't take it, Kurt. Just shut the fuck up about that, all right?'

I'd never taken a drink in my life. 'I don't drink, Mrs Gurney.'

'I don't drink, Mrs Gurney,' she repeated. 'You prig.'

I wondered what time it was, and how long we'd been gone.

'Do you know how suddenly life can turn?' Mrs Gurney asked. 'How bad it can get?'

At first I didn't say anything. This kind of conversation didn't lead anywhere. Mrs Gurney was drunk and belligerent. She was looking for an enemy. 'We need to get you home, Mrs Gurney,' I said. 'That's my only concern.'

'Your only concern,' Mrs Gurney said, imitating me again. 'Lucky you.'

I stood there, slightly behind Mrs Gurney. I was getting tired, but sitting down in the sand might indicate to her that where we were was okay, and it wasn't. We needed to get beyond this stage, this tricky stage of grovelling in the sand and feeling depressed, and go to sleep.

'We're not getting anywhere like this,' I said.

'I've got cottonmouth,' Mrs Gurney said. She made fish movements with her mouth. She was shivering, too. She clasped her knees and tucked her head between her legs, trying to ball herself up like a potato bug.

'Kurt,' Mrs Gurney said, looking up at me, 'do you think I'm beautiful?'

I switched the sandals I was holding to the other hand. First I'll tell you what I said, and then I'll tell you what I was thinking. I said yes, and I said it immediately. And why? Because I sensed that questions that didn't receive an immediate response fell away into silence and were never answered. They got sucked into the black hole. I'd observed this, and I knew the trick was to close the gap in Mrs Gurney's mind, to bridge that spooky silence between the question and the answer. There she was, drunk, sick, shivering, loveless, sitting in the sand and asking me, a mere boy, if I thought she was beautiful. I said yes, because I knew it wouldn't hurt, or cost me anything but one measly breath, though that wasn't really my answer. The answer was in the immediacy, the swiftness of my response, stripped of all uncertainty and hesitation.

'Yes,' I said.

Mrs Gurney lay down again in the sand. She unbuttoned her blouse and unfastened her brassiere.

I scanned the dark, and fixed my eyes on a tug hauling a barge north through the Passage, up to the San Juans.

Mrs Gurney sat up. She shrugged out of her blouse and slipped her bra off and threw them into the wind. Again, I fetched her things from where they fell, and held the bundle at my side, waiting.

'That's better,' Mrs Gurney said, arching her back and stretching her hands in the air, waggling them as if she were some kind of dignitary in a parade. 'The wind blowing, it's like a spirit washing over you.'

'We should go, Mrs Gurney.'

'Sit, Kurt, sit,' she said, patting the wet sand. The imprint of her hand remained there a few seconds, then flattened and vanished. The tide was coming in fast, and it would be high tonight, with the moon full.

I crouched down, a few fet away.

'So you think I'm beautiful?' Mrs Gurney said. She stared ahead, not looking at me, letting the words drift in the wind.

'This really isn't a question of beauty or not beauty, Mrs Gurney.'

'No?'

'No,' I said. 'I know your husband doesn't love you, Mrs Gurney. That's the problem here.'

'Beauty,' she sang.

'No. Like they say, beauty is in the eye of the beholder. You don't have a beholder anymore, Mrs Gurney.'

'The moon and the stars,' she said, 'the wind and the sea.'

Wind, sea, stars, moon: we were in uncharted territory, and it was my fault. I'd let us stray from the goal, and now it was nowhere in sight. I had to steer this thing back on course, or we'd end up talking about God.

'Get dressed, Mrs Gurney; it's cold. This isn't good. We're going home.'

She clasped her knees, and rocked back and forth. She moaned, 'It's so far.'

'It's not far,' I said. 'We can see it from here.'

'Someday I'm leaving all this to you,' Mrs Gurney said, waving her hands around in circles, pointing at just about everything in the world. 'When I get it from my husband, after the divorce, I'm leaving it to you. That's a promise, Kurt. I mean that. It'll be in my will. You'll get a call. You'll get a call and you'll know I'm dead. But you'll be happy, you'll be very happy, because all of this will belong to you.'

Her house was only a hundred yards away. A wind sock, full of the air that passed through it, whipped back and forth on a tall white pole. Her two kids had been staying in town most of that summer. I wasn't sure if they were up this weekend. She'd left the porch light on for herself.

'You'd like all this, right?' Mrs Gurney asked.

'Now is not the time to discuss it,' I said.

Mrs Gurney lay back down in the sand. 'The stars have tails,' she said. 'When they spin.'

I looked up; they seemed fixed in place to me.

'The first time I fell in love I was fourteen. I fell in love when I was fifteen, I fell in love when I was sixteen, seventeen, eighteen. I just kept falling, over and over,' Mrs Gurney said. 'This eventually led to marriage.' She packed a lump of wet sand on her chest. 'It's so stupid – you know where I met him?'

I assumed she was referring to Jack, to Mr Gurney. 'No,' I said.

'On a golf course, can you believe it?'

'Do you golf, Mrs Gurney?'

'No! Hell no.'

'Does Jack?'

'No.'

I couldn't help her – it's the stories that don't make sense that drunks like to repeat. From some people, I'd been hearing the same stories every summer for the last three years – the kind everyone thinks is special, never realizing how everyone tells pretty much the same one, never realizing how all those stories blend, one to the next, and bleed into each other.

'I'm thirsty,' Mrs Gurney said. 'I'm so homesick.'

'We're close now,' I said.

'That's not what I mean,' she said. 'You don't know what I mean.'

'Maybe not,' I said. 'Please put your shirt on, Mrs Gurney.'

'I'll kill myself,' Mrs Gurney said. 'I'll go home and I'll kill myself.'

'That won't get you anywhere.'

'It'll show them.'

'You'd just be dead, Mrs Gurney. Then you'd be forgotten.'

'Crutchfield isn't forgotten. Poor Crutchfield. The flag's at halfmast.'

'This year,' I said. 'Next year it'll be back where it always is.'

'My boys wouldn't forget.'

That was certainly true, I thought, but I didn't want to get into it.

Mrs Gurney sat up. She shook her head back and forth, wildly, and sand flew from it. Then she stood, wobbling. I held the shirt out to her, looking down. She wiggled her toes, burrowing them into the sand.

'Look at me,' Mrs Gurney said.

'I'd rather not, Mrs Gurney,' I said. 'Tomorrow you'll be glad I didn't.'

For a moment we didn't speak, and into that empty space rushed the wind, the waves, the moaning seal out on the diving raft. I looked up, into Mrs Gurney's eyes, which were dark green, and floating in tears. She stared back, but kind of vaguely, and I wondered what she saw.

I had the feeling that the first to flinch would lose.

She took the shirt from my hand.

I looked.

In this, I had no experience, but I knew what I saw was not young flesh. Her breasts sagged away like sacks of wet sand, slumping off to either side. They were quite enormous, I thought, although I had nothing to compare them with. There were long whitish scars on them, as if a wild man or a bear had clawed her. The nipples were purple in the moonlight, and they puckered in the cold wind. The gold, squiggling loops of chain shone against the dark of her neck, and the V of her tan line made everything else seem astonishingly white. The tan skin of her chest looked like parchment, like the yellowed, crinkled page of some ancient text, maybe the Bible, or the Constitution, the original copy, or even the rough draft.

Mrs Gurney slipped the shirt over her shoulders and let it flap there in the wind. It blew off and tumbled down the beach. She sighed. Then she stepped closer and leaned toward me. I could smell her – the pepper, the bananas.

'Mrs Gurney,' I said, 'let's go home now.' The tide was high enough for us to feel the first foamy white reaches of the waves wash around our feet. The receding waves dragged her shirt into the sea, and then the incoming waves flung it back. It hung there in the margin, agitated. We were looking into each other's eyes. Up so close, there was nothing familiar in hers; they were just glassy and dark and expressionless.

It was then, I was sure, that her hand brushed the front of my trunks. I don't remember too much of what I was thinking, if I was, and this, this not thinking too clearly, might have been my downfall. What is it out there that indicates the right way? I might have gone down all the way. I might have sunk right there. I knew all the words for it, and they were all short and brutal. Fuck, poke, screw. A voice told me I could get away with it. Who will know the difference, the voice asked. It said, Go for it. And I knew the voice, knew it was the same voice that told Mr Crutchfield to go ahead, fuck around. We were alone – nothing out there but the moon and the sea. I looked at Mrs Gurney, looked into her eyes, and saw two black lines pouring out of them and running in crazy patterns down her cheeks.

I felt I should be gallant, or tender, and kiss Mrs Gurney. I felt I should say something, then I felt I should be quiet. It seemed as if the moment were poised, as if everything were fragile, and held together with silence.

We moved up the beach, away from the shore and the incoming tide, and the sand beneath the surface still held some of the day's warmth.

I took off my T-shirt. 'Put this on,' I said.

She tugged it on, inside out, and I gathered up her sandals and stockings and her bra. We kept silent. We worked our way over the sand, over the tangle of driftwood, the wind heaving at us from the north.

We crossed the boardwalk, and I held Mrs Gurney's elbow as we went up the steps of her house. Inside, I found the aspirin and poured a glass of apple cider, and brought these to her in bed, where she'd already curled up beneath a heavy Mexican blanket. She looked like she was sleeping underneath a rug. 'I'm thirsty,' she said, and drank down the aspirin with the juice. A lamp was on. Mrs Gurney's silver hair splayed out against the pillow, poking like bike spokes, every which way. I knelt beside the bed, and she touched my hand and parted her lips to speak, but I squeezed her hand and her eyes closed. Soon she was asleep.

As I was going downstairs, her two boys, Mark and Timmy, came out of their bedroom, and stared at me from the landing.

'Mommy home?' asked Timmy, who was three.

'Yeah,' I said. 'She's in bed, she's sleeping.'

They stood there on the lighted landing, blinking and rubbing knuckles in their eyes, and I stood below them on the steps in the dark.

'Where's the sitter?' I asked.

'She fell asleep,' Timmy said.

'You guys should be asleep, too.'

'I can't sleep,' Timmy said. 'Tell a bedtime.'

'I don't know any bedtime stories,' I said.

Back home, inside our house, the bright light and smoke stung my eyes. The living-room was crowded, but I knew everybody – the Potters, the Shanks, the Capstands, etc. It was noisy and shrill, and someone had cranked up the Victrola, and one of my grandfather's old records was sending a sea of hissing static through the room. I could see on the mantel, through the curling smoke, the shrine Mother had made for Father: his Silver Star and Purple Heart, which he got in Lao Bao, up near Khe Sanh, near the DMZ when he was a medic. His diploma from medical school angled cockeyed off a cut nail. A foul ball he'd caught at a baseball game, his reading glasses, a pocketknife, a stethoscope, a framed Hippocratic oath with snakes wreathed around what looked like a barber pole. I saw Mother flit through the kitchen with a silver cocktail shaker, jerking it like a percussion instrument. She just kept pacing like a caged animal, rattling cracked ice in the shaker. I couldn't hear any distinct voices above the party noise. I stood there awhile. No one seemed to notice me until Fred, three sheets to the wind, as they say, hoisted his empty glass in the air, and said, 'Hey, Captain!'

I went into the kitchen. Mother set down the shaker and looked at me. I gave her a hug. 'I'm back,' I said.

Then I crossed into my room and stripped the sheets from my bed. I hung them out the window and shook the sand away. I tossed the sheets back on the bed and stretched out, but I couldn't get to sleep. I got up and pulled one of Father's old letters out from under my mattress. I went out the back door. It was one of those nights on the Point when the blowing wind, the waves breaking in crushed white lines against the shore, the grinding sand, the moonwashed silhouettes of the huddled houses, the slapping of buoys offshore – when all of this seems to have been going on for a long, long time, and you feel eternity looking down on you. I sat on the swing. The letter was torn at the creases, and I opened it carefully, tilting it into the moonlight. It was dated 1966, and written to Mother. The print was smudged and hard to see.

First, the old news: thank you for the necktie. I'm not sure when I'll get a chance to wear it, but thanks. Now for my news. I've been wounded, but don't worry. I'm okay.

For several days a company had been deployed on the perimeter of this village – the rumor was that somehow the fields had been planted with VC mines. The men work with tanks – picture tanks moving back and forth over a field like huge lawnmowers. They clear the way by exploding the mines. Generally VC mines are anti-personnel, and the idea is that the tanks are supposed to set off the mines and absorb the explosions. Tanks can easily sustain the blows, and the men inside are safe. A textbook operation. Simple. Yesterday they set off twelve mines. Who knows how they got there?

Clearing the perimeter took several days. Last night they thought they were done. But as the men were jumping off the tanks, one of them landed right on a mine. I was the first medic to reach him. His feet and legs were blown off, blown away up to his groin. I've never seen anything so terrible, but here's what I remember most clearly: a piece of shrapnel had penetrated his can of shaving cream, and it was shooting a stream of white foam about five feet in the air. Blood spilling everywhere, and then this fountain of white arcing out of his back. The pressure inside the can kept hissing. The kid was maybe nineteen. 'Doc, I'm a mess,' he said. I called in a medevac. I started packing dressings, then saw his eyes lock up, and tried to revive him with heart massage. The kid died before the shaving cream was done spraying.

Everything became weirdly quiet, considering the havoc, and then suddenly the LZ got hot and we took fire – fifteen minutes of artillery and incoming mortar fire, then quiet again. Nothing, absolutely nothing. I took a piece of shrapnel in my back, but don't worry. I'm all right, though I won't have occasion to wear that tie soon. I didn't even know I was wounded until I felt the blood, and even then I thought it was someone else's.

Strange, during that fifteen minutes of action I felt no fear. But there's usually not much contact with the enemy. Often you don't see a single VC the whole time. Days pass without any contact. They're out there, you know, yet you never see them. Just mines, booby traps. I'm only a medic, and my contact with the enemy is rarely direct –

what I see are the wounded men and the dead, the bodies. I see the destruction, and I have begun to both fear and hate the Vietnamese – even here in South Vietnam, I can't tell whose side they're on. Every day I visit a nearby village and help a local doctor vaccinate children. The morning after the attack I felt the people in the village were laughing at me because they knew an American had died. Yesterday I returned to the same village. Everything quiet, business as usual, but I stood there, surrounded by hooches, thinking of that dead kid, and for a moment I felt the urge to even the score somehow.

What am I saying, sweetie? I'm a medic, trained to save lives. Every day I'm closer to death than most people ever get, except in their final second on earth. It's a world of hurt – that's the phrase we use – and things happen over here, things you just can't keep to yourself. I've seen what happens to men who try. They're consumed by what they've seen and done, they grow obsessive, and slowly they lose sight of the job they're supposed to be doing. I have no hard proof of this, but I think in this condition men open themselves up to attack. You've got to talk things out, get everything very clear in your mind. Lucky for me I've got a buddy over here who's been under fire too, and can understand what I'm feeling. That helps. I'm sorry to write like this, but in your letter you said you wanted to know everything. It's not in my power to say what this war means to you or anyone back home, but I can describe what happens, and if you want, I'll continue doing that. For me, at least, it's a comfort to know someone's out there, far away, who can't really understand, and I hope is never able to. I'll write again soon.

> *All love,*
> *Henry*

I'd snagged this letter from a box Mother kept in her room, under the bed. There were other kinds of letters in the box, letters about love and family and work, but I didn't think Mother would miss this one, which was just about war. Father never talked much about his tours in Vietnam, but he would if I asked. Out of respect, I learned not to ask too much, but I knew about Zippo raids, trip flares, bouncing bettys, hand frags, satchel charges and such, and when he was angry, or sad, Father often peppered his speech with slang he'd picked up, like *titi*, which means 'little', and *didi mow*, which means 'go quickly', and *xin loi*, meaning 'sorry about that'.

I tucked the letter away. I got the swing going real good, and I rose up, then fell, rose and fell, seeing, then not seeing. When the swing was going high enough I let go, and sailed through the open air, landing in an explosion of soft sand. I wiped the grains out of my eyes. My eyes watered, and everything was unclear. Things toppled and blew in the wind. A striped beach umbrella rolled across the playfield, twirling like a pinwheel. A sheet from someone's clothesline flapped loose and sailed away. I thought of my nightmare, of Father's balloon tied to a stringbean. I looked up at the sky, and it was black, with some light. There were stars, millions of them like tiny holes in something, and the moon, like a bigger hole in the same thing. White holes. I thought of Mrs Gurney and her blank eyes and the black pouring out of them. Was it the wind, a sudden gust kicking up and brushing my trunks? It happened so quickly. Had she tried to touch me? Had she? I stretched out in the sand. The wind gave me goose bumps. Shivering, I listened. From inside the house, I heard the men laughing, the ice clinking, the women shrieking. Everything in there was still hysterical. I'd never get to sleep. I decided to stay awake. They would all be going home, but until then I'd wait outside.

I lay there, very quietly. I brushed some sand off me. I waited.

It was me who found Father, that morning. I'd gone up to get some creosote out of the trunk of his car. It was a cold, gray, misty morning, the usual kind we have, and in the grass field above the parking lot there was a family of deer, chewing away, looking around, all innocent. And there he was, sitting in the car. I opened the passenger door. At first my eyes kind of separated from my brain, and I saw everything, real slow, like you might see a movie, or something far away that wasn't happening to you. Some of his face was gone. One of his eyes was staring out. He was still breathing, but his lungs worked like he'd swallowed a yard of chunk gravel or sand. He was twitching. I touched his hand and the fingers curled around mine, gripping, but it was just nerves, an old reaction or something, because he was brain-dead already. My imagination jumped right out of its box when he grabbed me. I knew right away I was being grabbed by a dead man. I got away. I ran away. In our house I tried to speak, but there were no words. I started pounding the walls and kicking over the furniture and breaking stuff. I couldn't see, I heard falling. I ran around the house holding and ripping at my head. Eventually Mother caught me. I just pointed up to the car. You understand, I miss Father, miss having him around to tell me what's right and what's wrong, or to talk about *boom-boom*, which is sex, or just to go salmon fishing out by Hat Island, and not worry about things, either way, but I also have to say, never again do I want to see anything like what I saw that morning. I never, as long as I live, want to find another dead person. He wasn't even a person then, just a blown-up thing, just crushed-up garbage. Part of his head was blasted away, and there was blood and hair and bone splattered on the windshield. It looked like he'd just driven the car through something awful, like he needed to use the windshield wipers, needed to switch the blades on high and clear the way, except that the wipers wouldn't do him any good, because the mess was all on the inside.

D. J. Durnam
I Know Some Things

Andrew, the man my mother married a month ago, always wants me to call him 'Dad', and I can never bring myself to do it. I suppose I'd feel different if my real father was dead. But he's alive and kicking and trying to make a living as a drummer in a back-up band for a no-name country singer who opens shows in Reno. Actually, that's not all exactly true. The singer has a name: Tully Washington, and he opens shows in other places, too. My real dad sent me a fur coat three and a half years ago when Tully and the band played a gig in Tahoe. 'Little girl,' he said in the card that came with it (I was only nine then). 'This had your name written all over it. I thought of you a hundred times today like always and I asked myself, does my Bobbie have a good warm winter coat? I asked myself that because it's been so damn cold here for the last two days I nearly froze my ****s (ask your mother – ha, ha) off.' The coat was really really beautiful. It was made out of rabbit fur, real brown rabbit fur and it had pink satin lining in the hood. It was so soft I wanted to wear it inside out at first but I couldn't get the sleeves to work right.

If I had that coat now, I'd wear it all the time just to bug Andrew. 'I don't believe in fur coats.' That's what he said to me when I tried to describe it to him. Andrew is the most serious person I've ever known or ever want to know. He's serious about every little thing: the kind of bread he eats, the color of the shoes he wears jogging, the silly orchid plants he moved into our apartment which he says haven't bloomed since he bought them. He's all business even when it comes to jokes. When you tell him a riddle, he tries too hard to get the answer. 'No, don't tell me,' he says, 'let me guess, let me guess,' until it isn't any fun at all. He's serious about that Dad thing, too, and just to prove it, he insists on calling me Bobbie. A couple of times I tell him as polite as I can, 'Andrew, only my *real* father and mother call me Bobbie. I'm Roberta to everybody else.' But I think he's got the shortest memory in the world because even after I tell him that, it's still Bobbie this and Bobbie that. So finally I can't stand it and when Mom's not around I say to him, 'It's Roberta, okay? R-O-B-E-R-T-A. Roberta. Do you think you can handle that?' I say, 'Do you think you can get a grip on three syllables instead of two?' Then he doesn't call me anything for almost a week.

I can tell Andrew's the *most* serious about being a grad student at Cal. He's older than a lot of the other students and he says that means he's got to try harder. He's older because he was in the Peace Corps for a while and had a job after that in a bookstore on Telegraph Avenue. The Peace Corps is positively the most interesting thing about Andrew. So naturally, it's the one thing he won't talk about much. I don't even know exactly what country it was he went to in Africa or how long he was there. He only says he went there to teach them to grow food better and that it was very very hot. I could've figured it out for myself that his work in the Peace Corps had something to do with plants because that's what he studies at the university and he knows a lot. He's always trying to teach me the Latin names of flowers. He's always pointing to some perfectly ordinary daisy or lily and reeling off a long complicated name that makes it sound like a disease. He knows fancy names for leaves and stems and petals, too, and one afternoon in the Co-op food store he tells me and Mom that a strawberry isn't just a strawberry. It's an achene. And a peach turns out not to be just a peach. It's a drupe.

So the next morning I get the giggles cutting up strawberries into the cereal for our breakfast. Mom is sitting there at the kitchen table in her old yellow bathrobe, one bare foot on the floor, one tucked underneath her on the chair. Her black hair hangs half way down her back and she's raking the fingers of her left hand through it over and over again which is a habit she has. In her other hand, she's holding a cigarette even though she promised Andrew two weeks ago that she would quit smoking. She's staring out the window and every time she flicks off the ash on the tip of her cigarette, she misses the ashtray.

Andrew's sitting across the table from Mom and his red hair is still wet and shiny from his shower. His freckles have been scrubbed to a darker shade of red and you can tell that the pale pale skin underneath the freckles is going to be a healthy pink for a few more minutes. (God, he must've burned and peeled a thousand times in

Africa.) I know he'd like to say something to Mom about the ashtray but he doesn't. He turns to watch me cut up the berries.

'Well, my goodness,' I say. 'These *achenes* sure look tasty.'

I laugh. I can see Mom start to smile and take a drag off her cigarette to stop herself. Andrew takes a sip of coffee.

'Jeez, I wish I had a big ol' *drupe* to cut up, too. Yum.'

I laugh harder and Mom is just about to crack up. I can tell.

Andrew puts his coffee cup down slowly. 'You think you're pretty funny, don't you?' he says. What a baby.

I say, 'Hey, no shit, Dick Tracy.'

'Bobbie!' Mom says like she's horrified but she doesn't mean it.

I wink at her and wait for her to wink back at me. She doesn't.

Andrew sits there and stares at Mom like he's expecting her to make me apologize. But she doesn't do that either. So he picks up his hands off the table and looks at them and lays them back down again.

I put the bowls of cereal on the table and wait until Andrew starts to eat. Then I lean over and rub Mom's knee. I wink again. This time I'm positive she sees me because she frowns and starts to eat, too. I understand then that winking will go onto the list I'm keeping of things we don't do together anymore since Andrew came.

Mom says we have to watch our step a little with Andrew in the family. The main thing he's not supposed to find out about is the time we went on welfare. I don't know why he would give a damn one way or the other. We were only on it for six months. But Mom is extra hyper about the subject and even hearing about it on the evening news with Andrew in the room makes her nervous. It happened right about the time Dad sent me that fur coat. He had already been out touring around for two years, every once in a while sending Mom some cash taped to the back of a picture of the band. There was Dad in the picture sitting behind his drums but you could see he was wearing a plaid shirt and cowboy boots and a cowboy hat like everybody else in the band. Naturally, Tully himself had the fanciest hat of all of them with a big chunk of turquoise set in silver on the front of it to match his belt buckle. The second prettiest hat, the baby blue one, was tilted at an angle on the head of Miss Virginia Lou DuPree. She was a singer with the band then and she had hair that was so blond it looked white in the picture. Mom called her Old Skinny Ginny and Old Chicken Legs, and sometimes she called her That Goddamn Bitch.

It was not a good time for either of us, Mom or me. I remember that Mom cried a lot, at first only when she thought I wasn't looking and later any time she felt like it. She slept all the time, too. After a while, I began to feel more and more tired myself. Some days I just couldn't get up the energy to go to school, so we'd sit around the apartment and play cards. Crazy Eights, Seven Up, Double Solitaire, and we bet on the games. We played for things we *didn't* want to do. It went like this, that whenever I was ahead by the end of the day, I wouldn't have to brush my teeth or set and clear the table or go to bed when Mom did. And when she won, she always got me to promise I'd be the one to walk to the store next time we needed something. She hated to be seen using food stamps to buy stuff. It didn't bother me at all. At least not until my real dad sent me the rabbit coat.

I still have the clearest picture in my head of everything that happened the only time I wore that coat to the store. I see Mom lying on the couch with the old striped afghan bundled around her feet. She's won at cards by twenty-six points the way we keep count and she says, 'You go, sweetie, okay? Pot pies, I guess.' Then she thinks about it for a second. She says, 'And what the hell, get something good for dessert, too. My purse is on the kitchen table.'

Next I see myself walking real slow down the street. It's only about four blocks to the store but I take some wrong turns and make it six or seven blocks that afternoon to give everybody a chance to check out my new coat. I'm dawdling inside the store, too. I'm looking at every single item in the frozen food section before I grab two chicken pot pies. And I'm picking up and putting down cake mixes and cans of frosting and bags of cookies before I decide on a quart of mint chip ice cream for dessert.

The store is a small one with two checkout counters and just one of them is open when I get into line. But that day I don't mind waiting. Pretty soon a short bald guy walks up and smiles. Noticing my coat, I think, and I smile back until I see him wave at the guy working the cash register.

'Hey, Wally, how's tricks?' the guy at the register says. He's bald, too, so it's no wonder they like each other.

'Can't complain,' the one behind me says. Then he says, 'Well, I suppose I could, but you know it wouldn't do me a damn bit of good.'

They get a real kick out of this and both of them laugh as I slide the two pot pies and the ice cream onto the counter.

'I guess your old lady must be doing a helluva job fixing you dinner,' the one behind me, Wally, says, patting his stomach and grinning.

'I swear to God,' the guy behind the counter says. 'It's all muscle.' But you could tell he's just big and soft. And round in places where even fat people usually have some kind of point or angle, like the chin or the elbows. The front of the white apron he has on is dirty only where his stomach sticks out. Still looking at Wally, he says, 'Three sixty-four.'

Jesus, I'm thinking, I've never known anybody that weighed that much.

'That'll be three sixty-four,' he says, looking down at me now.

'What?'

'Three dollars and sixty-four cents. Sheese,' he says to Wally. 'It's been one of those days.'

I lay the food stamps next to the ice cream.

He picks them up and sighs. 'You only got two seventy-five here.'

I'm not sure I've heard him right.

'I bet you got some honest-to-God money some place in that pretty coat of yours,' he says.

By this time I've forgotten all about the coat. Now I feel two things happening. The coat getting bigger and hotter and bigger. Myself getting smaller.

'No real money?' he says. 'Well, what'll it be then? The pot pies or the ice cream?' He turns to Wally. 'I'll lay you five to one it's the ice cream.'

And I *do* want the ice cream. It's like he's reading my mind. Then he reaches his soft round hand out and touches the sleeve of my coat and even though I want to back away, I can't move. I see for the first time he has a long purple bruise running down the inside of his arm. Later I will remember it and hope that it gets worse, hope even that he dies from it.

'Real fur,' he says. 'Real goddamn fur.' He's still holding the food stamps in his other hand. 'I see this kind of crap all the time,' he says. 'I bet her mama got a mink to match it.' He leans over to Wally and under his breath he says, 'Or a beaver.'

The sharp crack of Wally's laugh makes me jump. I push the ice cream to one side and the pot pies forward. The man at the register, laughing, too, holds out the piece of paper that is my change but I wait until he lays it on the counter. I will not touch his hand.

And then I run straight home and I catch my breath in the underground garage of the apartment building next to ours and when Mom asks about dessert I just tell her I forgot.

Two weeks later, I have to go to the store again. This time I make sure I have plenty of food stamps and even though it's damp and windy outside and we've had frost three nights in a row, I take off my rabbit coat once I'm out of the apartment and drop it rolled up into the only drawer left in the old dresser at the far end of the under-ground garage. I check between the cars where sometimes street people drink or sleep. And outside I look up and down the block for anybody that might be hanging around, anybody with sharp eyes and time to kill. I'm not taking any chances that somebody's seen me hide my coat.

I race to the store, thinking about my coat the whole way like I can make it safe somehow by just concentrating hard enough. The store is warm and crowded and there's only one register open again. But the guy working it is skinny and has long hair. The fat man in the apron isn't anywhere around. I get into the line that stretches back into one of the aisles. I'm still thinking hard about my coat, still working on keeping some kind of strong mental link between me and it as the line moves forward slowly. Then the high school chick two people ahead of me gets to the counter and she must think the skinny guy's cute because she starts up one of those giggly getting-to-know-you conver-sations. And he must think she's OK, too, because it takes him longer than forever to ring up a jar of spaghetti sauce and a package of egg noodles. The woman in front of me clears her throat in a meaningful way. After a few seconds, I do the same. The lovebirds at the counter give us a long hard look. The girl knows how to say fuck you real good with just her eyes. Finally she heads out the door.

As soon as I'm out of the store, I run back to the garage so fast my stomach aches. My legs are shaking and my fingers, the tips of my ears and nose, are numb from the cold. I rush over to the dresser, panting, yank open the drawer. I put my hand into it and I don't remember that I'm even breathing as my fingers cover every inch of the inside surface corner to corner to corner. The coat is gone.

You can believe that I honestly thought it was the worst thing that could ever happen to me (which considering Mom's marriage to Andrew just goes to show how wrong a person can be). And you could say that it turned out to be a sort of turning point. Not just because I lost my coat, although that was bad enough. I cried so hard it took me over an hour to tell Mom what happened, and I cried off and on for a long time afterwards and missed a whole week of school. But it turned out to be a turning point because Mom promised to buy me another coat just like the other one as soon as she could afford it and then three weeks later, she landed a job at the university. (In the stockroom on the fourth floor of the Life Sciences Building where two years later *Andrew* would be a graduate student in the Botany Department. The rest, as they say, is history.) Even more important though when Mom takes this job is the woman she gets to stay with me in the afternoons: a Mrs Willa Birden. It's pretty weird at first to get home every day from school at 2:30 and see some strange woman sitting on the couch watching TV. But later that spring when we get an assignment in art class to pick a famous saying and illustrate it, I think about how I lost my coat. I decide to do 'Every cloud has a silver lining.' And then I draw Willa Birden.

I draw her hair wavy and long, even longer than Mom's, and half way between dark blond and gray. I leave it hanging loose in the picture even though she wears it mostly in a braid or braids which she lets me pull apart and twist back together again like rope and which I sometimes wind crisscrossed around the back of her head or on top of it. I draw her wide high forehead and the cheeks that match it, both of them smooth and tan even in the winter because, Willa says, she has a fair-sized streak of Indian blood in her (and although one week it's Blackfoot and the next it might be Shoshoni, Sioux or Crow, I've never doubted her word about any of it). I try to give her eyes that are hazel in the afternoon but closer to brown in the evening, eyes that don't miss a thing. I put in a big stubborn-looking nose (Willa told me that when she was a young girl her face was working itself towards something sweet and pretty until her nose decided it had a mind of its own) and a mouth which might also look oversized on anybody else's face but only looks comfortable and right at home near the bottom of Willa's. I draw in the little bit of loose skin under her chin that quivers when she sings. Then I give her broad straight shoulders because Willa is what Mom calls big-boned and from the shoulders I hang a long dress that hasn't got a lot of shape to it and I make the dress a kind of deep quiet blue like the color of the sky overhead just after the sun goes down and I can almost hear Willa telling me, 'You know, I'll wear just about any color as long as it's blue.'

This picture I draw is of Willa on one of her good days. It doesn't take me long to figure out that she has both good days (most of the time) and days that we don't talk about or try to remember so that even after knowing Willa months and months and months, the bad days still catch me a little by surprise.

On the very best days, we go out together to shop or to pretend to shop. I come home from school, drop my books on the couch. 'RIP,' I'll say, looking down at them to make Willa laugh, and she'll tell me where we're headed that afternoon. A lot of times it's up to Telegraph Avenue to talk to the people selling pottery or jewelry along the sidewalk. The people that are busy just nod and smile at us, but at the stands where business is slow, somebody is bound to say, 'How you doin' Willa?' or 'Watcha been thinkin' Willa?'

And she'll say, 'I been having some thoughts about Montana lately. Born and raised there, you know.'

They'll say something to encourage her.

And she'll say, 'On a ranch. A real big spread.'

Sometimes she says it was a reservation. Sometimes she is the daughter of a doctor who lived in Montana, the only one for a whole territory, the only one for miles around.

Or she might start out, 'I been thinking of writing a letter to my husband. But who in the world knows where I should send it? The last I saw of him was on a fishing trip on the Bighorn River.' Or at the Pendleton Roundup, the Calgary Stampede. Or when he took that temporary job in Butte.

Willa starts out like this telling the Chinese woman who runs the fresh fruit and vegetable store a real long story all about the house she and her husband built by themselves after they were married. But she seems to lose track of it all right in the middle. She looks at the plastic name tag pinned to the woman's sweater and she says, 'What's Tai-yu stand for?'

The woman smiles like she's been waiting years for somebody to ask. 'Black Jade,' she says.

Willa points to the baby asleep in a car seat in the chair near Tai-yu's knees.

'Clarence,' Tai-yu says. She smiles again. 'His father, too.'

'He has beautiful hair,' Willa says. And it's true. The baby has lots and lots of hair so black it shines blue where the light hits it whenever anybody comes through the door. He has on new red baby-sized overalls. New shoes, too, with a metal rod like a skinny silver bridge hooked up from foot to foot. I can't help staring at it.

'No pigeon toes,' Tai-yu says.

Willa is buying two temple oranges for us to eat later. 'My son had that,' she says, 'when he was a baby. Those shoes will do the trick alright. He grew up fine.' Tai-yu nods and nods. But then the next Thursday Willa says it was her daughter that had the shoes.

'No problem,' Willa says. 'She grew up fine.'

I look at Tai-yu's face to see if she's noticed. But she nods at Willa again and smiles at me this time and says, 'Yes, I believe so, too,' and she watches my feet when we walk to the door.

That woman Tai-yu believes. And I believe, too, when Willa tells me she's heard Tully Washington singing on the radio.

'So your father plays the drums,' she says when I show her one of the pictures he sent us. 'Well, I see where you get your good looks.'

Willa knows everything I know about my real father. I tell her everything about my rabbit coat, too, and of course when Andrew starts showing up more and more I give her all the dope on him and Mom.

'Picture this,' I say. 'Mom spending a whole hour trying on a ton of different outfits and just so she can look cool for creepy old Andrew.' I stand in the middle of the living-room and I make like I'm trying on clothes and checking myself out in the mirror.

'And get this,' I say. 'On Saturday morning before he got here she used the mouthwash three times so he wouldn't find out she smokes. She was walking around going – ' and I cup my hands over my mouth and blow into them and take a big sniff of my breath.

Willa grins. Then she puts on a serious face. 'You really shouldn't poke fun at your own mother, you know,' she says. But there's this little humming sound, the one Willa makes when she's trying not to laugh.

So I imitate Andrew. 'How do you do?' I say, sticking my hand straight out at Willa the way he stuck his out to me. Willa laughs out loud.

'How do you do?' That's exactly what he says to Willa, too, the first time they meet. Only he snuffles it because he's got a cold. You can tell he's been blowing his nose all day long. It looks sore and red, almost the color of his hair. He smells like cherry cough drops.

'Oh, perfectly well,' Willa says. Then, 'You ought to see a doctor about that cold,' and pretty soon she's into a story about her father. The one about how he got pneumonia from driving seventy miles in below zero weather with the heat broken in his car to deliver a baby which had already been born when he got there.

All the time she's talking, Andrew keeps looking over at the bathroom where Mom's supposed to be 'freshening up' as she's put it. 'Umm,' he says every couple of minutes. He's picking at a hole in the cushion of the chair he's sitting in, pulling little pieces of stuffing out, rolling them into balls with his fingers. 'Umm.'

Finally Mom comes waltzing out of the bathroom in a cloud of hair spray and the Windsong perfume I got her for Christmas, and what does Andrew do? He gives his head a little jerk in Willa's direction and raises his eyebrows at Mom, not even giving a damn if Willa sees him or not.

Mom stops short. Embarrassed, I can tell, and maybe getting her first real good look at the *true* Andrew.

But then she turns to Willa. 'Oh, God, Willa,' she says breaking right into the story. 'I'm sorry to keep you waiting. I completely forgot this was Friday.' She takes fifteen dollars out of her purse and hands it to Willa. Then she goes over and stands by Andrew and she reaches down and fixes his collar where it's turned up funny on one side. She says, 'Why don't we go into the kitchen? You look like you could use something good and hot to drink.'

They leave me and Willa on the couch, Willa holding out the money in front of her like she's never seen money before in her whole life. I lean on her and she puts her other hand on top of my hand. Her fingers are rough and almost twice as long as mine. They're darker than the back of her hand, darker than the skin on her wrist. 'I hate him,' I whisper.

'Shh-h-h,' Willa whispers back, pressing her fingers down harder on mine. 'You don't hate anybody.' She waits for me to answer. When I don't, she whispers it again, 'You don't hate anybody.'

'C'mon,' she says. 'Walk me part ways home. You'll feel better.'

Out in the stairwell though, I stop and sigh. I feel like crying. I say, 'In two weeks they're going to be married.'

'I know,' she says. 'I know.'

We sit on the steps by the second floor landing. Willa puts her arm around me and I push my face into the folds of her blue dress. I take deep breaths, deeper than Willa's because I can feel her stomach rising and falling lightly under my head. I take deep breaths and I'm breathing in a kind of spiciness that is Willa's special smell and it reminds me of her bad days. It makes me think of those days when I come home and find her curled up on the couch under the afghan with the TV off and the curtains pulled shut. She lies there without talking, staring straight ahead, and sometimes she rubs the fingers of one hand slowly back and forth across her forehead and across her cheek. Her head is pressed against the couch the way mine is pressed into her dress and against her stomach that evening when we're sitting by the landing. But on the couch Willa doesn't breathe deeply. She hardly seems to breathe at all and I have knelt on the floor and laid my head on the couch, sliding my face closer and closer to Willa's until our noses almost touch and my eyes are looking into her eyes which don't seem to see me or anything. And I have listened for her breath holding my own until I catch a faint puff from Willa.

On the stairs I push myself closer to Willa, my head still in her lap, and I remember how scared I was on the very first bad day, thinking Willa was sick or even dying. Get somebody, get help, I kept saying to myself, but some stronger feeling kept telling me at the same time, *Don't go*. Don't let anybody else see Willa like this. So I just sat there and shook her by the shoulder with both my hands and whispered her name over and over, Willa, Willa, Willa, and when she blinked her eyes I shook her harder and helped her sit up. After a long time, when she noticed the look on my face, I mean when she really *saw* it, she hung her head and said, 'I'm alright. I'm fine.' But I could tell she wasn't really herself until I saw her the next day and then she smiled at me in a way that made me understand we wouldn't ever be talking about what had happened.

And after a while that's all the bad days are, just something that happens once or twice a month that we don't talk about. Pretty soon I even stop shaking Willa awake as soon as I get home. Instead, I lay my books down quietly and go out again. Maybe I go to the university and sit by the fountain in Sproul Plaza and look at all the students walking by. Or I go over and sit way high up in the stands at the track and watch people jog around and around. Even better is when I get up the nerve to go down into the handball courts. It just kills me the way those guys throw themselves around those tiny little rooms with one hand stuck out like a claw. Sometimes I think they play better because I'm watching but sometimes they yell, 'Get lost,' and 'Hey would you get the hell outa here,' and the older ones, the gray-haired professors, say, 'Do you mind?' and they frown.

So then I might go over to the Tower record store on Durant and check out the high school crowd, the way they kind of jerk their butts and feet around to the music that's playing while they flip through the albums. I look for records by Tully Washington under T and W and

C&W, MISC in the country section. I never find any. Sometimes if the record store looks empty and boring, I call up this girl I know who can get us into the movie at the University Theatre for free. The guy at the ticket counter has the hots for her. There's almost never anybody around the theatre late in the afternoon and he always gets this girl into the corner of the lobby and pokes her in the chest where she's got the smallest boobs in the world and he says, 'What's happnin', Beebites?' She always says, 'Shit, don't touch the merchandise.' Then they giggle and giggle like they haven't said the very same things to each other a hundred times before, and when she kisses him she does it with her eyes closed and her mouth wide open. But when I kiss him I keep my lips pressed tight together over my teeth and I keep my eyes open because hey, I know some things. Then we walk into the theatre and try to figure out what's going on in the movie.

And when I get back to the apartment again I know Willa will be waiting, curled up on the couch with the afghan pulled way up to her chin and off her feet. Sometimes she's completely quiet but usually one hand is moving. I kneel down next to the couch. Her fingers look just like they're floating over her face, like they're tracing some kind of strange invisible pattern or smoothing it away. (Once I touched her fingers to my own face but when they began to glide across my cheek back and forth, back and forth along the bone under my eye, such a hard shiver went down my spine that I never did it again.) So when I'm kneeling by the couch, the first thing I do is take and hold this hand of hers in one of my own and with my other hand I stroke her shoulder. I give it a little shake and then another one. 'Willa,' I begin to whisper. 'Willabird . . . Willa . . .' I push the hair back from her face. 'Willa.'

'Willabird,' I say out loud just to hear the sound of it that evening when we're sitting in the stairwell. When I look up at her, she's smiling.

'You look so *serious*,' she says. 'Listen to me . . . I have this feeling . . . a good strong feeling that everything is going to work out for the best. You wait and see.'

I nod and try to smile back at her. But for the first time I can ever remember I have trouble believing what Willa's telling me and somehow this seems even sadder to me than Mom and Andrew's wedding.

For a while after their first meeting, Andrew doesn't say anything about Willa. He waits until after the wedding. Then one afternoon he sees my school books on the floor in a corner of the living-room and he says, 'Does Willa ever help you with your homework?'

'Sure,' I say. 'All the time. She knows *everything*,' and that shuts him up.

But then a few days later, he's at it again. 'What do you and Willa talk about?' and in another couple of days, 'Does Willa spend more time with you in the summer?' It's not like he asks these questions constantly or anything, but you can tell he's got something on his mind, something to do with Willa, and it's like this something, whatever it is, kind of itches his brain every once in a while and his silly questions are his way of scratching it.

I tell myself there's nothing to worry about, but I get a little nervous anyway. Without making it a real big deal, I start to try and get Willa out of the apartment every afternoon before 5:30 which is usually the time Mom and Andrew get home. I figure, out of sight, out of mind (as Mom used to say about my real father). But even though I try my best, they still meet once or twice a week. Things even go real bad for Willa one evening when Mom walks in sneezing and Willa gets going again on that pneumonia story. Only she says the patient her father was driving seventy miles to see was an old Indian woman who was already dead when he got there.

Naturally Andrew has to say, 'I thought it was a baby.'

Willa opens her eyes real wide. 'What?'

'A few weeks ago,' Andrew says, 'you told us he was driving out to deliver a baby. I distinctly remember that it was a *baby*.'

'What?' Willa says again very softly. She lays a hand on her chest where usually she has on an agate pendant but she isn't wearing it that evening. I'm sure I feel her tremble just a little.

Maybe Andrew notices this, too. He says, 'Oh, never mind. It's not important.' But then he looks at Mom *like I told you so*, or *that's that*, like he's come to some final decision, and I can see that he and Mom are having some kind of important conversation without speaking a word. 'Never mind,' he says.

After that I really start to worry. I worry so hard sometimes it seems like I can barely breathe, and at night I get these awful pictures of Andrew in my head. Sometimes he's sitting in the chair across from the couch. His eyes are closed and his lips are moving but not making a sound and he's memorizing every story Willa's ever told, repeating them over and over, just waiting to trip her up. Sometimes he's bent over the kitchen table writing all the stories down, recording them day by day in a diary he keeps locked up so Willa can never go back to check on what she's told him. And once I even see him like some prissy tight-assed angel sitting on a big cloud adding up black marks against Willa on some long heavenly scroll.

Crazy. But what's worse is when I imagine Andrew sneaking home from work early and catching Willa on a bad day. When I think of that happening, I swear to myself, I make a solemn vow, that I will never go out and leave Willa alone again in the apartment when I come back and find her curled up and silent on the couch. I begin to watch her more carefully, too, thinking maybe I'll see some signs of when a bad day's coming on. And sometimes just out of the blue I'll give her a hug to keep her spirits up, to make her laugh and hug me back, which seems to work because Willa doesn't have a single bad day for weeks, and every Friday evening when I know she's made it through another week OK, I'm so proud of her I could shout.

So on the Friday which is the month anniversary of Mom and Andrew's wedding, I'm feeling great. Willa's still in the apartment at 6:00 because it's her pay day. We're sitting side by side on the couch, and we know Mom and Andrew are home even before they get to the door. We hear them laughing all the way up the stairs.

'Sounds like they started celebrating already,' I say just as the door opens. Mom and Andrew try to walk through it at the same time and get stuck for a second, banging their shoulders against one another, laughing some more. Finally Mom steps back. 'After you my dear,' she says and Andrew walks into the living-room and plops down into the chair across from the couch. Mom giggles and perches herself on one of his knees, so Andrew gives out this big fake groan like Mom weighs two tons and she laughs, 'Very funny,' and grabs Andrew's special sprayer bottle off the shelf near the chair. *Pssst, pssst, pssst.* She gets off three good shots, misting Andrew the way he's always misting his orchids, and then he wrestles the bottle away from her.

All this time I can hear that little humming noise in Willa's throat and the first chance she gets, she begins laughing, too, and talking a mile a minute about her own wedding. It makes me nervous but Andrew doesn't seem to mind. He's busy letting his fingers do the walking down one of Mom's legs. At the first break though, he jiggles the knee under Mom and raises an eyebrow.

She looks at Willa and then at me. 'Guess what, sweetie,' she says and for no reason I could name I get this sinking feeling. 'A professor in Andrew's department is going away to live in England for a year.

Out of *all* the grad students he asked Andrew if he'd like to rent his house. We can have it real cheap.

'But that's not the best part,' she says hardly stopping to catch a breath and putting one of those isn't-broccoli-delicious smiles on her face, like I'm six years old or something. 'It's a *big* house so you could have your very own bedroom. For a *whole* year. With a real bed . . . Just think . . . you wouldn't have to sleep on that crummy old couch anymore.' She starts describing the house like she's got a perfect picture of every room in her head. 'And get this,' she says. 'Get this, there's a fireplace in the den *and* one in the living-room, too. And a piano! You could take lessons maybe.'

'And a big backyard,' Andrew puts in. He's grinning like he owns the place, like he built the place himself even.

Willa's smiling, too. She leans over, pokes me in the side with her elbow, and whispers. 'See I told you. Didn't I tell you?'

'Yeah,' Mom says. 'A real backyard and there's even a little green-house stuck onto the side of the garage where Andrew could keep his orchids.'

Willa. Andrew. Mom. Every one of them is looking at me, waiting for my reaction. I know that for the second time in my life I'm really truly the center of attention. It makes me shiver.

'Is the house around here?' I ask.

Andrew jiggles his knee and Mom again. Willa reaches for my hand.

'So I thought we'd kinda celebrate tonight,' Mom says but I know she heard my question. She gets up off Andrew's knee and pushes her blouse back into her skirt. 'I thought you and I could walk over to the store and pick out something extra special for dinner. OK?'

Two giant hands are twisting and squeezing and pulling on my stomach. And my throat is so dry I can barely say, 'The house isn't around here, is it.'

'Well, . . .' Mom turns toward Andrew but he's staring at the plants that are crowded around the living-room window. 'Well,' she says, 'actually, sweetie, it's in El Cerrito.'

El Cerrito. All the way on the other side of town. Miles from this apartment. Miles from Willa. I shiver again and then Willa does, too. It's like she's answering me. I feel the trembling pass over her fingers, and when I look at her face, I expect to see her squinting at Mom like she can't quite make her out. But Willa is watching Andrew. Now he's watching her right back.

I try not to shout. 'How's Willa supposed to get over to El Cerrito?' And I think, if she would just say something. Anything. I want her to cry or shake or curse.

But keeping up eye contact with Andrew for so long seems to have taken all her strength because when Willa lifts her hand off mine, she does it slowly, very slowly. Then she holds it in the air a second like she can't think what to do with it before she pats my knee, real absent-minded, the way you pet a dog when you've got something more important to wonder about. 'The house sounds charming,' she says, sounding herself like nobody I've ever met in my life.

This must be the kind of signal Andrew's been waiting for. Frowning and trying not to frown, he says, 'You can always take the bus to El Cerrito, Mrs Birden. You're welcome to visit Bobbie any time it's convenient. Of course, with us living out so far, it most likely won't be every day . . .'

I press my leg against Willa's leg and my arm against her arm. No response. Nothing doing.

'I promise I'll come see you,' she says instead. 'You can lay money on that. You won't be rid of this old Indian so easily.' But she says this last part to me, not Andrew. To *me*. She says it like it's supposed to be a joke, and when I don't laugh, she does – some dizzy little laugh I've never heard before. Then she stops and sighs, 'Anyhow, you're too big to be needing a babysitter anymore. You know that.'

A babysitter. I have *never* thought of Willa as a babysitter. And a promise. What good is a promise? How many times did I listen to Mom talking on and on and on – don't worry, Bobbie, it'll be alright, I'll get a job at the university, I promise we'll buy you another coat, a brand new coat, rabbit, better than that old one, just wait, you'll see . . .

What I see is Andrew across the living-room with his head tipped back so that his chin juts up. It only twitches when he asks, 'Bobbie . . . Roberta . . . Are you going to walk over to the store with your mom?'

'No,' I say. 'I'm not going anywhere.'

Mom has been leaning on the wall, dragging her fingers through her hair. 'Then you come with me, honey,' she says to Andrew. 'OK?'

Walking to the door, they move like people who are very tired but in a hurry. Willa and I, stuck side by side on the couch, listen to the door shut behind them.

'You might as well go with them,' I tell her.

She doesn't have a word to say to that.

By now the sun is going down. The pink light from the window makes Willa's dress purple. Her hands and arms are rosy, but I won't look at her face, and when I curl up on my half of the couch, I make sure my feet don't touch her.

I have a sideways view of the chair where Andrew was sitting with Mom on his knee. Imagining the two of them in that professor's house, that 'charming' house, is almost too easy. Mom's pulling Andrew all around a kitchen big enough to hold a circus, admiring every shiny bit of it, planning fancy dinners, a party, or even two or three parties. In the greenhouse, Andrew shows her how to mix fertilizer in a bucket and whistles as he points to a flower stalk on every single orchid plant. They fall in love with the dishwasher, a king-sized bed, with chairs in the living-room that match each other and the couch. Andrew takes one bedroom for his study. Mom says she'll use another for a sewing room and learn how to knit, too. I can see them so clearly every evening after dinner settling down together in front of a fire even on the warmest nights.

But I'm not in any of these scenes, not in any room, on any piece of furniture. I am not in this future, not in the past either, because when I try instead to remember Willa and me on Telegraph Avenue, all I get is a picture of the people selling jewelry, T-shirts, pottery along the sidewalk. There's Willa, alone, laughing and carrying on as usual, and everybody's just as glad to see her without me, just as happy to hear all those stories of hers again. For a minute I'm sure if I tried harder to imagine it I would be there in the picture, too. I reach my hand up, touch my face, but sliding my fingers down my forehead, I float them over a stranger's nose, across a stranger's lips and chin.

Willa stops my hand as she lies down, fitting herself somehow between me and the back of the couch. I think I should jump up and away but I can't do anything but lie very still and shut my eyes. Willa folds her arm around me then. Her knees move up to touch the backs of my knees. I feel her fingers on my wrist. They close around my hand so that the tips are pressed into my palm. And I know she's taking long slow breaths because they're warm on my neck.

Louise Erdrich
Saint Marie

Marie Lazarre

So when I went there, I knew the dark fish must rise. Plumes of radiance had soldered on me. No reservation girl had ever prayed so hard. There was no use in trying to ignore me any longer. I was going up there on the hill with the black robe women. They were not any lighter than me. I was going up there to pray as good as they could. Because I don't have that much Indian blood. And they never thought they'd have a girl from this reservation as a saint they'd have to kneel to. But they'd have me. And I'd be carved in pure gold. With ruby lips. And my toenails would be little pink ocean shells, which they would have to stoop down off their high horse to kiss.

I was ignorant. I was near age fourteen. The length of sky is just about the size of my ignorance. Pure and wide. And it was just that – the pure and wideness of my ignorance – that got me up the hill to Sacred Heart Convent and brought me back down alive. For maybe Jesus did not take my bait, but them Sisters tried to cram me right down whole.

You ever see a walleye strike so bad the lure is practically out its back end before you reel it in? That is what they done with me. I don't like to make that low comparison, but I have seen a walleye do that once. And it's the same attempt as Sister Leopolda made to get me in her clutch.

I had the mail-order Catholic soul you get in a girl raised out in the bush, whose only thought is getting into town. For Sunday Mass is the only time my father brought his children in except for school, when we were harnessed. Our soul went cheap. We were so anxious to get there we would have walked in on our hands and knees. We just craved going to the store, slinging bottle caps in the dust, making fool eyes at each other. And of course we went to church.

Where they have the convent is on top of the highest hill, so that from its windows the Sisters can be looking into the marrow of the town. Recently a windbreak was planted before the bar 'for the purposes of tornado insurance.' Don't tell me that. That poplar stand was put up to hide the drinkers as they get the transformation. As they are served into the beast of their burden. While they're drinking, that body comes upon them, and then they stagger or crawl out the bar door, pulling a weight they can't move past the poplars. They don't want no holy witness to their fall.

Anyway, I climbed. That was a long-ago day. There was a road then for wagons that wound in ruts to the top of the hill where they had their buildings of painted brick. Gleaming white. So white the sun glanced off in dazzling display to set forms whirling behind your eyelids. The face of God you could hardly look at. But that day it drizzled, so I could look all I wanted. I saw the homelier side. The cracked whitewash and swallows nesting in the busted ends of eaves. I saw the boards sawed the size of broken windowpanes and the fruit trees, stripped. Only the tough wild rhubarb flourished. Goldenrod rubbed up their walls. It was a poor convent. I didn't see that then but I know that now. Compared with others it was humble, ragtag, out in the middle of no place. It was the end of the world to some. Where the maps stopped. Where God had only half a hand in the creation. Where the Dark One had put in thick bush, liquor, wild dogs, and Indians.

I heard later that the Sacred Heart Convent was a catchall place for nuns that don't get along elsewhere. Nuns that complain too much or lose their mind. I'll always wonder now, after hearing that, where they picked up Sister Leopolda. Perhaps she had scarred someone else, the way she left a mark on me. Perhaps she was just sent around to test her Sisters' faith, here and there, like the spot-checker in a factory. For she was the definite most-hard trial to anyone's endurance, even when they started out with veils of wretched love upon their eyes.

I was that girl who thought the black hem of her garment would help me rise. Veils of love which was only hate petrified by longing – that was me. I was like those bush Indians who stole the holy black hat of a Jesuit and swallowed little scraps of it to cure their fevers. But the hat itself carried smallpox and was killing them with belief. Veils of faith! I had this confidence in Leopolda. She was different. The other Sisters had long ago gone blank and given up on Satan. He slept for them. They never noticed his comings and goings. But Leopolda kept track of him and knew his habits, minds he burrowed in, deep spaces where he hid. She knew as much about him as my grandma, who called him by other names and was not afraid.

In her class, Sister Leopolda carried a long oak pole for opening high windows. It had a hook made of iron on one end that could jerk a patch of your hair out or throttle you by the collar – all from a distance. She used this deadly hook-pole for catching Satan by surprise. He could have entered without your knowing it – through your lips or your nose or any one of your seven openings – and gained your mind. But she would see him. That pole would brain you from behind. And he would gasp, dazzled, and take the first thing she offered, which was pain.

She had a stringer of children who could only breathe if she said the word. I was the worst of them. She always said the Dark One wanted me most of all, and I believed this. I stood out. Evil was a common thing I trusted. Before sleep sometimes he came and whispered conversation in the old language of the bush. I listened. He told me things he never told anyone but Indians. I was privy to both worlds of his knowledge. I listened to him, but I had confidence in Leopolda. She was the only one of the bunch he even noticed.

There came a day, though, when Leopolda turned the tide with her hook-pole.

It was a quiet day with everyone working at their desks, when I heard him. He had sneaked into the closets in the back of the room. He was scratching around, tasting crumbs in our pockets, stealing buttons, squirting his dark juice in the linings and the boots. I was the only one who heard him, and I got bold. I smiled. I glanced back and smiled and looked up at her sly to see if she had noticed. My heart jumped. For she was looking straight at me. And she sniffed. She had a big stark bony nose stuck to the front of her face for smelling out brimstone and evil thoughts. She had smelled him on me. She stood up. Tall, pale, a blackness leading into the deeper blackness of the slate wall behind her. Her oak pole had flown into her grip. She had seen me glance at the closet. Oh, she knew. She knew just where he was. I watched her watch him in her mind's eye. The whole class was watching now. She was staring, sizing, following his scuffle. And all of a sudden she tensed down, posed on her bent kneesprings, cocked her arm back. She threw the oak pole singing over my head, through my braincloud. It cracked through the thin wood door of the back closet, and the heavy pointed hook drove through his heart. I turned. She'd speared her own black rubber overboot where he'd taken refuge in the tip of her darkest toe.

Something howled in my mind. Loss and darkness. I understood. I was to suffer for my smile.

He rose up hard in my heart. I didn't blink when the pole cracked. My skull was tough. I didn't flinch when she shrieked in my ear. I only shrugged at the flowers of hell. He wanted me. More than anything he craved me. But then she did the worst. She did what broke my mind to her. She grabbed me by the collar and dragged me, feet flying, through the room and threw me in the closet with her dead black overboot. And I was there. The only light was a crack beneath the door. I asked the Dark One to enter into me and boost my mind. I asked him to restrain my tears, for they was pushing behind my eyes. But he was afraid to come back there. He was afraid of her sharp pole. And I was afraid of Leopolda's pole for the first time, too. I felt the cold hook in my heart. How it could crack through the door at any minute and drag me out, like a dead fish on a gaff, drop me on the floor like a gutshot squirrel.

I was nothing. I edged back to the wall as far as I could. I breathed the chalk dust. The hem of her full black cloak cut against my cheek. He had left me. Her spear could find me any time. Her keen ears would aim the hook into the beat of my heart.

What was that sound?

It filled the closet, filled it up until it spilled over, but I did not recognize the crying wailing voice as mine until the door cracked open, brightness, and she hoisted me to her camphor-smelling lips.

'He *wants* you,' she said. 'That's the difference. I give you love.'

Love. The black hook. The spear singing through the mind. I saw that she had tracked the Dark One to my heart and flushed him out into the open. So now my heart was an empty nest where she could lurk.

Well, I was weak. I was weak when I let her in, but she got a foothold there. Hard to dislodge as the year passed. Sometimes I felt him – the brush of dim wings – but only rarely did his voice compel. It was between Marie and Leopolda now, and the struggle changed. I began to realize I had been on the wrong track with the fruits of hell. The real way to overcome Leopolda was this: I'd get to heaven first.

And then, when I saw her coming, I'd shut the gate. She'd be out! That is why, besides the bowing and the scraping I'd be dealt, I wanted to sit on the altar as a saint.

To this end, I went up on the hill. Sister Leopolda was the consecrated nun who had sponsored me to come there.

'You're not vain,' she said. 'You're too honest, looking into the mirror, for that. You're not smart. You don't have the ambition to get clear. You have two choices. One, you can marry a no-good Indian, bear his brats, die like a dog. Or two, you can give yourself to God.'

'I'll come up there,' I said, 'but not because of what you think.'

I could have had any damn man on the reservation at the time. And I could have made him treat me like his own life. I looked good. And I looked white. But I wanted Sister Leopolda's heart. And here was the thing: sometimes I wanted her heart in love and admiration. Sometimes. And sometimes I wanted her heart to roast on a black stick.

She answered the back door where they had instructed me to call. I stood there with my bundle. She looked me up and down.

'All right,' she said finally. 'Come in.'

She took my hand. Her fingers were like a bundle of broom straws, so thin and dry, but the strength of them was unnatural. I couldn't have tugged loose if she was leading me into rooms of white-hot coal. Her strength was a kind of perverse miracle, for she got it from fasting herself thin. Because of this hunger practice her lips were a wounded brown and her skin deadly pale. Her eye sockets were two deep lashless hollows in a taut skull. I told you about the nose already. It stuck out far and made the place her eyes moved even deeper, as if she stared out the wrong end of a gun barrel. She took the bundle from my hands and threw it in the corner.

'You'll be sleeping behind the stove, child.'

It was immense, like a great furnace. There was a small cot close behind it.

'Looks like it could get warm there,' I said.

'Hot. It does.'

'Do I get a habit?'

I wanted something like the thing she wore. Flowing black cotton. Her face was strapped in white bandages, and a sharp crest of starched white cardboard hung over her forehead like a glaring beak. If possible, I wanted a bigger, longer, whiter beak than hers.

'No,' she said, grinning her great skull grin. 'You don't get one yet. Who knows, you might not like us. Or we might not like you.'

But she had loved me, or offered me love. And she had tried to hunt the Dark One down. So I had this confidence.

'I'll inherit your keys from you,' I said.

She looked at me sharply, and her grin turned strange. She hissed, taking in her breath. Then she turned to the door and took a key from her belt. It was a giant key, and it unlocked the larder where the food was stored.

Inside there was all kinds of good stuff. Things I'd tasted only once or twice in my life. I saw sticks of dried fruit, jars of orange peel, spice like cinnamon. I saw tins of crackers with ships painted on the side. I saw pickles. Jars of herring and the rind of pigs. There was cheese, a big brown block of it from the thick milk of goats. And besides that there was the everyday stuff, in great quantities, the flour and the coffee.

It was the cheese that got to me. When I saw it my stomach hollowed. My tongue dripped. I loved that goat-milk cheese better than anything I'd ever ate. I stared at it. The rich curve in the buttery cloth.

'When you inherit my keys,' she said sourly, slamming the door in my face, 'you can eat all you want of the priest's cheese.'

Then she seemed to consider what she'd done. She looked at me. She took the key from her belt and went back, sliced a hunk off, and put it in my hand.

'If you're good you'll taste this cheese again. When I'm dead and gone,' she said.

Then she dragged out the big sack of flour. When I finished that heaven stuff she told me to roll my sleeves up and begin doing God's labor. For a while we worked in silence, mixing up the dough and pounding it out on stone slabs.

'God's work,' I said after a while. 'If this is God's work, then I've done it all my life.'

'Well, you've done it with the Devil in your heart then,' she said. 'Not God.'

'How do you know?' I asked. But I knew she did. And I wished I had not brought up the subject.

'I see right into you like a clear glass,' she said. 'I always did.'

'You don't know it,' she continued after a while, 'but he's come around here sulking. He's come around here brooding. You brought him in. He knows the smell of me, and he's going to make a last ditch try to get you back. Don't let him.' She glared over at me. Her eyes were cold and lighted. 'Don't let him touch you. We'll be a long time getting rid of him.'

So I was careful. I was careful not to give him an inch. I said a rosary, two rosaries, three, underneath my breath. I said the Creed. I said every scrap of Latin I knew while we punched the dough with our fists. And still, I dropped the cup. It rolled under that monstrous iron stove, which was getting fired up for baking.

And she was on me. She saw he'd entered my distraction.

'Our good cup,' she said. 'Get it out of there, Marie.'

I reached for the poker to snag it out from beneath the stove. But I had a sinking feel in my stomach as I did this. Sure enough, her long arm darted past me like a whip. The poker lighted in her hand.

'Reach,' she said. 'Reach with your arm for that cup. And when your flesh is hot, remember that the flames you feel are only one fraction of the heat you will feel in his hellish embrace.'

She always did things this way, to teach you lessons. So I wasn't surprised. It was playacting, anyway, because a stove isn't very hot underneath right along the floor. They aren't made that way. Otherwise a wood floor would burn. So I said yes and got down on my stomach and reached under. I meant to grab it quick and jump up again, before she could think up another lesson, but here it happened. Although I groped for the cup, my hand closed on nothing. That cup was nowhere to be found. I heard her step toward me, a slow step. I heard the creak of thick shoe leather, the little *plat* as the folds of her heavy skirts met, a trickle of fine sand sifting, somewhere, perhaps in the bowels of her, and I was afraid. I tried to scramble up, but her foot came down lightly behind my ear, and I was lowered. The foot came down more firmly at the base of my neck, and I was held.

'You're like I was,' she said. 'He wants you very much.'

'He doesn't want me no more,' I said. 'He had his fill. I got the cup!'

I heard the valve opening, the hissed intake of breath, and knew that I should not have spoke.

'You lie,' she said. 'You're cold. There is a wicked ice forming in your blood. You don't have a shred of devotion for God. Only wild cold dark lust. I know it. I know how you feel. I see the beast . . . the beast watches me out of your eyes sometimes. Cold.'

The urgent scrape of metal. It took a moment to know from where. Top of the stove. Kettle. Lessons. She was steadying herself with the iron poker. I could feel it like pure certainty, driving into the wood floor. I would not remind her of pokers. I heard the water as it came, tipped from the spout, cooling as it fell but still scalding as it struck. I must have twitched beneath her foot, because she steadied me, and then the poker nudged up beside my arm as if to guide. 'To warm your cold ash heart,' she said. I felt how patient she would be. The water came. My mind went dead blank. Again. I could only think the kettle would be cooling slowly in her hand. I could not stand it. I bit my lip so as not to satisfy her with a sound. She gave me more reason to keep still.

'I will boil him from your mind if you make a peep,' she said, 'by filling up your ear.'

Any sensible fool would have run back down the hill the minute Leopolda let them up from under her heel. But I was snared in her black intelligence by then. I could not think straight. I had prayed so hard I think I broke a cog in my mind. I prayed while her foot squeezed my throat. While my skin burst. I prayed even when I heard the wind come through, shrieking in the busted bird nests. I didn't stop when pure light fell, turning slowly behind my eyelids. God's face. Even that did not disrupt my continued praise. Words came. Words came from nowhere and flooded my mind.

Now I could pray much better than any one of them. Than all of them full force. This was proved. I turned to her in a daze when she let me up. My thoughts were gone, and yet I remember how surprised I was. Tears glittered in her eyes, deep down, like the sinking reflection in a well.

'It was so hard, Marie,' she gasped. Her hands were shaking. The kettle clattered against the stove. 'But I have used all the water up now. I think he is gone.'

'I prayed,' I said foolishly. 'I prayed very hard.'

'Yes,' she said. 'My dear one, I know.'

We sat together quietly because we had no more words. We let the dough rise and punched it down once. She gave me a bowl of mush, unlocked the sausage from a special cupboard, and took that in to the Sisters. They sat down the hall, chewing their sausage, and I could hear them. I could hear their teeth bite through their bread and meat. I couldn't move. My shirt was dry but the cloth stuck to my back, and I couldn't think straight. I was losing the sense to understand how her mind worked. She'd gotten past me with her poker and I would never be a saint. I despaired. I felt I had no inside voice, nothing to direct me, no darkness, no Marie. I was about to throw that cornmeal mush out to the birds and make a run for it, when the vision rose up blazing in my mind.

I was rippling gold. My breasts were bare and my nipples flashed and winked. Diamonds tipped them. I could walk through panes of glass. I could walk through windows. She was at my feet, swallowing the glass after each step I took. I broke through another and another. The glass she swallowed ground and cut until her starved insides were only a subtle dust. She coughed. She coughed a cloud of dust. And then she was only a black rag that flapped off, snagged in bob wire, hung there for an age, and finally rotted into the breeze.

I saw this, mouth hanging open, gazing off into the flagged boughs of trees.

'Get up!' she cried. 'Stop dreaming. It is time to bake.'

Two other Sisters had come in with her, wide women with hands like paddles. They were evening and smoothing out the firebox beneath the great jaws of the oven.

'Who is this one?' they asked Leopolda. 'Is she yours?'

'She is mine,' said Leopolda. 'A very good girl.'

'What is your name?' one asked me.

'Marie.'

'Marie. Star of the Sea.'

'She will shine,' said Leopolda, 'when we have burned off the dark corrosion.'

The others laughed, but uncertainly. They were mild and sturdy French, who did not understand Leopolda's twisted jokes, although they muttered respectfully at things she said. I knew they wouldn't believe what she had done with the kettle. There was no question. So I kept quiet.

'*Elle est docile*,' they said approvingly as they left to starch the linens.

'Does it pain?' Leopolda asked me as soon as they were out the door.

I did not answer. I felt sick with the hurt.

'Come along,' she said.

The building was wholly quiet now. I followed her up the narrow staircase into a hall of little rooms, many doors. Her cell was the quietest, at the very end. Inside, the air smelled stale, as if the door had not been opened for years. There was a crude straw mattress, a tiny bookcase with a picture of Saint Francis hanging over it, a ragged palm, a stool for sitting on, a crucifix. She told me to remove my blouse and sit on the stool. I did so. She took a pot of salve from the bookcase and began to smooth it upon my burns. Her hands made slow, wide circles, stopping the pain. I closed my eyes. I expected to see blackness. Peace. But instead the vision reared up again. My chest was still tipped with diamonds. I was walking through windows. She was chewing up the broken litter I left behind.

'I am going,' I said. 'Let me go.'

But she held me down.

'Don't go,' she said quickly. 'Don't. We have just begun.'

I was weakening. My thoughts were whirling pitifully. The pain had kept me strong, and as it left me I began to forget it; I couldn't hold on. I began to wonder if she'd really scalded me with the kettle. I could not remember. To remember this seemed the most important thing in the world. But I was losing the memory. The scalding. The pouring. It began to vanish. I felt like my mind was coming off its hinge, flapping in the breeze, hanging by the hair of my own pain. I wrenched out of her grip.

'He was always in you,' I said. 'Even more than in me. He wanted you even more. And now he's got you. Get thee behind me!'

I shouted that, grabbed my shirt, and ran through the door throwing it on my body. I got down the stairs and into the kitchen, even, but no matter what I told myself, I couldn't get out the door. It wasn't finished. And she knew I would not leave. Her quiet step was immediately behind me.

'We must take the bread from the oven now,' she said.

She was pretending nothing happened. But for the first time I had gotten through some chink she'd left in her darkness. Touched some doubt. Her voice was so low and brittle it cracked off at the end of her sentence.

'Help me, Marie,' she said slowly.

But I was not going to help her, even though she had calmly buttoned the back of my shirt up and put the big cloth mittens in my hands for taking out the loaves. I could have bolted for it then. But I didn't. I knew that something was nearing completion. Something was about to happen. My back was a wall of singing flame. I was turning. I watched her take the long fork in one hand, to tap the loaves. In the other hand she gripped the black poker to hook the pans.

'Help me,' she said again, and I thought, Yes, this is part of it. I put the mittens on my hands and swung the door open on its hinges. The oven gaped. She stood back a moment, letting the first blast of heat rush by. I moved behind her. I could feel the heat at my front and at my back. Before, behind. My skin was turning to beaten gold. It was coming quicker than I thought. The oven was like the gate of a personal hell. Just big enough and hot enough for one person, and that was her. One kick and Leopolda would fly in headfirst. And that would be one-millionth of the heat she would feel when she finally collapsed in his hellish embrace.

Saints know these numbers.

She bent forward with her fork held out. I kicked her with all my might. She flew in. But the outstretched poker hit the back wall first, so she rebounded. The oven was not so deep as I had thought.

There was a moment when I felt a sort of thin, hot disappointment, as when a fish slips off the line. Only I was the one going to be lost. She was fearfully silent. She whirled. Her veil had cutting edges. She had the poker in one hand. In the other she held that long sharp fork she used to tap the delicate crusts of loaves. Her face turned upside down on her shoulders. Her face turned blue. But saints are used to miracles. I felt no trace of fear.

If I was going to be lost, let the diamonds cut! Let her eat ground glass!

'Bitch of Jesus Christ!' I shouted. 'Kneel and beg! Lick the floor!'

That was when she stabbed me through the hand with the fork, then took the poker up alongside my head, and knocked me out.

It must have been a half an hour later when I came around. Things were so strange. So strange I can hardly tell it for delight at the remembrance. For when I came around this was actually taking place. I was being worshiped. I had somehow gained the altar of a saint.

I was laying back on the stiff couch in the Mother Superior's office. I looked around me. It was as though my deepest dream had come to life. The Sisters of the convent were kneeling to me. Sister Bonaventure. Sister Dympna. Sister Cecilia Saint-Claire. The two French with hands like paddles. They were down on their knees. Black capes were slung over some of their heads. My name was buzzing up and down the room, like a fat autumn fly lighting on the tips of their tongues between Latin, humming up the heavy blood-dark curtains, circling their little cosseted heads. Marie! Marie! A girl thrown in a closet.

Who was afraid of a rubber overboot. Who was half overcome. A girl who came in the back door where they threw their garbage. Marie! Who never found the cup. Who had to eat their cold mush. Marie! Leopolda had her face buried in her knuckles. Saint Marie of the Holy Slops! Saint Marie of the Bread Fork! Saint Marie of the Burnt Back and Scalded Butt!

I broke out and laughed.

They looked up. All holy hell burst loose when they saw I'd woke. I still did not understand what was happening. They were watching, talking, but not to me.

'The marks . . .'

'She has her hand closed.'

'*Je ne peux pas voir.*'

I was not stupid enough to ask what they were talking about. I couldn't tell why I was laying in white sheets. I couldn't tell why they were praying to me. But I'll tell you this: it seemed entirely natural. It was me. I lifted up my hand as in my dream. It was completely limp with sacredness.

'Peace be with you.'

My arm was dried blood from the wrist down to the elbow. And it hurt. Their faces turned like flat flowers of adoration to follow that hand's movements. I let it swing through the air, imparting a saint's blessing. I had practiced. I knew exactly how to act.

They murmured. I heaved a sigh, and a golden beam of light suddenly broke through the clouded window and flooded down directly on my face. A stroke of perfect luck! They had to be convinced.

Leopolda still knelt in the back of the room. Her knuckles were crammed halfway down her throat. Let me tell you, a saint has senses honed keen as a wolf. I knew that she was over my barrel now. How it happened did not matter. The last thing I remembered was how she flew from the oven and stabbed me. That one thing was most certainly true.

'Come forward, Sister Leopolda.' I gestured with my heavenly wound. Oh, it hurt. It bled when I reopened the slight heal. 'Kneel beside me,' I said.

She kneeled, but her voice box evidently did not work, for her mouth opened, shut, opened, but no sound came out. My throat clenched in noble delight I had read of as befitting a saint. She could not speak. But she was beaten. It was in her eyes. She stared at me now with all the deep hate of the wheel of devilish dust that rolled wild within her emptiness.

'What is it you want to tell me?' I asked. And at last she spoke.

'I have told my Sisters of your passion,' she managed to choke out. 'How the stigmata . . . the marks of the nails . . . appeared in your palm and you swooned at the holy vision. . . .'

'Yes,' I said curiously.

And then, after a moment, I understood.

Leopolda had saved herself with her quick brain. She had witnessed a miracle. She had hid the fork and told this to the others. And of course they believed her, because they never knew how Satan came and went or where he took refuge.

'I saw it from the first,' said the large one who put the bread in the oven. 'Humility of the spirit. So rare in these girls.'

'I saw it too,' said the other one with great satisfaction. She sighed quietly. 'If only it was me.'

Leopolda was kneeling bolt upright, face blazing and twitching, a barely held fountain of blasting poison.

'Christ has marked me,' I agreed.

I smiled the saint's smirk into her face. And then I looked at her. That was my mistake.

For I saw her kneeling there. Leopolda with her soul like a rubber overboot. With her face of a starved rat. With the desperate eyes drowning in the deep wells of her wrongness. There would be no one else after me. And I would leave. I saw Leopolda kneeling within the shambles of her love.

My heart had been about to surge from my chest with the blackness of my joyous heat. Now it dropped. I pitied her. I pitied her. Pity twisted in my stomach like that hook-pole was driven through me. I was caught. It was a feeling more terrible than any amount of boiling water and worse than being forked. Still, still, I could not help what I did. I had already smiled in a saint's mealy forgiveness. I heard myself speaking gently.

'Receive the dispensation of my sacred blood,' I whispered.

But there was no heart in it. No joy when she bent to touch the floor. No dark leaping. I fell back into the white pillows. Blank dust was whirling through the light shifts. My skin was dust. Dust my lips. Dust the dirty spoons on the ends of my feet.

Rise up! I thought. Rise up and walk! There is no limit to this dust!

Max Garland
Signs and Wonders

What Uncle Kelvin's sermons lacked in theological precision, they more than made up for in downright fervor. I don't mean that he was one of those religious idiots, one of those fire-breathers trying to work their way into a television ministry. It's just that he was, as more than one member of the congregation put it, 'the savingest white preacher in Irene County'. The crucial moment of a typical service would find Uncle Kelvin bounding from behind the pulpit in midquotation, full of the fire of the Pentecost, flapping about like a robin and calling upon the seventeen or eighteen names of the Lord to shower a little mercy upon the hard-working men and women of the Mount Olive Pentecostal Assembly – who were more than likely standing by this time, raising their arms in the air and waiting for the first waves of glossolalia to kick in. It was not the performance of a zealot, though it might have been hard to tell the difference if you were standing too far outside the Spirit.

The sermons themselves were liberal mixtures of local anecdote and specific Biblical reference. Uncle Kelvin leaned heavily on Genesis, Exodus, the four Gospels, Acts, I Corinthians and Hebrews. But he always started in Irene County, Kentucky: 'There was a certain man in town who had just lost his wife. You all know him. I don't want to mention any names. This poor man came to me after service one Sunday night, tears streaming down his face, and he said to me . . .'

After the scene setting and the undeniable establishment of the local angle, Uncle Kelvin's message would begin gradually ascending by way of Biblical quotation and scriptural analogy. His pacing grew more frantic. He removed his glasses and wiped them with the exaggerated motion of a man drying a dinner plate.

'The wind bloweth where it listeth, and thou hearest the sound thereof, but canst not tell whence it cometh, and whither it goeth: so is every one that is born of the Spirit.' By the time Uncle Kelvin had worked his way up to direct quotes from Jesus, the sermon was in full flower. His necktie was loosened. The women were fanning faster and faster with the cardboard fans depicting the Sermon on the Mount and the Last Supper, scenes that were increasingly reduced to blurs and abstractions by the quickening motions of their wrists. And then the bounding forth began, and the holy peregrinations. The poor soul who had lost his wife had, by the grace of God, managed to crawl out of the pit of earthly despair and was now 'a living habitation for the power that dredged this little county of ours up out of the waters on the third day of creation'.

What had happened was the Holy Ghost. What always happened was the Holy Ghost. The man whose wife had died so painfully and needlessly, the child whom no one loved, the petty thief, the rich man with the empty heart – what happened to all of them eventually was that the Holy Ghost came down and lifted them at precisely the moment they realized, after long bouts of intransigence, that their own efforts were limited, their own powers relatively small.

You could always depend upon a trembling handful of the faithful to come forward at the end of the service and more or less deliver themselves into the arms of God. Uncle Kelvin would embrace them one by one, cue the choir into a whispered rendition of 'Softly and Tenderly', and then lead them through the recitations of repentance and salvation. It didn't matter that most, if not all, of them were already converted, saved, sanctified, and blessed several times over. The coming forward was understood as a gesture of appreciation for Uncle Kelvin's efforts, the choir's bone-chilling harmonies, the array of hairdos and clean shaves and modest costume jewelry, even the summer light glazing the relatively unadorned windows of the church. Everyone was aware that in the ordinary Baptist and Methodist churches of the county one salvation was enough. But Uncle Kelvin's theory was that it didn't cost the Holy Ghost a nickel to descend a second or even a third or fourth time if a man got shaky about the predicament of his soul. If he had to save a man every Sunday of the man's life, that's exactly what my uncle would do. Along with attendance figures and collection-plate totals, a chalk-board in the vestibule kept the tally of souls saved, and by the end of the liturgical year the figures not only exceeded the entire church membership, but approached the population of the county itself.

The Reverend Kelvin Stone wasn't really my uncle. He was my second cousin, son of my grandfather's brother. Our fifty-two-year age difference, however, hoisted him into that category of men I always regarded as uncles, men to whom you didn't owe absolute obedience, and therefore obeyed without the accumulation of hidden rage that shadowed the usual father-son relationship. The authority of uncles was generally exercised within the pose of neglect, and whatever was learned was learned because the teaching was too loose and casual to resist.

This was true of even so professionally flamboyant a man as Uncle Kelvin. When the two of us were alone together, he left the animations of the pulpit behind him, so that, with the exception of a little practical fishing instruction, Uncle Kelvin's influence on me was as subtle as a noon breeze. He also took no particular pains to invoke a picture of holiness in my presence. As a matter of fact, he kept a hand in most of the popular vices, especially tobacco (which was almost a patriotic indulgence for a Kentuckian) and bourbon (taken at the onset of certain maladies, after particularly weighty meals, and as a punctuation to the long, icebound February evenings). Sunday-afternoon fishing, automobile worship and overeating were the other natural failings that allowed Uncle Kelvin to walk in the company of men and boys.

'That's it, just plop it in near the willow.' Actually, I had tossed my line into the uninhabited green void at the middle of the pond, nowhere near the willow. The red-and-white bobber wobbled and floated over the deep water like a tiny buoy. The fact that Uncle Kelvin considered my cast to be in the vicinity of the desired willow was a throwaway encouragement, a gesture a father could not have made in good conscience.

'Now just leave it alone awhile. Just sit back and let the worm do the work. If he's hungry, he'll come to you. A real fisherman has to learn what not to do, and you're a born fisherman, that's as plain as day.'

Uncle Kelvin had a half-acre stock pond left over from before the fall of the cattle market. Cattail, reed, birch and willow had grown up around the edges, but there was an abundance of small bluegill, a few striped bass, schools of minnows, and the rumor of a great catfish lurking somewhere in the wallow of silt along the pond floor. Whatever fish we caught were placed on a stringer until the end of the day, then generally tossed back into the water to be caught again.

Uncle Kelvin's wife Agnes had died long before I was born, and before they had managed to have any children of their own. He had never remarried and never resumed serious farming after Agnes's death. The pastures surrounding the pond were rented to members of the congregation as grazing land for quarter horses and Tennessee Walkers. The shallow bank of the pond was stamped and decorated with their deep hoofprints.

'Jesus was a fisherman himself. You know that, don't you?' Uncle Kelvin asked, tossing his own line within inches of the overhanging sweep of willow branches along the east bank. Uncle Kelvin didn't usually bring Jesus into the fishing.

'I thought he was a carpenter.' I couldn't resist tugging on my line a little. The bobber lurched forward a few inches, leaving a brief trail in the algae. I figured the worm might appear a little healthier, a little more like fresh goods, if I jiggled him around.

'A fisher of men, son. The Bible says a fisher of men, but in my own personal opinion, I think he might have started out with regular fish, then moved on up. What do you think?'

It was a real question. Most of his questions to me were real ones, not just gestures of inclusion. We were two men fishing for bluegill, maybe bass, maybe even the apocryphal catfish who was by this time older and wiser than several members of the immediate family. We were two men who believed in heaven and hell and a Jesus between them. I never caught Uncle Kelvin watching to see that the barb of the bluegill hook didn't lodge itself in the soft flesh of my finger. Likewise, I never saw the faintest shade of worry cross his face when I leaned out from the tangle of willow roots to investigate the ferocity of a water snake with the tip of my fishing rod. We were two men far back in the field who knew in our hearts that fishing was pure unadulterated laziness, and that laziness was just a cozy word for the sin of sloth.

'Maybe he was a fisherman,' I said. 'I mean, I'm not sure, but I guess he could have done some real fishing. I don't know.' I didn't know, but it occurred to me that if Jesus had done a little ordinary fishing, then maybe it wasn't the sin of sloth after all.

Of course Uncle Kelvin and I weren't really two men. We were a young boy and his honorary uncle, a Pentecostal minister, a man fully capable of elevating the spirits of tobacco farmers, distillery workers, sheriff's deputies, mothers of ten, stock-car drivers and emerging high-school beauties. We were a nine-year-old boy and a sixty-two-year-old childless widower who had eaten far too many helpings of far too many meals at the invitation of grateful members of his congregation. He was, in fact, a man who was fully aware that he was only a stroke or two away from the end of what he considered a lucky and blessed and ordinary life.

'What would you say to a sandwich?' meant Uncle Kelvin was already reaching into the paper bag and was about to hand over the bologna and cheese with the worm-scented thumbprint embedded in the cellophane. Uncle Kelvin always made three sandwiches for himself and two for me, and he kept four large Pepsis half submerged in the shade of the willow roots until lunch. The sandwiches were made with airy white bread which by lunchtime had lost much of its corporality and begun to degenerate into a wet sponge of delicious dough.

'What would you say to a sandwich, buddy?' Uncle Kelvin repeated. Sometimes his questions weren't real questions after all.

'Howdy, sandwich.' I had almost forgotten my cue and the punchline answer I had learned from the Red Skelton character, Freddie the Freeloader. We were a couple of men far back in the field eating sandwiches, cracking jokes. Like shadowy props, the Tennessee Walkers grazed on the distant rise of rye and alfalfa.

'I'll tell you a little secret, son.' I had just asked Uncle Kelvin about the tongues. 'I'll tell you a little secret. Personally I can take the tongues or leave them. But a lot of people, a lot of good people, wouldn't think they'd been to church unless they spoke in tongues. They want to be sure the Holy Ghost has arrived, and one way to be sure is to feel themselves letting loose with a stream of something that couldn't have come from their lips alone.'

'But how do you do it? I mean how do you know if you're supposed to do it?' Neither of my parents spoke in tongues. The most visible evidence of my mother's reaction to the sermon and hymn singing was a kind of mistiness which she softly dabbed away with my father's handkerchief. My father's reaction was confined to a congratulatory handshake at the church door after the service ended.

'Some of the Pentecostals say I'm dead wrong about this, but since they're not here right now, let me tell you something: I wouldn't worry too much about the tongues. If that's the gift you're given, you'll know it. If it's not, well, remember what St Paul said.'

'What did he say?'

' "For if I pray in an unknown tongue, my spirit prayeth, but my understanding is unfruitful." He also said, "Yet in the church I had rather speak five words with my understanding, that by my voice I might teach others also, than ten thousand words in an unknown tongue." '

'But *you* do it. Lots of people do it. All the old people speak in tongues.' It was as close to a full-fledged theological debate as we would ever come. I *was* worried about the tongues – sometimes in church I felt something warm happening in my stomach and chest.

'Signs and wonders, son. Sometimes people need signs and wonders. That's why I steer clear of those verses of St Paul's in my sermons. A lot of good people need the tongues.'

After the sandwiches and Pepsis, Uncle Kelvin took out his pipe, nestled a few pinches of tobacco into the bowl, cupped his hands around the lit match in a ceremonial gesture impossible not to admire, and watched the wisps of aromatic smoke begin to curl upward and then launch themselves strand by strand onto the pre-vailing breeze. Every time the ritual was the same. Whether the fish stringer was empty or jostling in the shallow water with the frus-trations of the morning's catch of bluegill, Uncle Kelvin with his folding chair and his propped-up fishing rod and his pipe was the very portrait of a happy man. And this was the quality, I think, that enabled him to elevate the souls that even the fire-breathers and the doomsdayers couldn't lift an inch.

Uncle Kelvin was a man so comfortable with the affections of the living God, he could simply do as he pleased. He didn't have to preach the Judgment. He didn't have to bully the guilt-ridden with visions of Hell memorized from Isaiah and Revelation. He merely loosened up the members of the congregation with a little exuberance, a little show of life, then carried them along on the Shakespearean cadences of the King James Bible and let the Holy Ghost do the rest. He just set the stage, a little extravagantly sometimes, and then tried to maneuver himself out of the way and let the Spirit come in.

Once you subtracted the emotion and the timing, the foot shuffling and the face reddening, most of Uncle Kelvin's sermons were about simple human suffering, lives gone wrong for any number of ordinary reasons. The anecdotal endings always provided deliverance, which was achieved by leaning on the power that set the world in motion in the first place – and not on the power that would strangle, eternally harangue and vilify the creatures of that world.

True, sometimes the congregation got a little friskier than Uncle Kelvin, prancing about and speaking with the tongues of Ezekiel and Jeremiah, and sometimes a little fever crept in – some trembling and barking and teeth-chattering left over from the nearby Shaker community that had died out earlier in the century. But most of the time the Spirit effectively worked his way down the emotional ladder, rung by rung, from ecstasy to joy to common happiness, then finally settled into something like a simple presence: a strength that didn't always have to exert itself in dramatic ways, but which nevertheless didn't seem to have a bottom; a strength that could be drawn up like well water by the grief-torn and lonely.

My own religious ideas whirled around the rhythms of King James, the Pentecostal experience, and the figure of Uncle Kelvin. God I understood as the enormous being who preceded the world and probably resembled the portrait of Moses in my illustrated Old Testament. His only son, Jesus, could be visualized in three ways: the infant in the manger, innocent and emanating holiness from the first cry; the Good Shepherd, a grown-up Jesus who comforted and healed and taught by enigma and example; and finally, the suffering Jesus, the one who took on pain with such genuine conviction that he even mouthed my own fears of abandonment from the cross itself.

It was easy enough to visualize the figure of God and the three Jesuses, but much harder to concoct an image of the Holy Ghost, the force that drove the passions of Uncle Kelvin's flock. There was no portrait of the Holy Ghost, no way to hold him in mind that didn't grow hazy and drift off like the wisps of smoke from Uncle Kelvin's pipe. In fact, sometimes the Holy Ghost was represented in my mind by just that, a smokelike figure or a creature of fog rising from the bluegill pond. The image would be of early morning, late September, the sun low and silvery, the Holy Ghost summoning a vague shape from the mist, rising and moving against the background of willows like a skater. At other times the Holy Ghost would be even less tangible – the small motion of night wind meandering through the folds of the bedroom curtain, for example. Then there were the stars, the powdery ribbons of the Milky Way on a clear night in summer. Maybe a storm had swept through earlier in the day, and the faint river of stars filled in the space between horizons. On these nights, the pulse of cicadas and the unnerving rhythm of field crickets helped enliven the gathering image of the Ghost.

At the outermost fringe of my imagination I thought of the Holy Ghost as Jesus with a body of vapor: a Jesus whose body could sift right through the walls of the house. A Jesus who could stroll into the confines of a man and haunt the man and allow him to speak in the antique syllables of Ezekiel and Jeremiah, to lose the fear of earthly death, or simply to lead a decent life within the limits of the flesh – which Uncle Kelvin said was made, after all, of ordinary, garden-variety dust.

But saying that, Uncle Kelvin then departed from the Hardshell Baptists and the Mountain Baptists and the unlikely Kentucky order of Trappist monks, all of whom believed that since the body was dust it should be honored no more than dust. Once the Holy Ghost according to Uncle Kelvin moved in, our dust was divinely animated dust that could dance around, and pray, and have second helpings of country ham and biscuits, and love other dust. He never preached the body as a snare or a pitfall.

'There are two ways to go wrong,' Uncle Kelvin proclaimed in one of his sermons. 'You can hate the world in order to love God, which won't work for the simple reason that God made the world, a fact you don't have to read any further than the first page of Genesis to learn; or you can love the world so much and be so dazzle-eyed and blinded by the things of the world that you forget who made them and start imagining that maybe you can hoard them or take them with you or twist them into a semblance of everlasting life.'

Uncle Kelvin's body could never have been mistaken for that of an ascetic. When he lowered himself into the driver's seat of the Cadillac Coupe de Ville furnished by the congregation of Mount Olive, the great car rocked and dipped and settled as slowly as a rowboat. In fact, the last time I saw Uncle Kelvin alive he had just pushed himself away from my mother's table after a double dose of catfish, okra and hush puppies all rolled and fried in the same thick batter of pancake mix.

'If I could preach the way you cook, there wouldn't be an empty seat in the church, Elizabeth.' Uncle Kelvin was in the second stage of rising from the table.

'I'm glad you enjoyed it, Brother Stone.' My mother generally spoke to Uncle Kelvin with mock formality. 'But you don't have any empty seats now.'

'How about a look at the garden, Uncle Kelvin?' my father asked. They were already heading for the door. The question was a formalized code emptied of secrecy years ago. 'How about a look at the garden?' meant that my father and Uncle Kelvin would sit in the two rust-flecked metal lawn chairs at the edge of the garden and drink one small glass of bourbon apiece. The bourbon was local and very sweet and needed only a quick cold drink from the garden hose as a chaser.

After the glasses were returned to the garage I was free to wander toward the garden and settle along the fringes of their conversation, which generally progressed from gardening to weather and finally reached a plateau and settled on the subject of automobiles. Sometimes for my sake a little fishing or baseball would be tossed in, but on my home terrain I was content to be the boy. I could wait until the next fishing expedition with Uncle Kelvin for my brief elevation into manhood.

Sometimes the conversation had already reached the automobile stage by the time I came to the garden. 'They spoil me like a baby,' Uncle Kelvin would say. 'I'm just an old-fashioned Cadillac man and they all know it and they spoil me like a baby.' Every three years the congregation paid the trade-in difference between Uncle Kelvin's old Cadillac and a new one. Although my father was also a member of the congregation, Uncle Kelvin always referred to the congregation as 'they', conferring upon my father a special intimacy. He knew my father would argue for the virtues of the top-of-the-line Buicks and Oldsmobiles.

'You can't tell the difference with your eyes closed,' my father declared. 'If I were a betting man, which the Lord knows I'm not, I'd bet half the farm you couldn't tell the difference between the ride of a nice Olds sedan and that Cadillac of yours with your eyes closed.' My father believed in the up-and-coming, but Uncle Kelvin was a Cadillac man, and the debate was all form and pastime, riding on the small warm wave of the bourbon. The chairs were placed at the west edge of the garden, and the vegetable rows ascended according to height from west to east. From the chairs you could look over the leaves of the radishes to the frill of the carrots, then beyond to the pointed tips of the onions, the broad leaves of squash, the double row of potatoes, the furred and mysterious okra, and finally the rows of tomatoes, pole beans and sweet corn. It was like a broad green staircase. The night would be falling, the fireflies blinking through the garden, and the catalpa trees beginning to rattle with cicadas.

But the last night I didn't follow them into the garden. I remember Uncle Kelvin pushing himself from the table, lifting himself in stages, and heading for the kitchen door just ahead of my father. Later there was the sound of Uncle Kelvin at the screen door, saying goodnight to my mother and sending a farewell into the television room – from which I answered without looking up. Then came the vaultlike sound of the Cadillac door closing, and Uncle Kelvin backing out and away toward the two quick strokes that killed him: the first one dividing him for two days into the man he was and a shadow of that man, and the second 'sending him home', as the minister said at the funeral.

'By the grace of God he didn't suffer long,' the minister also said, referring to the speed of the two strokes. 'He never breathed a complaint, and by the grace of God he didn't suffer at the end.'

No one I loved had ever died before. The figure in the coffin was small and pale and seemed dwarfed by the flowers, and had nothing to do with Uncle Kelvin as far as I could see. For a long time afterwards I thought of the minister's statements about the suffering. I knew nothing about it except that some people wore it on their sleeves and some kept it inside.

'Sometimes the Lord answers *no*' was from another of Uncle Kelvin's sermons. 'The Lord always answers, but I have to tell you folks, sometimes the Lord answers *no*, and that's when you need the Holy Ghost to come down and give you the strength to bear that *no*.'

Uncle Kelvin had married at nineteen and lived with Aunt Agnes for thirty-four years before watching her dwindle away over the course of a single winter. The recognizable part of her, the *Agnes*, began to hide in the farthest corners of her body until it became clear to Uncle Kelvin which way his prayers for her were going to be answered.

Uncle Kelvin's reaction to her death became part of the local legend about the Reverend Kelvin Stone – and part of the force that brought even the already saved and sanctified down the aisle of Mount Olive for second and third helpings of the Holy Ghost. He had missed only one Sunday, the Sunday after they buried her, and his sermons didn't change a mote afterwards. He indulged in the normal vices no more or less, and although he did give up serious farming, he kept the house and lawn as clean as any woman.

But it's hard to know about the suffering. If, under the pose of easiness and equality exhibited when Uncle Kelvin and I fished together, was a suffering hard to bear – and if I was the son he never had, the unattainable namesake – I never felt the awkward weight of that love.

My mother had hoped for a short time that my mornings and afternoons with Uncle Kelvin might lead me toward the calling myself. She had felt the stirrings as I sat beside her in church, and she knew there were worse livings to be made, and worse troubles than the troubles of a Pentecostal minister. You only had to read the headlines in the paper to see what could happen to a boy who wandered too far in the world.

But in spite of the nudging and my bald admiration, I had begun to realize even before he died that I would not be following too closely in Uncle Kelvin's footsteps. In spite of the strange warmth that started in my stomach and rose through my chest at the highest pitch of the Sunday service, I was beginning to understand even then that what I valued most about Uncle Kelvin was coming from the direction of the bluegill pond. It had mostly to do with morning and patience. It had to do with waiting and fidgeting into place and watching, and then with the quick splash of adrenalin as the bobber shook and the rod tip wavered.

And there were damselflies, a brief iridescence among the reeds. There were the redwings fuming and swaying on the brown wicks of the cattails. It didn't matter that an hour might pass, that the morning was lifting. The trick was to keep the restlessness corralled and let the worm do the work. The trick was to let the nibble become the full-fledged strike, and even then to let the bluegill run with the hook until it lodged itself in the thin translucent doom of the mouth. You had waited and he had come, out of curiosity or hunger, and the rod tip bent with the exaggerated pull of the small fish and you had him, and all you had to do was bring him up, small and thrashing, bright as a prism or a live jewel – blue, green, violet, red. And if the last of the mist had skated away, and if you had been taught by Uncle Kelvin, that's when adrenalin turned to pity: when you held the fish, shining and gasping in your hand, as if he had come from a place much farther away than the ordinary waters of the pond.

Ellen Gilchrist
Victory Over Japan

When I was in the third grade I knew a boy who had to have fourteen shots in the stomach as the result of a squirrel bite. Every day at two o'clock they would come to get him. A hush would fall on the room. We would all look down at our desks while he left the room between Mr Harmon and his mother. Mr Harmon was the principal. That's how important Billy Monday's tragedy was.

Mr Harmon came along in case Billy threw a fit. Every day we waited to see if he would throw a fit but he never did. He just put his books away and left the room with his head hanging down on his chest and Mr Harmon and his mother guiding him along between them like a boat.

'Would you go with them like that?' I asked Letitia at recess. Letitia was my best friend. Usually we played girls chase the boys at recess or pushed each other on the swings or hung upside down on the monkey bars so Joe Franke and Bobby Saxacorn could see our underpants but Billy's shots had even taken the fun out of recess. Now we sat around on the fire escape and talked about rabies instead.

'Why don't they put him to sleep first?' Letitia said. 'I'd make them put me to sleep.'

'They can't,' I said. 'They can't put you to sleep unless they operate.'

'My father could,' she said. 'He owns the hospital. He could put me to sleep.' She was always saying things like that but I let her be my best friend anyway.

'They couldn't give them to me,' I said. 'I'd run away to Florida and be a beachcomber.'

'Then you'd get rabies,' Letitia said. 'You'd be foaming at the mouth.'

'I'd take a chance. You don't always get it.' We moved closer together, caught up in the horror of it. I was thinking about the Livingstons' bulldog. I'd had some close calls with it lately.

'It was a pet,' Letitia said. 'His brother was keeping it for a pet.'

It was noon recess. Billy Monday was sitting on a bench by the swings. Just sitting there. Not talking to anybody. Waiting for two o'clock, a small washed-out-looking boy that nobody paid any attention to until he got bit. He never talked to anybody. He could hardly even read. When Mrs Jansma asked him to read his head would fall all the way over to the side of his neck. Then he would read a few sentences with her having to tell him half the words. No one would ever have picked him out to be the center of a rabies tragedy. He was more the type to fall in a well or get sucked down the drain at the swimming pool.

Fourteen days. Fourteen shots. It was spring when it happened and the schoolroom windows were open all day long and every afternoon after Billy left we had milk from little waxy cartons and Mrs Jansma would read us chapters from a wonderful book about some children in England that had a bed that took them places at night. There we were, eating graham crackers and listening to stories while Billy was strapped to the table in Doctor Finley's office waiting for his shot.

'I can't stand to think about it,' Letitia said. 'It makes me so sick I could puke.'

'I'm going over there and talk to him right now,' I said. 'I'm going to interview him for the paper.' I had been the only one in the third grade to get anything in the Horace Mann paper. I got in with a story about how Mr Harmon was shell-shocked in the First World War. I was on the lookout for another story that good.

I got up, smoothed down my skirt, walked over to the bench where Billy was sitting and held out a vial of cinnamon toothpicks. 'You want one,' I said. 'Go ahead. She won't care.' It was against the rules to bring cinnamon toothpicks to Horace Mann. They were afraid someone would swallow one.

'I don't think so,' he said. 'I don't need any.'

'Go on,' I said. 'They're really good. They've been soaking all week.'

'I don't want any,' he said.

'You want me to push you on the swings?'

'I don't know,' he said. 'I don't think so.'

'If it was my brother's squirrel, I'd kill it,' I said. 'I'd cut its head off.'

'It got away,' he said. 'It's gone.'

'What's it like when they give them to you?' I said. 'Does it hurt very much?'

'I don't know,' he said. 'I don't look.' His head was starting to slip down onto his chest. He was rolling up like a ball.

'I know how to hypnotize people,' I said. 'You want me to hypnotize you so you can't feel it?'

'I don't know,' he said. He had pulled his legs up on the bench. Now his chin was so far down into his chest I could barely hear him talk. Part of me wanted to give him a shove and see if he would roll. I touched him on the shoulder instead. I could feel his little bones beneath his shirt. I could smell his washed-out rusty smell. His head went all the way down under his knees. Over his shoulder I saw Mrs Jansma headed our way.

'Rhoda,' she called out. 'I need you to clean off the blackboards before we go back in. Will you be a sweet girl and do that for me?'

'I wasn't doing anything but talking to him,' I said. She was beside us now and had gathered him into her wide sleeves. He was starting to cry, making little strangled noises like a goat.

'Well, my goodness, that was nice of you to try to cheer Billy up. Now go see about those blackboards for me, will you?'

I went on in and cleaned off the blackboards and beat the erasers together out the window, watching the chalk dust settle into the bricks. Down below I could see Mrs Jansma still holding on to Billy. He was hanging on to her like a spider but it looked like he had quit crying.

That afternoon a lady from the PTA came to talk to us about the paper drive. 'One more time,' she was saying. 'We've licked the Krauts. Now all we have left is the Japs. Who's going to help?' she shouted.

'I am,' I shouted back. I was the first one on my feet.

'Who do you want for a partner?' she said.

'Billy Monday,' I said, pointing at him. He looked up at me as though I had asked him to swim the English Channel, then his head slid down on the desk.

'All right,' Mrs Jansma said. 'Rhoda Manning and Billy Monday.

Team number one. To cover Washington and Sycamore from Calvin Boulevard to Conner Street. Who else?'

'Bobby and me,' Joe Franke called out. He was wearing his coonskin cap, even though it was as hot as summer. How I loved him! 'We want downtown,' he shouted. 'We want Dirkson Street to the river.'

'Done,' Mrs Jansma said. JoEllen Scaggs was writing it all down on the blackboard. By the time Billy's mother and Mr Harmon came to get him the paper drive was all arranged.

'See you tomorrow,' I called out as Billy left the room. 'Don't forget. Don't be late.'

When I got home that afternoon I told my mother I had volunteered to let Billy be my partner. She was so proud of me she made me some cookies even though I was supposed to be on a diet. I took the cookies and a pillow and climbed up into my treehouse to read a book. I was getting to be more like my mother every day. My mother was a saint. She fed hoboes and played the organ at early communion even if she was sick and gave away her ration stamps to anyone that needed them. She had only had one pair of new shoes the whole war.

I was getting more like her every day. I was the only one in the third grade that would have picked Billy Monday to help with a paper drive. He probably couldn't even pick up a stack of papers. He probably couldn't even help pull the wagon.

I bet this is the happiest day of her life, I was thinking. I was lying in my treehouse watching her. She was sitting on the back steps putting liquid hose on her legs. She was waiting for the Episcopal minister to come by for a drink. He'd been coming by a lot since my daddy was overseas. That was just like my mother. To be best friends with a minister.

'She picked out a boy that's been sick to help her on the paper drive,' I heard her tell him later. 'I think it helped a lot to get her to lose weight. It was smart of you to see that was the problem.'

'There isn't anything I wouldn't do for you, Ariane,' he said. 'You say the word and I'll be here to do it.'

I got a few more cookies and went back up into the treehouse to finish my book. I could read all kinds of books. I could read Book-of-the-Month Club books. The one I was reading now was called *Cakes and Ale*. It wasn't coming along too well.

I settled down with my back against the tree, turning the pages, looking for the good parts. Inside the house my mother was bragging on me. Above my head a golden sun beat down out of a blue sky. All around the silver maple leaves moved in the breeze. I went back to my book. *She put her arms around my neck and pressed her lips against mine. I forgot my wrath. I only thought of her beauty and her enveloping kindness.*

'You must take me as I am, you know,' she whispered.

'All right,' I said.

Saturday was not going to be a good day for a paper drive. The sky was gray and overcast. By the time we lined up on the Horace Mann playground with our wagons a light rain was falling.

'Our boys are fighting in rain and snow and whatever the heavens send,' Mr Harmon was saying. He was standing on the bleachers wearing an old baseball shirt and a cap. I had never seen him in anything but his gray suit. He looked more shell-shocked than ever in his cap.

'They're working over there. We're working over here. The Germans are defeated. Only the Japs left to go. There're canvas tarps from Gentilly's Hardware, so take one to cover your papers. All right now. One grade at a time. And remember, Mrs Winchester's third grade is still ahead by seventy-eight pounds. So you're going to have to go some to beat that. Get to your stations now. Get ready, get set, go. Everybody working together . . .'

Billy and I started off. I was pulling the wagon, he was walking along beside me. I had meant to wait awhile before I started interviewing him but I started right in.

'Are you going to have to leave to go get it?' I said.

'Go get what?'

'You know. Your shot.'

'I got it this morning. I already had it.'

'Where do they put it in?'

'I don't know,' he said. 'I don't look.'

'Well, you can feel it, can't you?' I said. 'Like, do they stick it in your navel or what?'

'It's higher than that.'

'How long does it take? To get it.'

'I don't know,' he said. 'Till they get through.'

'Well, at least you aren't going to get rabies. At least you won't be foaming at the mouth. I guess you're glad about that.' I had stopped in front of a house and was looking up the path to the door. We had come to the end of Sycamore, where our territory began.

'Are you going to be the one to ask them?' he said.

'Sure,' I said. 'You want to come to the door with me?'

'I'll wait,' he said. 'I'll just wait.'

We filled the wagon by the second block. We took that load back to the school and started out again. On the second trip we hit an attic with bundles of the *Kansas City Star* tied up with string. It took us all afternoon to haul that. Mrs Jansma said she'd never seen anyone as lucky on a paper drive as Billy and I. Our whole class was having a good day. It looked like we might beat everybody, even the sixth grade.

'Let's go out one more time,' Mrs Jansma said. 'One more trip before dark. Be sure and hit all the houses you missed.'

Billy and I started back down Sycamore. It was growing dark. I untied my Brownie Scout sweater from around my waist and put it on and pulled the sleeves down over my wrists. 'Let's try that brick house on the corner,' I said. 'They might be home by now.' It was an old house set back on a high lawn. It looked like a house where old people lived. I had noticed old people were the ones who saved things. 'Come on,' I said. 'You go to the door with me. I'm tired of doing it by myself.'

He came along behind me and we walked up to the door and rang the bell. No one answered for a long time although I could hear footsteps and saw someone pass by a window. I rang the bell again.

A man came to the door. A thin man about my father's age.

'We're collecting papers for Horace Mann School,' I said. 'For the war effort.'

'You got any papers we can have?' Billy said. It was the first time he had spoken to anyone but me all day. 'For the war,' he added.

'There're some things in the basement if you want to go down there and get them,' the man said. He turned a light on in the hall and we followed him into a high-ceilinged foyer with a set of winding stairs going up to another floor. It smelled musty, like my grandmother's house in Clarksville. Billy was right beside me, sticking as close as a burr. We followed the man through the kitchen and down a flight of stairs to the basement.

'You can have whatever you find down here,' he said. 'There're papers and magazines in that corner. Take whatever you can carry.'

There was a large stack of magazines. Magazines were the best thing you could find. They weighed three times as much as newspapers.

'Come on,' I said to Billy. 'Let's fill the wagon. This will put us over the top for sure.' I picked up a bundle and started up the stairs. I went in and out several times carrying as many as I could at a time. On the third trip Billy met me at the foot of the stairs. 'Rhoda,' he said. 'Come here. Come look at this.'

He took me to an old table in a corner of the basement. It was a walnut table with grapes carved on the side and feet like lion's feet. He laid one of the magazines down on the table and opened it. It was a photograph of a naked little girl, a girl smaller than I was. He turned the page. Two naked boys were standing together with their legs twined. He kept turning the pages. It was all the same. Naked children on every page. I had never seen a naked boy. Much less a photograph of one. Billy looked up at me. He turned another page. Five naked little girls were grouped together around a fountain.

'Let's get out of here,' I said. 'Come on. I'm getting out of here.' I headed for the stairs with him right behind me. We didn't even close the basement door. We didn't even stop to say thank you.

The magazines we had collected were in bundles. About a block from the house we stopped on a corner, breathless from running. 'Let's see if there's any more,' I said. We tore open a bundle. The first magazine had pictures of naked grown people on every page.

'What are we going to do?' he said.

'We're going to throw them away,' I answered, and started throwing them into the nandina bushes by the Hancocks' vacant lot. We threw them into the nandina bushes and into the ditch that runs into Mills Creek. We threw the last ones into a culvert and then we took our wagon and got on out of there. At the corner of Sycamore and Wesley we went our separate ways.

'Well, at least you'll have something to think about tomorrow when you get your shot,' I said.

'I guess so,' he replied.

'Look here, Billy. I don't want you to tell anyone about those magazines. You understand?'

'I won't.' His head was going down again.

'I mean it, Billy.'

He raised his head and looked at me as if he had just remembered something he was thinking about. 'I won't,' he said. 'Are you really going to write about me in the paper?'

'Of course I am. I said I was, didn't I? I'm going to do it tonight.'

I walked on home. Past the corner where the Scout hikes met. Down the alley where I found the card shuffler and the Japanese fan. Past the yard where the violets grew. I was thinking about the boys with their legs twined. They looked like earthworms, all naked like that. They looked like something might fly down and eat them. It made me sick to think about it and I stopped by Mrs Alford's and picked a few irises to take home to my mother.

Billy finished getting his shots. And I wrote the article and of course they put it on page one. BE ON THE LOOKOUT FOR MAD SQUIRREL, the headline read. By Rhoda Katherine Manning. Grade 3.

> We didn't even know it was mean, the person it bit said. That person is in the third grade of our school. His name is William Monday. On April 23 he had his last shot. Mrs Jansma's class had a cake and gave him a pencil set. Billy Monday is all right now and things are back to normal.
>
> I think it should be against the law to keep dangerous pets or dogs where they can get out and get people. If you see a dog or squirrel acting funny go in the house and stay there.

I never got around to telling my mother about those magazines. I kept meaning to but there never seemed to be anywhere to start. One day in August I tried to tell her. I had been to the swimming pool and I thought I saw the man from the brick house drive by in a car. I was pretty sure it was him. As he turned the corner he looked at me. *He looked right at my face.* I stood very still, my heart pounding inside my chest, my hands as cold and wet as a frog, the smell of swimming pool chlorine rising from my skin. What if he found out where I lived? What if he followed me home and killed me to keep me from telling on him? I was terrified. At any moment the car might return. He might grab me and put me in the car and take me off and kill me. I threw my bathing suit and towel down on the sidewalk and started running. I ran down Linden Street and turned into the alley behind Calvin Boulevard, running as fast as I could. I ran down the alley and into my yard and up my steps and into my house looking for my mother to tell her about it.

She was in the living-room, with Father Kenniman and Mr and Mrs DuVal. They lived across the street and had a gold star in their window. Warrene, our cook, was there. And Connie Barksdale, our cousin who was visiting from the Delta. Her husband had been killed on Corregidor and she would come up and stay with my mother whenever she couldn't take it anymore. They were all in the living-room gathered around the radio.

'Momma,' I said. 'I saw this man that gave me some magazines . . .'

'Be quiet, Rhoda,' she said. 'We're listening to the news. Something's happened. We think maybe we've won the war.' There were tears in her eyes. She gave me a little hug, then turned back to the radio. It was a wonderful radio with a magic eye that glowed in the dark. At night when we had blackouts Dudley and I would get into bed with my mother and we would listen to it together, the magic eye glowing in the dark like an emerald.

Now the radio was bringing important news to Seymour, Indiana. Strange, confused, hush-hush news that said we had a bomb bigger than any bomb ever made and we had already dropped it on Japan and half of Japan was sinking into the sea. Now the Japs had to surrender. Now they couldn't come to Indiana and stick bamboo up our fingernails. Now it would all be over and my father would come home.

The grown people kept on listening to the radio, getting up every now and then to get drinks or fix each other sandwiches. Dudley was sitting beside my mother in a white shirt acting like he was twenty years old. He always did that when company came. No one was paying any attention to me.

Finally I went upstairs and lay down on the bed to think things over. My father was coming home. I didn't know how to feel about that. He was always yelling at someone when he was home. He was always yelling at my mother to make me mind.

'What do you mean, you can't catch her,' I could hear him yelling. 'Hit her with a broom. Hit her with a table. Hit her with a chair. But, for God's sake, Ariane, don't let her talk to you that way.'

Well, maybe it would take a while for him to get home. First they had to finish off Japan. First they had to sink the other half into the sea. I curled up in my soft old eiderdown comforter. I was feeling great. We had dropped the biggest bomb in the world on Japan and there were plenty more where that one came from.

I fell asleep in the hot sweaty silkiness of the comforter. I was dreaming I was at the wheel of an airplane carrying the bomb to Japan. Hit 'em, I was yelling. Hit 'em with a mountain. Hit 'em with a table. Hit 'em with a chair. Off we go into the wild blue yonder, climbing high into the sky. I dropped one on the brick house where the bad man lived, then took off for Japan. Down we dive, spouting a flame from under. Off with one hell of a roar. We live in flame. Buckle down in flame. For nothing can stop the Army Air Corps. Hit 'em with a table, I was yelling. Hit 'em with a broom. Hit 'em with a bomb. Hit 'em with a chair.

Spalding Gray
Sex and Death to the Age 14

I can remember riding beside the Barrington River on the back of my mother's bicycle and she was shouting out and celebrating because we had just dropped the bomb on the Japs in Hiroshima, and that meant that her two brothers were coming home. A lot of people died in World War II. I didn't know any.

The first death which occurred in *our* family was a cocker spaniel. Jill. Jealous Jill. We called her that because she was very jealous when my little brother was born. Jill died of distemper, which I thought meant bad temper because she was always jealous. But before she died, she bit me. Not *just* before she died, but some time before. I was harassing her with a rubber submarine, as I often did in the pantry of our house in Barrington, Rhode Island, and she turned on me and took a chunk out of my wrist; it looked like a bite out of an apple from my point of view. I guess it wasn't because I don't have a scar. I ran to my mother and she said, 'You had it coming to you, dear, for harassing the dog with a rubber submarine.'

When we were 14, a group of us used to try to knock ourselves out. Organically. By taking 20 deep breaths, head held between our legs, and then coming up real fast and blowing on our thumbs without letting out any air. Then all the blood would rush up or down, I don't know which, but it would rush somewhere, fast. And we would hope to pass out, but it never worked. Then we'd spin in circles until we all got so dizzy that we fell down. Then we went home.

So one day I was in the bathtub taking a very hot bath. It was a cold day and the radiator was going full blast. I got out of the tub and thought, well, this is a good time to knock myself out, I'm so dizzy, I'm halfway there. So I took 20 deep breaths and went right out, and on my way out I hit my head on the sink, which was kind of a double knockout. When I landed my arm fell against the radiator. I must have been out quite a long time because when I came to, I lifted my arm up and it was like this dripping-rare-red roast beef, third-degree burn. Actually it didn't hurt at all because I was in shock, a steam burn on my finger would have hurt more. I ran downstairs and showed it to my mother and she said, 'Put some soap in it, dear, and wrap it in gauze.' She was a Christian Scientist, so she had a distance on those things.

The next day when I got to school, the burn began to drip through the gauze. I went down to the infirmary, and when the nurse saw it she screamed, 'What, you haven't been to a doctor with this? That's a third-degree burn. You've got to get to a doctor right away.' So I went back home and told my mother what the nurse had said, and my mother said, 'Well, it's your choice, dear. It's your choice.' Anyway, Jill died of distemper and I can remember I was wearing a T-shirt with a little red heart on it, and after the dog died I remember seeing the heart – my heart, the dog's heart, a heart – float up against a very clear blue sky. There was no pollution then in Barrington, Rhode Island. My mother told me that I stopped talking for a long time after that. She said they were thinking of taking me to a psychiatrist, but I don't know where they were going to find a psychiatrist in Barrington, Rhode Island, in 1946. Maybe they were thinking of Providence.

After Jill died, we got another dog, a beagle. We named the beagle Bugle because he made a sound like a bugle when he followed a scent. And Bugle would often get a scent in the fields behind our house where we used to play. We had a particular little grassy area we called 'Hitler's hideout', inspired by World War II, where we would play Korean war games on weekends. My mother forbade them on Sundays and discouraged them on weekdays, so Saturdays were usually pretty intense.

We had toy rifles and used a galvanized metal garden bug sprayer for a flame thrower, which one of us would wear on his back. It was attached to a long hose which led to a little pump handle, and instead of DDT we would shoot water out of it. Also, Ralston Russell's father had brought back a German Luger from the war, as well as a German helmet, complete with swastikas. The Luger had had its firing pin removed, but it was very real. The helmet seemed even more real. You could almost smell the dead German's sweat on the leather band inside. I assumed someone had taken this helmet right off a dead soldier, but I couldn't imagine Mr Russell doing that. He was a Christian Science practitioner during the war and I didn't think he'd seen much combat. I had always thought of him as a gray flannel mystic in his little office off their basement rec room where he went every day, dressed in a three-piece suit, to pray for sick people. They didn't even have to be there. He just sat and concentrated real hard on knowing 'the truth' and sent out all his thoughts to wherever his patients were lying, waiting to get better. But maybe Mr Russell did see action. Maybe he was in the field trying to bring dead GIs back to life. But the gun and helmet were very real. I was sure I could smell the enemy on them.

Judy Griggs was the only girl in the neighborhood and she lived next door to us. Her father was my father's boss at the screw-machine plant, and I remember that they had a very big yard with an apple orchard at the end of it. Judy played a game with us in her yard called 'Ice Lady'. The Griggses had a clothesline shaped like the Pentagon, and Mrs Griggs would hang her sheets out to dry on it. Judy, who was the Ice Lady, would chase us through the rows of clean sheets until she touched one of us, and we had to freeze and stand still like a statue. Judy was queen of her backyard, but she wanted more. She wanted to be a member of our gang, which had only four of us in it, all boys. Judy tried to prove to us that she was a boy by putting a garden hose between her legs while her sister, Bethany, turned on the water. Once she used a turkey baster, but that still wasn't enough to convince us. We forced her to go into the fields with us and pull down her pants to show us that she really was a boy. Instead of a tinkler we saw her, well, I don't think we had a name for it actually, but I remember it as this very small fleshy slit where her tinkler might have been if she had one. Then we took her into our chicken coop and tortured her mildly by tying her to a post and stirring up all the dust from the dirt floor with a broom. We'd leave her there until the dust settled, and she seemed to like it. At least she gave every sign of liking it.

The Griggses had hired an Italian yard man named Tony Pazzulo. Tony was lots of fun – he used to pick us up and swing us around and bury us under piles of raked leaves. The most fun was being thrown around by him. Our fathers, Dad and Mr Griggs, never touched us in that rough, playful way, and we all loved it. One day Tony took the cover off the cesspool for some reason and we all looked down into it.

It was a great dark pool of 'grunts' and 'doots' (we called the big ones 'grunts' and the small ones 'doots'), and suddenly the Griggses' yard took on a new dimension, even after Tony put the cesspool cover back on.

Shortly after Tony uncovered the cesspool, Mr Griggs bought a whole bunch of chickens. One Saturday he cut off all their heads while we watched. He used the stump of a big tree for a chopping block and held the chickens' heads down on it while he cut them off with an ax. Then the chickens ran headless around the yard with blood spurting from their necks until they flopped down on the ground and died.

Soon after Judy Griggs pulled her pants down, houses began to grow in the back fields. We played in the foundations and among the electrical wires and saw wallboards go on and the houses get finished and the new neighbors move in. I can remember once being up on some scaffolding and seeing some boards lying against a house, and I just decided to push them down on my friend Tim Morton. I didn't think about it. I just pushed and they fell and crushed him. I thought I had killed him, not only because of the way he was lying down there, but also because of the way his father ran, jumping over the hedge, to pick up Tim's limp body in his arms. I was terrified. I ducked back in through the window of the unfinished house to hide, and my older brother, Rocky, who stayed out on the scaffolding, had to take the blame. Tony Morton just stood there with his son's broken body in his arms, yelling up at Rocky, 'I'll be back to deal with you, my friend.' I felt scared for Rocky. I felt scared for all of us.

Not long after that, Tim died of lung cancer. He was very young and no one seemed able to diagnose it. They thought it was what they called a lung fungus that had been brought back by American soldiers from the Korean War. Tim's death was a strange kind of relief because we'd always heard that one in four would have to die of something – cancer, tuberculosis, polio, whatever – so I always wondered who would be the *one* of the four of us who hung out together. That was often on my mind.

We lost Bugle the beagle in the back fields during hunting season. My mother told me not to worry about it, this was something that happened. Hunters often stole dogs during the hunting season, so probably some nice, loving hunter had given Bugle a good warm home.

Shortly after Bugle disappeared we got a cocker spaniel that chased cars. I don't remember its name, but I do remember it chased cars and Harvey Flynt said we could cure this if we filled a squirt gun with vinegar and shot the spaniel in the eye with it every time it chased our car. But before we could try this, the dog was run over by a truck bringing cement to one of the new houses in the back fields.

Then we got another dog which we called Roughy because it was so rough with us. Soon after we got it, Dad said, 'I'm sorry boys, but we're going to have to give Roughy away because he's too rough.' By then my brother Rocky had become very attached to Roughy and didn't want to see him go. He wanted to save some memory of the dog, so he took one of Roughy's fresh 'doots' and put it in a jelly jar with a tight cap and kept it by his bed next to the little radio that had a Bob Hope decal on it and a white plastic dial that looked like a poached egg when it was lit.

Some time after that my mother took us out into the yard. It was summer and we sat in the shade of a big elm while she read to us from a book about the reproduction of cows.

We gave up at last on dogs and switched to cats. Our first cat's name was Kitzel. All I remember about Kitzel was that she was a calico who lived a long time and liked to eat corn-on-the-cob. After Kitzel grew up, I wanted a kitten, so I got a kitten from the Griggses that I called Mittens. I named her Mittens because she had little white markings on her front paws. And I had this relationship with Mittens: I would make a sound, kind of a half-blow, half-whistle (we called it a *wumple*), and Mittens would come running. Then one weekend she didn't come and I looked everywhere for her. The only place I did not look was the cellar of our barn. My brother Rocky told me that he had seen footprints of the Blain brothers down there. The Blain brothers were ten-foot-tall hairy men who roamed the Rhode Island countryside and were known to jump over eight-foot-high hurricane fences with a deer under each arm, or a child, because they were running out of deer in Rhode Island. Rocky told me the brothers had last been seen at the Boy Scout camp, Camp Yiago, not too far from where we lived.

At the end of the weekend, my mother said that she had seen the trash truck pick up Mittens's little body on Friday by the side of Rumstick Road, and she hadn't had the heart to tell me. Mom cheered me up by telling me that I could get another kitten.

And I did. I got another kitten and I named it Mittens, Mittens the Second. That Mittens was killed on Rumstick Road by Mrs Jessup driving a large black Chrysler at dusk. I saw it happen and began to run away, and Mrs Jessup ran after me to try to apologize and comfort me, but I ran ahead of her because I didn't want to see her. I ran into my house and up to my bedroom. I couldn't catch my breath and felt like I was suffocating.

This reminded me of the time when I woke up in the middle of the night and saw my brother Rocky standing on his bed, blue in the face and gasping for air, crying out that he was dying. My mother and father were standing beside the bed trying to quiet him, and Mom said, 'Calm down, dear, it's all in your mind.' And after he calmed down, my father went back to bed, and my mother turned out the light and sat on the edge of Rocky's bed in the dark. The only illumination in the room was a cluster of fluorescent decals on the ceiling, of the Big Dipper, the Little Dipper, Saturn and the Moon. We were all there very quiet, in the dark, and then Rocky would start in, 'Mom, when I die, is it forever?' and Mom said, 'Yes.' And then Rocky said, 'Mom, when I die is it forever and ever?' And she said, 'Yes, dear.' And then he said, 'Mom, when I die is it forever and ever and ever?' And she said, 'Uh-huh, dear.' And he said, 'Mom, when I die is it forever and ever and ever and ever . . .' I just went right off to this.

Rocky used to take me into the bottom of his bed – he called it Noss Hall, a foreign land under the blankets – and tell me that he loved me over and over again. I can remember the smell of his feet and how his sweat made a yellow ring around his collar – *yellow sweat*. Shortly after that, he left me for my Gram Gray, who lived with us. On Sundays I was allowed to go into their room and get into bed with my gramma, just to listen to Jack Benny and 'Allen's Alley'. I can remember the smell of my gramma – the smell of her flesh and the way it hung so soft and old – and the feel of her silk nightgown. I can remember that better than any contact with my mother.

My mother and I had two physical rituals that I clearly recall. One was the cleaning of my tinkler. We called it a tinkler then. Since I'm not circumcised, she would clean it every Saturday with cotton and baby oil and she would turn me quite firmly over her knee and go at it like a cleaning woman with a Chore Girl. She would do it very hard and it would hurt and I'd squirm in her arms.

The other ritual was 'making a path' – she'd sit at the edge of my bed and I'd stick out my arm and she'd make a path with her finger up the inside of my arm. She'd do this until I was almost hypnotized and went right out. Sometimes, my friend Ralston Russell would stay overnight, and my mother would sit in between our twin beds and we'd both stick out our arms and she'd made double paths.

After Mittens the Second died I got a third kitten that I named Mittens, which I think might have been a mistake. I found this Mittens's body one cold February day during double sessions. In the seventh grade we had double sessions because there weren't enough teachers to go around, so I went to school in the afternoons and got the mornings off to play. I'd go out and play and leave my math homework for my gramma to do, and then I'd come in and copy it over. I never learned how to add as a result. Gram smoked Viceroys and blew the smoke in my face. It went in blue and came out gray, and I liked the smell.

I would play outside with Patrick Scully and Scott Tarbox. Patrick Scully's father had a very good collection of pornographic pictures. He was in real estate and often had reason to go to Tijuana on business, and he would send back these picture postcards of matadors and bulls to his wife saying, 'Hi, having a lovely time at the bullfights in Tijuana.' And we thought, bullfights, yeah I bet. His entire bureau drawer was overflowing with these pornographic pictures, which he made no attempt to hide. Patrick and I would take out our favorite pictures, roll them up, put them in a jar, and bury them in Patrick's backyard. Then when we wanted to look at them again we'd just go dig them up. They were old and kind of yellowed, like tintypes. I used to imagine that the naked people in the pictures were very old or dead by the time I was looking at them, and somehow that added some spice to it.

Our favorite picture was an odd one, and that's why it was our favorite, I'm sure. We couldn't figure out what was going on in it. It was a picture of a man standing naked with this huge semierection (anything was huge to us, at 11 years old), and this semierection was just sort of lobbing down into a glass of water which made it look even bigger because the glass magnified it. Then there was this naked woman kneeling in front of the glass who was either about to drink out of it or had just finished drinking, I don't know which, but we found this photo fascinating because we couldn't imagine our parents doing this to have us. (Was that what sex was all about?) So we'd just look at it and then roll it up again, put it back in the jar, and bury it.

We didn't talk about this because we didn't have much of a vocabulary then. A penis was a tinkler, a dick, or a boner if it was hard, and my mother's breasts we called pontoons. That was about it, at 11 years old. Then one day Mrs Tarbox caught us changing into our bathing suits to go for a swim. We were all naked, Patrick, Scott and me, and we clutched our suits over our tinklers and Mrs Tarbox said, 'What, are you modest?' And we didn't know what *that* meant and we weren't the kind to go look it up. But all of us were stamp collectors, and we each had something called 'The Modern Stamp Album'. So we equated the word *modest* with *modern*. It became the key sexy phrase – kind of a catchall – that we used whenever we wanted to talk about something dirty. We'd giggle and ask, 'Is that a Modern Stamp Album picture?' 'It that a Modern Stamp Album house?' 'Is that a Modern Stamp Album movie?' Then we'd burst into hysterics and laugh until we fell down.

So it was during double sessions that I found Mittens the Third frozen in the backyard, just frozen solid like a package of green beans. My mother said the cat must have gotten into some rat poison. She had an explanation for every death. It was never mysterious.

I never knew what happened to the bodies. Someone took care of them. I don't remember any funerals; in the Christian Science Church there are no funerals at all. But, come to think of it, we did have a little graveyard with popsicle-stick crosses out behind the outhouse. That was the graveyard where we buried the little wild animals like mice and sparrows. Once I found a mouse near our back steps and it was *alive* with maggots, so many maggots that its whole body was moving as though it were alive. We didn't bury that one. It was gone in three days.

As for domestic animals, most of them were buried out by the currant bushes in the apple orchard behind our house.

Shortly after we made the popsicle-stick graveyard, the polio epidemic came to town. I was terrified of ending up in an iron lung. We'd see pictures of them on TV. Paul Winchell and Jerry Mahoney were always trying to raise money for the March of Dimes, and we'd see them standing by an iron lung with huge rearview mirrors, and I'd think, God, how hideous. It would be like being buried alive.

Mrs Brinch, our fifth-grade science teacher, didn't help. She was obsessed with polio. At the end of the year she showed us pictures of polio victims she was taking care of and said, 'Now get plenty of rest this summer, drink a lot of water, be careful where you swim, don't go into any crowded movie theaters and remember, you can contract polio at any time.'

In the Christian Science Church you had to go to Sunday School until you were 20. There were a number of Sunday School teachers but the one I remember best is Chad Oswald. He always had a number of wonderful healings to tell about.

Each week we were asked to bring in a healing story of our own. This meant that each week something bad had to happen to us so we could be healed. For instance, I would say, 'I came down our back steps, tripped and fell and hit my head on the cement, and I knew the Truth and I was healed.' Then Ralston Russell, who was also in that class, would say, 'Oh, *that* cement, that's cheap cement. It's not hard – it's like rubber.' And I knew that was a class thing because the Russells had more money and could afford a firmer cement.

When I stayed over at Ralston's, we talked to each other in the dark from the twin beds. We pulled down our pajama bottoms and talked about how it felt to be naked against the cotton sheets. One time, Mrs Russell, who was listening at the door, burst in and said, 'You both pull up your pants right now!'

Once I had this little piece of flesh growing off my nose. It was like a little stalactite, and it wouldn't go away. It was very embarrassing because it looked like a piece of snot and all my friends kept telling me to wipe my nose. My mother asked the Christian Science practitioner to pray for the stalactite to drop off. I got impatient and wanted to have a doctor burn it off, but Mom said, 'Please give it one more day, dear,' so I agreed. On that last day I was being tutored in math (since my gramma had done all my math homework for me, I couldn't add without doing it on my fingers), my tutor said, 'It looks like you need to wipe your nose. Let me get you some Kleenex.' And I thought, oh, no, here we go again. So I pretended to be wiping my nose and the little stalactite just dropped right off.

Being Christian Scientists we had to work very hard in order to keep a hot line to God. If we let this hot line down, there was a chance that the polio germs might get in, so I was working overtime. When we got tired of working we could call the practitioner who would take over and pray for us while we rested up. We thought the polio germs were everywhere. Once Chan, my little brother, came home from kindergarten with his rest blanket, and on it were some little red threads. He said, 'Look, these are polio germs; they're so big you can seen them,' and I believed him. Ralston Russell told me that he knew someone who stuck out his tongue and got polio instantly – the tongue just stayed out there, paralyzed. So I was getting fearful. I was washing my hands with rubbing alcohol and staying out of crowded movie theaters in August and swimming with my head very high above water. And I made it through the polio epidemic.

After I found the third Mittens dead, I sort of gave up on cats and started to get involved with birds. Eddie Potter and I both bought ducks for Easter. He named his Carl Duck, after our seventh-grade teacher Carl Caputo. I don't remember what I named mine. Eddie and I were close friends. Eddie was the kind of guy who would laugh at anything. He would buy an orange popsicle, eat half of it, and then instead of offering it to me or another friend, he'd throw the other half in the sand and stamp on it and laugh. Another thing he laughed at was cars that got stuck in the sand, particularly those old double-ended Studebakers. He would stand there, screaming with laughter, pointing at the back tires spinning in the sand.

Eddie and I used to play strip poker together; I would usually win, so Eddie would end up naked. The rule was that the loser would have to go through some mild ordeal, some little punishment, nothing very big. One of my punishments was to make Eddie crawl down between his twin beds. Most of Barrington, Rhode Island, was made up of twin beds. I don't think I saw a double bed until I got to Boston. My parents had twin beds that were very close together. When I was feeling anxious and no one was home I would go into my mother's walk-in closet, look at all her dresses, look at the line of shoes, and look at myself in her full-length mirror on the door. I liked that very much. Then, dressed only in my underwear, I would crawl between my parents' beds and hang there, just hang there until I felt all right.

My mother's parents, who lived down the street, had twin beds also, but theirs were wider apart because they had a larger bedroom. They fell in love at Hope High School and got married right after graduation. They had a good marriage and three children. My gramma's two sisters were not so lucky in love. There was Aunt Tud, who was jilted early on by a coffee plantation owner and never got involved with men after that. She became very plump. She'd always cook the meal bread and mince pies at Christmas and Thanksgiving. And then there was my Aunt Belle, who married Bob Budlong. They never had any children, but Bob made up for that because he was kind of like a half-child, half-man who ran a little grocery store in Scituate, Rhode Island. He could never stand collecting money from his customers, the poor people of Scituate, so he finally gave the whole store away and they ended up living in a trailer. It was very cold in that trailer, so when my grandparents went down to Florida for the winter, they'd invite Bob and Belle to stay in their home. This house was immaculate, like a joyful funeral parlor, with wall-to-wall carpeting.

At Christmas and Thanksgiving, Bob would blow up great long balloons that he brought from his store. He'd let them loose in my gramma's house and we'd all laugh as they sputtered around the room spraying juice over my grampa's bald head until at last they withered and dove into the after-dinner mints. Then Bob would fall asleep with his hands clasped over his belly and his stubby cigar stuck between his lips.

Bob would often take me for driving lessons. We'd drive all around Barrington waving at friends. I could barely see over the wheel or reach the clutch, never mind the brakes, and I loved it. After my driving lesson we'd come back to the house to watch *Queen for a Day*. I don't know where Aunt Belle was all this time, maybe upstairs reading *Science and Health*. *Queen for a Day* was Uncle Bob's favorite TV show. We'd watch it together and he would weep and clap to try to make the applause meter go up for his favorite contestant. Then, exhausted from all his clapping, he would fall asleep, leaving his cigar balanced on my gramma's coffee table, flaking ashes on her rug. Next *The Mickey Mouse Club* would come on, and I'd stay very awake because I had a crush on Annette Funicello at the time. Sometime during the final song, Bob would wake up and say, 'When is *Queen for a Day* going to be on?' And I'd say, 'Uh, Bob. We just saw *Queen for a Day*.' And he'd say, 'Well, tell me all about it, tell me who won.' Then we'd go down to the Barrington shopping center, and he'd stick little hard candies down the backs of children. But I don't remember whether Bob and Belle had twin beds or a double bed in their trailer.

So Eddie's little punishment for losing at strip poker was to slip down between the twin beds and crawl naked over the little dustballs, fuzzies we called them. Then he'd come up the other side of the bed smiling, covered with fuzzies and looking for more. I couldn't think of any more punishments, it wasn't my specialty, so he'd begin making up his own. I would be the witness. He'd take a little cocktail dish, the kind you'd use for pigs-in-the-blanket or smoked clams, and he would put his dick on it – still connected of course. Then he'd go downstairs and display it to Rita Darezzo, the cleaning woman, as though it were a rare hors d'oeuvre, calling, 'Rita, it's cocktail time!'

Anyway, the ducks were growing up; they were reaching puberty and my duck's quack was getting deeper. Winter was coming, and I was keeping the duck in the playroom so that it wouldn't mess up the house and would go on the linoleum. I put a little game board, a Karom board, in the doorway of the playroom to keep it in there. One Sunday I went up to get ready for Sunday School. I had to wear this woolen suit, which I hated, and to keep it from itching I'd put on my pajamas first. I was very thick. When I came downstairs, the board had fallen down and the duck was gone. I searched the house, but I couldn't find it anywhere. Then I walked over and lifted up the board and there it was, flat, like pressed duck, like Daffy Duck after the steamroller has run over him. It didn't look real. It didn't look like any duck I'd known. I couldn't figure out how a board that thin could have done something like that. I thought my father must have stepped on it, by accident. I thought he must have come into the playroom and stepped on the board, but I didn't want to think that. I don't know who took care of the little body, but I went off to Sunday School.

After the duck, I continued with the birds and got a parakeet that I called Budgy. This parakeet was one of the blue ones – there were two kinds, blue and green – and it cost $7.50. I had a wonderful relationship with Budgy for about a year. I would whistle from my room and he would whistle back from downstairs. Then I would run down, feed him, change his water and clean the bottom of his cage. About a year went by and one day I whistled and whistled and . . . you know the rest. I went downstairs and there he was, on his back on the bottom of the cage with his little claws curled up. I thought he must have died of a heart attack or pneumonia because I was told these little tropical birds were not used to the New England climate.

After a short break with no pets, or maybe just a random turtle or two in between, a next-door neighbor offered me an empty 50-gallon fish tank. I thought, why not, they're 90 percent water and I won't give them names. I bought every kind of tropical fish. I had the black mollies, the zebra fish, the neons, the swordtails, the guppies, the catfish, the angel fish and the Siamese fighters, who bit the tails off the angel fish. And they died. They died often. The proliferation of death made me more indifferent to it, I think. I would take the little white net and scoop them up and ride them down on my bike to one of the lots in the neighborhood that hadn't been developed yet. I'd give them an outdoor burial by flicking them out of the net and into the grass.

About a mile down the road from that vacant lot lived the Lillows, who had the first television in the neighborhood, and we would go there to watch *Howdy Doody*. One day a group of us were coming out of the house and we looked up and saw Stokes Lillow hanging from a pine tree, showing us his asshole. We were standing there looking up and he was just hanging there like a little koala bear, spreading his cheeks. I had never seen anything like that before. I don't think I had even seen my own.

Shortly after Stokes Lillow showed us his asshole, that vacant lot was developed and a German family with a strange name moved in – the Lindbergers. Now this seemed odd to us, like they were from some other side of some other tracks. We hadn't seen any Germans, we hadn't seen any blacks, we hadn't seen any Jews, we hadn't seen anything but Rhode Island WASPs. So in came the Lindbergers, and they were a strange family. First of all, there were more than three children in the family, that was the first odd thing. The second odd thing was that Mr Lindberger was having an affair with his secretary. Mrs Lindberger told my mother this, and my mother told me. (My mother and I were very close – actually we dated all the way through college – and so she'd tell me these intimate things.) I didn't know anything about affairs. I thought they only happened in New Hampshire because my grandmother had lent me her copy of *Peyton Place*. It was the first real novel I ever read, and it got me started. After that I went on to Jack Kerouac and Thomas Wolfe. My mother said to me, 'Mr Lindberger is having an affair with his secretary because every time Mr Lindberger touches Mrs Lindberger she gets an electric shock.' So they were having these electric shock treatments, but they weren't having any kind of love life. But he was a good provider. He would always come home late at night in his Lincoln Continental, a big black Lincoln Continental with the spare tire built into the trunk. He took very good care of his children – he had five of them – and he was a good father. He'd see his secretary at night and come home late.

I made friends with Larry Lindberger, who was a couple of years older and had a parakeet. But he had a completely different relationship with his parakeet than I did. He would let it out of the cage, let it fly around the dining-room, then take a wet towel, twist it up and snap the bird right out of the air. And the bird would go like a feather bullet, ricochet off the window, and then flutter around with its tail dragging like an overloaded B-49 trying to take off. He'd snap it maybe one more time and then he'd put it back in its cage so it could rest up for the next day. When I saw this, I knew Larry and I had a different aesthetic. But I didn't stop him from hitting the bird, I just watched and took it in.

So the fish died out and the tank got emptied and I gave up on animals and started to get interested in people. I had been putting this off as long as possible. But before I got involved with people I went on what you might call a shooting spree. I got a pellet pistol, went outside and started shooting everything in sight. All the songbirds on telephone wires, frogs, and one squirrel, which we ate – it tasted like a rat. The frog legs we ate too. They were very skinny, not what like you'd get in a French restaurant, but tasty.

I wanted to buy a shotgun so I could go duck hunting, but my father said no. And I knew by then that when my father said no it meant yes, so I kept at him. At last I got a single-barrel Winchester 20 gauge and began to hunt for black ducks. I wasn't a very good shot and would often only wound them and have to finish them off with my switchblade. I'd hold them down and slit their throats. It was awful.

Then one day when I was out on my paper route down near Potter's Cove I heard mallard ducks quacking and got very excited because I'd never shot a mallard before. So I got up real early the next morning and went down to Potter's Cove. Just when I got there a huge flock of mallards took off in this spectacular V-formation, and I just stood there and watched. I don't know why I didn't pull the trigger. I wanted to think it was against the law to shoot ducks before dawn.

Shortly after that I sold my gun to my father and he put it away in a closet.

Then I started going to dancing school on Friday nights. That meant Friday-night baths, after which I put on my pajamas and my blue wool suit over them, and my white gloves – then I went downstairs to wait for the car pool to pick me up. While I was waiting I would look for sexy pictures in any magazine I could find. We didn't have any *National Geographics*. The only sexy pictures in our house besides the underwear ads in the Sears Roebuck catalog were to be found in *Life* magazine, which arrived every Friday, just in time.

I found two erotic pictures in *Life* magazine that I kept going back to. One was of Prince Charles jumping over hurdles as a young boy, which I kept under the bed and used to look at every time I was anxious. The other was of the collapse of Rome, with everyone crawling around in the streets half naked. Maybe they had the plague. I thought, this is really sexy: anything goes now because there are no more rules. Everyone can just do what they want sexually.

I'd be looking at this picture when the car pool would come and take me away to dancing school and I'd have to snap into the box step. I would dance with Sue Wheelock, my partner, and they would play 'Sweet Sue' on the piano. I had a recording of 'Sweet Sue' on a Paul Whiteman record. It was one of those painted records with a picture of the whole Paul Whiteman band that spun into a blur of color when I turned the record player on. I loved that song; it went, 'Every star above, reminds me of the one I love, Sweet Sue, it's you' in one of those high, 1920s crooner voices. And I would say to Sue Wheelock, 'Isn't it a coincidence that they're playing "Sweet Sue"?' as though it implied that we were meant for each other. That chance and destiny had smiled down from above. But she thought I was just trying to put the make on her at an early age, so that didn't get me very far.

I had a relationship on another dancefloor with Sally Funk. We were in every jitterbug contest in the canteen in seventh grade. We were real good jitterbuggers, but it never went beyond the dance-floor. Then I fell in love with Julie Brooks, and Julie Brooks I can only describe as an angel – very full lips, olive skin, long brown hair. Julie and I and a bunch of us who were hanging out together would have kissing contests. We would all get together and see how long two people could hold a kiss. Someone would time it while the rest of us stood around watching, smoking Lucky Strike Regulars. Julie and I used to kiss for about 20 minutes just holding our lips pressed tight with no movement at all. I was very uncomfortable because it was hard to breathe. The other thing we'd do is have make-out sessions in Julie's house when her mother wasn't there, playing 'Sha-Boom, Sha-Boom' on her little automatic 45-record player. Then we got into dry humping in the field behind Julie's house in September in the sun. I always liked it in the sun. Six of us would go out there, three boys and three girls, and we'd make different spots in the grass and make out. Julie was always wearing those madras Bermuda shorts that were so popular in the late fifties, and I would get my hand up on her right thigh, and that was enough. I'd never go any further, in my mind the rest was a jungle. Once I did touch the jungle, briefly, and I told my friend Ryan Ryder about it. He said, 'What, you touched the place she pees out of?' That brought me down and fast. I think he was jealous, but I didn't know about jealousy then. I didn't know about jealousy until two weeks later. So I went back to keeping my hand on her thigh, dry humping until I would come. I would come in my jeans and then we'd go have vanilla Cokes. I was happy and I thought she was happy, too; things were going fine until one of the girls, Linda Chipperfield, asked her mother if she could get pregnant through her clothes, and we never saw Linda again. I think her mother kept her in forever. So that broke up our club.

Around that time I told Julie that I was going to fuck her; we had just gotten up the courage to say 'fuck' in public. It was probably more exciting than the actual act, although none of us in the neighborhood had even done it yet. Ryan always warned us to be careful about saying it on the streets. He said that we could be brought up on a morals charge and we'd get our driver's licenses revoked. But none of us had our driver's licenses yet.

Telling Julie I was going to fuck her was kind of like a threat and a promise, a threat to me and a promise to her. I thought it was time. I gave her two weeks, I don't know why it was two, but it was going to be the second Saturday in October. I didn't know how I was going to do it.

The Saturday before the Saturday that I was going after Julie my father said that we should go play golf. This was odd to me, we had never played golf before. Later I found out from my gramma that my father's father, Grampa Gray, told him the facts of life out on a golf course. But we didn't even belong to a country club. In Barrington, Rhode Island, there were two classes of people, those who belonged to the Rhode Island Country Club and those who didn't. We didn't. So my father and I had to play golf at the Wampanaug public course, just over the border in Seekonk, Massachusetts. It was a little nine-hole course that we called Swampanaug because when it rained it was mostly under water. When we got to about the fourth hole, my father said, 'You know, there was a gal at our plant . . .' (he meant his factory – he worked at a very conservative factory that made screw machines and they didn't even allow Coca-Cola until the old boss retired) ' . . . there was this gal at our office who had a turkey in the oven, and she wouldn't admit it because she wasn't married. Everyone knew she had a turkey in the oven, it was a plain as the nose on her face. Everyone was looking at it. It was disgusting. She stayed around until she had this turkey, and then she left.'

After a long silence, he said, 'You know, there are diseases that make you blind.' Now I knew that sex and blindness somehow went together because Ray Strite told me that if you got sperm in your eyes, you could go temporarily blind and that men on Devil's Island would rub sperm in their eyes in the morning to get out of a particularly difficult work shift. So I did have that equation in my head.

Then I began to get paranoid. I suspected that there might be a plot afoot, that Mrs Brooks had called my father and said, 'You know, your son is going to fuck my daughter and you better take him out on a golf course and tell him he's going to go blind if he does that.' Also Reverend Quigley's wife had seen Julie and me wrestling in the backyard and had come out and slapped a part of Julie's anatomy and said that people our age do not wrestle, boys and girls do not wrestle together, this was a rule in our neighborhood. I thought that maybe Mrs Quigley had told Mrs Brooks. I saw that my father was as nervous as I was, or more so, so I tried to relieve him by saying, 'I won't do it, I won't do whatever it is that you're talking about. I won't do it.'

That Saturday I went to see Julie. And I found out that Julie had played Spin the Bottle with Billy Patterson the night before and that they had ended up exchanging shirts. That meant that he had seen Julie in her bra and she had seen his skinny bare chest. So that was it with Julie. That was pretty much it until I was 25, it was a heavy rejection. I went off with Ryan, the one who told me not to touch the place she pees out of, to see *Heaven Knows, Mr Allison* in Providence.

Some weeks later I tried to get Julie back. I began to force myself on her. I would hold her down and try to kiss her, and she would push me away. And no one was around to tell me that this was not the way to win someone back. No one was giving me any information. They were telling me about turkeys and going blind, but they were not telling me how to get Julie Brooks back, which was the advice I was looking for.

Shortly after that masturbation took hand. I'm not saying that it was Julie's fault – actually I had discovered it while I was going out with her. Thurston Beckingham had told me that if you took a piece of animal fur and rubbed your dick real fast it would feel good. That's all, just rub it and it would feel good. I didn't have any animal fur around the house and I wasn't the type of kid to go out and buy some just to do that. But there were a lot of Davy Crockett hats in the neighborhood. Then one night I just began doing it with my right hand (we called it Madam Palm and her five lovely daughters), just instinctively, like a monkey. I didn't expect anything to come of it, but after about half an hour I had an ejaculation. That was a surprise, no one had told me that I could do it on my own. I think I kept at it just because it felt good. Then it became a kind of . . . I wouldn't call it a habit exactly, but it was something that I practiced often at night. I would read *Sexology* magazine to try to find out if I was going to grow hair on my palms or go crazy.

Eventually, the masturbation became more elaborate, the way those things do. There was a big mansion across the street from our house that the president of Blackstone Valley Gas and Electric owned, and I would run around in his backyard, naked under a full moon, swinging from pine trees like a monkey, over marble statues of women in the nude. That was one of the excitements. The other was mirrors.

I began to like to masturbate in front of mirrors. The mirror was very important because, being a Christian Scientist, I kind of lost track of my body; for many years it was denied me. So it became important for me to look at what was there, to get a good sense of it. Also, my father had a deck of playing cards with naked women on them, airbrush jobs, like the photo of Marilyn Monroe naked on that red velvet spread. When my parents weren't home I would go into their room and take these cards out of his bureau drawer and look at them. Just look at them. This would get me excited and then I would cross the room to my mother's full-length mirror. On the way I would have to pass her bureau, on top of which were pictures of all my relatives: my grampa in his business suit, my aunt in her wedding dress and my two uncles in their navy uniforms. They all had incredibly serious looks and their eyes seemed to follow me as I passed. I was young enough to maintain an erection past that, get to the mirror, and masturbate in front of it, catching glimpses over my shoulder of my uncles, my grampa and my aunt.

There were no real private places to masturbate in the neighborhood, and no one had locks on their bedroom doors. Friends would sometimes report getting caught by their mothers, which I could not imagine. There was a bathhouse at the yacht club with private stalls, but my father would always rush me, calling out, 'Hurry up! What's taking you so long to change?' There was a hole in the wall where you could look through to the girls' side, which I did only once and no one was there. Then we'd have group masturbation, in Gill Leach's attic. It wasn't exactly a circle jerk, it was just to see who would come first. I don't think we kept score.

But once again something happened to make me paranoid. My parents decided to send me away to a religious camp for the summer, Camp Genesis on Cape Cod. I don't know why. The camp had nothing to do with Christian Science, it was more of a Holy-Roller-type fire-and-brimstone camp. It was coeducational. The boys and girls were divided by a cold, cold lake: the boys on the north shore, the girls on the south. It was there at Camp Genesis that I fell in love with Timmy Cox. Timmy was as pretty as Julie Brooks, only he was a boy, which was very confusing. I decided to keep a safe distance. I just looked at Timmy, endlessly. Then one day he hit me in the head with his shoe. He must have sensed something, he just threw the shoe across the tent and hit me, knocked me out. They took me to the infirmary, and I guess they gave me some sort of sleeping pill to make me relax. I started to go out, but never having had sleeping pills before I thought the nurse might have given me an overdose, and I began to fight to stay awake. After I got back to the tent, Timmy apologized, and I realized I had to do something else with my attraction to him.

That's when the spitting began. At night, after lights out, I would spit into my right hand and then fling it across the tent until someone cried out, 'Hey, who spit?' And I knew it had hit someone. They would always blame the person in the bed over them. I did this almost every night. I did this for a long time until my friend Ryan Ryder sent me a letter in which he asked how the spitting was going. Someone in the tent got ahold of the letter and threatened to tell our counselor. I was afraid of being punished by him. He was an ex-stockcar driver and a recent born-again Christian, and I had never been beaten before. I knew the guy who had read the letter was stealing live ammunition from Edwards Air Force Base, which was next to our camp. I threatened to tell on him if he told on me. We had a good blackmail relationship going and he never turned me in.

At the end of July, my mother came to camp to pick me up. The whole family was going to a reunion for my Grampa Gray, who lived in Holland, Michigan. Now Grampa Gray was an odd man. He was married three times, first to my Gram Gray. They got divorced shortly after my father was born. Gram Gray told me that she had stayed with Curtis for as long as she did because the sex life was so good. For 10 years. And she never got involved with another man after that.

I had been out to Holland, Michigan, to visit Grampa Gray once before, when I was much younger, and I can remember only one thing about it. One morning I was sitting downstairs at the breakfast table and he came down wearing a Harpo Marx wig and said, 'Come here, boy, come here and sit on my lap.' I sat on his lap and he said, 'You be a good boy or I'll pour this whiskey down your neck.' I said, 'Oh, you wouldn't dare.' And he did, he poured the whole glass down the back of my neck, and I started to cry.

But this time, as we were driving away from Camp Genesis, my mother said to me, 'Spalding dear, I have some bad news. Grampa Gray has passed away. He died of a heart attack. Lois called up and said to come out anyway for a party. Curtis would have loved it.' Lois was Grampa Gray's third wife. Dad called her a real card, a hell of a gal, and Mom said she was the life of the party. Once when she came to visit us she got drunk and put on a rubber Mortimer Snerd mask. We all laughed and went to the Fore 'n Aft steak house, and on the way Grampa Gray tried to feel up Gram Gray, his first wife, while Lois sat in the back.

When we got out to Michigan, we had a big party. I played boogie-woogie on the piano while Dad danced into the night with a tall blond relative I'd never seen before. Mom went to bed early because she didn't drink. I remember masturbating in an upstairs closet and reading about a sex slaying in *True Detective* magazine in which the naked bodies of two 11-year-old boys were found in the trunk of a car not far from Grampa Gray's farm.

As soon as I got home from Michigan, my friend Spike Claxton came over to see me. He had just gotten his driver's license and had bought a '49 Ford coupe. He asked me if I wanted to go over to Dirty Dick Dixon's to have my tubes cleaned. I didn't know what he was talking about, but I wanted to get out of the house and I was curious. We drove over to Dirty Dick's, which was on the other side of town where all the tract houses with lawns like golf greens were. Dirty Dick Dixon's was right in the middle of this little development, surrounded by trees and overgrown hedges to prevent people from looking in. We pulled into the clamshell driveway and went through the side door into the kitchen, where there was a table with whiskey bottles on it. Dirty Dick was there and some guys from Bay Springs – Tony De Luca, Izzie de Rosa, Mickey de Silva – all in their dungaree jackets. There were some porn pictures spread out on the table. Not very good ones – mostly close-ups, mostly hair. And in the corner by the refrigerator stood Chad Oswald, my old Sunday School teacher. I could only see this as a coincidence. Here we were face-to-face and I thought he should leave. But instead of leaving he just went into the living-room and sat down. Then Spike turned to me and said, 'Hey, you see that guy who just went into the living-room? I saw him here last night, he had his schlong out on the table and it was *huge*. It was like a piece of Polish sausage.' And I said, 'Oh, really?'

So we all went into the living-room to wait to get our tubes cleaned in the tube-cleaning room, or whatever it was, the guest bedroom. And Dirty Dick kept coming out to take us in one at a time. At that point I'd given up on the idea of having my tubes cleaned, in fact, I didn't even feel like I had any tubes to be cleaned. I just sat there looking across at the Sunday School teacher, when suddenly a fight broke out. Spike Claxton hit Tony De Luca. Over went a chair. Over went a lamp. And the Sunday School teacher raced for the front door and we ran for the back. Spike and I jumped into his car, spun rubber, spun clamshells, got out of there, got home. I didn't tell anyone about it. I decided to keep it a secret.

The next day Spike called up and said, 'Hey, Dirty Dick called me this morning and told me never to bring that Gray boy over again. What's the problem? What did you say to him? What's up?' I just said, 'I don't know, Spike, I don't know.' Then a week later my mother said to me, 'Oh, I saw Chad Oswald at a concert with his mother. He'd make some gal a real good husband. Why do you think he doesn't get married?' And I just said, 'I don't know, Mom, I don't know.'

At the time I was getting straight Es in school. E was for failure, and they wrote it in red. So I was failing everything. I really wanted to transfer into the automobile mechanics course, but they only let Italians take that. I ended up in the business course, but I didn't do very well there either, since my gramma had always done all my math homework. So instead of adding and subtracting I began to systematically destroy the school.

I would get rotten eggs from in back of the supermarket. I'd bring them to school with me in the morning, and when the halls were crowded, I'd lob them into the Latin teacher's room. Other times I'd break off the lead from a pencil in the lock of Mrs Brumage's door so we wouldn't have to go into her all-boys English class to stand and recite Portia's speech, 'The quality of mercy is not strained. . . .'

At last I began building bombs. I'd take a birthday candle and stick it in a wad of clay, lay a big cherry bomb firecracker at the bottom of the candle, and put it behind a toilet in the boys' room. It's not as though I never thought someone might sit on that toilet – I did think about it, I did think that would be bad. Then I'd light the candle and head for English class from where, exactly 15 minutes later, I'd hear this enormous explosion and all the teachers would run out to try to catch the mad bomber. They'd round up all the boys, whose ears were still ringing from the blast, and take them down to be interrogated in the principal's office, but no one ever knew anything. Finally, Mr Balducci, the science teacher, offered a $5 reward for any information leading to the identity of this mad bomber. No one turned me in.

My older brother, Rocky, also tried to wreck the high school. At last, he was suspended for jumping up and down on the roof during a band concert. He really wanted to be a Maine guide, and once he tried to run away to Maine. But he did it the hard way, by crawling out his bedroom window, inching along the gutter, and climbing down a pine tree. He only got as far as Pawtucket. When he got back, he couldn't stand living in the big house anymore, so he stole some lumber and built a shack in our backyard.

Rocky used to have this problem. When he was out on his paper route, he would see trucks dumping dirt into the new foundations of the big houses and he'd hallucinate a child being covered over by the dirt. He would come home and tell my mother, 'I just saw someone being buried alive.' My mother would say, 'It's only your imagination, dear. Sit down.' Then she'd read to him from the Bible or from *Science and Health* to ground his imagination. In the winter when he was out on his paper route riding alongside the Barrington River, he'd see a hole in the ice and imagine that a child was falling through it. He'd come back and tell my mother, 'I saw a child falling through the ice, it's drowning! We've got to call the police.' And she'd say, 'Sit down, dear, let me read to you from the Bible.' Finally, my parents thought Rocky should go away to school to straighten out and buckle down. They sent him to Fitchton Academy in New Hampshire, and he hated it there. He would call my father up and say, 'You've got to get me out of this school, I'm very unhappy.' Then my father would go up and get him and when they'd get as far as the Howard Johnson's at the Portsmouth rotary my father would say, 'Let's stop here and get a clam roll.' But Rocky was paralyzed. He couldn't go in. He was convinced that he was going to kill someone in the restaurant. They drove all the way back to Barrington on empty stomachs.

So my father said to me, 'We're thinking of sending you to Fitchton Academy. It's time to buckle down or you'll end up in the Navy. It's shape up or ship out for you, my friend.'

Fitchton was run by a rabble-rouser, Colton W. Cartwright. He would have 'squirm sessions' on Sundays with the students, at which he made these Cotton Mather speeches. He would start by holding up a water glass saying, 'Eighty percent of the Coca-Cola glasses in America have active syphilis germs on the edge.' That was just the opener. He'd go on from there for an hour. He'd say, 'Today it is the jungles of Laos. Tomorrow it will be the cornfields of Fitchton!' This was the school that they were thinking of sending me to, and I had to go up there for an interview.

My mother drove. It was about a four-, five-hour trip up to Fitchton, New Hampshire. I might have been thinking about Susan Tice, the first girl in our neighborhood to get a two-piece, leopard-skin bathing suit. I was constantly dreaming of being on a desert island with Susan, just the two of us. I would dream of her in school, and I'd get an erection. Then I'd have to go up to the board to do some math, and I'd have to kind of force it down and then walk bent over like a cripple. So, I guess I was thinking of Susan Tice all the way up to Fitchton.

We got up there, walked in, and C. W. Cartwright in his three-piece suit looked at us from under his bushy eyebrows and said, 'Well, my friend, what's going on with you? Look at this report card. Straight Es. Why aren't you buckling down? What's the problem?' Now, no one had asked me anything like this before, just straight out. He just took me aside, a stranger. It was kind of sobering. I wasn't ready for it.

Out of nowhere, I said. 'Well, since *they* have invented the hydrogen bomb, there is no future. Not only does it negate my consciousness, it negates that of Beethoven's.' There was a long pause. He looked back at me and said, 'That what *they* said when *they* invented the crossbow.' Now I knew there was a difference between the hydrogen bomb and the crossbow, but I didn't know how to tell him because I was too intimidated by his three-piece suit and his bushy eyebrows. I just looked back at him, and Mom and I drove back in a kind of funk.

Later we got a letter from Fitchton Academy, and my father said, 'This is awful. They are not going to accept you because of your attitude. You're going to end up in the Navy.' Which frightened me. I believed him this time. So my father said, 'I'm going to write C. W. Cartwright a letter and request that he give you a second interview. Do you think you can promise me that you'll cooperate with him this time?' So I said, 'All right, yes, I'll give it a try.' And my mother drove me all the way up again. I walked into C. W. Cartwright's office, and he said, 'Well, my friend, can you promise us that you'll buckle down?' And I said, 'Yes, yes. I'll buckle down. I'll buckle down. I'll do it, I'll buckle down.'

Romesh Gunesekera
Kolla

'Mister Salgado is a real gentleman. You must do whatever the hell he tells you.' My uncle pulled my ear. 'You understand, *kolla*? Just do it.' I was eleven years old. It was 1962: the year of the bungled coup. My uncle was escorting me to a house in town I had never been to before.

The two columns at the front of the house plunged into beds of scarlet *rathmal* and white jasmine. The big bay between them, and the front windows, were shielded by cane tats painted in mildewy green. They were skew-whiff, unthreaded in places and splattered with bird-droppings. The roof was a line of reddish clay curls. A colossal white tree with tiny flecks of flame presided over the garden.

My uncle took me into the back of the house through a side entrance.

Inside, a door with a long grey metal spring attached to it squeaked behind us, closing automatically. A crumpled old woman was sitting on a small wooden stool with her feet in the sun. She looked up. 'You are back again?' she said to my uncle. 'What is this coming and going so much?' Her mouth collapsed around her empty gums.

My uncle told her we were there to see Mister Salgado.

She got up, wincing, and slowly made her way into the main part of the house. 'I will ask,' she mumbled.

We sat on the floor and waited. My ear hurt from my uncle's tug. When the sun sank behind the rooftops, we were summoned: '*Ko?*' a voice called from somewhere deep inside the house. *Where?* The polished syllable echoed. The last rays of light splintered through the trees. My uncle pushed me forward, 'Let's go.'

At first Mister Salgado said nothing. My uncle too was a man of few words. They were both silent for a while, simply wagging their heads at each other like puppets in the air. Eventually Mister Salgado nodded towards me: 'So, this is the boy?'

'Yes, this is the boy.' My uncle shifted his weight from one foot to the other, leaning towards the wall. One hand groped for support, the other proffered a bag of green mangoes we had brought. To him, Mister Salgado was probably not much more than a boy, but a boy whom history had favoured – a product of modern feudalism – whereas my uncle was a road-runner, a driver for an oil company. 'This is the one I was telling about. He is the boy. He can learn very quickly.'

A smooth untroubled face stared at me. 'School? Did you go?'

'Yes,' I blurted out. 'I went to school. Fifth Standard. I can read and write.' I had even learned some English from my poor, tormented schoolmaster, still under the spell of a junglified Victoria. He lived in a limewashed bungalow near my father's fields.

'And now?'

My uncle wriggled next to me. 'As I told before, he can learn quickly but he cannot live at home any more. That trouble . . .'

I had burned the thatched roof of a hut in the schoolyard by accident. I only dropped a single match flaring down the mouth of my father's almost-empty arrack bottle: a whistle of blue flame shot out and climbed the *cadjan* fronds. My father went mad; I ran away to my uncle who promised to arrange a new life for me. He told me I would never have to go back again. 'I am doing this only because I think your mother – if she were alive – would have wanted me to. Understand?'

Mister Salgado sighed. He was thin and had a curved spine. He often twisted himself into the most awkward postures, his long legs intertwined and his neck alarmingly cricked. The sad expression of a hurt heron would struggle in his face. He spoke slowly, almost hesitantly, politely changing the subject and asking my uncle about the failed coup as if it were some unseasonable rain. I had never heard language so gently spoken. My uncle's speech, in comparison, was a strangulation of the spirit. Ever after, when Mister Salgado spoke, I would be captivated. I could lose myself in his voice; this happened not only on that first day, but frequently over many years. Sometimes I would miss the instructions he was trying to give me, but he didn't always notice. I think he himself was sometimes entranced by his voice and lost the sense of what he had started out to convey. Perhaps that was why he sometimes preferred to be silent. I could understand that. My head also sometimes seemed more full of words than could ever pass my lips.

Mister Salgado, Ranjan Salgado, was a bachelor. A sweet smell clung to him, heady and unnatural, derived from an ivory bottle shaped like a bell and impossible to open properly. He would shake tiny, powerful drops out of the metal clasp at the top of its narrow neck and rub them on his hands, or his face or body. The scent made me think of cinnamon bushes, but it was the nature of the town to deceive. Even in Mister Salgado's house deceit had found a nest, especially in the head of his servant Joseph.

Mister Salgado would sit in his chair after his meal and rest his cheek, or his chin, or sometimes even his whole head on a thin finger or on a cupped palm – inviting misfortune – and stare with his huge eyes into nothing as if all he wanted was to grow old. He sat at the head of the dark mahogany table that I learned to polish to a deep and brilliant shine. At night, when alone, he usually liked to eat bread and western food: *courses*. Small discs of fried meat and creamy mashed potatoes that disappeared without a trace into his body. Corned beef was a favourite. He ate it with a *seeni-sambol* that burned the roof of your mouth. When, eventually, I became his cook as well as everything else, I created a special hash: crispy corned beef roasted with potatoes, onions and green chilli, dappled with soy sauce and brown sugar. I relished it too.

At first my job was simply to take the young master his morning tea and then sweep the front veranda and steps. Until I proved myself I was not allowed even to make tea, or dust or sweep inside the rooms. I was glad. I did not want to break anything.

The broom I was given was enormous. I was terrified that I would knock something over and so I would use the side door from the kitchen to go around the outside of the house to get to the front. I didn't dare go through the sitting-room or dining-room with it. One day I had a brilliant idea: I cut the handle short. That was the start of the trouble with Joseph.

'Stupid idiot, you chicken-head bumpkin, you pumpkin-face. Have you no respect for property? You are here to look after things, not destroy them.'

I was meant to help Joseph, but he resented me right from the beginning. Perhaps because, despite my circumstances, I was not of his kind. Joseph had come to work for Mister Salgado two years earlier. He was from Kosgahapola, a small brackish village on the other side of Ambalangoda beyond the mask-makers. He had wriggled his way into a job in a government Rest House until a by-election resulted in his being kicked out. The opposition had won, and the local party workers were being paid off, or at least that's what he had said to Lucy-*amma*, the very first person I had met in the house, Mister Salgado's cookwoman. More likely he was caught pilfering. Despite his high-horse ranting he could never hold back; he had been born with the moral equivalent of a sweet tooth – no temptation was too small. I despised him for this defect: I felt he sullied Mister Salgado's house.

But that day it was as though I were the one who had disfigured the place, as if the broom were some living creature I had dismembered, a scion of a dynasty instead of a wooden pole with a worn-out coir head. We never replaced brush-heads in that house until the bristles completely disappeared: it was a household trait. Mister Salgado, priding himself on his skills of measurement, never even replaced a toothbrush until there was practically nothing left but the plastic handle. I would watch the bristles get shorter and more squashed day after day, until sometimes I myself would go and buy him a new one and place it in his mug. I would hide the old one in the bathroom cabinet – I never quite had the courage to throw it out – but invariably it would appear again the next day in its usual place, unusurped. But I was right to cut the broom handle and Joseph was wrong to scold me. Our young master heard the commotion and came out of his room. Joseph complained vociferously but my Mister Salgado said, 'No, it's all right. The boy needs a shorter broom.' Then I knew I was in the right place; *he*, at least, did not think I was stupid.

Joseph laid down the rules. He told me where I could sleep at night, 'Under that small, round hole' – a window in the alcove of the sitting-room – and what time I should get up. At night after he had turned out all the main lights and locked the front door, I would bolt the concertina doors in the sitting-room – one bolt into a dimple in the cold cement floor, the other into a cross-beam – and curl up on my mat under the porthole. I usually positioned myself so that I could look out while waiting for sleep to overcome me. I would imagine a star-chart in the sky that would cause the fall of Joseph – some terrible mishap, preferably preceded by disgrace before the master – and my own meteoric rise in the household. Early in my childhood I had convinced myself that I had a *deviya*'s divine ability to control my dreams, and so each night I would dream of revenge.

One night I decided to turn Joseph into a frog. I went to sleep sweet with anticipation. But in the middle of the night I woke up in a sweat. Something had gone wrong. I could not move. I was locked into position, petrified. My heart was pounding: a demon had entered the house. I prayed for it to go away and promised to be good and obey everyone around me and worship the god of all the gods if only the monster would go. Hours later, or minutes later, when there had been no sound inside the room, I began to feel brave again. I rolled off the mat and jumped to my feet. Nothing happened. No dagger flashed down; no demon pounced. There was no one to wrestle, only my own shadow from the half-moon and the scuttle of a startled gecko. I crouched and waited. Slowly, as I realized that there really was no one there, I began to play a game where all kinds of marauders entered the house and I, alone, repelled them. But in the end all that happened was that I overslept. When I opened my eyes it was morning. Joseph was nudging me with his foot. 'Get up,' he was saying. 'Get up, you stupid bastard.' The blue-and-white Chinese vase floating on the dark sideboard shook. I thought it was going to fall and break. But it was I – my body – that was shaking, not the vase. I rolled away again but without the energy I had had in the middle of the night. Sleep had wasted me.

'Tea! Tea!' Joseph was furious. 'Take tea to master. Get up, you lazy cow, take the tea!'

Fumbling with my sarong, I struggled to my feet. I could not stop rubbing my eyes. Without a word I rushed to the kitchen. Lucy-*amma* had put the tea to brew and even got the tray out for me. I quickly wiped the cup with the edge of my sarong and poured the tea. Milk and half a spoonful of sugar. It had always been that: just enough milk to turn the clear brown into creamy mud, and half a teaspoon of white sugar to fortify it. I knotted my sarong again, tight, and took the tea in.

Mister Salgado was in bed snoring lightly in the heat. The over-sheet was crumpled up on a side, and his sarong lay sloughed off his slim hips. His banyan revealed a few strands of black hair on a narrow boyish chest.

I went in and placed the tray on the side-table, 'Sir, tea!'

He was awake but he kept his eyes closed. He pretended to be asleep so that he did not have to acknowledge me. Early in the morning he was always very particular about maintaining his privacy. His *Einstein-time*, as he would call it later in life. I had learned that he liked me to leave the tea and disappear without a word. Then he would get out of bed and go to the chair by the window to sip his tea as if he were never comfortable in his large, dreamily soft bed with its padding and coir and coiled springs. But this morning I stayed on. I felt guilty for being late; I also wanted to do something to protect my standing from the criticisms that I knew Joseph would make later in the morning.

'Sir,' I declared, 'last night someone tried to break into the house. Sir, I chased them away, really . . .'

He groaned softly and turned. The bed creaked under him. On the headboard a small lamp rocked. I felt the whole room turn with his movement. He was tall, and when he was lying down he seemed to go on forever. His feet stuck out over the end of the bed, uncovered; he had high insteps that seemed to bunch his toes and shorten his feet. They looked like the feet of a woman.

'Sir, might have been *thieves*.'

I could see only half his face; one side was buried in the pillow. He opened an enormous brown eye and stared at me. A bare shoulder rose and dropped with each warm breath. Two inoculation scars like patched-up bullet holes flattened the skin of his upper arm. His sleep seemed luxurious. He made a sound like a hum, an all-purpose grunt. It was not a question, neither was it a statement, but it acknowledged my existence and the fact that I had said my piece. The dark, dreamy eye slowly closed, the pupil furling fast; the audience was over.

'What happened?' Joseph asked when I got back.

'Nothing,' I said. 'I gave the tea.'

'Still asleep?'

I deliberately did not answer. Let him imagine the worst, the worst for him. It made my blood boil just to think of him contaminating the world with his foul breath, controlling my destiny. I turned my head as if I were hiding something and ducked into the kitchen.

Lucy-*amma* was cutting onions, Bombay onions. The beards sliced off each onion were heaped on one side. She worked the knife like a stern goddess – a *devatara* – slicing translucent, perfect semicircles. She was always cutting onions. I learned something from that: the omnipresence of the onion, constantly appearing like the heart's throb of our kitchen life. For breakfast, for lunch, for dinner, for every meal it turned up: sliced or chopped.

I learned about cutting onions mostly by watching Lucy-*amma*, but she also taught me by getting me to do it. I became her kitchen assistant – an apprentice onion-cutter. I was grateful for that role even though at first, I suppose because I was young and small and near to the cutting-surface, I would weep as I did it. I could do nothing about that except grow older and taller. Only much later did I learn the tricks to minimize the effects: like washing the onion, sticking bread on the tip of the knife, winding a damp cloth around my hand. But even now, most of the time I still do none of these: I just cut, crying cathartically.

In those early days my interest in onions had nothing to do with my ambition to be a cook. It started as a refuge; an escape from Joseph. He could not stand the fumes of a good strong onion. When we were cutting onions, and especially when we were frying them, he did not come anywhere near the kitchen. He would flee to the bottom of the garden. I became more and more embroiled in cooking onions simply to avoid him.

That morning, after my late start, I found Lucy-*amma* chopping at high speed with her eyes half-closed. She had been cooking since the turn of the century. The place where she had been born had turned from village to jungle and back to village, time and again, over her seventy-odd years. The whole country had been turned from jungle to paradise to jungle again, as it has been even more barbarically in my own life. Some nights I would sit on the floor beside her and listen to stories of the old days. She had known Mister Salgado as a child while she was bringing up her own, and his father as a child when she was one. She had served Mister Salgado's grandfather whisky and coffee during the riots of 1915. She had seen politicians with handlebar moustaches and tortoiseshell topknots, morning coats and gold-thread sarongs, barefoot and church-shod. She had seen monkey-suits give way to Nehru shirts; Sheffield silver replaced by coconut spoons. But her cooking and her wood-stove – two black stones outside the kitchen – remained timeless. The rice still took twenty minutes to cook, and if the lid was lifted before the dimples appeared all would be lost; and, she explained, you still could not tell a fresh coconut without shaking it, and you could not make a *pol-sambol* without breaking it. Culinary taste was not fickle, she would say, and the way you swallow food, like the way you make babies, has not changed throughout the history of mankind.

'You need this one?' I asked, picking up a small red onion. The dry papery skin crackled. She did not answer. Her eyes were half-closed, protected against the vapours; her knife was a blur of steel.

I took the onion and cut it in half, and then neatly cut each half in half again. It was a small onion and the quarters fitted in the hollow of my hand; rattling, in a muffled sort of way, like dice in a gambler's fist.

I was not entirely sure what I would do with the onion quarters, but I knew that I wanted to bring the two – the onion and Joseph – uncomfortably together.

Mister Salgado's house was the centre of the universe, and everything in the world took place within its enclosure. Even the sun seemed to rise out of the garage and sleep behind the *del* tree at night. Red-beaked parrots and yellow-eared *salaleenas* came and sang in the garden. Bullfrogs croaked by the gate. On Monday the greengrocer turned up with his basket of okra and beans; on Tuesday the butcher with oxtail and a hunk of goat-meat; on Wednesday the fishmonger came balancing sprats and prawns in two baskets on a pole calling out,

> *Isso, isso,*
> *thora malu,*
> *para malu,*
> *ku-nis-so-o.*

And on Thursday the haberdasher appeared with a cardboard trunk on his head. There was no point in his coming to our house – he sold only to women and the only woman in our house was Lucy-*amma* who never even looked at what he had to offer. But the man was a friend of Joseph and he came to gossip. His lips were splayed out, permanently parted, as if continuously spewing a web of intrigue.

He was due at mid-morning. I decided to wait for his arrival because Joseph would chat to him for at least half an hour and that would give me time to get into his room with my raw onion and do something diabolical: rub onion juice all over his sleeping-mat. Until then I busied myself on the front veranda, sweeping dust from one end to the other and into the garden, making a cloud of red motes puff out of my broom head.

The haberdasher had a little handbell which he rang as he criss-crossed his way down the lane. Each time he rang the bell the crows on the road scrambled into the air. The whole place echoed with their cawing, his tinkling and the cooing of our neighbour's brainless doves. It was the march of a wizard. There was a house on the other side of our lane where he always stopped: number eight. Mr Pando's house. It was a mysterious fortress with high walls. From the lane nothing could be seen of the house except the edge of the roof; the haberdasher always got in but I never did, even though years later we got to know Mr Pando quite well. The tinkling of the bell would suddenly stop and there would be silence punctuated by the occasional shrill exclamation of Mrs Pando – the *nona* – discovering gold brocade, or the price of a fake emerald bangle. But this morning when he stopped outside the barricade and the tinkling died there was something missing. The massive door in the wall did not ease open: the whole lane tensed up. Then to my surprise the bell began to tinkle again. At first rather tentatively, as if the ringer were unsure as to what he should do. Then more insistently, as if he were trying to force the door open with the peals of his tiny bell. It was furious enough to wake the dead, but there was no response from number eight. He shouted out '*badu badu badu . . .*' goods and goodies, and then his voice trailed into a kind of puzzled anxiety. No sale at number eight today. He rang his bell slightly less enthusiastically and came towards our house.

'So, so?' I heard Joseph say to the vendor when he appeared. He was leaning over the gate, swinging to and fro.

'Those people must have gone somewhere.'

'Can't be. I heard them earlier in the morning. Big commotion was going on there with that Pando-*nona*.'

I had heard it too but had taken no notice. Joseph wiped his face with a corner of his sarong and waved the haberdasher in. His friend was a stocky man whose dark, round face was always dripping with sweat. When he squatted and eased the cardboard trunk down, he looked like a toad. The top of his head was flat and disfigured without the huge trunk on it. The flatness came from a cloth ring he wore on his head as a cushion. He took that off too and fanned himself, slowly rocking back and forth on his haunches. 'She even asked me to bring lace today.' He snapped open the brassy locks of the trunk and poked at a bundle inside. 'And look, georgette.' He cleared his ugly throat.

'What she want lace for?'

'Same as anybody. Why not? What do you think she wants?'

Joseph sniggered.

I turned to go to Joseph's room, but suddenly there was the most terrible howl I had ever heard: starting as a rumble in the bowels of the earth it erupted somewhere beyond the garden, filling the air with pain and fury; a bestial sound, demonic in its anguish like the screech of some gut-roasted bird, or the squeal of a punctured pig; a sickly sound stretched by a rack and wound around the boreholes of a drill, searing the nerve-ends of every jellified maggoty head in the neighbourhood. This was a howl loud enough to dwarf the history of sound in our lane, maybe the whole town, even the whole country.

Joseph and his friend ran out into the middle of the lane. I darted back into the garden. We all looked at Mr Pando's house: the source of the howl. Someone – a woman – started shouting. Doors banged. Glass shattered. More screaming and screeching. I climbed to the top of the white tree in the front garden.

The whole of Mr Pando's front yard had turned powdery red as if covered with dust from Mars. The steps were strewn with small plastic bags. A woman hurried out and swept the powder off the steps. Then there was another howl from the house and she scampered back inside. There was more shouting, voices rising higher and higher. The crows were distraught, cawing and circling above the house. The sky turned black. Pando-*nona* rushed out and looked at the sky, and then rushed back in swearing. The howling carried on in huge, long, unearthly moans, rising and falling to a rhythm of its own.

Joseph and his friend and all our other neighbours gathered outside the house. The haberdasher was the one, in the end, who went in after the police smashed the door down.

When he came back he was hopping up and down. '*Miris, machang* – chillies! Those two witches tried to kill Pando-*mahathaya* with chillies. Hot, dry, red chillies and chilli powder. Place is covered all over with it.' His face streamed with sweat, his eyes brightened over every word. 'Pando-*mahathaya* was tied up in the bath. To see him, *appo*!' he banged the side of his head. 'His face, his arms, his balls, even his prick, all swollen like balloons. *Big*, man. They'd rubbed chilli powder all over. He was howling in agony. *Nona*-lady was screaming at him and pouring buckets of chilli powder. And that servant woman was rubbing it in. Up his arse!' Our witness laughed, prodding himself with his finger and wriggling about.

When the police dragged the two women out, Pando-*nona* was still screaming at her husband. 'I'll give you the hots, you *bathala*-poker.' It seemed she had discovered her recently wed husband frolicking in the bathroom with a girl from the famous Hothouse Bodega. His howling and her screaming ring-marked everything in the whole neighbourhood: stones, trees, buildings, people. Poor Pando's skin retained a reddish tinge ever after, and he was always mopping himself with a big white handkerchief as if he were permanently too hot.

I went back into the kitchen and chucked my onion quarters into a bowl; they seemed too tame, but I was not ready to use chilli yet.

The next year, in September, Mister Salgado had planned to go away for a few days to his cousin's tea-estate. Joseph was to be left in charge of the house. I had to stay with him as there was nowhere else for me to go. I had been in the house for more than a year, but I was not happy. As long as Joseph presided over me I could not be, and if I stayed in that condition I knew, eventually, I too would become corrupted and mean-spirited.

In preparation for Mister Salgado's absence, we closed up the house and fitted white linen sheets over the furniture in the sitting-room and the dining-room. Joseph supervised. I tugged and pulled and tucked and smoothed, and turned the whole place into a funeral parlour. I was given instructions on a huge new range of duties: polishing the brass, the copper, the silver; oiling door hinges, locks, pulley-wheels on the tats; making all kinds of inventories. I had to count the cutlery, count the china, count the linen, count the number of bulbs in the house, the books in the bookcases. These counting jobs came straight from the master himself. The night before he left, every time he saw me, his eyes would widen and he would ask me to count yet another thing. Catching sight of me down the corridor, carrying out some earlier instruction such as taking the silver goblets to their treasure chest, he would say, 'Ah!' and ensnare me with his voice. 'This . . .' Everything would stop. I would wait while he paused to clear his throat and find the word he was looking for. 'Yes, I think you must count all the different glasses we have. You must learn to distinguish between the types, the shape you know, and how many.

Not now, but while I am away.' Then he would lift his head questioningly like a teacher – a *gurunanse*.

'Yes, Sir.'

I had to go and write down all these different tasks. Early on I learned the value of making lists from watching Mister Salgado. He was a great one for lists. He would listen to *The Mikado* and write page after page of lists: shopping lists, laundry lists, book lists, betting lists, things-to-do lists, things-not-to-do lists, diary lists, repair lists, packing lists, record lists, larder lists, letters-to-write lists. I would find these on his desk, in the pockets of the clothes I had to put away, sometimes by the telephone and sometimes in his bag, like charms or favourite poems.

My lists, at that time, were always small ones: a scrap of paper – usually the one-inch margin of an old newspaper, torn from an inside page. I used to feel guilty about even that – my furtive attempts to emulate him and better myself – because the old newspapers in the house were sold to a collector who came once a month. My scraps for learning were a small loss in income for him. He came with a basket on his head and scales folded in a cloth in his hand. The newspapers were stacked in neat square piles and tied crosswise with dirty twine. Each bundle would be weighed and paid for. Then with a month's news neatly placed on top of his head, he would rise and waddle away. The knowledge that could be packed into that basket was humbling; everything that happened in the world for a whole month. Sometimes I would use an old envelope retrieved from the straw basket in the study. I would write my list with a pencil and keep it in my shirt pocket.

On the evening I was asked to count the glasses I was getting increasingly anxious; my list was becoming unwieldy. I liked to keep it neat, writing just on one side with careful, evenly spaced letters. It was the way I learned to write. I didn't like squeezing in words or adding a line where there really ought not to be one. And because newspapers were so thin, I didn't much like writing on both sides. I press too hard when I write and the other side of the paper tends to become embossed. I also do not like having more than one list – unlike Mister Salgado. But that night rushing about, listening for his awkward signals – his Ahs and Hmms, the pauses, the instructions – I ended up with too many things to do. If these were exercises to stimulate me, to develop skills of classification and mathematics, they were in danger of failing completely.

Although he had been to the best of Colombo's schools, Mister Salgado regarded himself as largely self-educated. He came from a line of people who believed in making their own future. To him there were no boundaries to knowledge. He studied mosquitoes, swamps, sea corals and the whole bloated universe, and right from the early days wrote long articles about all of them. He wrote about the legions under the sea, the transformation of water into rock – the cycle of light, plankton, coral and limestone – the yield of beach to ocean. I sometimes burst in on him in his study when, pen in hand, he was poised on the brink of some miraculous calculation. 'Sorry, Sir,' I would say and he would motion me to be quiet. 'Listen, do you know how many stars there are in the sky?' I would shake my head, 'No, Sir.' He would nod and smile to himself. 'They have been counted, you know, but nobody can count how many polypifers surround us in the sea.'

The morning he was due to leave for up-country I was allowed to serve breakfast. I brought him his plantain, his soft-boiled egg, his toast and butter and pineapple jam, in real trepidation. He was deep in thought. When I came to take his plate away, he looked up at the ceiling fan and spoke like a sage, 'You must look after this place.'

'Sir?' But before I could say anything else Joseph appeared, rubbing his head with the heel of his palm nervously. 'Everything ready, Sir.'

Later that morning Lucy-*amma* also went away, on her annual visit home. 'Now, make sure you eat some rice every day. Joseph will give you food. There is money in the biscuit tin to get something from the *kadé*,' she said, tying up her belongings in an old tablecloth.

'He won't, I know he won't.' I hated the idea of being dependent on him. 'He is jealous of me, he'll want me to starve.'

'Don't be stupid, child.'

I carried her bundle down to the gate. It smelled of boiled rice and coconut milk, just as she did. She lifted it up on top of her head like the paper-collector, the bottleman, the haberdasher, and disappeared down our magic road. I felt trapped. Blood pounded in my head at the thought that there was nobody else in the house – in the world – except Joseph and me. I felt like running around and around the garden in a never-ending circle like a mad dog, spinning faster and faster so that Joseph would never catch me, but instead I waited at the gate, as far away as possible from the house, and rubbed my elephant-hair bracelet for good luck.

What I disliked most about Joseph was the power he had over me, the power to make me feel powerless. He was not a big man but he had a long rectangular head shaped like a devil-mask. His face was heavy and his lower jaw jutted out, making his head look detached from his body. A sullen heart compressed the muscles beneath the skin of his face in a permanent grimace. He had big hands that would appear out of nowhere. And as I was always trying to avoid him and never looked up at him, the sight of his hands suddenly on a doorknob or reaching for a cloth was terrifying. The hands, like the head, always seemed disembodied. I expected to find them around my throat one day. The nails were in good shape though; he took good care of his nails. I don't know where he learned to look after them, but maybe he too learned something from our Mister Salgado.

When the clouds came and I smelled rain loosening in the air, I headed back up to the house. I didn't know what else to do: he would be there somewhere, waiting, gloating.

The kitchen was in darkness. The small windows by the sink did not let in much light, and because the place was empty the other doors were closed. I didn't want to turn on the lights and attract attention to myself; instead I groped along the edge of the side-table until I got to the counter where Lucy-*amma* did her cutting. Underneath I found a small basket of red onions. I quickly bit one open and rubbed it all over my hands. Then I put it inside my shirt for my protection. If he was to come anywhere near me I would fling it in his face, or smear it all over him. It was not chilli powder, but it would keep him away. I had to be prepared for anything. I hid in the back. Our part of the house – the kitchen, the storeroom, Lucy's room, Joseph's room, the spaces between the servants' warren and the back veranda – was always full of junk: old battle-worn chairs, empty cargo boxes, a buckled cupboard jammed against the wall where I hid my few belongings, a blistered chrome refrigerator, bald brushes and rust-eaten dustpans, a mangled electric blender, a wireless with its face punched in and a big, blackened iron. All the leftovers of city living washed up like driftwood. But it was comfortable.

The rain fell in small pellets ripping the petals off the flowers in the garden. I imagined Joseph outside, pierced by the drops, drenched to the bone, catching a chill, pneumonia, something deadly: an illness of the mind. In each needle line of rain, I saw a message for him from the gods, my gods. I could see them in the sky crowded on a bamboo raft on a blue lake surrounded by rolling hills, holding silver spears and peering through peep-holes in the clouds, searching for Joseph, determined to destroy him.

'Here, eat this.' Joseph threw a ready-made packet of rice and curry on to the chair next to me. 'I will be out tonight.' I had not heard him come up behind me because of the noise of the rain. 'I'm going when the rain stops. You close the doors and keep guard. Sleep inside.'

Where he had to go I could not imagine, but I was overjoyed. I wished the rain would stop immediately: instead it poured down even harder. The sound rose to a crescendo. Water drilling into the ground. The gutters were spilling over and waves seemed to wash down the sides of the veranda; the drain had turned into a river. Joseph disappeared into his room, and I reversed my prayers; I tried to will the rain to stop. 'Give us a break: let him go, leave the house, then come down as hard as hard can be so he will never ever return. Let him drown as he walks slurping in the rain with that spoony jaw of his.'

At nightfall the rain stopped. Joseph left wearing a stylish pink shirt. The first thing I did was tuck into my rice-packet; I was starving but I had not wanted to eat while he was around. I did not want to give him the satisfaction of seeing me drool over food that he provided, but drool I did. I had eaten nothing since early morning when Lucy-*amma* gave me some bread which I had with a bit of butter left over on a breakfast plate. I stuffed my face, fist over fist.

That night was the first time I stayed alone in the house: our big town house with its cane blinds, Formica surfaces and nylon mats. It was a dark house; the lights never quite reached everywhere even when they were all turned on. Even the biggest bulb, a huge clear globe in the dining-room, seemed to be overshadowed by the space it had to illuminate: the ceiling barely discernible and some of the corners, the oblongs of shadow behind pieces of boxy furniture, indistinct. I always felt the place was bigger than its form, that each room extended beyond what I could see, that the house itself extended beyond what I could know, as if each room had a shadow room which only shadows could enter and where secret rituals of peculiar sciences – oceanography, sexology – were practised.

I sat out on the front steps and checked through the list of things to do for my Mister Salgado. For the first time I felt at peace in the house. Not only because of the quietness inside, the quiet of an empty house, but also because of the knowledge that Joseph was not roaming about inside. Knowing that I would not bump into him around a dark corner. Or see him glowering under some light, smirking. Not having his presence spoiling my life.

In the end I didn't do any of the jobs I should have. I planned out what I needed to do but then drifted away, imagining life in the house forever without Joseph. I felt I could spend my life growing in the house, making something of myself. I had the feeling that my Mister Salgado would help me. I also felt, even then, that Mister Salgado could do better with just me by his side. Joseph was not the man for him. Joseph should be stuck up some palm tree, high on *toddy*, keeping the demons happy like the rest of his people. He made the house seem awkward and unbalanced. I felt he wanted to abuse everything in Mister Salgado's house like a drunk who resented what he could not reach, especially the sobriety of those who could stand where he would fall. I felt I could change that; smooth the house and cultivate our lives to some fruition. Perfection even. It seemed possible in those days.

I felt safer than I had ever felt before in my life. The silhouettes of the trees and bushes in the garden, the glow in the sky from the gas lamps on the main road seemed mine and only mine, embellished by familiarity. I didn't know what happened much beyond our lane. I knew the *kadé* – the tea kiosk at the top of the road, a few shops at the junction, and I had been to the market, but the rest of the city – what it means to be in a city – was a mystery to me. I had no idea how much I did not know about the city – Mister Salgado's *sleepy town* – beyond the few roads I had seen. I could not imagine where Joseph had gone. Was it some place in the heart of Pettah? A brothel? A den in the harbour area? What kind of place? In those days we had no television, and I had not read any books about life in the town we lived in. Only the newspapers gave some inkling, but not enough to give shape or sense to the place. I read about brawls in taverns, drug trafficking; courtroom dramas about the price of onions; the Profumo scandal rocking England; but I could not visualize the lie of the land, the real geography of the city or the sea between countries. The few grainy black-and-white pictures in the newspapers formed a shadow world of petrified garlands, smiling stupefied politicians and gnomic sorcerers' boxes. I had no real opening to the outside world; only walls everywhere, sometimes painted, sometimes with frescos – people, narratives, icons – or a mural to fool me completely, but nothing real. I was trapped inside what I could see, what I could hear, what I could walk to without straying from my undefined boundaries, and in what I could remember from what I learned in my mud-walled school. My head was like a balloon that had only a few puffs of air in it. Not enough to float up in the sky; not helium but a sadder more mortal air that only allowed it to loll about bumping into chairs and footstools and sleep huddled on the floor. But at least it had not been completely deformed by the spite so prevalent in our surroundings, the whole of our world. 'The politics of envy is the master of all our industry,' Mister Salgado used to say to characterize the times and the tussle everywhere for power.

The next morning was the best I had woken to, ever. The sun warmed my face. There was no sound in the house. No one was shouting at me. No pounding of flour, no coconut-scraping, no onion-chopping. Nothing even from our neighbours, no radios, no slap and slurp of washing. No hawking and spitting. I opened my eyes and stayed still. I did not have to do anything for anyone. The house was completely and utterly empty. Delicious, complete cow-head nirvana. It was as if Joseph had never been there.

But inevitably he intruded into my thoughts. I imagined him in some despicable hole in the most wretched part of the city, devoured by sorcerers and thieves. Even murdered: some miracle whereby my wishes had been picked up by the spirits of the city and been executed by some other agent. Had I stumbled on a deadly mantra? An inadvertent curse? When by mid-morning I still had not seen him, I was jubilant. I was sure the gods had intervened on my behalf.

If Joseph was dead then everything was really up to me. There was only a day before Mister Salgado was due to come back and there was a lot to be done. I realized I had better finish all the jobs he had given me to prove myself the right and proper successor to Joseph. I started by polishing the silver. It was a big job: Mister Salgado had a teak canteen full of cutlery which had belonged to his grandfather. It served a dozen people and had been the bedrock of that generation's grander socializing. He also had cups and school trophies and a silver-plated jug. I laid everything out like a picnic on newspaper spread out underneath the frangipani in the garden and set to work. The polish was almost nourishing to inhale: a rich odour of fenugreek and red lentils. The liquid worked itself under my fingernails as I rubbed it on the metal, coating it in a powdery flaking white skin, and removed it all black on a rag, then a newspaper, then another cloth, polishing and rubbing, sweating, until the pieces shone like molten sun on the lawn. If only my master would come now he could see me doing so well with the things he wanted done. I would do anything for him, if only I could remain in the house on my own – without Joseph.

My life until then had been the same as the lives of all those who leave their unhappy homes, their squabbling families, their claustrophobic riverbank asylums, and break out into a clear world beckoning from beyond the edge of their dreams, there to make at least a moment sparkle like a star in the night. But with my Mister Salgado I thought I might find something more, something that would really change the world and make our lives worthwhile. I polished the silver, I counted the cutlery, I did everything he asked me to, wishing I could see Joseph's corpse. What colour would it be? Bloodless? Grey? Without all that water and stuffing inside, would it be like a collapsed and empty bag? Take the blood away, the stuff that seeps out, and the soul that must leave it like any other parasite, what's left – in the case of Joseph – must be pretty pointless: a shrunken leather pouch. Bone, cartilage, rotting flesh and blubber. I had never seen a corpse in its natural state. It was not common in our countryside in those days. Our barbarities were startling but domestic: the dismembering of an adulterous husband, drunken homicide; occasionally acid thrown in a fit of jealousy near the more urban areas where the community had no hold, or political privilege gave protection. But there were no death squads then, no thugs so callous in their killing that they felt no pleasure until they saw someone twitch against a succession of bullets. In my childhood no one dreamed of leaving a body to rot where it had been butchered, as people have had to learn to do more recently.

In the afternoon the sun was hotter than it had been for some time; I went back into the house. I sat in the front bay with the bamboo tats half rolled up. The floor in the house was cool except where the sun fell directly on it. The breeze blew over the low parapet walls and under the greenish tubes of the tats. The sound of the breeze passing was in itself cooling. It was our version of the water gardens that are found in more rarefied countries, or back in our own more refined archaeological past. In the shade, I watched ants crawling across a warm step; small black beetles scurrying across a wilderness; soldiers marching up into the hills and warriors from some heavenly bush paradise descending to protect the roots of a croton hedge. I remembered the coconut trees of my childhood, the sound of the breeze through the fronds. Simple, pure, deathless air.

Most of all I missed the closeness of the tank – the reservoir. The lapping of the dark water, flapping lotus leaves, the warm air rippling over it and the cormorants rising, the silent glide of a hornbill. And then those very still moments when the world would stop and only colour move like the blue breath of dawn lightening the sky, or the darkness of night misting the globe; a colour, a ray of curved light and nothing else. The water would be unbroken like a mirror, and the moon would gleam in it. At twilight when the forces of darkness and the forces of light were evenly matched and in balance there was nothing to fear. No demons, no troubles, no carrion. An elephant swaying to a music of its own. A perfect peace that seemed eternal even though the jungle might unleash its fury at any moment. The tank was a sea made safe by human imagination, a vast expanse of water that ensured the health of our bodies and our minds and soothed our graceless lives. The city lacked such water. Mister Salgado's house had no visible body of water except when it rained. But even the rain quickly ran off; within an hour the place would be baking. A tank or a river provided a place with a kind of majesty that I felt the house – we – needed. A year later I convinced him – the young *mahathaya* – to build a small pond, a tin tank, in a corner of the garden. But it was not a success. The idea was good, and he perked up when I described it. '*Nelum* flowers and lilies, some gold-fish to look at in the evening.' He was happy. 'Right,' he said, 'put it in the corner near the jam tree.' The idea fired his imagination but when it came down to it he was all theory, no practice. I had to be the engineer even though I had no training. My mistake was in the positioning. The jam tree shed so much fruit that the pond was soon full of rotting berries and dead leaves. And the fruit bats came to it every night. The lily-pads were spattered with their droppings, and the water turned filthy. It became the breeding ground for a vicious strain of mosquito. They fed on me. Huge monsters with suckers like elephant trunks. But Mister Salgado found the whole thing increasingly interesting: especially the mosquitoes. He made a study of their development and wrote a paper about insects and bat-droppings. Later he expounded his theories to a small circle of students. 'The mosquito . . .' he would say, and you would think he was invoking a god in heaven. I would cup my ears to catch every reverberation of each word he would utter. 'The mosquito is a much-neglected beast. If we fail to study it and simply rely on DDT, we do so at our peril.'

Peril . . . DDT . . . beast. It was poetry to me. He made even the drone of a mosquito, which he mimicked in his discourses, as sensuous as the hum of a hummingbird.

But that day, sitting alone on the floor of the front bay, I had no notion of the future. I did not really believe that Joseph was dead, or that my life would improve. I wanted it to and I convinced myself that if I acted as though these things had happened and were happening, then they truly would. That some mischievous little godling would intervene with a triple-pronged arrow and prick fate towards my desires. The garden shimmered and I could even see mirages of our jewelled river, maybe that small *takarang* tank that was to come – our pond – hovering on the hot driveway. I drifted away in the heat of the afternoon, swelling and stretching, overcoming my unease.

I was woken by a sound in the house. I thought it might be one of the cats. The neighbourhood was full of strays. They were mangy, full of fleas and disaffected spirits. And they chased the birds that made their homes with us. My argument against them was that they pissed all over our bushes. Once I found an orange tom in the study. I shouted at it, and instead of going out of the window it jumped for the door. The stupid cat almost knocked itself out because I had shut the door behind me when I had entered. I had my belt in my hand to crack like a whip, but all I had to do was pick the animal up by the scruff of its neck and fling it out. Its eyes flared, the slits widening in the topaz, and it spat and hissed and yowled but never came back.

The sitting-room was as I had left it earlier: a morgue of white-sheeted furniture. I went down the corridor to the bedrooms. Mister Salgado's bedroom door was closed. I opened it.

Joseph was by the mirror. His face was pallid; his red eyes bulged. He had unbuttoned his shirt and was rubbing Mister Salgado's cologne on his chest. Talcum powder had settled on the tabletop. He looked up and saw me across the room, reflected in the mirror. He hissed something under his breath and turned quickly around. He came towards me locking me with his gaze. I couldn't move. I swallowed and swallowed but my mouth was dry. I couldn't get anything to move from inside. Joseph had his mouth open and his tongue thickened between his teeth. I could see the spittle on his lips bubbling. He lunged forward and grabbed me. I lashed out with my hand. If I could hit his jaw his tongue would fall out, but his arms were like steel belts around me. He pushed me down on the big soft bed. He was on top of me, twice my size, squeezing the life out of me and the breath out of my chest. His fist digging in between my legs and punching a hole in me. The more I struggled, the stronger he became. I bit his arm, and he nearly broke my back. In the end I gave up and died. I let the life out of my body, and he froze. Then with one hand he undid his sarong and pulled at his dribbling warped prick. He looked down at it, and I slipped out from under him down on to the floor. He rolled over still holding himself. He was breathing hard; his body was pumping. I found a shoe under the bed and flung it at him. I wanted to scream but I couldn't. I had no voice. I jumped up and ran out of the house.

I wanted to keep running, all the way up to the shops at the junction. But I knew if I did that, and if Joseph didn't chase me, I would not know where he was. I would not know when I could go back. I stopped at the gate. Every breath I took seemed to be fire; everything inside me was charged up. But I could do nothing. I waited for him to appear.

Eventually he came down the driveway and let himself out. He disappeared down the lane. I followed him up to the main road and then along it towards the sea. I had never been up that way. A bus came by, and I lost him.

Back in the bedroom the bed had been straightened out, but not as well as it should have been. I could still smell him there.

That night I learned to identify every tiny sound of the dark. Every creak in the garden, every hum on the main road, every flap of every bat that screamed into the jam tree. I listened even though I knew that footsteps could hardly be heard on our hard driveway. I wished I had scattered newspapers or dry leaves all around the place, or set up trip-wires four inches above the ground and attached to a bell. But I had not. And I could not now in the dark when he could pounce again.

Mister Salgado parked his car under the porch and, putting his hand on the roof, hauled himself out. The car creaked as his weight shifted; the side tipped, and he unravelled his long legs. 'Where's Joseph?'

I said I did not know.

'Get him here.'

'He's not in the house, Sir.'

'What?'

I had not searched the house, but I was sure I would have sensed it if he had returned. 'He hasn't been here since yesterday.'

From the way Mister Salgado looked at me, I might have been talking gibberish. 'What do you mean, he hasn't been here?'

'He went somewhere, Sir. He didn't tell me anything.'

Mister Salgado's eyes narrowed, and a small vertical furrow appeared in his broad forehead sucking in the skin where his eyebrows met. 'Unload this then.' He opened the boot of the car. It was full of fruit and coconuts. 'Take all this . . .' he waved his hand about, 'take it to the back.' He went inside the house deep in thought.

I wondered what he really knew about Joseph.

I took the smooth, polished, pinkish coconuts and a small carriage of plantains into the kitchen. His bag I took to his bedroom.

'Some tea, Sir? Shall I bring?'

He looked up at me as if I were a total stranger. Then something ignited in his head. 'Yes. Bring tea.'

It was strange being the only person around to look after him, but I knew what to do. Nobody had to tell me.

When I went back to him with the tea-tray, he asked me, 'So, where did Joseph go?'

'He went somewhere in a bus.'

'A bus came here?'

'No, Sir, on the main road. He went and got on one.'

'You went with him?'

'No, Sir, I saw him. I was going to the *kadé*.' I don't know why I lied, but sometimes I start saying the wrong thing and find I cannot stop. I wanted to tell him exactly what I had seen and what had happened. But the words were impossible to get out. I did not want to be tarnished by telling – by putting into words – what had gone on. It would have spoiled everything. We would have had Joseph between us forever. It was not what I wanted. It was better, I thought, to leave it untold. That way maybe the event would fade. It would disappear. Without words to sustain it, the past would die. But I was wrong. It does not go away; what has happened *has* happened. It hangs on the robes of the soul. Maybe putting it into words can trap it. Separate it. Afterwards maybe it can go in a box, like a letter, and be buried. Or maybe nothing can ever be buried. I felt tense thinking of what to say. There was no way I could tell him the truth, however much I wished.

Late in the afternoon I heard the metal hasp on the gate clang back on its heels. Joseph came up the driveway with a slight swagger. A flock of feeding birds scattered out of his way. Everything about him suggested defiance. He had a small parcel wrapped in a newspaper tucked under his arm; his sarong was hitched up a few inches to let him stride like a *chandiya*.

The closer he got, the louder the crows cackled. I felt the wind blow towards the house, the branches of the big white tree bent towards us and the spirits of the garden gathered around.

I wanted to shout out that Joseph was here, but I did not need to: Mister Salgado was in the front bay watching him walk up.

'Where did you go?' I heard him ask.

'Pettah, Sir.'

Mister Salgado was standing on the step. One hand was up to his face, gripping his chin between two long curled fingers, the other hand supported his arm. He looked at Joseph silently for a moment. 'So, what did you get?'

'Nothing, Sir.'

'What is the parcel then?'

Joseph seemed a little unsteady. From the garden I could not see his face until he shrugged and turned away from Mister Salgado. Then I could see he was drunk. His eyes were shining.

'You'd better go,' Mister Salgado said quietly. So quietly that I barely heard him. Joseph probably didn't hear him at all – being drunk. But the tone of Mister Salgado's voice, the angle of his head, the look in his eyes made the message clear. He meant really go. *Clear out. Roll your mat and disappear.* Mister Salgado in his quiet undemonstrative sober way was giving our Joseph the push. He was fired. Joseph did not understand.

'You'd better be out of this house before dark. Take your things and go. I don't want to see you here again.' Mister Salgado turned and went back into the house. Before he disappeared he shoved a hand in his pocket and pulled out a roll of notes. He dropped it on the table next to him: one month's severance pay, Joseph's notice. The course of Joseph's life had changed with those three short sentences. He looked like a buffalo whose head had been severed with one stroke of a Kali sword: it was dead but the head had yet to fall, a microsecond of illusion and reality conjoined. Alive and dead. Time melted, dripping with every breath he took.

I felt sorry for Joseph even though I hated him; the moment he began to fail, my feelings began to change. Like when you are pushing hard against a stubborn door which suddenly opens and gives way, and you have to pull back, just to regain your balance and not go falling headlong into nothing. I felt like that with Joseph. With those few quiet words, barely audible, Mister Salgado had reversed everything in our world. Not just for Joseph but for me too. We would undergo a revolution. In the light of this knowledge Joseph seemed to change in front of my eyes from a spumy barrel full of stunted frogs into a pitiful little man obsessed by the small world that he had lorded over and was now too stinking drunk even to understand what was happening to it. Eventually he scratched his ear, picked up the money and shuffled off towards our part of the house. He hardly noticed me.

Joseph had developed his taste for numbness, I think, smoking cigarette butts and draining the dregs of beer and liquor left by visitors to the Rest House where he worked before he came to Mister Salgado. He was the type who could dilute the bottle even as he poured the shots. But he didn't know what his limitations were; he thought just because he knew the habits of his superiors he could become one. It was his frustration, knowing there was no future for the likes of him in the kind of service he dreamed of, that turned him into a monster. The dream just ate him up: first the brain, then the eyes, the throat, then the prick. As he grew older he grew thicker-skinned until he was all bone and meat: there was no space inside for a conscience, for morality, for any inner life. He grew into a numbskull, a stupid monster. Malign spirits wormed into his heart. My Mister Salgado was too innocent to understand, but that day at least he had a glimmering and intuitively knew what he had to do.

I didn't say a word to Joseph. He went to his room and I heard him pack his things. A little later he went back into the house. I could hear him talking to Mister Salgado; I couldn't make out the words. Mister Salgado didn't seem to say anything in return. When Joseph came back out, he spat at my feet. 'You bastards, you are going to eat shit one day, shit.' He turned and disappeared, cursing the house, swearing to bury monkey skulls and pig entrails in our garden.

Mister Salgado called for me later that night. He was going out to eat; Lucy-*amma* had not returned yet. He asked me whether Joseph had gone.

'Yes, Sir,' I said. 'Took all his things and went.'

'He will not be coming back.' Mister Salgado looked at me. 'Can you do everything?'

I nodded, not even knowing what he meant, except that my dream was coming true.

'You will see to the whole house then.'

I felt overwhelmed by the responsibility. 'Sir, don't know how to do *everything*. May need *some* help.'

He lowered his head and let his voice envelop us both. 'Lucy will cook, but you'd better learn from her,' he said. 'You will have no problem learning. I can see that. You are a smart *kolla*. Really, you should go to school . . .'

'No, Sir.' I was sure, at that time, that there was nothing a crowded, bewildering school could offer me that I could not find in his gracious house. 'All I have to do is watch you, Sir. Watch what you do. That way I can really learn.'

He sighed, slowly releasing us into the future. 'Let's see.'

So I watched him, I watched him unendingly, all the time, and learned to become what I am.

Kirsty Gunn
Tinsel Bright

Years before Moma divorced my Dad he used to dress up as a fairy for the hospital every Christmas Day. In that role he was truly beautiful to see. A blond man, and delicately made, he stunned all the patients with his wide variety of fairy outfits, a froth of tulle and sequins in colours that I would have chosen if I could have been a fairy too.

This, of course, would never happen. Only doctors were allowed to wear the fairy tutus and the tight spangled bodice with fitted bra. It was the custom at Victoria Grand, the hospital where my father worked as a heart surgeon, for the men to transform themselves this way. For more than fifty years they had tripped the bright wards as elves and pixies on December the 25th, spreading cheer and good humour to even those so ill they couldn't laugh out loud, couldn't leave their beds. It was my Dad's arrival at the hospital, however, that made the event really special. From his first parade he'd seen the limitations in the green cotton costumes, his red elf tights had chafed him badly and carried the smell of too many wearings.

'As there is no doubt that the annual parade is of enormous benefit to all the patients at Victoria Grand, I would like to suggest we make the event even more entertaining,' he'd announced to the Social Board, quite soon after his first time. 'Therefore, if you'll let me, I'd like to make our parade a Spectacular. I'd like to be in charge of costumes from now on.'

I was perhaps five or six then. I remember it well as being a time of outfits. My new school required that I be dressed in a variety of uniforms, pale blue linen dresses for summer, serge pinafores with blue flannel blouses when the months were cool. My mother took me shopping in a special uniform shop and I came home with boxes of blue blazers, coats, hats. There were brown socks and white socks and three different kinds of shoes. Yet, though I loved taking the things from their paper packets, smelling the newness of fabric and leather, none of the clothes pleased me as much, when I put them on, as I hoped. None of them were fairy.

In the meantime, my Dad toiled at the sewing-machine, and was planning, planning. What I know now, is that the magic of these Christmases past, in the sparkle of a sequined bodice, in the stiffened folds of a sugar-pink gown, came from it being a time when doctors were men and men only. Girls didn't dress up and play this game. Even the pretty nurses looked lumpen and unhappy when compared with the sight of senior staff on parade. Giggling, they nudged each other when my Dad darted past them with his tinsel wand. They knew that, with his first Spectacular, 'Fairies from Foreign Lands', he'd started something different. It was only the beginning. 'Fairy Friends of Aladdin' he announced the next year. Then 'Winter Fairies in the Snow'.

'See this trimming, Francie?' He'd lengthen out a piece of bright silver for me to see, but never touch. 'I'm going to stitch it to the hems so it looks like ice . . .' Still, even though things may have looked like a hospital romance movie, with handsome men treading the wards and a nurse for a woman by their side, my own mother was no sister. She was a painter, just starting out when I was born, but there were big plans for her career, I know. All through the 1960s she was friends with Clement Greenberg and Franz Kline and Helen Frankenthaler, as well as some big gallery dealers in Paris and Berlin. We called her MOMA after the gallery in New York City, her favourite place in the whole wide world. I think she liked that. I think it helped her believe things would work out all right for her in the end.

Whatever, it was surely her tenderness with colour that got my Dad falling in love. He'd always wanted to work in the theatre. The heart doctoring was his father's idea, he said, not his, and it had saddened him ever since that he'd let himself be bullied into following a career he didn't care for.

'Don't ever listen to what parents say,' he used to tell me.

'That's my advice. You've got your own life to live and your mother and I don't feature in it, believe me. Follow your instincts, Francie. I wanted costumes! Costumes! The smell of greasepaint in the air! Now all I have is a Christmas show once a year. I'm a sad man . . .'

Oh, but I didn't believe him. My Dad smiled too much, tickled me too much, to be unhappy. Besides, he'd invented the Victoria Grand Fairy Day, hadn't he? How could the sight of more than twenty doctors, all fully outfitted by the skill of his hands, be sad? Even when Christmas was months away I'd come into his study and find him with the wooden chest out, armloads of fabric and stockings and tinsel wings spread around him. He used to do his own make-up too, practising different 'looks' well in advance of the big day. In all my life I have never known a person to possess more cosmetics and lotions than he; he almost had too many bottles, jars, creams.

Still, these kinds of thoughts did not flourish then; these were the fine days of my mother's talent. Her studio seemed always filled with light and the pleasant sound of her humming as she worked. Moma wore a yellow smock for painting, we were all three of us in costume of one sort or another. Blotched bright all over her front were the colours she used: vermilion, emerald, clear sea blue. They formed a pattern there, as if she herself were a pretty canvas. Her cheeks too might be smudged with paint; she would have stepped back from her work to consider it, resting her face in her hands, thinking. I knew that gesture well. She was so calm and lovely then. When she took her hands away, colour was there.

How different that careless mark upon her from the painstaking detail that went into my father's Christmas face. First he creamed his whole face in, smoothing the shadows away from under his eyes and carrying the pale colour all the way down from temple to jawline. Only when his features were as blank and perfect as one of my mother's canvases did he begin the detailed work: drawing in the fine line of black that outlined his eyes, painting over the lids a film of shimmering blue. He filled his pale eyebrows in until they were dark and exciting-looking and after he had coloured his lips a juicy red he used Vaseline to make them shiny and wet. 'Cherry ripe,' he used to say.

By contrast, Moma in her studio worked earnestly in flat colours. With a broad knife she scooped up the thick oil from her palette and spread it like softened butter across the canvas, working the pigment in with the palm of her hand until the whole surface was deeply stained. The clean scent of her work rose from the floor where she was crouched over it, painting the last quick lines that were her signature. Without looking up she'd say 'Hi' when I came in. 'Had a good day at school?'

These things, as I remember them, seem like nice times for a girl. Even my Dad working late most nights didn't disturb the impression that we three were happy together. Moma and I ate our supper at the big table in the dining-room, waiting, listening, like a TV family, for the sound of his car in the driveway. Then, when he walked in the door we both ran up and kissed him and he put his arms around us and called us 'my girls'.

'What have my two girls been doing today?'

'How's my big girl?'

'How's my little girl?'

As he sat at the table, eating the meal Moma had kept warm for him in the hostess tray, I watched my parents together. My mother, changed into a new dress for the evening, the scent of linseed warm like fragrance on her skin and my Dad sometimes reaching out to take her hand, to stroke it. How I loved it when he did that to Moma, and how she seemed to need it too. She put her own hand over his, then leaned over and kissed him with her mouth.

Cherry ripe.

All wives were behaving that way towards husbands in the early '60s. That was what my mother said, much later, when everything had changed.

'We were putting up, honey. We were dealing, but that's all we were doing. I was an innocent when you were young. I had no idea your father was the way he was. No one will understand this now but when I married him I really believed he would be a husband. All the fairy days were nothing to me, I believed, I believed . . .'

I was grown up by then but still I put my hands to my ears and ran from the room like a little girl. I too had glimpsed my father beneath his white doctor's coat, knew how manly his dark suit had been.

'All the time he was lying to me,' my mother, in the next room, talked on. I put a pillow over my head, but even then could hear the sound of her, talking to herself maybe, but the words coming out to find rest in me. 'I never knew . . . I never guessed. Now my life is over and I feel like such a fool . . .'

From now on, I guess she'll always be that kind of woman. Yet there was a time when she had a family, a career and a turkey to slice when my Dad's Fairy Parade was done. It took me to change all that, the quiet daughter you should never trust. We could have had

Christmas Days the same for ever had it not been for that one day, the last, had it not been for me.

I was ten years old. I remember because the parade dresses were based on *Swan Lake*, which my Dad had taken me to see earlier in the year for a birthday treat. When we came out of the dark matinée theatre into the brightness of the afternoon, his eyes were shining. 'That's it, Francie! This year I'll do white tulle and swansdown. I'll make the dresses ankle length and petticoat them so they come out to here . . .' He swept his arms around him in a circle. 'What do you think?'

In the months that followed he worked hard on the idea, in the evenings drawing up patterns for different designs, then experimenting with cloth, cut and sewing right up to the weekend before Christmas Day when suddenly the dresses were nearly done and he was stitching white beads on to the bodices, a thick crust of them like frost, and all by hand. Although when they were finished they were not to me as beautiful on the bulky forms of the doctors as they had been on the ballerinas in the theatre, still my Dad was so slim in his gown he was dainty. He'd put on a special cream that looked plain white in the jar until he dipped his fingers in and they came out sparkling with a million trillion glittery bits. Gently, he applied these to his cheekbones, his throat, his shoulders, patting the cream down so the tiny stars became affixed. When he took up his wand, and turned, twinkling in the light, my heart stopped. If a real fairy had asked me what I wanted most in the world, I would have wished for a pot of that glitter. More than any of my Dad's outfits or silver shoes, I wanted my fingers deep in the jar, to bring them out rich with stars.

Christmas that year we had a guest in the house. He was a colleague, my Dad said, 'on loan'. He came all the way from another hospital up north and it was my Dad's job to show him around Victoria Grand, teach him about hearts. He was a tall man, I remember, and completely bald, the skin stretched tight over his forehead so his whole head was as taut and shiny as a sheath.

'Your Dad looks great, doesn't he?'

I was watching the parade with him in the hospital. I was even holding his hand. Across the ward, my Dad was running around the beds with the other doctors just like they did every year.

'Twinkle, twinkle!' they called out to the sick and dying.

As usual, it seemed everyone was laughing, even if they couldn't sit up in bed properly, patients loved my Dad's Christmas show.

'I'll make your wish come true!' one fairy doctor said to an old lady lying on her back. 'I'm your little bit of Christmas magic . . .' He pirouetted for her and, though she couldn't move her head at all, I saw that she was smiling. 'Happy Christmas to you . . .'

In the midst of all the swan dresses and the dancing I saw my Dad looking around, looking for me, I thought, at first, but it was the man whose hand I held he was seeking. When he found him, their eyes met. He smiled. For seconds, it seemed a lifetime to me, they were held together in stillness amidst all the bright whirl of the room, the swirl of white organza skirts, the laughter. Then my Dad came running over to us and tapped us both upon the shoulder with his tinsel wand. That was all he did. Yet, though I was left bare of his touch, a fragment of the wand's silver stayed on the man's jacket, glittering. Then I knew. Knew enough to watch them for the rest of the morning, watch them when we went home to my mother's turkey meal, watch them in the bathroom together, my father pretending to take his make-up off, the other following. Through the crack of the door I saw them with each other, the expert speed of their hands, placement of kisses, my Dad's wet mouth.

Cherry ripe.

I'm the guilty one who told my Moma all.

Today, I don't call her Moma. I use her real name, Marjorie, when we talk on the telephone. She tells me about her job in the art supplies shop, the people she meets. Her own painting she gave up on years ago, I'm not sure that she writes letters to Clement Greenberg or to any of those people any more. Even so, she seems pleased enough with her life. 'Contented,' she says.

She still wants to talk about her marriage years with me but even now I can't hear any of it.

'You should get in touch with your father,' she tells me. 'You know, he and I have found friendship over the years, I'm sure you could too . . .'

After my Dad left home I couldn't talk to anyone for a long time. Now I understand why he so loved the theatre, the costumes and disguise . . . It took me a while to discover that. The more layers you can put on to yourself the safer you become, and quieter. Years later, and, like him, I've become a doctor; I specialize in hearts. When I started out in medical school I couldn't so much as dissect a soft mouse or a round sheep's eye, but now that I'm fully adult, in my own dark suits, white coat, I can cut and cut. Although I have many friends, play golf, and go out on dinner dates most weekends, I am actually a very lonely person: unlike my Dad, I lack the real ability to transform. When he sent for his clothes, he left behind all the dresses he'd made, the trunk full of petal skirts and wings, the tinsel trims, even the little pot of glittery cream he left for me to play with.

'Let Francie be the Christmas fairy from now on,' his letter said.

But I threw all the lovely things away.

Jamaica Kincaid
Gwen

On opening day, I walked to my new school alone. It was the first and last time that such a thing would happen. All around me were other people my age – twelve years – girls and boys, dressed in their school uniforms, marching off to school. They all seemed to know each other, and as they met they would burst into laughter, slapping each other on the shoulder and back, telling each other things that must have made for much happiness. I saw some girls wearing the same uniform as my own, and my heart just longed for them to say something to me, but the most they could do to include me was to smile and nod in my direction as they walked on arm in arm. I could hardly blame them for not paying more attention to me. Everything about me was so new: my uniform was new, my shoes were new, my hat was new, my shoulder ached from the weight of my new books in my new bag; even the road I walked on was new, and I must have put my feet down as if I weren't sure the ground was solid. At school, the yard was filled with more of these girls and their most sure-of-themselves gaits. When I looked at them, they made up a sea. They were walking in and out among the beds of flowers, all across the fields, all across the courtyard, in and out of classrooms. Except for me, no one seemed a stranger to anything or anyone. Hearing the way they greeted each other, I couldn't be sure that they hadn't all come out of the same woman's belly, and at the same time, too. Looking at them, I was suddenly glad that because I had wanted to avoid an argument with my mother I had eaten all my breakfast, for now I surely would have fainted if I had been in any more weakened a condition.

I knew where my classroom was, because my mother and I had kept an appointment at the school a week before. There I met some of my teachers and was shown the ins and outs of everything. When I saw it then, it was nice and orderly and empty and smelled just scrubbed. Now it smelled of girls milling around, fresh ink in inkwells, new books, chalk and erasers. The girls in my classroom acted even more familiar with each other. I was sure I would never be able to tell them apart just from looking at them, and I was sure that I would never be able to tell them apart from the sound of their voices.

When the school bell rang at half past eight, we formed ourselves into the required pairs and filed into the auditorium for morning prayers and hymn-singing. Our headmistress gave us a little talk, welcoming the new students and welcoming back the old students, saying that she hoped we had all left our bad ways behind us, that we would be good examples for each other and bring greater credit to our school than any of the other groups of girls who had been there before us. My palms were wet, and quite a few times the ground felt as if it were seesawing under my feet, but that didn't stop me from taking in a few things. For instance, the headmistress, Miss Moore. I knew right away that she had come to Antigua from England, for she looked like a prune left out of its jar a long time and she sounded as if she had borrowed her voice from an owl. The way she said, 'Now, girls . . .' When she was just standing still there, listening to some of the other activities, her gray eyes going all around the room hoping to see something wrong, her throat would beat up and down as if a fish fresh out of water were caught inside. I wondered if she even smelled like a fish. Once when I didn't wash, my mother had given me a long scolding about it, and she ended by saying that it was the only thing she didn't like about English people: they didn't wash often enough, or wash properly when they finally did. My mother had said, 'Have you ever noticed how they smell as if they had been bottled up in a fish?' On either side of Miss Moore stood our other teachers, women and men – mostly women. I recognized Miss George, our music teacher; Miss Nelson, our homeroom teacher; Miss Edward, our history and geography teacher; and Miss Newgate, our algebra and geometry teacher. I had met them the day my mother and I were at school. I did not know who the others were, and I did not worry about it. Since they were teachers, I was sure it wouldn't be long before, because of some misunderstanding, they would be thorns in my side.

We walked back to our classroom the same way we had come, quite orderly and, except for a few whispered exchanges, quite silent.

But no sooner were we back in our classroom than the girls were in each other's laps, arms wrapped around necks. After peeping over my shoulder left and right, I sat down in my seat and wondered what would become of me. There were twenty of us in my class, and we were seated at desks arranged five in a row, four rows deep. I was at a desk in the third row, and this made me even more miserable. I hated to be seated so far away from the teacher, because I was sure I would miss something she said. But, even worse, if I was out of my teacher's sight all the time, how could she see my industriousness and quickness at learning things? And, besides, only dunces were seated so far to the rear, and I could not bear to be thought a dunce. I was now staring at the back of a shrubby-haired girl seated in the front row – the seat I most coveted, since it was directly in front of the teacher's desk. At that moment, the girl twisted herself around, stared at me, and said, 'You are Annie John? We hear you are very bright.' It was a good thing Miss Nelson walked in right then, for how would it have appeared if I had replied, 'Yes, that is completely true' – the very thing that was on the tip of my tongue.

As soon as Miss Nelson walked in, we came to order and stood up stiffly at our desks. She said to us, 'Good morning, class,' half in a way that someone must have told her was the proper way to speak to us and half in a jocular way, as if we secretly amused her. We replied, 'Good morning, Miss,' in unison and in a respectful way, at the same time making a barely visible curtsy, also in unison. When she had seated herself at her desk, she said to us, 'You may sit now,' and we did. She opened the roll book, and as she called out our names each of us answered, 'Present, Miss.' As she called out our names, she kept her head bent over the book, but when she called out my name and I answered with the customary response she looked up and smiled at me and said, 'Welcome, Annie.' Everyone, of course, then turned and looked at me. I was sure it was because they could hear the loud racket my heart was making in my chest.

It was the first day of a new term, Miss Nelson said, so we would not be attending to any of our usual subjects; instead, we were to spend the morning in contemplation and reflection and writing something she described as an 'autobiographical essay'. In the afternoon, we would read aloud to each other our autobiographical essays. (I knew quite well about 'autobiography' and 'essay', but reflection and contemplation! A day at school spent in such a way! Of course, in most books all the good people were always contemplating and reflecting before they did anything. Perhaps in her mind's eye she could see our future and, against all prediction, we turned out to be good people.) On hearing this, a huge sigh went up from the girls. Half the sighs were in happiness at the thought of sitting and gazing off into clear space, the other half in unhappiness at the misdeeds that would have to go unaccomplished. I joined the happy half, because I knew it would please Miss Nelson, and my own selfish interest aside, I liked so much the way she wore her ironed hair and her long-sleeved blouse and box-pleated skirt that I wanted to please her.

The morning was uneventful enough: a girl spilled ink from her ink-well all over her uniform; a girl broke her pen nib and then made a big to-do about replacing it; girls twisted and turned in their seats and pinched each other's bottoms; girls passed notes to each other. All this Miss Nelson must have seen and heard, but she didn't say anything – only kept reading her book: an elaborately illustrated edition of *The Tempest*, as later, passing by her desk, I saw. Midway in the morning, we were told to go out and stretch our legs and breathe some fresh air for a few minutes; when we returned, we were given glasses of cold lemonade and a slice of bun to refresh us.

As soon as the sun stood in the middle of the sky, we were sent home for lunch. The earth may have grown an inch or two larger between the time I had walked to school that morning and the time I went home to lunch, for some girls made a small space for me in their little band. But I couldn't pay much attention to them; my mind was on my new surroundings, my new teacher, what I had written in my nice new notebook with its black-all-mixed-up-with-white cover and smooth lined pages (so glad was I to get rid of my old notebooks, which had on their covers a picture of a wrinkled-up woman wearing a crown on her head and a neckful and armfuls of diamonds and pearls – their pages so coarse, as if they were made of cornmeal). I flew home. I must have eaten my food. I flew back to school. By half past one, we were sitting under a flamboyant tree in a secluded part of our schoolyard, our autobiographical essays in hand. We were about to read aloud what we had written during our morning of contem-plation and reflection.

In response to Miss Nelson, each girl stood up and read her compo-sition. One girl told of a much revered and loved aunt who now lived in England and of how much she looked forward to one day moving to England to live with her aunt; one girl told of her brother studying medicine in Canada and the life she imagined he lived there (it seemed quite odd to me); one girl told of the fright she had when she dreamed she was dead, and of the matching fright she had when she woke and found that she wasn't (everyone laughed at this, and Miss Nelson had to call us to order over and over); one girl told of how her oldest sister's best friend's cousin's best friend (it was a real rigmarole) had gone on a Girl Guide jamboree held in Trinidad and met someone who millions of years ago had taken tea with Lady Baden-Powell; one girl told of an excursion she and her father had made to Redonda, and of how they had seen some booby birds tending their chicks. Things went on in that way, all so playful, all so imaginative. I began to wonder about what I had written, for it was the opposite of playful and it was the opposite of imaginative. What I had written was heart-felt, and, except for the very end, it was all too true. The afternoon was wearing itself thin. Would my turn ever come? What should I do, finding myself in a world of new girls, a world in which I was not even near the center?

It was a while before I realized that Miss Nelson was calling on me. My turn at last to read what I had written. I got up and started to read, my voice shaky at first, but since the sound of my own voice had always been a calming potion to me, it wasn't long before I was reading in such a way that, except for the chirp of some birds, the hum of bees looking for flowers, the silvery rush-rush of the wind in the trees, the only sound to be heard was my voice as it rose and fell in sentence after sentence. At the end of my reading, I thought I was imagining the upturned faces on which were looks of adoration, but I was not; I thought I was imagining, too, some eyes brimming over with tears, but again I was not. Miss Nelson said that she would like to borrow what I had written to read for herself, and that it would be placed on the shelf with the books that made up our own class library, so that it would be available to any girl who wanted to read it. This is what I had written:

'When I was a small child, my mother and I used to go down to Rat Island on Sundays right after church, so that I could bathe in the sea. It was at a time when I was thought to have weak kidneys and a bath in the sea had been recommended as a strengthening remedy. Rat Island wasn't a place many people went to anyway, but by climbing down some rocks my mother had found a place that nobody seemed to have ever been. Since this bathing in the sea was a medicine and not a picnic, we had to bathe without wearing swimming costumes. My mother was a superior swimmer. When she plunged into the seawater, it was as if she had always lived there. She would go far out if it was safe to do so, and she could tell just by looking at the way the waves beat if it was safe to do so. She could tell if a shark was nearby, and she had never been stung by a jellyfish. I, on the other hand, could not swim at all. In fact, if I was in water up to my knees I was sure that I was drowning. My mother had tried everything to get me swimming, from using a coaxing method to just throwing me without a word into the water. Nothing worked. The only way I could go into the water was if I was on my mother's back, my arms clasped tightly around her neck, and she would then swim around not too far from the shore. It was only then that I could forget how big the sea was, how far down the bottom could be, and how filled up it was with things that couldn't understand a nice hallo. When we swam around in this way, I would think how much we were like the pictures of sea mammals I had seen, my mother and I, naked in the seawater, my mother sometimes singing to me a song in a French patois I did not yet understand, or sometimes not saying anything at all. I would place my ear against her neck, and it was as if I were listening to a giant shell, for all the sounds around me – the sea, the wind, the birds screeching – would seem as if they came from inside her, the way the sounds of the sea are in a seashell. Afterward, my mother would take me back to the shore, and I would lie there just beyond the farthest reach of a big wave and watch my mother as she swam and dove.

'One day, in the midst of watching my mother swim and dive, I heard a commotion far out at sea. It was three ships going by, and they were filled with people. They must have been celebrating something, for the ships would blow their horns and the people would cheer in response. After they passed out of view, I turned to look at my mother, but I could not see her. My eyes searched the small area of water where she should have been, but I couldn't find her. I stood up and started to call out her name, but no sound would come out of my throat. A huge black space then opened up in front of me and I fell inside it. I couldn't see what was in front of me and I couldn't hear anything around me. I couldn't think of anything except that my mother was no longer near me. Things went on in this way for I don't know how long. I don't know what, but something drew my eye in one direction. A little bit out of the area in which she usually swam was my mother, just sitting and tracing patterns on a large rock. She wasn't paying any attention to me, for she didn't know that I had missed her. I was glad to see her and started jumping up and down and waving to her. Still she didn't see me, and then I started to cry, for it dawned on me that, with all the water between us and I being unable to swim, my mother could stay there forever and the only way I would be able to wrap my arms around her again was if it pleased her or if I took a boat. I cried until I wore myself out. My tears ran down into my mouth, and it was the first time that I realized tears had a bitter and salty taste. Finally, my mother came ashore. She was, of course, alarmed when she saw my face, for I had let the tears just dry there and they left a stain. When I told her what had happened, she hugged me so close that it was hard to breathe, and she told me that nothing could be farther from the truth – that she would never ever leave me. And though she said it over and over again, and though I felt better, I could not wipe out of my mind the feeling I had had when I couldn't find her.

'The summer just past, I kept having a dream about my mother sitting on the rock. Over and over I would have the dream – only in it my mother never came back, and sometimes my father would join her. When he joined her, they would both sit tracing patterns on the rock, and it must have been amusing, for they would always make each other laugh. At first, I didn't say anything, but when I began to have the dream again and again, I finally told my mother. My mother became instantly distressed; tears came to her eyes, and, taking me in her arms, she told me all the same things she had told me on the day at the sea, and this time the memory of the dark time when I felt I would never see her again did not come back to haunt me.'

I didn't exactly tell a lie about the last part. That is just what would have happened in the old days. But actually the past year saw me launched into young-ladyness, and when I told my mother of my dream – my nightmare, really – I was greeted with a turned back and a warning against eating certain kinds of fruit in an unripe state just before going to bed. I placed the old days' version before my classmates because, I thought, I couldn't bear to show my mother in a bad light before people who hardly knew her. But the real truth was that I couldn't bear to have anyone see how deep in disfavor I was with my mother.

As we walked back to the classroom, I in the air, my classmates on the ground, jostling each other to say some words of appreciation and congratulation to me, my head felt funny, as if it had swelled up to the size of, and weighed no more than, a blown-up balloon. Often I had been told by my mother not to feel proud of anything I had done and in the next breath that I couldn't feel enough pride about something I had done. Now I tossed from one to the other: my head bowed down to the ground, my head high up in the air. I looked at these girls surrounding me, my heart filled with just-sprung-up love, and I wished then and there to spend the rest of my life only with them.

As we approached our classroom, I felt a pinch on my arm. It was an affectionate pinch, I could tell. It was the girl who had earlier that day asked me if my name was Annie John. Now she told me that her name was Gweneth Joseph, and reaching into the pocket of her tunic, she brought out a small rock and presented it to me. She had found it, she said, at the foot of a sleeping volcano. The rock was black, and it felt rough in my hands, as if it had been through a lot. I immediately put it to my nose to see what it smelled like. It smelled of lavender, because Gweneth Joseph had kept it wrapped in a handkerchief doused in that scent. It may have been in that moment that we fell in love. Later, we could never agree on when it was. That afternoon, we walked home together, she going a little out of her usual way, and we exchanged likes and dislikes, our jaws dropping and eyes widening when we saw how similar they were. We separated ourselves from the other girls, and they, understanding everything, left us alone. We cut through a tamarind grove, we cut through a cherry-tree grove, we passed down the lane where all the houses had elaborate hedges growing in front, so that nothing was visible but the upstairs windows. When we came to my street, parting was all but unbearable. 'Tomorrow,' we said, to cheer each other up.

Gwen and I were soon inseparable. If you saw one, you saw the other. For me, each day began as I waited for Gwen to come by and fetch me for school. My heart beat fast as I stood in the front yard of our house waiting to see Gwen as she rounded the bend in our street. The sun, already way up in the sky so early in the morning, shone on her, and the whole street became suddenly empty so that Gwen and everything about her were perfect, as if she were in a picture. Her panama hat, with the navy blue and gold satin ribbon – our school colors – around the brim, sat lopsided on her head, for her head was small and she never seemed to get the correct-size hat, and it had to be anchored with a piece of elastic running under her chin. The pleats in the tunic of her uniform were in place, as was to be expected. Her cotton socks fit neatly around her ankles, and her shoes shone from just being polished. If a small breeze blew, it would ruffle the ribbons in her short, shrubby hair and the hem of her tunic; if the hem of her tunic was disturbed in that way, I would then be able to see her knees. She had bony knees and they were always ash-colored, as if she had just finished giving them a good scratch or had just finished saying her prayers. The breeze might also blow back the brim of her hat, and since she always walked with her head held down I might then be able to see her face: a small, flattish nose; lips the shape of a saucer broken evenly in two; wide, high cheekbones; ears pinned back close against her head – which was always set in a serious way, as if she were going over in her mind some of the many things we had hit upon that were truly a mystery to us. (Though once I told her that about her face, and she said that really she had only been thinking about me. I didn't look to make sure, but I felt as if my whole skin had become covered with millions of tiny red boils and that shortly I would explode with happiness.) When finally she reached me, she would look up and we would both smile and say softly, 'Hi.' We'd set off for school side by side, our feet in step, not touching but feeling as if we were joined at the shoulder, hip and ankle, not to mention heart.

As we walked together, we told each other things we had judged most private and secret: things we had overheard our parents say, dreams we had had the night before, the things we were really afraid of; but especially we told of our love for each other. Except for the ordinary things that naturally came up, I never told her about my changed feeling for my mother. I could see in what high regard Gwen held me, and I couldn't bear for her to see the great thing I had had once and then lost without an explanation. By the time we got to school, our chums often seemed overbearing, with their little comments on the well-pressedness of each other's uniforms, or on the neatness of their schoolbooks, or on how much they approved of the way Miss Nelson was wearing her hair these days. A few other girls were having much the same experience as Gwen and I, and when we heard comments of this kind we would look at each other and roll up our eyes and toss our hands in the air – a way of saying how above such concerns we were. The gesture was an exact copy, of course, of what we had seen our mothers do.

My life in school became just the opposite of my first morning. I went from being ignored, with hardly a glance from anyone, to having girls vie for my friendship, or at least for more than just a passing acquaintanceship. Both my classmates and my teachers noticed how quick I was at learning things. I was soon given responsibility for overseeing the class in the teacher's absence. At first, I was a little taken aback by this, but then I got used to it. I indulged many things, especially if they would end in a laugh or something touching. I would never dillydally with a decision, always making up my mind right away about the thing in front of me. Sometimes, seeing my old frail self in a girl, I would defend her; sometimes, seeing my old frail self in a girl, I would be heartless and cruel. It all went over quite well, and I became very popular.

My so recently much-hated body was now a plus: I excelled at games and was named captain of a volleyball team. As I was favored by my classmates inside and outside the classroom, so was I favored by my teachers – though only inside the classroom, for I had become notorious to them for doing forbidden things. If sometimes I stood away from myself and took a look at who I had become, I couldn't be more surprised at what I saw. But since who I had become earned me the love and devotion of Gwen and the other girls, I was only egged on to find new and better ways to entertain them. I don't know what invisible standard was set, or by whom or exactly when, but eight of us met it, and soon to the other girls we were something to comment on favorably or unfavorably, as the case might be.

It was a nook of some old tombstones – a place discovered by girls going to our school long before we were born – shaded by trees with trunks so thick it would take four arm's lengths to encircle them, that we would sit and talk about the things we said were on our minds that day. On our minds every day were our breasts and their refusal to budge out of our chests. On hearing somewhere that if a boy rubbed your breasts they would quickly swell up, I passed along this news. Since in the world we occupied and hoped forever to occupy boys were banished, we had to make do with ourselves. What perfection we found in each other, sitting on these tombstones of long-dead people who had been the masters of our ancestors! Nothing in particular really troubled us except for the annoyance of a fly colliding with our lips, sticky from eating fruits; a bee wanting to nestle in our hair; the breeze suddenly blowing too strong. We were sure that the much-talked-about future that everybody was preparing us for would never come, for we had such a powerful feeling against it, and why shouldn't our will prevail this time? Sometimes when we looked at each other, it was all we could do not to cry out with happiness.

My own special happiness was, of course, with Gwen. She would stand in front of me trying to see into my murky black eyes – a way, she said, to tell exactly what I was thinking. After a short while, she would give up, saying, 'I can't make out a thing – only my same old face.' I would then laugh at her and kiss her on the neck, sending her into a fit of shivers, as if someone had exposed her to a cold draft when she had a fever. Sometimes when she spoke to me, so overcome with feeling would I be that I was no longer able to hear what she said, I could only make out her mouth as it moved up and down. I told her that I wished I had been named Enid, after Enid Blyton, the author of the first books I had discovered on my own and liked. I told her that when I was younger I had been afraid of my mother's dying, but that since I had met Gwen this didn't matter so much. Whenever I spoke of my mother to her, I was always sure to turn the corners of my mouth down, to show my scorn. I said that I could not wait for us to grow up so that we could live in a house of our own. I had already picked out the house. It was a gray one, with many rooms, and it was in the lane where all the houses had high, well-trimmed hedges. With all my plans she agreed, and I am sure that if she had had any plans of her own I would have agreed with them also.

On the morning of the first day I started to menstruate, I felt strange in a new way – hot and cold at the same time, with horrible pains running up and down my legs. My mother, knowing what was the matter, brushed aside my complaints and said that it was all to be expected and I would soon get used to everything. Seeing my gloomy face, she told me in a half-joking way all about her own experience with the first step in coming of age, as she called it, which had happened when she was as old as I was. I pretended that this information made us close – as close as in the old days – but to myself I said, 'What a serpent!'

I walked to school with Gwen feeling as I supposed a dog must feel when it has done something wrong and is ashamed of itself and trying to get somewhere quick, where it can lie low. The cloth between my legs grew heavier and heavier with every step I took and I was sure that everything about me broadcast, 'She's menstruating today. She's menstruating today.' When Gwen heard what had happened, tears came to her eyes. She had not yet had the wonderful experience, and I could see that she cried for herself. She said that, in sympathy, she would wear a cloth, too.

In class, for the first time in my life, I fainted. Miss Nelson had to revive me, passing her smelling salts, which she had in a beautiful green vial, back and forth under my nose. She then took me to Nurse, who said that it was the fright of all the unexpected pain that had caused me to faint, but I knew that I had fainted after I brought to my mind a clear picture of myself sitting at my desk in my own blood.

At recess, among the tombstones, I of course had to exhibit and demonstrate. None of the others were menstruating yet. I showed everything without the least bit of flourish, since my heart wasn't in it. I wished instead that one of the other girls were in my place and that I were just sitting there in amazement. How nice they all were, though, rallying to my side, offering shoulders on which to lean, laps in which to rest my weary, aching head, and kisses that really did soothe. When I looked at them sitting around me, the church in the distance, beyond that our school, with throngs of girls crossing back and forth in the schoolyard, beyond that the world, how I wished that everything would fall away, so that suddenly we'd be sitting in some different atmosphere, with no future full of ridiculous demands, no need for any sustenance save our love for each other, with no hindrance to any of our desires, which would, of course, be simple desires – nothing, nothing, just sitting on our tombstones forever. But that could never be, as the tolling of the school bell testified.

We walked back to class slowly, as if going to a funeral. Gwen and I vowed to love each other always, but the words had a hollow ring, and when we looked at each other we couldn't sustain the gaze. It had been decided by Miss Nelson and Nurse that I was not to return to school after lunch, with Nurse sending instructions to my mother to keep me in bed for the rest of the day.

When I got home, my mother came toward me, arms outstretched, concern written on her face. My whole mouth filled up with a bitter taste, for I could not understand how she could be so beautiful even though I no longer loved her.

Richard McCann
My Mother's Clothes: The School of Beauty and Shame

Like every corner house in Carroll Knolls, the corner house on our block was turned backward on its lot, a quirk introduced by the developer of the subdivision, who, having run short of money, sought variety without additional expense. The turned-around houses, as we kids called them, were not popular, perhaps because they seemed too public, their casement bedroom windows cranking open onto sun-struck asphalt streets. In actuality, however, it was the rest of the houses that were public, their picture windows offering dioramic glimpses of early-American sofas and Mediterranean-style pole lamps whose mottled globes hung like iridescent melons from wrought-iron chains. In order not to be seen walking across the living-room to the kitchen in our pajamas, we had to close the venetian blinds. The corner house on our block was secretive, as though it had turned its back on all of us, whether in superiority or in shame, refusing to acknowledge even its own unkempt yard of yellowing zoysia grass. After its initial occupants moved away, the corner house remained vacant for months.

The spring I was in sixth grade, it was sold. When I came down the block from school, I saw a moving van parked at its curb. 'Careful with that!' a woman was shouting at a mover as he unloaded a tiered end table from the truck. He stared at her in silence. The veneer had already been splintered from the table's edge, as though someone had nervously picked at it while watching TV. Then another mover walked from the truck carrying a child's bicycle, a wire basket bolted over its thick rear tire, brightly colored plastic streamers dangling from its handlebars.

The woman looked at me. 'What have you got there? In your hand.'

I was holding a scallop shell spray-painted gold, with imitation pearls glued along its edges. Mrs Eidus, the art teacher who visited our class each Friday, had showed me how to make it.

'A hatpin tray,' I said. 'It's for my mother.'

'It's real pretty.' She glanced up the street as though trying to guess which house I belonged to. 'I'm Mrs Tyree,' she said, 'and I've got a boy about your age. His daddy's bringing him tonight in the new Plymouth. I bet you haven't sat in a new Plymouth.'

'We have a Ford.' I studied her housedress, tiny blue and purple flowers imprinted on thin cotton, a line of white buttons as large as Necco Wafers marching toward its basted hemline. She was the kind of mother my mother laughed at for cutting recipes out of *Woman's Day*. Staring from our picture window, my mother would sometimes watch the neighborhood mothers drag their folding chairs into a circle on someone's lawn. 'There they go,' she'd say, 'a regular meeting of the Daughters of the Eastern Star!' 'They're hardly even *women*,' she'd whisper to my father, 'and their *clothes*.' She'd criticize their appearance – their loud nylon scarves tied beneath their chins, their disintegrating figures stuffed into pedal pushers – until my father, worried that my brother, Davis, and I could hear, although laughing himself, would beg her, 'Stop it, Maria, please stop; it isn't funny.' But she wouldn't stop, not ever. 'Not even thirty and they look like they belong to the DAR! They wear their pearls inside their bosoms in case the rope should break!' She was the oldest mother on the block but she was the most glamorous, sitting alone on the front lawn in her sleek kick-pleated skirts and cashmere sweaters, reading her thick paperback novels, whose bindings had split. Her hair was lightly hennaed, so that when I saw her pillowcases piled atop the washer, they seemed dusted with powdery rouge. She had once lived in New York City.

After dinner, when it was dark, I joined the other children congregated beneath the streetlamp across from the turned-around house. Bucky Trueblood, an eighth-grader who had once twisted the stems off my brother's eyeglasses, was crouched in the center, describing his mother's naked body to us elementary school children gathered around him, our faces slightly upturned, as though searching for a distant constellation, or for the bats that Bucky said would fly into our hair. I sat at the edge, one half of my body within the circle of light, the other half lost to darkness. When Bucky described his mother's nipples, which he'd glimpsed when she bent to kiss him goodnight, everyone giggled; but when he described her genitals, which he'd seen by dropping his pencil on the floor and looking up her nightie while her feet were propped on a hassock as she watched TV, everyone huddled nervously together, as though listening to a ghost story that made them fear something dangerous in the nearby dark. 'I don't believe you,' someone said; 'I'm telling you,' Bucky said, '*that's what it looks like.*'

I slowly moved outside the circle. Across the street a cream-colored Plymouth was parked at the curb. In a lighted bedroom window Mrs Tyree was hanging café curtains. Behind the chain link fence, within the low branches of a willow tree, the new child was standing in his yard. I could see his white T-shirt and the pale oval of his face, a face deprived of detail by darkness and distance. Behind him, at the open bedroom window, his mother slowly fiddled with a valance. Behind me the children sat spellbound beneath the light. Then Bucky jumped up and pointed in the new child's direction – 'Hey, you, you want to hear something really *good*?' – and even before the others had a chance to spot him, he vanished as suddenly and completely as an imaginary playmate.

The next morning, as we waited at our bus stop, he loitered by the mailbox on the opposite corner, not crossing the street until the yellow school bus pulled up and flung open its door. Then he dashed aboard and sat down beside me. 'I'm Denny,' he said. Denny: a heavy, unbeautiful child, who, had his parents stayed in their native Kentucky, would have been a farm boy, but who in Carroll Knolls seemed to belong to no particular world at all, walking past the identical ranch houses in his overalls and Keds, his whitish-blond hair close-cropped all around except for the distinguishing, stigmatizing feature of a wave that crested perfectly just above his forehead, a wave that neither rose nor fell, a wave he trained with Hopalong Cassidy hair tonic, a wave he tended fussily, as though it were the only loveliness he allowed himself.

What in Carroll Knolls might have been described by someone not native to those parts – a visiting expert, say – as *beautiful*, capable of arousing terror and joy? The brick ramblers strung with multicolored Christmas lights? The occasional front-yard plaster Virgin entrapped within a chicken-wire grotto entwined with plastic roses? The spring

Denny moved to Carroll Knolls, I begged my parents to take me to a nightclub, had begged so hard for months, in fact, that by summer they finally agreed to a Sunday matinee. Waiting in the backseat of our Country Squire, a red bow tie clipped to my collar, I watched our house float like a mirage behind the sprinkler's web of water. The front door opened, and a white dress fluttered within the mirage's ascending waves: slipping on her sunglasses, my mother emerged onto the concrete stoop, adjusted her shoulder strap, and teetered across the wet grass in new spectator shoes. Then my father stepped out and cut the sprinkler off. We drove – the warm breeze inside the car sweetened by my mother's Shalimar – past ranch houses tethered to yards by chain link fences; past the Silver Spring Volunteer Fire Department and Carroll Knolls Elementary School; past the Polar Bear Soft-Serv stand, its white stucco siding shimmery with mirror shards; past a bulldozed red-clay field where a weathered billboard advertised IF YOU LIVED HERE YOU'D BE HOME BY NOW, until we arrived at the border – a line of cinder-block discount liquor stores, a traffic light – of Washington, D.C. The light turned red. We stopped. The breeze died and the Shalimar fell from the air. Exhaust fumes mixed with the smell of hot tar. A drunk man stumbled into the crosswalk, followed by an old woman shielding herself from the sun with an orange umbrella, and two teenaged boys dribbling a basketball back and forth between them. My mother put down her sun visor. 'Lock your door,' she said.

Then the light changed, releasing us into another country. The station wagon sailed down boulevards of Chinese elms and flowering Bradford pears, through hot, dense streets where black families sat on wooden chairs at curbs, along old streetcar tracks that caused the tires to shimmy and the car to swerve, onto Pennsylvania Avenue, past the White House, encircled by its fence of iron spears, and down 14th Street, past the Treasury Building, until at last we reached the Neptune Room, a cocktail lounge in the basement of a shabbily elegant hotel.

Inside, the Neptune Room's walls were painted with garish mermaids reclining seductively on underwater rocks, and human frogmen who stared longingly through their diving helmets' glass masks at a loveliness they could not possess on dry earth. On stage, leaning against the baby grand piano, a *chanteuse* (as my mother called her) was singing of her grief, her wrists weighted with rhinestone bracelets, a single blue spotlight making her seem like one who lived, as did the mermaids, underwater.

I was transfixed. I clutched my Roy Rogers cocktail (the same as a Shirley Temple, but without the cheerful, girlish grenadine) tight in my fist. In the middle of 'The Man I Love' I stood and struggled toward the stage.

I strayed into the spotlight's soft-blue underwater world. Close up, from within the light, the singer was a boozy, plump peroxide blonde in a tight black cocktail dress; but these indiscretions made her yet more lovely, for they showed what she had lost, just as her songs seemed to carry her backward into endless regret. When I got close to her, she extended one hand – red nails, a huge glass ring – and seized one of mine.

'Why, what kind of little sailor have we got here?' she asked the audience.

I stared through the border of blue light and into the room, where I saw my parents gesturing, although whether they were telling me to step closer to her microphone or to step farther away, I could not tell. The whole club was staring.

'Maybe he knows a song!' a man shouted from the back.

'Sing with me,' she whispered. 'What can you sing?'

I wanted to lift her microphone from its stand and bow deeply from the waist, as Judy Garland did on her weekly TV show. But I could not. As she began to sing, I stood voiceless, pressed against the protection of her black dress; or, more accurately, I stood beside her, silently lip-syncing to myself. I do not recall what she sang, although I do recall a quick, farcical ending in which she falsettoed, like Betty Boop, 'Gimme a Little Kiss, Will Ya, Huh?' and brushed my forehead with pursed red lips.

That summer, humidity enveloping the landfill subdivision, Denny, 'the new kid', stood on the boundaries, while we neighborhood boys played War, a game in which someone stood on Stanley Allen's front porch and machine-gunned the rest of us, who one by one clutched our bellies, coughed as if choking on blood, and rolled in exquisite death throes down the grassy hill. When Stanley's father came up the walk from work, he ducked imaginary bullets. 'Hi, Dad,' Stanley would call, rising from the dead to greet him. Then we began the game again: whoever died best in the last round got to kill in the next. Later, after dusk, we'd smear the wings of balsa planes with glue, ignite them, and send them flaming through the dark on kamikaze missions. Long after the streets were deserted, we children sprawled beneath the corner streetlamp, praying our mothers would not call us – '*Time to come in*!' – back to our ovenlike houses; and then sometimes Bucky, hoping to scare the elementary school kids, would lead his solemn procession of junior high 'hoods' down the block, their penises hanging from their unzipped trousers.

Denny and I began to play together, first in secret, then visiting each other's houses almost daily, and by the end of the summer I imagined him to be my best friend. Our friendship was sealed by our shared dread of junior high school. Davis, who had just finished seventh grade, brought back reports of corridors so long that one could get lost in them, of gangs who fought to control the lunchroom and the bathrooms. The only safe place seemed to be the Health Room, where a pretty nurse let you lie down on a cot behind a folding screen. Denny told me about a movie he'd seen in which the children, all girls, did not have to go to school at all but were taught at home by a beautiful governess, who, upon coming to their rooms each morning, threw open their shutters so that sunlight fell like bolts of satin across their beds, whispered their pet names while kissing them, and combed their long hair with a silver brush. 'She never got mad,' said Denny, beating his fingers up and down through the air as though striking a keyboard, 'except once when some old man told the girls they could never play piano again.'

With my father at work in the Pentagon and my mother off driving the two-tone Welcome Wagon Chevy to new subdivisions, Denny and I spent whole days in the gloom of my living-room, the picture window's venetian blinds closed against an August sun so fierce that it bleached the design from the carpet. Dreaming of fabulous prizes – sets of matching Samsonite luggage, French Provincial bedroom suites, Corvettes, jet flights to Hawaii – we watched Jan Murray's 'Treasure Hunt' and Bob Barker's 'Truth or Consequences' (a name that seemed strangely threatening). We watched 'The Loretta Young Show', worshipping yet critiquing her elaborate gowns. When '*The Early Show*' came on, we watched old Bette Davis, Gene Tierney and Joan Crawford movies – *Dark Victory, Leave Her to Heaven, A Woman's Face*. Hoping to become their pen pals, we wrote long letters to fading movie stars, who in turn sent us autographed photos we traded between ourselves. We searched the house for secrets, like contraceptives, Kotex and my mother's hidden supply of Hershey bars. And finally, Denny and I, running to the front window every few minutes to make sure no one was coming unexpectedly up the side-walk, inspected the secrets of my mother's dresser: her satin nightgowns and padded brassieres, folded atop pink drawer liners and scattered with loose sachets; her black mantilla, pressed inside a shroud of lilac tissue paper; her heart-shaped candy box, a flapper doll strapped to its lid with a ribbon, from which spilled galaxies of cocktail rings and cultured pearls. Small shrines to deeper intentions, private grottoes of yearning: her triangular cloisonné earrings, her brooch of enameled butterfly wings.

Because beauty's source was longing, it was infused with romantic sorrow; because beauty was defined as 'feminine', and therefore as 'other', it became hopelessly confused with my mother: Mother, who quickly sorted through new batches of photographs, throwing unflattering shots of herself directly into the fire before they could be seen. Mother, who dramatized herself, telling us and our playmates, 'My name is Maria Dolores; in Spanish, that means "Mother of Sorrows".' Mother, who had once wished to be a writer and who said, looking up briefly from whatever she was reading, 'Books are my best friends.' Mother, who read aloud from Whitman's *Leaves of Grass* and O'Neill's *Long Day's Journey Into Night* with a voice so grave I could not tell the differences between them. Mother, who lifted cut-glass vases and antique clocks from her obsessively dusted curio shelves to ask, 'If this could talk, what story would it tell?'

And more, always more, for she was the only woman in our house, a 'people-watcher', a 'talker', a woman whose mysteries and moods seemed endless: Our Mother of the White Silk Gloves; Our Mother of the Veiled Hats; Our Mother of the Paper Lilacs; Our Mother of the Sighs and Heartaches; Our Mother of the Gorgeous Gypsy Earrings; Our Mother of the Late Movies and the Cigarettes; Our Mother whom I adored and who, in adoring, I ran from, knowing it 'wrong' for a son to wish to be like his mother; Our Mother who wished to influence us, passing the best of herself along, yet who held the fear common to that era, the fear that by loving a son too intensely she would render him unfit – 'Momma's boy', 'tied to apron strings' – and who therefore alternately drew us close and sent us away, believing a son needed 'male influence' in large doses, that female influence was pernicious except as a final finishing, like manners; Our Mother of the Mixed Messages; Our Mother of Sudden Attentiveness; Our Mother of Sudden Distances; Our Mother of Anger; Our Mother of Apology.

The simplest objects of her life, objects scattered accidentally about the house, became my shrines to beauty, my grottoes of romantic sorrow: her Revlon lipstick tubes, 'Cherries in the Snow'; her Art Nouveau atomizers on the blue mirror top of her vanity; her pastel silk scarves knotted to a wire hanger in her closet; her white handkerchiefs blotted with red mouths. Voiceless objects; silences. The world halved with a cleaver: 'masculine', 'feminine'. In these ways was the plainest ordinary love made complicated and grotesque. And in these ways was beauty, already confused with the 'feminine', also confused with shame, for all these longings were secret, and to control me all my brother had to do was to threaten to expose that Denny and I were dressing ourselves in my mother's clothes.

Denny chose my mother's drabbest outfits, as though he were ruled by the deepest of modesties, or by his family's austere Methodism: a pink wraparound skirt from which the color had been laundered, its hem almost to his ankles; a sleeveless white cotton blouse with a Peter Pan collar; a small straw summer clutch. But he seemed to challenge his own primness, as though he dared it with his 'effects': an undershirt worn over his head to approximate cascading hair; gummed hole-punch reinforcements pasted to his fingernails so that his hands, palms up, might look like a woman's – flimsy crescent moons waxing above his fingertips.

He dressed slowly, hesitantly, but once dressed he was a manic Proteus metamorphosing into contradictory, half-realized forms, throwing his 'long hair' back and balling it violently into a French twist; tapping his paper nails on the glass-topped vanity as though he were an important woman kept waiting at a cosmetics counter; stabbing his nails into the air as though he were an angry teacher assigning an hour of detention; touching his temple as though he were a shy schoolgirl tucking back a wisp of stray hair; resting his fingertips on the rim of his glass of Kool-Aid as though he were an actress seated over an ornamental cocktail – a Pink Lady, say, or a Silver Slipper. Sometimes, in an orgy of jerky movement, his gestures overtaking him with greater and greater force, a dynamo of theatricality unleashed, he would hurl himself across the room like a mad girl having a fit, or like one possessed; or he would snatch the chenille spread from my parents' bed and drape it over his head to fashion for himself the long train of a bride. 'Do you like it?' he'd ask anxiously, making me his mirror. 'Does it look *real*?' He wanted, as did I, to become something he'd neither yet seen nor dreamed of, something he'd recognize the moment he saw it: himself. Yet he was constantly confounded, for no matter how much he adorned himself with scarves and jewelry, he could not understand that this was himself, as was also and at the same time the boy in overalls and Keds. He was split in two pieces – as who was not? – the blond wave cresting rigidly above his close-cropped hair.

'He makes me nervous,' I heard my father tell my mother one night as I lay in bed. They were speaking about me. That morning I'd stood awkwardly on the front lawn – 'Maybe you should go help your father,' my mother had said – while he propped an extension ladder against the house, climbed up through power lines he separated with his bare hands, and staggered across the pitched roof he was re-shingling. When his hammer slid down the incline, catching on the gutter, I screamed, 'You're falling!' Startled, he almost fell.

'He needs to spend more time with you,' I heard my mother say.

I couldn't sleep. Out in the distance a mother was calling her child home. A screen door slammed. I heard cicadas, their chorus as steady and loud as the hum of a power line. *He needs to spend more time with you*. Didn't she know? Saturday mornings, when he stood in his rubber hip boots fishing off the shore of Triadelphia Reservoir, I was afraid of the slimy bottom and could not wade after him; for whatever reasons of his own – something as simple as shyness, perhaps – he could not come to get me. I sat in the parking lot drinking Tru-Ade and reading *Betty and Veronica*, wondering if Denny had walked alone to Wheaton Plaza, where the weekend manager of Port-o'-Call allowed us to Windex the illuminated glass shelves that held Lladró figurines, the porcelain ballerina's hands so realistic one could see tiny life and heart lines etched into her palms. *He needs to spend more time with you*. Was she planning to discontinue the long summer afternoons that she and I spent together when there were no new families for her to greet in her Welcome Wagon car? 'I don't feel like being alone today,' she'd say, inviting me to sit on their chenille bedspread and watch her model new clothes in her mirror. Behind her an oscillating fan fluttered nylons and scarves she'd heaped, discarded, on a chair. 'Should I wear the red belt with this dress or the black one?' she'd ask, turning suddenly toward me and cinching her waist with her hands.

Afterward we would sit together at the rattan table on the

screened-in porch, holding cocktail napkins around sweaty glasses of iced Russian tea and listening to big-band music on the Zenith.

'You look so pretty,' I'd say. Sometimes she wore outfits I'd selected for her from her closet – pastel chiffon dresses, an apricot blouse with real mother-of-pearl buttons.

One afternoon she leaned over suddenly and shut off the radio. 'You know you're going to leave me one day,' she said. When I put my arms around her, smelling the dry carnation talc she wore in hot weather, she stood up and marched out of the room. When she returned, she was wearing Bermuda shorts and a plain cotton blouse. 'Let's wait for your father on the stoop,' she said.

Late that summer – the summer before he died – my father took me with him to Fort Benjamin Harrison, near Indianapolis, where, as a colonel in the U.S. Army Reserves, he did his annual tour of duty. On the propjet he drank bourbon and read the newspapers while I made a souvenir packet for Denny: an airsickness bag, into which I placed the Chiclets given me by the stewardess to help pop my ears during takeoff, and the laminated white card that showed the location of emergency exits. Fort Benjamin Harrison looked like Carroll Knolls: hundreds of acres of concrete and sun-scorched shrubbery inside a cyclone fence. Daytimes I waited for my father in the dining mess with the sons of other officers, drinking chocolate milk that came from a silver machine, and desultorily setting fires in ashtrays. When he came to collect me, I walked behind him – gold braid hung from his epaulets – while enlisted men saluted us and opened doors. At night, sitting in our BOQ room, he asked me questions about myself: 'Are you looking forward to seventh grade?' 'What do you think you'll want to be?' When these topics faltered – I stammered what I hoped were the right answers – we watched TV, trying to preguess lines of dialogue on reruns of his favorite shows, *The Untouchables* and 'Rawhide'. 'That Della Street,' he said as we watched *Perry Mason*, 'is almost as pretty as your mother.' On the last day, eager to make the trip memorable, he brought me a gift: a glassine envelope filled with punched IBM cards that told me my life story as his secretary had typed it into the office computer. Card One: *You live at 10406 Lillians Mill Court, Silver Spring, Maryland.* Card Two: *You are entering seventh grade.* Card Three: *Last year your teacher was Mrs Dillard.* Card Four: *Your favorite color is blue.* Card Five: *You love the Kingston Trio.* Card Six: *You love basketball and football.* Card Seven: *Your favorite sport is swimming.*

Whose son did these cards describe? The address was correct, as was the teacher's name and the favorite color; and he'd remembered that one morning during breakfast I'd put a dime in the jukebox and played the Kingston Trio's song about 'the man who never returned'. But whose fiction was the rest? Had I, who played no sport other than kickball and Kitty-Kitty-Kick-the-Can, lied to him when he asked me about myself? Had he not heard from my mother the outcome of the previous summer's swim lessons? At the swim club a young man in black trunks had taught us, as we held hands, to dunk ourselves in the water, surface, and then go down. When he had told her to let go of me, I had thrashed across the surface, violently afraid I'd sink. But perhaps I had not lied to him; perhaps he merely did not wish to see. It was my job, I felt, to reassure him that I was the son he imagined me to be, perhaps because the role of reassurer gave me power. In any case, I thanked him for the computer cards. I thanked him the way a father thanks a child for a well-intentioned gift he'll never use – a set of handkerchiefs, say, on which the embroidered swirls construct a monogram of no particular initial, and which thus might be used by anyone.

As for me, when I dressed in my mother's clothes, I seldom moved at all: I held myself rigid before the mirror. The kind of beauty I'd seen practiced in movies and in fashion magazines was beauty attained by lacquered stasis, beauty attained by fixed poses – 'ladylike stillness', the stillness of mannequins, the stillness of models 'caught' in mid-gesture, the stillness of the passive moon around which active meteors orbited and burst. My costume was of the greatest solemnity: I dressed like the *chanteuse* in the Neptune Room, carefully shimmying my mother's black slip over my head so as not to stain it with Brylcreem, draping her black mantilla over my bare shoulders, clipping her rhinestone dangles to my ears. Had I at that time already seen the movie in which French women who had fraternized with German soldiers were made to shave their heads and walk through the streets, jeered by their fellow villagers? And if so, did I imagine myself to be one of the collaborators, or one of the villagers, taunting her from the curb? I ask because no matter how elaborate my costume, I made no effort to camouflage my crew cut or my male body.

How did I perceive myself in my mother's triple-mirrored vanity, its endless repetitions? I saw myself as doubled – both an image and he who studied it. I saw myself as beautiful, and guilty. The lipstick made my mouth seem the ripest rose, or a wound; the small rose on the black slip opened like my mother's heart disclosed, or like the Sacred Heart of Mary, aflame and pierced by arrows; the mantilla transformed me into a Mexican penitent or a Latin movie star, like Dolores Del Rio. The mirror was a silvery stream: on the far side, in a clearing, stood the woman who was icily immune from the boy's terror and contempt; on the close side, in the bedroom, stood the boy who feared and yet longed after her inviolability. (Perhaps, it occurs to me now, this doubleness is the source of drag queens' vulnerable ferocity.) Sometimes, when I saw that person in the mirror, I felt as though I had at last been lifted from that dull, locked room, with its mahogany bedroom suite and chalky blue walls. But other times, particularly when I saw Denny and me together, so that his reality shattered my fantasies, we seemed merely ludicrous and sadly comic, as though we were dressed in the garments of another species, like dogs in human clothes. I became aware of my spatulate hands, my scarred knees, my large feet; I became aware of the drooping, unfilled bodice of my slip. Like Denny, I could neither dispense with images nor take their flexibility as pleasure, for the idea of self I had learned and was learning still was that one was constructed by one's images – '*When boys cross their legs, they cross one ankle atop the knee*' – so that one finally sought the protection of believing in one's own image and, in believing in it as reality, condemned oneself to its poverty.

(That locked room. My mother's vanity; my father's highboy. If Denny and I, still in our costumes, had left that bedroom, its floor strewn with my mother's shoes and handbags, and gone through the darkened living-room, out onto the sunstruck porch, down the sidewalk, and up the street, how would we have carried ourselves? Would we have walked boldly, chattering extravagantly back and forth between ourselves, like drag queens refusing to acknowledge the stares of contempt that are meant to halt them? Would we have walked humbly, with the calculated, impervious piety of the condemned walking barefoot to the public scaffold? Would we have walked simply, as deeply accustomed to the normalcy of our own strangeness as Siamese twins? Or would we have walked gravely, a solemn procession, like Bucky Trueblood's gang, their manhood hanging from their unzipped trousers?

(We were eleven years old. Why now, more than two decades later, do I wonder for the first time how we would have carried ourselves through a publicness we would have neither sought nor dared? I am six feet two inches tall; I weigh 198 pounds. Given my size, the question I am most often asked about my youth is 'What football position did you play?' Overseas I am most commonly taken to be a German or a Swede. Right now, as I write this, I am wearing L. L. Bean khaki trousers, a LaCoste shirt, Weejuns: the anonymous American costume, although partaking of certain signs of class and education, and most recently, partaking also of certain signs of sexual orientation, this costume having become the standard garb of the urban American gay man. Why do I tell you these things? Am I trying – not subtly – to inform us of my 'maleness', to reassure us that I have 'survived' without noticeable 'complexes'? Or is this my urge, my constant urge, to complicate my portrait of myself to both of us, so that I might layer my selves like so many multicolored crinoline slips, each rustling as I walk? When the wind blows, lifting my skirt, I do not know which slip will be revealed.)

Sometimes, while Denny and I were dressing up, Davis would come home unexpectedly from the bowling alley, where he'd been hanging out since entering junior high. At the bowling alley he was courting the protection of Bucky's gang.

'Let me in!' he'd demand, banging fiercely on the bedroom door, behind which Denny and I were scurrying to wipe the makeup off our faces with Kleenex.

'We're not doing anything,' I'd protest, buying time.

'Let me in this minute or I'll tell!'

Once in the room, Davis would police the wreckage we'd made, the emptied hatboxes, the scattered jewelry, the piled skirts and blouses. 'You'd better clean this up right now,' he'd warn. 'You two make me *sick.*'

Yet his scorn seemed modified by awe. When he helped us rehang the clothes in the closet and replace the jewelry in the candy box, a sullen accomplice destroying someone else's evidence, he sometimes handled the garments as though they were infused with something of himself, although at the precise moment when he seemed to find them loveliest, holding them close, he would cast them down.

After our dress-up sessions Denny would leave the house without good-byes. I was glad to see him go. We would not see each other for days, unless we met by accident; we never referred to what we'd done the last time we'd been together. We met like those who have murdered are said to meet, each tentatively and warily examining the other for signs of betrayal. But whom had we murdered? The boys who walked into that room? Or the women who briefly came to life within it? Perhaps this metaphor has outlived its meaning. Perhaps our shame derived not from our having killed but from our having created.

In early September, as Denny and I entered seventh grade, my father became ill. Over Labor Day weekend he was too tired to go fishing. On Monday his skin had vaguely yellowed; by Thursday he was severely jaundiced. On Friday he entered the hospital, his liver rapidly failing; Sunday he was dead. He died from acute hepatitis, possibly acquired while cleaning up after our sick dog, the doctor said. He was buried at Arlington National Cemetery, down the hill from the Tomb of the Unknown Soldier. After the twenty-one-gun salute, our mother pinned his colonel's insignia to our jacket lapels. I carried the flag from his coffin to the car. For two weeks I stayed home with my mother, helping her write thank-you notes on small white cards with black borders; one afternoon, as I was affixing postage to the square, plain envelopes, she looked at me across the dining room table. 'You and Davis are all I have left,' she said. She went into the kitchen and came back. 'Tomorrow,' she said, gathering up the note cards, 'you'll have to go to school.'

Mornings I wandered the long corridors alone, separated from Denny by the fate of our last names, which had cast us into different homerooms and daily schedules. Lunchtimes we sat together in silence in the rear of the cafeteria. Afternoons, just before gym class, I went to the Health Room, where, lying on a cot, I'd imagine the Phys. Ed. coach calling my name from the class roll, and imagine my name, unclaimed, unanswered to, floating weightlessly away, like a balloon that one jumps to grab hold of but that is already out of reach. Then I'd hear the nurse dial the telephone. 'He's sick again,' she'd say. 'Can you come pick him up?' At home I helped my mother empty my father's highboy. 'No, we want to save that,' she said when I folded his uniform into a huge brown bag that read GOODWILL INDUSTRIES; I wrapped it in a plastic dry-cleaner's bag and hung it in the hall closet.

After my father's death my relationship to my mother's things grew yet more complex, for as she retreated into her grief, she left behind only her mute objects as evidence of her life among us: objects that seemed as lonely and vulnerable as she was, objects that I longed to console, objects with which I longed to console myself – a tangled gold chain, thrown in frustration on the mantel; a wineglass, its rim stained with lipstick, left unwashed in the sink. Sometimes at night Davis and I heard her prop her pillow up against her bedroom wall, lean back heavily, and tune her radio to a call-in show: '*Nightcaps, what are you thinking at this late hour?*' Sunday evenings, in order to help her prepare for the next day's job hunt, I stood over her beneath the bare basement bulb, the same bulb that first illuminated my father's jaundice. I set her hair, slicking each wet strand with gel and rolling it, inventing gossip that seemed to draw us together, a beautician and his customer.

'You have such pretty hair,' I'd say.

'At my age, don't you think I should cut it?' She was almost fifty.

'No, never.'

That fall Denny and I were caught. One evening my mother noticed something out of place in her closet. (Perhaps now that she no longer shared it, she knew where every belt and scarf should have been.)

I was in my bedroom doing my French homework, dreaming of one day visiting Au Printemps, the store my teacher spoke of so excitedly as she played us the Edith Piaf records that she had brought back from France. In the mirror above my desk I saw my mother appear at my door.

'Get into the living-room,' she said. Her anger made her small, reflected body seem taut and dangerous.

In the living-room Davis was watching TV with Uncle Joe, our father's brother, who sometimes came to take us fishing. Uncle Joe was lying in our father's La-Z-Boy recliner.

'There aren't going to be any secrets in this house,' she said. 'You've been in my closet. What were you doing there?'

'No, we weren't,' I said. 'We were watching TV all afternoon.'

'*We*? Was Denny here with you? Don't you think I've heard about that? Were you and Denny going through my clothes? Were you wearing them?'

'No, Mom,' I said.

'Don't lie!' She turned to Uncle Joe, who was staring at us. 'Make him stop! He's lying to me!'

She slapped me. Although I was already taller than she, she slapped me over and over, slapped me across the room until I was backed against the TV. Davis was motionless, afraid. But Uncle Joe jumped up and stood between my mother and me, holding her until her rage turned to sobs. 'I can't, I can't be both a mother and a father,' she said to him. 'I can't do it.' I could not look at Uncle Joe, who, although he was protecting me, did not know I was lying.

She looked at me. 'We'll discuss this later,' she said. 'Get out of my sight.'

We never discussed it. Denny was outlawed. I believe, in fact, that it was I who suggested he never be allowed in our house again. I told my mother I hated him. I do not think I was lying when I said this. I truly hated him – hated him, I mean, for being me.

For two or three weeks Denny tried to speak with me at the bus stop, but whenever he approached, I busied myself with kids I barely knew. After a while Denny found a new best friend, Lee, a child despised by everyone, for Lee was 'effeminate'. His clothes were too fastidious; he often wore his cardigan over his shoulders, like an old woman feeling a chill. Sometimes, watching the street from our picture window, I'd see Lee walking toward Denny's house. 'What a queer,' I'd say to whoever might be listening. 'He walks like a *girl*.' Or sometimes, at the junior high school, I'd see him and Denny walking down the corridor, their shoulders pressed together as if they were telling each other secrets, or as if they were joined in mutual defense. Sometimes when I saw them, I turned quickly away, as though I'd forgotten something important in my locker. But when I felt brave enough to risk rejection, for I belonged to no group, I joined Bucky Trueblood's gang, sitting on the radiator in the main hall, and waited for Lee and Denny to pass us. As Lee and Denny got close, they stiffened and looked straight ahead.

'Faggots,' I muttered.

I looked at Bucky, sitting in the middle of the radiator. As Lee and Denny passed, he leaned forward from the wall, accidentally disarranging the practiced severity of his clothes, his jeans puckering beneath his tooled belt, the breast pocket of his T-shirt dropping with the weight of a pack of Pall Malls. He whistled. Lee and Denny flinched. He whistled again. Then he leaned back, the hard lines of his body reasserting themselves, his left foot striking a steady beat on the tile floor with the silver V-tap of his black loafer.

Peter Meinke
The Ponoes

When I was ten years old I couldn't sleep, because the minute I closed my eyes the ponoes would get me. The ponoes were pale creatures about two feet tall, with pointed heads and malevolent expressions, though they never actually said anything. What they did was to approach me, slowly, silently, in order to build up my fear (because I knew what they were going to do); then they would tickle me. I was extremely ticklish in those days, in fact I could hardly bear to be touched by anybody, and the ponoes would swarm over me like a band of drunken and sadistic uncles, tickling me till I went crazy, till I almost threw up, flinging my legs and arms around in breathless agony. I would wake up soaked, my heart banging in my chest like the bass drum in the school marching band. This lasted almost an entire year, until the Murphy brothers got rid of them for me. Because the ponoes would come whenever I fell asleep, I hated to go to bed even more than most children. My parents were not particularly sympathetic; ponoes did not seem that frightening to them, nor were they sure, for a long time, that I wasn't making them up. Even my best friend, Frankie Hanratty, a curly-haired black-eyed boy of unbounded innocence, was dubious. No one else (including myself) had ever heard of them; they seemed like some sort of cross between elves, dwarves, and trolls. But where did I get the name? I think my parents felt that there was something vaguely sexual about them, and therefore distasteful.

'Now no more talk about these, um, ponoes, young man. Right to bed!'

'I'm afraid!' That year – 1942 – I was always close to tears, and my bespectacled watery eyes must have been a discouraging sight, especially for my father, who frequently would take me to the Dodger games at Ebbett's Field, and introduce me to manly players like

Cookie Lavagetto and Dixie Walker. I had a collection of signed baseballs that my father always showed to our guests.

Because I was terrified, I fought sleep with all my might. I read through most of the night, by lamplight, flashlight, even moonlight, further straining my already weak eyes. When I *did* fall asleep, from utter exhaustion, my sleep was so light that when the ponoes appeared on the horizon – approaching much like the gangs in *West Side Story*, though of course I didn't know that then – I could often wake myself up before they reached me. I can remember wrestling with my eyelids, lifting them, heavy as the iron covers of manholes we'd sometimes try to pry open in the streets, bit by bit until I could see the teepee-like designs of what I called my 'Indian blanket'. Often I would get just a glimpse of my blanket and then my eyelids would clang shut and the ponoes were upon me. It is possible, I suppose, that I only *dreamed* I was seeing my blanket, but I don't think so.

Sometimes I would give up trying to open my eyes, give up saying to myself, *This is only a dream*, and turn and run. My one athletic skill was, and remains still, running. There were few who could catch me, even at ten, and today, premature white hair flying, I fill our game room with trophies for my age bracket in the 5,000- and 10,000-meter races along the Eastern seaboard. Often, toward the end of a race, I hear footsteps behind me and I remember the ponoes; the adrenaline surges again, and the footsteps usually fall back. But in my dreams the ponoes would always gain and my legs would get heavier and heavier and I'd near a cliff that I would try to throw myself over but it was like running through waist-deep water with chains on, and I would be dragged down at the edge. This, I suppose, with variations and without ponoes, is a common enough dream.

My mother was more compassionate to me because at that time she was also suffering from a 'classical' recurring dream: the empty room. She would be in a large hotel, walking down a long corridor where all the doors were exactly the same, and unnumbered. She would go along, fear bubbling in her throat, looking at the doors until she stopped in front of one that she knew, for some reason, was hers. Slowly, inch by inch, she would open the door, see the empty room, and scream in terror, waking herself up. Sometimes she would scream only in the dream and sometimes she would scream in actuality as well. But since her dream would only come once a week, or even less frequently, she didn't have the problem with sleeping that I did. Even she would lose patience with me, mainly because my schoolwork, along with everything else, suffered. Mother was very high on education and was determined – as I was a reader – that I was going to be the first member of our family to go to college. Norman Vincent Peale preached regularly at a nearby church and the neighborhood was awash with positive thinking.

During this year, since I scarcely slept in bed, I fell asleep everywhere else: in the car, at the movies, even at dinner, a true zombie. In the winter I liked to curl up on the floor near the silver-painted radiators, whose clanking seemed to keep the ponoes away. I constantly dropped off at my desk at school, once actually clattering to the floor and breaking my glasses, like some pratfall from *The Three Stooges*, whom we would see regularly on Saturday matinees at the Quentin Theatre. Eleven cents for a double feature, it was another world! But Miss McDermott was not amused and would rap my knuckles sharply with her chalkboard pointer. She was a stout and formidable old witch and when she first came at me, aiming her stick like an assassin from *Captain Blood*, I had thought she was going to poke my eyes out and leaped from my seat, to the delight of my classmates, who for weeks afterward liked to charge at me with fingers pointed at my nose.

We had moved from the Irish section of Boston to the Irish section of Brooklyn, and my father, Little Jack Shaughnessy, liked to hang around the tough bars of Red Hook where – he told me – there was a cop on every corner looking for an Irish head to break. My father was Little Jack and I was Little Jim (or Littlejack and Littlejim) because we were both short, but he was husky, a warehouse worker at Floyd Bennett Airport. Though he was not a chronic brawler, he liked an occasional fight, and was disappointed in my obvious fear of physical violence.

'Come on, Jimmy, keep the left up.' He'd slap me lightly on the face, circling around me. 'Straight from the shoulder now!'

I'd flail away, blinking back the tears, the world a blur without my glasses, like a watercolor painting left in the rain. To this day, when I take off my glasses, I have the feeling that someone is going to hit me. Oddly enough, it was fighting that made me fall in love with the Murphy brothers, Tom and Kevin, though love may not be exactly the right word.

I was a natural-born hero worshiper. Perhaps I still am, as I believe unequivocally that our country has gone steadily to the dogs since President Kennedy was shot in 1963, despite all the revelations of character flaws and administrative blunders. When I was young, most of my heroes came from books – D'Artagnan, Robin Hood – or movies: characters like the Green Hornet and Zorro, or real actors like Nelson Eddy whose romantic scenes with Jeanette MacDonald made my classmates whoop and holler. I would whoop and holler too, so as not to give myself away, but at night, fending off the ponoes, I would lie in bed in full Royal Canadian Mountie regalia singing, in my soaring tenor, 'For I'm falling in love with someone, someone . . .' while Jeanette would stand at the foot of my bed shyly staring down at her incredibly tiny feet, or petting my noble horse, which was often in the room with us. This fantasy was particularly ludicrous as I was unable to carry a tune, and had been firmly dubbed a 'listener' by Miss McDermott in front of the whole music class, after which I spent the term moving my mouth to the words without uttering a sound.

The Murphy brothers were tough, the scourge of P.S. 245; extorters of lunch money, fist fighters, hitters of home runs during gym class, they towered over most of us simply because they were older, having been left back several times. Tom was the older and meaner; Kevin was stronger but slow-witted, perhaps even retarded. Tom pushed him around a lot but was careful not to get him really mad, because there was nothing that Kevin would not do when in a rage, which became increasingly evident as they grew older. Pale, lean, black-haired, they wore white shirts with the sleeves rolled up and black pants and shiny black shoes: for brawlers they were very neat dressers, early examples of the Elvis Presley look, though they never looked so soft as Elvis. Most of the rest of us wore corduroy knicker-bockers, whistling down the halls as we walked, with our garters dangling and our socks humped around our ankles. Small and weak, I wanted nothing more than to be like the two fighting brothers, who seemed to me to resemble the pictures of tough soldiers, sailors, and marines that were posted everywhere.

The Murphys had strong Brooklyn accents (they actually called themselves the Moifys), but the whole neighborhood was heading that way, and the schools fought valiantly against it: accents were bad in 1942. I still remember the poem we all had to recite:

> *There once was a turtle*
> *Whose first name was Myrtle*

Swam out to the Jersey shore ...

Tom Murphy would get up in front of the class (like many of the others), grinning insolently, scratching obscenely, ducking spitballs, and mutter:

> *Aah dere wunce wuz a toitle*
> *Whoze foist name wuz Moitle*
> *Swam out to da Joizey shaw ...*

We would applaud and Tom would clasp his hands above his head like a winning prizefighter and swagger back to his seat. Miss McDermott never hit the Murphys, but tried to minimize their disturbance (distoibance!) by pretending they weren't there.

But there they were: they had the cigarettes, they had the playing cards with the photographs that made us queasy, they wrote on the bathroom walls and the schoolyard sidewalks. Of course they must have written obscenities but in the fall of 1942 they mainly wrote things like KILL THE KRAUTS and JAPS ARE JERKS: they were fiercely patriotic. I thought of the change when I recently visited my daughter's high school: painted on the handball court was YANKEE GET OUT OF NORTH AMERICA.

And, suddenly, Tom Murphy adopted me. It was like the lion and the mouse, the prince and the pauper. Like a German submarine, he blew me out of the water and I lost all sense of judgment, which was, in 1942, a very small loss. Perhaps it was because I was so sleepy.

On rainy days, when we couldn't go outside to play softball or touch football, we stayed in the gym and played a vicious game the Murphys loved, called dodge ball. We divided into two sides and fired a soccer-sized ball at each other until one side was eliminated. The Murphys, always on the same side, firing fastballs the length of the tiny gymnasium, would knock boys down like tin soldiers. I was usually one of the last to go as I was so small and hard to hit, but no one worried about me because I was absolutely incapable of hitting anyone else, and eventually would get picked off. But one rainy September week, while our Marines were digging in on Guadalcanal and Rommel was sweeping across Egypt, they had to call the game off twice in a row because the brothers couldn't hit me before the next class started. They stood on the firing line and boomed the ball off the wall behind me while I jumped, ducked, slid in panic, like a rabbit in front of the dogs, sure that the next throw would splatter my head against the wall. Even when the coach rolled in a second ball they missed me, throwing two at a time. The truth was, I suppose, that the Murphys were not very good athletes, just bigger and stronger than the rest of us.

The next day was Saturday, and I was out in front of our house flipping war cards with Frankie, who lived next door, when the brothers suddenly loomed above us, watching. Kevin routinely snatched Frankie's cap and he and Tom tossed it back and forth while we crouched there, waiting, not even thinking, looking from one brother to the other.

Finally, Tom said, 'Littlejim, go get me a licorice stick,' and stuck a penny in my hand. 'Fast, now, get a leg on.' Mostroni's Candy Store was three blocks away, and I raced off, gasping with relief. The thought had crossed my mind that they were going to break my glasses because I had frustrated them in dodge ball. I'm sure I set an East Thirty-second Street record for the three-block run, returning shortly with the two sticks: two for a penny, weep for what is lost. Tom took the sticks without thanks and gave one to his brother, who had pulled the button off Frankie's new cap. Frankie still squatted there, tears in his eyes, looking at the three of us now with hatred. He could see I was on the other side. I sold Frankie down the river and waited for new orders.

'Can you get us some potatoes?'

'No,' I said, 'I don't think so.' Tom glared at me. 'Maybe one.'

'Make it a big one,' he said. 'I feel like a mickey.' Mickeys were what we called potatoes baked in open fires; all over Flatbush you could smell the acrid aroma of charred potatoes.

'My cap,' said Frankie. Kevin dropped it in a puddle from yesterday's rain and stepped on it. Ruined. Frankie picked it up, blindly, holding it with two fingers, and stumbled up the steps to his front door. We lived in a row of attached two-story brick houses, quite respectable, though sliding, with a few steps in front (on which we played stoop ball) and a handkerchief-patch of lawn, usually surrounded by a small hedge. In front of our house was the lamppost by which I could read at night, and next to it a slender young maple tree, which my father would tie to the lamppost during strong winds.

I went through the alley to our back entrance, and found my mother working in our Victory Garden of Swiss chard, carrots, radishes, beets. My father went fishing in Sheepshead Bay every Saturday, a mixed blessing as he would come back loaded with fish but in a generally unstable condition so we never knew what to expect. Today I was glad, as it would make my theft easy.

My mother looked up as I passed. 'Littlejim, are you all right?' My mother has always been able to look right into my heart as if it were dangling from my nose, a gift for which I frequently wished to strangle her.

'Of course,' I said with scorn in my lying voice, 'I'm just thirsty.'

'Well, have a nice glass of milk, sweetheart,' she said, wiping her forehead and looking at me closely. I trotted into the kitchen and looked in the potato pail beneath the sink. There were around ten left so I took a large one and a small one, stuck them in my shirt, and went out the front door. The Murphys were waiting down the street by the vacant lot, the fire already going.

Thus began my life of crime, which lasted almost eight months, well into 1943, for which I showed natural gifts, except temperamentally. I was always trembling but never caught. I graduated from potatoes to my mother's purse, from packs of gum at the candy store ('that Nazi wop,' said Tom) to packs of cigarettes at the delicatessen: the owners watched the Murphys while my quick hands stuffed my pockets full of contraband. Under the protection of the Murphy brothers, who beat up a German boy so badly that he was hospitalized, who dropped kittens into the sewers, who slashed the tires of cars owned by parents who tried to chastise them, I collected small sums of money from boys much larger than myself. Like Mercury, god of cheats and thieves, I was the swift messenger for Tom and Kevin Murphy.

I loved them. They needed me, I thought, not reading them very well. What they really needed was temporary diversion, and for a while I provided that. Kevin was virtually illiterate, so, beginning with the Sunday comics one afternoon, I became his official reader. He read (looked at) nothing but comic books – *Plastic Man, Superman, Captain Marvel, The Katzenjammer Kids; Sheena Queen of the Jungle* was his particular favorite because of her lush figure and scanty clothing.

'Get a load of that,' he'd squeak (Kevin, and to a lesser extent Tom, had a high nasal whine). 'What the freak is she saying?'

' "Stand back," ' I'd read, ' "There's something in there!" '

'Freaking A!' Kevin would shout. He got terrifically excited by these stories.

It was not long before I was talking like the Murphys, in a high squeaky voice with a strong Brooklyn accent, punctuated (in school) by swear words and (at home) by half-swear words that I didn't understand. My mother was horrified.

'What the freak is this?' I'd shrill at some casserole she was placing on the table.

'Jimmy! Don't use language like that!'

'Freak? What's wrong with that?' I'd say in truly abysmal ignorance. 'Freak, freaky, freaking. It doesn't mean *anything*, everyone says it.' This is 1943, remember.

'I don't care what everyone says,' my father would shout, turning red. 'You watch your lip around here, and fast!'

On weekends we sat around a fire in the vacant lot, smoking cigarettes I had stolen (the Murphys favored the Lucky Strike red bull's-eye pack, which showed through the pockets of their white shirts) and eating mickeys which I had scooped up from in front of Tietjen's Grocery. About six of us were generally there – the Murphys, myself, and two or three of the tougher kids on the block whose faces have faded from my memory.

One spring day, when rains had turned the lot into trenches of red clay among the weeds and abandoned junk – people dumped old stoves, broken bicycles, useless trash there – Tom Murphy had the idea for The Lineup. This was based on a combination of dodge ball from school and firing squads from the daily news. The idea was to catch kids from the neighborhood, line them up like enemy soldiers against the garage that backed on to the lot, and fire clay balls at them. They would keep score and see who was the best shot.

'Go get Frankie and his little brother,' Tom told me. To Tom, almost everyone was an enemy. 'They're playing Three Steps to Germany in front of his house. Tell him you want to show him something.'

Since the cap incident, Frankie had become much more alert, darting into his house whenever the Murphys appeared on the block. He often looked at me with reproach during the past months, but never said anything, and I simply dropped him like a red hot mickey, though he had been my only real friend.

'He won't come,' I said. 'He won't believe me.'

'He'll believe you,' Tom said. Kevin stepped on my foot and pushed me heavily into the bushes. It was the first time he had turned on me and I couldn't believe it. I looked at Tom for help.

'Go get Frankie and Billy,' he repeated. 'We'll hide in the bushes.'

I walked miserably down the block, sick at heart. Shouldn't I just duck into my own house? Shouldn't I tell Frankie to run? Somehow these alternatives seemed impossible. I was committed to the Murphy brothers. While my childhood went up in flames, I spoke through the blaze in my head and talked Frankie into coming to the lot for some mickeys. I was bright-eyed with innocence, knowing full well what I was doing, cutting myself off from my parents, my church, selling my friend for the love of the Murphy brothers, whom I wanted to love me back.

'My ma gave me two potatoes. They'll be ready in a couple of minutes. You and Billy can split one.'

Frankie wanted to believe me. 'Have you seen Tom or Kevin today?'

'They went crabbing,' I said, glib with evil. 'Their Uncle Jake took them out on the bay. They promised they'd bring me some blueclaws.'

The walk down the block to the lot, maybe two hundred yards, was the longest I've ever taken. I babbled inanely to keep Frankie from asking questions. Billy was saved by suddenly deciding to go play inside instead – he didn't like mickeys, anyway, a heresy admitted only by the very young. I didn't dare protest, for fear of making Frankie suspicious. The lot appeared empty and we were well into it when Kevin stood up from behind a gutted refrigerator; Frankie whirled around right into Tom, who twisted his thin arm and bent him to the ground.

'Lineup time!' shouted Kevin, 'Freaking A!', as they carried the kicking boy over to the wall. There, they threw him down and tore off his shoes, making it difficult for him to run, over the rusty cans, cinders, and thorny bushes. They had made a large pile of clay balls already, and the three other boys began firing them mercilessly at the cowering figure, their misses making red splotches on the garage wall. This was the first Lineup in our neighborhood, a practice that quickly escalated so that within a few months boys were scaling the lethal tin cans their parents flattened to support the war effort. The Murphy boys held back momentarily, looking down at me.

'Where's Billy, you little fag?' Tom asked.

'He wouldn't come. He doesn't like mickeys.' I was wincing at Frankie's cries as a clay ball would strike him.

'Maybe you ought to take his place,' Tom said. 'One target's not enough.' Kevin reached from behind and snatched off my glasses,

plunging me into the shadowy halfworld in which I was always terrified. Without my glasses I could hardly speak and I said nothing as
they pushed me back and forth like a rag doll.

'You see that hoop there?' one of them said. 'Bring it over to the
garage and stand in it, you four-eyed freak.' Squinting, I could barely
make out a whitish hoop lying near the fire. I bent down and grabbed
it with my right hand and went down on my knees with a piercing
scream that must have scared even the Murphy brothers. They had
heated the metal hoop in the fire until it was white hot and my hand
stuck briefly to it, branding me for life. The older boys whooped and
ran off, firing a few last shots at Frankie, Kevin not forgetting to drop
my glasses in the fire, where my father found them the next day.

I knelt doubled up, retching with pain and grief while Africa was
falling to the Allies and our soldiers battled through the Solomon
Islands: the tide had turned. I went home and had my hand attended
to – third-degree burns! – and slept dreamless as a baby for the first
time in years.

Leonard Michaels
Murderers

When my uncle Moe dropped dead of a heart attack I became expert in the subway system. With a nickel I'd get to Queens, twist and zoom to Coney Island, twist again toward the George Washington Bridge – beyond which was darkness. I wanted proximity to darkness, strangeness. Who doesn't? The poor in spirit, the ignorant and frightened. My family came from Poland, then never went any place until they had heart attacks. The consummation of years in one neighborhood: a black Cadillac, corpse inside. We should have buried Uncle Moe where he shuffled away his life, in the kitchen or toilet, under the linoleum, near the coffee pot. Anyhow, they were dropping on Henry Street and Cherry Street. Blue lips. The previous winter it was cousin Charlie, forty-five years old. Moe, Charlie, Sam, Adele – family meant a punch in the chest, fire in the arm. I didn't want to wait for it. I went to Harlem, the Polo Grounds, Far Rockaway, thousands of miles on nickels, mainly underground. Tenements watched me go, day after day, fingering nickels. One afternoon I stopped to grind my heel against the curb. Melvin and Arnold Bloom appeared, then Harold Cohen. Melvin said, 'You step in dog shit?' Grinding was my answer. Harold Cohen said, 'The rabbi is home. I saw him on Market Street. He was walking fast.' Oily Arnold, eleven years old, began to urge: 'Let's go up to our roof.' The decision waited for me. I considered the roof, the view of industrial Brooklyn, the Battery, ships in the river, bridges, towers, and the rabbi's apartment. 'All right,' I said. We didn't giggle or look to one another for moral signals. We were running.

The blinds were up and curtains pulled, giving sunlight, wind, birds to the rabbi's apartment – a magnificent metropolitan view. The rabbi and his wife never took it, but in the light and air of summer afternoons, in the eye of gull and pigeon, they were joyous. A bearded young man and his young pink wife, sacramentally bald. Beard and Baldy, with everything to see, looked at each other. From a water tank on the opposite roof, higher than their windows, we looked at them. In psychoanalysis this is 'The Primal Scene'. To achieve the primal scene we crossed a ledge six inches wide. A half-inch indentation in the brick gave us fingerholds. We dragged bellies and groins against the brick face to a steel ladder. It went up the side of the building, bolted into brick, and up the side of the water tank to a slanted tin roof which caught the afternoon sun. We sat on that roof like angels, shot through with light, derealized in brilliance. Our sneakers sucked hot slanted metal. Palms and fingers pressed to bone on nailheads.

The Brooklyn Navy Yard with destroyers and aircraft carriers, the Statue of Liberty putting the sky to the torch, the dull remote sky-scrapers of Wall Street, and the Empire State Building were among the wonders we dominated. Our view of the holy man and his wife, on their living-room couch and floor, on the bed in their bedroom, could not be improved. Unless we got closer. But fifty feet across the air was right. We heard their phonograph and watched them dancing. We couldn't hear the gratifications or see pimples. We smelled nothing. We didn't want to touch.

For a while I watched them. Then I gazed beyond into simmering nullity, gray, blue and green murmuring over rooftops and towers. I had watched them before. I could tantalize myself with this brief ocular perversion, the general cleansing nihil of a view. This was the beginning of philosophy. I indulged in ambience, in space like eons. So what if my uncle Moe was dead? I was philosophical and luxurious. I didn't even have to look at the rabbi and his wife. After all, how many times had we dissolved stickball games when the rabbi came home? How many times had we risked shameful discovery, scrambling up the ladder, exposed to their windows – if they looked. We risked life itself to achieve this eminence. I looked at the rabbi and his wife.

Today she was a blond. Bald didn't mean no wigs. She had ten wigs, ten colors, fifty styles. She looked different, the same, and very good. A human theme in which nothing begat anything and was gorgeous. To me she was the world's lesson. Aryan yellow slipped through pins about her ears. An olive complexion mediated yellow hair and Arabic black eyes. Could one care what she really looked like? What was *really*? The minute you wondered, she looked like something else, in another wig, another style. Without the wigs she was a baldy-bean lady. Today she was a blonde. Not blonde. A blonde. The phonograph blared and her deep loops flowed Tommy Dorsey, Benny Goodman, and then the thing itself, Choo-Choo Lopez. Rumba! One, two-three. One, two-three. The rabbi stepped away to delight in blond imagination. Twirling and individual, he stepped away snapping fingers, going high and light on his toes. A short bearded man, balls afling, cock shuddering like a springboard. Rumba! One, two-three. *Olé! Vaya*, Choo-Choo!

> *I was on my way to spend some time in Cuba.*
> *Stopped off at Miami Beach, la-la.*
> *Oh, what a rumba they teach, la-la.*
> *Way down in Miami Beach,*
> *Oh, what a chroombah they teach, la-la.*
> *Way-down-in-Miami-Beach.*

She, on the other hand, was somewhat reserved. A shift in one lush hip was total rumba. He was Mr Life. She was dancing. He was a naked man. She was what she was in the garment of her soft, essential self. He was snapping, clapping, hopping to the beat. The beat lived in her visible music, her lovely self. Except for the wig. Also a watch-band that desecrated her wrist. But it gave her a bit of the whorish. She never took it off.

Harold Cohen began a cocktail-mixer motion, masturbating with two fists. Seeing him at such hard futile work, braced only by sneakers, was terrifying. But I grinned. Out of terror, I twisted an encouraging face. Melvin Bloom kept one hand on the tin. The other knuckled the rumba numbers into the back of my head. Nodding like a defective, little Arnold Bloom chewed his lip and squealed as the rabbi and his wife smacked together. The rabbi clapped her buttocks, fingers buried in the cleft. They stood only on his legs. His back arched, knees bent, thighs thick with thrust, up, up, up. Her legs wrapped his hips, ankles crossed, hooked for constriction. 'Oi, oi, oi,' she cried, wig flashing left, right, tossing the Brooklyn Navy Yard, the Statue of Liberty and the Empire State Building to hell. Arnold squealed oi, squealing rubber. His sneaker heels stabbed tin to stop his slide. Melvin said, 'Idiot.' Arnold's ring hooked a nailhead and the ring and ring finger remained. The hand, the arm, the rest of him were gone.

We rumbled down the ladder. 'Oi, oi, oi,' she yelled. In a freak of ecstasy her eyes had rolled and caught us. The rabbi drilled to her quick and she had us. '*OI, OI,*' she yelled above congas going clop, doom-doom, clop, doom-doom on the way to Cuba. The rabbi flew to the window, a red mouth opening in his beard: 'Murderers.' He couldn't know what he said. Melvin Bloom was crying. My fingers were tearing, bleeding into brick. Harold Cohen, like an adding machine, gibbered the name of God. We moved down the ledge quickly as we dared. Bongos went tocka-ti-tocka, tocka-ti-tocka. The rabbi screamed, 'MELVIN BLOOM, PHILLIP LIEBOWITZ, HAROLD COHEN, MELVIN BLOOM,' as if our names screamed this way, naming us where we hung, smashed us into brick.

Nothing was discussed.

The rabbi used his connections, arrangements were made. We were sent to a camp in New Jersey. We hiked and played volleyball. One day, apropos of nothing, Melvin came to me and said little Arnold had been made of gold and he, Melvin, of shit. I appreciated the sentiment, but to my mind they were both made of shit. Harold Cohen never again spoke to either of us. The counselors in the camp were World War II veterans, introspective men. Some carried shrapnel in their bodies. One had a metal plate in his head. Whatever you said to them they seemed to be thinking of something else, even when they answered. But step out of line and a plastic lanyard whistled burning notice across your ass.

At night, lying in the bunkhouse, I listened to owls. I'd never before heard that sound, the sound of darkness, blooming, opening inside you like a mouth.

Susan Minot
Hiding

Our father doesn't go to church with us but we're all downstairs in the hall at the same time, bumbling, getting ready to go. Mum knuckles the buttons of Chicky's snowsuit till he's knot-tight, crouching, her heels lifted out of the back of her shoes, her nylons creased at the ankles. She wears a black lace veil that stays on her hair like magic. Sherman ripples by, coat flapping, and Mum grabs him by the hood, reeling him in, and zips him up with a pinch at his chin. Gut stands there with his bottom lip out, waiting, looking like someone's smacked him except not that hard. Even though he's nine, he still wants Mum to do him up. Delilah comes half-hurrying down the stairs, late, looking like a ragamuffin with her skirt slid down to her hips and her hair all slept on wrong. Caitlin says, 'It's about time.' Delilah sweeps along the curve of the banister, looks at Caitlin who's all ready to go herself with her pea jacket on and her loafers and bare legs, and tells her, 'You're going to freeze.' Everyone's in a bad mood because we just woke up.

Dad's outside already on the other side of the French doors, waiting for us to go. You can tell it's cold out there by his white breath blowing by his cheek in spurts. He just stands on the porch, hands shoved in his black parka, feet pressed together, looking at the crusty snow on the lawn. He doesn't wear a hat but that's because he barely feels the cold. Mum's the one who's warm-blooded. At skiing, she'll take you in when your toes get numb. You sit there with hot chocolate and a carton of french fries and the other mothers and she rubs your foot to get the circulation back. Down on the driveway the car is warming up and the exhaust goes straight up, disappearing in thin white curls.

'OK, Monkeys,' says Mum, filing us out the door. Chicky starts down the steps one red boot at a time till Mum whisks him up under a wing. The driveway is wrinkled over with ice so we take little shuffle steps across it, blinking at how bright it is, still only half-awake. Only the station wagon can fit everybody. Gus and Sherman scamper in across the huge backseat. Caitlin's head is the only one that shows over the front. (Caitlin is the oldest and she's twelve. I'm next, then Delilah, then the boys.) Mum rubs her thumbs on the steering wheel so that her gloves are shiny and round at the knuckles. Dad is doing things like checking the gutters, waiting till we leave. When we finally barrel down the hill, he turns and goes back into the house which is big and empty now and quiet.

We keep our coats on in church. Except for the O'Shaunesseys, we have the most children in one pew. Dad only comes on Christmas and Easter, because he's not Catholic. A lot of times you only see the mothers there. When Dad stays at home, he does things like cuts prickles in the woods or tears up thorns, or rakes leaves for burning, or just stands around on the other side of the house by the lilacs, surveying his garden, wondering what to do next. We usually sit up near the front and there's a lot of kneeling near the end. One time Gus got his finger stuck in the diamond-shaped holes of the heating vent and Mum had to yank it out. When the man comes around for the collection, we each put in a nickel or a dime and the handle goes by like a rake. If Mum drops in a five-dollar bill, she'll pluck out a couple of bills for her change.

The church is huge. Out loud in the dead quiet, a baby blares out DAH-DEE. We giggle and Mum goes *Ssshhh* but smiles too. A baby always yells at the quietest part. Only the girls are old enough to go to Communion; you're not allowed to chew it. The priest's neck is peeling and I try not to look. 'He leaves me cold,' Mum says when we leave, touching her forehead with a fingertip after dipping it into the holy water.

On the way home, we pick up the paper at Cage's and a bag of eight lollipops – one for each of us, plus Mum and Dad, even though Dad never eats his. I choose root beer. Sherman crinkles his wrapper, flicking his eyes around to see if anyone's looking. Gus says, 'Sherman, you have to wait till after breakfast.' Sherman gives a fierce look and shoves it in his mouth. Up in front, Mum, flicking on the blinker, says, 'Take that out,' with eyes in the back of her head.

Depending on what time of year it is, we do different things on the weekends. In the fall we might go to Castle Hill and stop by the orchard in Ipswich for cider and apples and red licorice. Castle Hill is closed after the summer so there's nobody else there and it's all covered with leaves. Mum goes up to the windows on the terrace and tries to peer in, cupping her hands around her eyes and seeing curtains. We do things like roll down the hills, making our arms stiff like mummies, or climb around on the marble statues which are really cold, or balance along the edge of the fountains without falling. Mum says *Be careful* even though there's no water in them, just red leaves plastered against the sides. When Dad notices us he yells *Get down*.

One garden has a ghost, according to Mum. A lady used to sneak out and meet her lover in the garden behind the grape trellis. Or she'd hide in the garden somewhere and he'd look for her and find her. But one night she crept out and he didn't come and finally when she couldn't stand it any longer, she went crazy and ran off the cliff and killed herself and now her ghost comes back and keeps waiting. We creep into the boxed-in place smelling the yellow berries and the wet bark and Delilah jumps – 'What was that?' – trying to scare us. Dad shakes the wood to see if it's rotten. We run ahead and hide in a pile of leaves. Little twigs get in your mouth and your nostrils; we hold still underneath listening to the brittle ticking leaves. When we hear Mum and Dad get close, we burst up to surprise them, all the leaves fluttering down, sputtering from the dust and tiny grits that get all over your face like grey ash, like Ash Wednesday. Mum and Dad just keep walking. She brushes a pine needle from his collar and he jerks his head, thinking of something else, probably that it's a fly. We follow them back to the car in a line all scruffy with leaf scraps.

After church, we have breakfast because you're not allowed to eat before. Dad comes in for the paper or a sliver of bacon. One thing about Dad, he has the weirdest taste. Spam is his favorite thing or this cheese that no one can stand the smell of. He barely sits down at all, glancing at the paper with his feet flat down on either side of him, ready to get up any minute to go back outside and sprinkle white fertilizer on the lawn. After, it looks like frost.

This Sunday we get to go skating at Ice House Pond. Dad drives. 'Pipe down,' he says into the back seat. Mum faces him with white fur around her hood. She calls him Uncs, short for Uncle, a kind of joke, I guess, calling him Uncs while he calls her Mum, same as we do. We are making a racket.

'Will you quit it?' Caitlin elbows Gus.

'What? I'm not doing anything.'

'Just taking up all the room.'

Sherman's in the way back. 'How come Chicky always gets the front?'

''Cause he's the baby.' Delilah is always explaining everything.

'I en not a baby,' says Chicky without turning around.

Caitlin frowns at me. 'Who said you could wear my scarf?'

I ask into the front seat, 'Can we go to the Fairy Garden?' even though I know we won't.

'Why couldn't Rummy come?'

Delilah says, 'Because Dad didn't want him to.'

Sherman wants to know how old Dad was when he learned how to skate.

Dad says, 'About your age.' He has a deep voice.

'Really?' I think about that for a minute, about Dad being Sheran's age.

'What about Mum?' says Caitlin.

This isn't his department so he just keeps driving. Mum shifts her shoulders more toward us but still looks at Dad.

'When I was a little girl on the Boston Common.' Her teeth are white and she wears fuchsia lipstick. 'We used to have skating parties.'

Caitlin leans close to Mum's fur hood, crossing her arms into a pillow. 'What? With dates?'

Mum bats her eyelashes. 'Oh sure. Lots of beaux.' She smiles, acting like a flirt. I look at Dad but he's concentrating on the road.

We saw one at a football game once. He had a huge mustard overcoat and bow tie and a pink face like a ham. He bent down to shake our tiny hands, half-looking at Mum the whole time. Dad was someplace else getting the tickets. His name was Hank. After he went, Mum put her sunglasses on her head and told us she used to watch him play football at BC. Dad never wears a tie except to work. One time Gus got lost. We waited until the last people had trickled out and the stadium was practically empty. It had started to get dark and the headlights were crisscrossing out of the parking field. Finally Dad came back carrying him, walking fast, Gus's head bobbing around and his face all blotchy. Dad rolled his eyes and made a kidding groan to Mum and we laughed because Gus was always getting lost. When Mum took him, he rammed his head onto her shoulder and hid his face while we walked back to the car, and under Mum's hand you could see his back twitching, trying to hide his crying.

We have Ice House Pond all to ourselves. In certain places the ice is bumpy and if you glide on it going *Aauuuuhhhh* in a low tone, your voice wobbles and vibrates. Every once in a while, a crack shoots across the pond, echoing just beneath the surface, and you feel something drop in the hollow of your back. It sounds like someone's jumped off a steel wire and left it twanging in the air.

I try to teach Delilah how to skate backwards but she's flopping all over the ice, making me laugh, with her hat lopsided and her mittens dangling out of her sleeves. When Gus falls, he just stays there, polishing the ice with his mitten. Dad sees him and says, 'I don't care if my son is a violin player,' kidding.

Dad played hockey in college and was so good his name is on a plaque that's right as you walk into the Harvard rink. He can go really fast. He takes off – *whooosh* – whizzing, circling at the edge of the pond, taking long strides, then gliding, chopping his skates, crossing over in little jumps. He goes zipping by and we watch him: his hands behind him in a tight clasp, his face as calm as if he were just walking along, only slightly forward. When he sweeps a corner, he tips in, then rolls into a hunch, and starts the long side-pushing again. After he stops, his face is red and the tears leak from the sides of his eyes and there's a white smudge around his mouth like frostbite. Sherman, copying, goes chopping forward on collapsed ankles and it sounds like someone sharpening knives.

Mum practices her 3s from when she used to figure skate. She pushes forward on one skate, turning in the middle like a petal flipped suddenly in the wind. We always make her do a spin. First she does backwards crossovers, holding her wrists like a tulip in her fluorescent pink parka, then stops straight up on her toes, sucking in her breath and dips, twisted, following her own tight circle, faster and faster, drawing her feet together. Whirring around, she lowers into a crouch, ventures out one balanced leg, a twirling whirlpool, hot pink, rises again, spinning, into a blurred pillar or a tornado, her arms going above her head and her hands like the eye of a needle. Then suddenly: stop. Hiss of ice shavings, stopped. We clap our mittens. Her hood has slipped off and her hair is spread across her shoulders like when she's reading in bed, and she takes white breaths with her teeth showing and her pink mouth smiling. She squints over our heads. Dad is way off at the car, unlacing his skates on the tailgate but he doesn't turn. Mum's face means that it's time to go.

Chicky stands in the front seat leaning against Dad. Our parkas crinkle in the cold car. Sherman has been chewing on his thumb and it's a pointed black witch's hat. A rumble goes through the car like a monster growl and before we back up Dad lifts Chicky and sets him leaning against Mum instead.

The speed bumps are marked with yellow stripes and it's like sea serpents have crawled under the tar. When we bounce, Mum says, 'Thank-you-Ma'am' with a lilt in her voice. If it was only Mum, the radio would be on and she'd turn it up on the good ones. Dad snaps it off because there's enough racket already. He used to listen to opera when he got home from work but not anymore. Now we give him hard hugs and he changes upstairs then goes into the TV room to the same place on the couch, propping his book on his crossed knees and reaching for his drink without looking up. At supper, he comes in for a handful of onion-flavored bacon crisps or a dish of miniature corn-on-the-cobs pickled. Mum keeps us in the kitchen longer so he can have a little peace and quiet. Ask him what he wants for Christmas and he'll say *No more arguing*. When Mum clears our plates, she takes a bite of someone's hot dog or a quick spoonful of peas before dumping the rest down the pig.

In the car, we ask Dad if we can stop at Shucker's for candy. When he doesn't answer, it means *No*. Mum's eyes mean *Not today*. She says, 'It's treat night anyway.' Treats are ginger ale and vanilla ice cream.

On Sunday nights we have treats and BLTs and get to watch Ted Mack and Ed Sullivan. There are circus people on almost every time, doing cartwheels or flips or balancing. We stand up in our socks and try some of it. Delilah does an imitation of Elvis by making jump rope handles into a microphone. Girls come on with silver shoes and their stomachs showing and do clappity tap dances. 'That's a cinch,' says Mum behind us.

'Let's see you then,' we say and she goes over to the brick in front of the fireplace to show us. She bangs the floor with her sneakers, pumping and kicking, thudding her heels in smacks, not like clicking at all, swinging her arms out in front of her like she's wading through the jungle. She speeds up, staring straight at Dad who's reading his book, making us laugh even harder. He's always like that. Sometimes for no reason, he'll snap out of it, going, 'What? What? What's all this? What's going on?' as if he's emerged from a dark tunnel, looking like he does when we wake him up and he hasn't put on his glasses yet, sort of angry. He sits there before dinner, popping black olives into his mouth one at a time, eyes never leaving his book. His huge glass mug is from college and in the lamplight you can see the liquid separate. One layer is beer, the rest is gin. Even smelling it makes you gag.

Dad would never take us to Shucker's for candy. With him, we do things outside. If there's a storm we go down to the rocks to see the waves – you have to yell – and get sopped. Or if Mum needs a nap, we go to the beach. In the spring it's wild and windy as anything, which I love. The wind presses against you and you kind of choke but in a good way. Sherman and I run, run, run! Couples at the end are so far away you can hardly tell they're moving. Rummy races around with other dogs, flipping his rear like a goldfish, snapping at the air, or careening in big looping circles across the beach. Caitlin jabs a stick into the wet part and draws flowers. Chicky smells the seaweed by smushing it all over his face. Delilah's dark bangs jitter across her forehead like magnets and she yells back to Gus lagging behind. Dad looks at things far away. He points out birds – a great blue heron near the breakers as thin as a safety pin or an osprey in the sky, tilting like a paper cutout. We collect little things. Delilah holds out a razor shell on one sandy palm for Dad to take and he says *Uh-huh* and calls Rummy. When Sherman, grinning, carries a dead seagull to him, Dad says, 'Cut that out.' Once in Maine, I found a triangle of blue and white china and showed it to Dad. 'Ah, yes, a bit of crockery,' he said.

'Do you think it's from the Indians?' I whispered. They had made the arrowheads we found on the beach.

'I think it's probably debris,' he said and handed it back to me. According to Mum, debris is the same thing as litter, as in Don't Be a Litter Bug.

When we get home from skating, it's already started to get dark. Sherman runs up first and beats us to the door but can't open it himself. We are all used to how warm it was in the car so everybody's going *Brrr*, or *Hurry up*, banging our feet on the porch so it thunders. The sky is dark blue glass and the railing seems whiter and the fur on Mum's hood glows. From the driveway Dad yells, 'I'm going downtown. Be right back,' slamming the door and starting the car again.

Delilah yells, 'Can I come?' and Gus goes, 'Me too!' as we watch the car back up.

'Right back,' says his deep voice through the crack in the window and he rounds the side of the house.

'How come he didn't stop on the way home?' asks Caitlin, sticking out her chin.

'Yah,' says Delilah. 'How come?' We look at Mum.

She kicks the door with her boot. 'In we go, Totsies,' she says instead of answering and drops someone's skate on the porch because she's carrying so much stuff.

Gus gets in a bad mood, standing by the door with his coat on, not moving a muscle. His hat has flaps over the ears. Delilah flops onto the hall sofa, her neck bent, ramming her chin into her chest. 'Why don't you take off your coat and stay awhile?' she says, drumming her fingers as slow as a spider on her stomach.

'I don't have to.'

'Yah,' Sherman butts in. 'Who says you're the boss?' He's lying on the marble tile with Rummy, scissor-kicking his legs like windshield wipers.

'No one,' says Delilah, her fingers rippling along.

On the piano bench, Caitlin is picking at her split ends. We can hear Mum in the kitchen putting the dishes away.

Banging on the piano fast because she knows it by heart, Caitlin plays 'Walking in a Winter Wonderland'. Delilah sits up and imitates her behind her back, shifting her hips from side to side, making us all laugh. Caitlin whips around, 'What?'

'Nothing.' But we can't help laughing.

'Nothing what?' says Mum coming around the corner, picking up mittens and socks from the floor, snapping on the lights.

Delilah stiffens her legs. 'We weren't doing anything,' she says.

We make room for Mum on the couch and huddle. Gus perches at the edge, sideways.

'When's Dad coming back?' he says.

'You know your father,' says Mum vaguely, smoothing Delilah's hair on her lap, daydreaming at the floor but thinking about something. When Dad goes to the store, he only gets one thing, like a can of black bean soup or watermelon rind.

'What shall we play?' says Sherman, strangling Rummy in a hug.

'Yah. Yah. Let's do something,' we say and turn to Mum.

She narrows her eyes into spying slits. 'All rightee. I might have a little idea.'

'What?' we all shout, excited. 'What?' Mum hardly ever plays with us because she has to do everything else.

She rises, slowly, lifting her eyebrows, hinting. 'You'll see.'

'What?' says Gus and his bottom lip loosens nervously.

Delilah's dark eyes flash like jumping beans. 'Yah, Mum. What?'

'Just come with me,' says Mum in a singsong and we scamper after her. At the bottom of the stairs, she crouches in the middle of us. Upstairs behind her, it's dark.

'Where are we going?' asks Caitlin and everybody watches Mum's face, thinking of the darkness up there.

'Hee hee hee,' she says in her witch voice. 'We're going to surprise your father, play a little trick.'

'What?' asks Caitlin again, getting ready to worry but Mum's already creeping up the stairs so we follow, going one mile per hour like her, not making a peep even though there's no one in the house to hear us.

Suddenly she wheels around. 'We're going to hide,' she cackles.

'Where?' we all want to know, sneaking along like burglars.

Her voice is hushed. 'Just come with me.'

At the top of the stairs it is dark and we whisper.

'How about your room?' says Delilah. 'Maybe under the bed.'

'No,' says Sherman breathlessly. 'In the fireplace.' We all laugh because we could never fit in there.

Standing in the hall, Mum opens the door to the linen closet and pulls the light string. 'How about right here?' The light falls across our faces. On the shelves are stacks of bed covers and rolled puffs, red and white striped sheets and pink towels, everything clean and folded and smelling of soap.

All of a sudden Caitlin gasps, 'Wait – I hear the car!'

Quickly we all jumble and scramble around, bumbling and knocking and trying to cram ourselves inside. Sherman makes whimpering noises like an excited dog. *Sshhh*, we say, or *Hurry, Hurry*, or *Wait*. I knee up to a top shelf and Sherman gets a boost after me and then Delilah comes grunting up. We play in here sometimes. Gus and Chicky crawl into the shelf underneath, wedging themselves in sideways. Caitlin half-sits on molding with her legs dangling and one hand braced against the door frame. When the rushing settles, Mum pulls out the light and hikes herself up on the other ledge. Everyone is off the ground then, and quiet.

Delilah giggles. Caitlin says *Ssshhhh* and I say *Come on* in a whisper. Only when Mum says *Hush* do we all stop and listen. Everyone is breathing; a shelf creaks. Chicky knocks a towel off and it hits the ground like a pillow. Gus says, 'I don't hear anything.'

Sshhh, we say. Mum touches the door and light widens and we listen. Nothing.

'False alarm,' says Sherman.

Our eyes start to get used to the dark. Next to me Delilah gurgles her spit.

'What do you think he'll do?' whispers Caitlin. We all smile, curled up in the darkness with Mum thinking how fooled he'll be, coming back and not a soul anywhere, standing in the hall with all the lights glaring not hearing a sound.

'Where will he think we've gone?' We picture him looking around for a long time, till finally we all pour out of the closet.

'He'll find out,' Mum whispers. Someone laughs at the back of his throat, like a cricket quietly ticking.

Delilah hisses, 'Wait – '

'Forget it,' says Caitlin who knows it's a false alarm.

'What will he do?' we ask Mum.

She's in the darkest part of the closet, on the other side of the light slant. We hear her voice. 'We'll see.'

'My foot's completely fallen asleep,' says Caitlin.

'Kick it,' says Mum's voice.

'Ssshhh,' lisps Chicky and we laugh at him copying everybody.

Gus's muffled voice comes from under the shelf. 'My head's getting squished.'

'Move it,' says Delilah.

'Quiet!'

And then we really do hear the car.

'Silence, Monkeys,' says Mum and we all hush, holding our breaths. The car hums up the hill.

The motor dies and the car shuts off. We hear the door crack, then clip shut. Footsteps bang up the echoing porch, loud, toe-hard and scuffing. The glass panes rattle when the door opens, resounding in the empty hall, and then the door slams in the dead quiet, reverberating through the whole side of the house. Someone in the closet squeaks like a hamster. Downstairs there isn't a sound.

'Anybody home?' he bellows, and we try not to giggle.

Now what will he do? He strides across the deep hall, going by the foot of the stairs, obviously wondering where everybody's gone, stopping at the hooks to hang up his parka.

'What's he doing?' whispers Caitlin to herself.

'He's by the mitten basket,' says Sherman. We all have smiles, our teeth like watermelon wedges, grinning in the dark.

He yells toward the kitchen, 'Hello?' and we hunch our shoulders to keep from laughing, holding onto something tight like our toes or the shelf, or biting the side of our mouths.

He starts back into the hall.

'He's getting warmer,' whispers Mum's voice, far away. We all wait for his footsteps on the stairs.

But he stops by the TV room doorway. We hear him rustling something, a paper bag, taking out what he's bought, the bag crinkling, setting something down on the hall table, then crumpling up the bag and pitching it in the wastebasket. Gus says, 'Why doesn't he – ?' *Ssshhh*, says Mum like spitting and we all freeze. He moves again – his footsteps turn and bang on the hollow threshold into the TV room where the rug pads the sound.

Next we hear the TV click on, the sound swelling and the dial switching *tick-ah tikka tikka tick* till it lands on a crowd roar, a football game. We can hear the announcer's voice and the hiss-breath behind it of cheering.

Then it's the only sound in the house.

'What do we do now?' says Delilah only half-whispering. Mum slips down from her shelf and her legs appear in the light, touching down.

Still hushed, Sherman goes, 'Let's keep hiding.'

The loud thud is from Caitlin jumping down. She uses her regular voice. 'Forget it. I'm sick of this anyway.' Everyone starts to rustle. Chicky panics, 'I can't get down,' as if we're about to desert him.

'Stop being such a baby,' says Delilah, disgusted.

Mum doesn't say anything, just opens the door all the way. Past the banister in the hall it is yellow and bright. We climb out of the closet, feet-feeling our way down backwards, bumping out one at a time, knocking down blankets and washcloths by mistake. Mum guides our backs and checks our landings. We don't leave the narrow hallway. The light from downstairs shines up through the railing and casts shadows on the wall – bars of light and dark like a fence. Standing in it we have stripes all over us. *Hey look*, we say whispering, with the football drone in the background, even though this isn't anything new – we always see this, holding out your arms and seeing the stripes. Lingering near the linen closet we wait. Mum picks up the tumbled things, restacking the stuff we knocked down, folding things, clinching a towel with her chin, smoothing it over her stomach and then matching the corners left and right, like crossing herself, patting everything into neat piles. The light gets like this every night after we've gone to bed and we creep into the hall to listen to Mum and Dad downstairs. The bands of shadows go across our nightgowns and pajamas and we press our foreheads against the railing trying to hear the mumbling of what Mum and Dad are saying down there. Then we hear the deep boom of Dad clearing his throat and look up at Mum. Though she is turned away, we can still see the wince on her face like when you are waiting to be hit or right after you have been. So we keep standing there, our hearts pounding, waving our hands through the flickered stripes, suddenly interested the way you get when it's time to take a bath and you are mesmerized by something. We're stalling, waiting for Mum to finish folding, waiting to see what she's going to do next because we don't want to go downstairs yet, where Dad is, without her.

Alice Munro
The Turkey Season

When I was fourteen I got a job at the Turkey Barn for the Christmas season. I was still too young to get a job working in a store or as a part-time waitress; I was also too nervous.

I was a turkey gutter. The other people who worked at the Turkey Barn were Lily and Marjorie and Gladys, who were also gutters; Irene and Henry, who were pluckers; Herb Abbott, the foreman, who superintended the whole operation and filled in wherever he was needed. Morgan Elliott was the owner and boss. He and his son, Morgy, did the killing.

Morgy I knew from school. I thought him stupid and despicable and was uneasy about having to consider him in a new and possibly superior guise, as the boss's son. But his father treated him so roughly, yelling and swearing at him, that he seemed no more than the lowest of the workers. The other person related to the boss was Gladys. She was his sister, and in her case there did seem to be some privilege of position. She worked slowly and went home if she was not feeling well, and was not friendly to Lily and Marjorie, although she was, a little, to me. She had come back to live with Morgan and his family after working for many years in Toronto, in a bank. This was not the sort of job she was used to. Lily and Marjorie, talking about her when she wasn't there, said she had had a nervous breakdown. They said Morgan made her work in the Turkey Barn to pay for her keep. They also said, with no worry about the contradiction, that she had taken the job because she was after a man, and that the man was Herb Abbott.

All I could see when I closed my eyes, the first few nights after working there, was turkeys. I saw them hanging upside down, plucked and stiffened, pale and cold, with the heads and necks limp, the eyes and nostrils clotted with dark blood; the remaining bits of feathers – those dark and bloody, too – seemed to form a crown. I saw them not with aversion but with a sense of endless work to be done.

Herb Abbott showed me what to do. You put the turkey down on the table and cut its head off with a cleaver. Then you took the loose skin around the neck and stripped it back to reveal the crop, nestled in the cleft between the gullet and the windpipe.

'Feel the gravel,' said Herb encouragingly. He made me close my fingers around the crop. Then he showed me how to work my hand down behind it to cut it out, and the gullet and windpipe as well. He used shears to cut the vertebrae.

'Scrunch, scrunch,' he said soothingly. 'Now, put your hand in.'

I did. It was deathly cold in there, in the turkey's dark insides.

'Watch out for bone splinters.'

Working cautiously in the dark, I had to pull the connecting tissues loose.

'Ups-a-daisy.' Herb turned the bird over and flexed each leg. 'Knees up, Mother Brown. Now.' He took a heavy knife and placed it directly on the knee knuckle joints and cut off the shank.

'Have a look at the worms.'

Pearly-white strings, pulled out of the shank, were creeping about on their own.

'That's just the tendons shrinking. Now comes the nice part!'

He slit the bird at its bottom end, letting out a rotten smell.

'Are you educated?'

I did not know what to say.

'What's that smell?'

'Hydrogen sulfide.'

'Educated,' said Herb, sighing. 'All right. Work your fingers around and get the guts loose. Easy. Easy. Keep your fingers together. Keep the palm inwards. Feel the ribs with the back of your hand. Feel the guts fit into your palm. Feel that? Keep going. Break the strings – as many as you can. Keep going. Feel a hard lump? That's the gizzard. Feel a soft lump? That's the heart. OK? OK. Get your fingers around the gizzard. Easy. Start pulling this way. That's right. That's right. Start to pull her out.'

It was not easy at all. I wasn't even sure what I had was the gizzard. My hand was full of cold pulp.

'Pull,' he said, and I brought out a glistening, liverish mass.

'Got it. There's the lights. You know what they are? Lungs. There's the heart. There's the gizzard. There's the gall. Now, you don't ever want to break that gall inside or it will taste the entire turkey.' Tactfully, he scraped out what I had missed, including the testicles, which were like a pair of white grapes.

'Nice pair of earrings,' Herb said.

Herb Abbott was a tall, firm, plump man. His hair was dark and thin, combed straight back from a widow's peak, and his eyes seemed to be slightly slanted, so that he looked like a pale Chinese or like pictures of the Devil, except that he was smooth-faced and benign. Whatever he did around the Turkey Barn – gutting, as he was now, or loading the truck, or hanging the carcasses – was done with efficient, economical movements, quickly and buoyantly. 'Notice about Herb – he always walks like he had a boat moving underneath him,' Marjorie said, and it was true. Herb worked on the lake boats, during the season, as a cook. Then he worked for Morgan until after Christmas. The rest of the time he helped around the poolroom, making hamburgers, sweeping up, stopping fights before they got started. That was where he lived; he had a room above the poolroom on the main street.

In all the operations at the Turkey Barn it seemed to be Herb who had the efficiency and honor of the business continually on his mind; it was he who kept everything under control. Seeing him in the yard talking to Morgan, who was a thick, short man, red in the face, an unpredictable bully, you would be sure that it was Herb who was the boss and Morgan the hired help. But it was not so.

If I had not had Herb to show me, I don't think I could have learned turkey gutting at all. I was clumsy with my hands and had been shamed for it so often that the least show of impatience on the part of the person instructing me could have brought on a dithering paralysis. I could not stand to be watched by anybody but Herb. Particularly, I couldn't stand to be watched by Lily and Marjorie, two middle-aged sisters, who were very fast and thorough and competitive gutters. They sang at their work and talked abusively and intimately to the turkey carcasses.

'Don't you nick me, you old bugger!'

'Aren't you the old crap factory!'

I had never heard women talk like that.

Gladys was not a fast gutter, though she must have been thorough; Herb would have talked to her otherwise. She never sang and certainly she never swore. I thought her rather old, though she was not as old as Lily and Marjorie; she must have been over thirty. She seemed offended by everything that went on and had the air of keeping plenty of bitter judgments to herself. I never tried to talk to her, but she spoke to me one day in the cold little washroom off the gutting shed. She was putting pancake makeup on her face. The color of the makeup was so distinct from the color of her skin that it was as if she were slapping orange paint over a whitewashed, bumpy wall.

She asked me if my hair was naturally curly.

I said yes.

'You don't have to get a permanent?'

'No.'

'You're lucky. I have to do mine up every night. The chemicals in my system won't allow me to get a permanent.'

There are different ways women have of talking about their looks. Some women make it clear that what they do to keep themselves up is for the sake of sex, for men. Others, like Gladys, make the job out to be a kind of housekeeping, whose very difficulties they pride themselves on. Gladys was genteel. I could see her in the bank, in a navy-blue dress with the kind of detachable white collar you can wash at night. She would be grumpy and correct.

Another time, she spoke to me about her periods, which were profuse and painful. She wanted to know about mine. There was an uneasy, prudish, agitated expression on her face. I was saved by Irene, who was using the toilet and called out, 'Do like me, and you'll be rid of all your problems for a while.' Irene was only a few years older than I was, but she was recently – tardily – married, and heavily pregnant.

Gladys ignored her, running cold water on her hands. The hands of all of us were red and sore-looking from the work. 'I can't use that soap. If I use it, I break out in a rash,' Gladys said. 'If I bring my own soap in here, I can't afford to have other people using it, because I pay a lot for it – it's a special anti-allergy soap.'

I think the idea that Lily and Marjorie promoted – that Gladys was after Herb Abbott – sprang from their belief that single people ought to be teased and embarrassed whenever possible, and from their interest in Herb, which led to the feeling that somebody ought to be after him. They wondered about him. What they wondered was: how can a man want so little? No wife, no family, no house. The details of his daily life, the small preferences, were of interest. Where had he been brought up? (Here and there and all over.) How far had he gone in school? (Far enough.) Where was his girlfriend? (Never tell.) Did he drink coffee or tea if he got the choice? (Coffee.)

When they talked about Gladys's being after him they must have really wanted to talk about sex – what he wanted and what he got. They must have felt a voluptuous curiosity about him, as I did. He aroused this feeling by being circumspect and not making the jokes some men did, and at the same time by not being squeamish or gentlemanly. Some men, showing me the testicles from the turkey, would have acted as if the very existence of testicles were somehow a bad joke on me, something a girl could be taunted about; another sort of man would have been embarrassed and would have thought he had to protect me from embarrassment. A man who didn't seem to feel one way or the other was an oddity – as much to older women, probably, as to me. But what was so welcome to me may have been disturbing to them. They wanted to jolt him. They even wanted Gladys to jolt him, if she could.

There wasn't any idea then – at least in Logan, Ontario, in the late forties – about homosexuality's going beyond very narrow confines. Women, certainly, believed in its rarity and in definite boundaries. There were homosexuals in town, and we knew who they were: an elegant, light-voiced, wavy-haired paperhanger who called himself an interior decorator; the minister's widow's fat, spoiled only son, who went so far as to enter baking contests and had crocheted a tablecloth; a hypochondriacal church organist and music teacher who kept the choir and his pupils in line with screaming tantrums. Once the label was fixed, there was a good deal of tolerance for these people, and their talents for decorating, for crocheting, and for music were appreciated – especially by women. 'The poor fellow,' they said. 'He doesn't do any harm.' They really seemed to believe – the women did – that it was the penchant for baking or music that was the determining factor, and that it was this activity that made the man what he was – not any other detours he might take, or wish to take. A desire to play the violin would be taken as more a deviation from manliness than would a wish to shun women. Indeed, the idea was that any manly man would wish to shun women but most of them were caught off guard, and for good.

I don't want to go into the question of whether Herb was homosexual or not, because the definition is of no use to me. I think that probably he was, but maybe he was not. (Even considering what happened later, I think that.) He is not a puzzle so arbitrarily solved.

The other plucker, who worked with Irene, was Henry Streets, a neighbor of ours. There was nothing remarkable about him except that he was eighty-six years old and still, as he said of himself, a devil for work. He had whiskey in his thermos, and drank it from time to time through the day. It was Henry who had said to me, in our kitchen, 'You ought to get yourself a job at the Turkey Barn. They need another gutter.' Then my father said at once, 'Not her, Henry. She's got ten thumbs,' and Henry said he was just joking – it was dirty work. But I was already determined to try it – I had a great need to be successful in a job like this. I was almost in the condition of a grownup person who is ashamed of never having learned to read, so much did I feel my ineptness at manual work. Work, to everybody I knew, meant doing things I was no good at doing, and work was what people prided themselves on and measured each other by. (It goes without saying that the things I was good at, like schoolwork, were suspect or held in plain contempt.) So it was a surprise and then a triumph for me not to get fired, and to be able to turn out clean turkeys at a rate that was not disgraceful. I don't know if I really understood how much Herb Abbott was responsible for this, but he would sometimes say, 'Good girl,' or pat my waist and say, 'You're getting to be a good gutter – you'll go a long ways in the world,' and when I felt his quick, kind touch through the heavy sweater and bloody smock I wore, I felt my face glow and I wanted to lean back against him as he stood behind me. I wanted to rest my head against his wide, fleshy shoulder. When I went to sleep at night, lying on my side, I would rub my cheek against the pillow and think of that as Herb's shoulder.

I was interested in how he talked to Gladys, how he looked at her or noticed her. This interest was not jealousy. I think I wanted something to happen with them. I quivered in curious expectation, as Lily and Marjorie did. We all wanted to see the flicker of sexuality in him, hear it in his voice, not because we thought it would make him seem more like other men but because we knew that with him it would be entirely different. He was kinder and more patient than most women, and as stern and remote, in some ways, as any man. We wanted to see how he could be moved.

If Gladys wanted this, too, she didn't give any signs of it. It is impossible for me to tell with women like her whether they are as thick and deadly as they seem, not wanting anything much but opportunities for irritation and contempt, or if they are all choked up with gloomy fires and useless passions.

Marjorie and Lily talked about marriage. They did not have much good to say about it, in spite of their feeling that it was a state nobody should be allowed to stay out of. Marjorie said that shortly after her marriage she had gone into the woodshed with the intention of swallowing Paris green.

'I'd have done it,' she said. 'But the man came along in the grocery truck and I had to go out and buy the groceries. This was when we lived on the farm.'

Her husband was cruel to her in those days, but later he suffered an accident – he rolled the tractor and was so badly hurt he would be an invalid all his life. They moved to town, and Marjorie was the boss now.

'He starts to sulk the other night and say he don't want his supper. Well, I just picked up his wrist and held it. He was scared I was going to twist his arm. He could see I'd do it. So I say, "You *what*?" And he says, "I'll eat it." '

They talked about their father. He was a man of the old school. He had a noose in the woodshed (not the Paris green woodshed – this would be an earlier one, on another farm), and when they got on his nerves he used to line them up and threaten to hang them. Lily, who was the younger, would shake till she fell down. This same father had arranged to marry Marjorie off to a crony of his when she was just sixteen. That was the husband who had driven her to the Paris green. Their father did it because he wanted to be sure she wouldn't get into trouble.

'Hot blood,' Lily said.

I was horrified, and asked, 'Why didn't you run away?'

'His word was law,' Marjorie said.

They said that was what was the matter with kids nowadays – it was the kids that ruled the roost. A father's word should be law. They brought up their own kids strictly, and none had turned out bad yet. When Marjorie's son wet the bed she threatened to cut off his dingy with the butcher knife. That cured him.

They said ninety per cent of the young girls nowadays drank, and swore, and took it lying down. They did not have daughters, but if they did and caught them at anything like that they would beat them raw. Irene, they said, used to go to the hockey games with her ski pants slit and nothing under them, for convenience in the snowdrifts afterward. Terrible.

I wanted to point out some contradictions. Marjorie and Lily themselves drank and swore, and what was so wonderful about the strong will of a father who would insure you a lifetime of unhappiness? (What I did not see was that Marjorie and Lily were not unhappy altogether – could not be, because of their sense of consequence, their pride and style.) I could be enraged then at the lack of logic in most adults' talk – the way they held to their pronouncements no matter what evidence might be presented to them. How could these women's hands be so gifted, so delicate and clever – for I knew they would be as good at dozens of other jobs as they were at gutting; they would be good at quilting and darning and painting and papering and kneading dough and setting out seedlings – and their thinking so slapdash, clumsy, infuriating?

Lily said she never let her husband come near her if he had been drinking. Marjorie said since the time she nearly died with a hemorrhage she never let her husband come near her, period. Lily said quickly that it was only when he'd been drinking that he tried anything. I could see that it was a matter of pride not to let your husband come near you, but I couldn't quite believe that 'come near' meant 'have sex'. The idea of Marjorie and Lily being sought out for such purposes seemed grotesque. They had bad teeth, their stomachs sagged, their faces were dull and spotty. I decided to take 'come near' literally.

The two weeks before Christmas was a frantic time at the Turkey Barn. I began to go in for an hour before school as well as after school and on weekends. In the morning, when I walked to work, the street lights would still be on and the morning stars shining. There was the Turkey Barn, on the edge of a white field, with a row of big pine trees behind it, and always, no matter how cold and still it was, these trees were lifting their branches and sighing and straining. It seems unlikely that on my way to the Turkey Barn, for an hour of gutting turkeys, I should have experienced such a sense of promise and at the same time of perfect, impenetrable mystery in the universe, but I did. Herb had something to do with that, and so did the cold snap – the series of hard, clear mornings. The truth is, such feelings weren't hard to come by then. I would get them but not know how they were to be connected with anything in real life.

One morning at the Turkey Barn there was a new gutter. This was a boy eighteen or nineteen years old, a stranger named Brian. It seemed he was a relative, or perhaps just a friend, of Herb Abbott's. He was staying with Herb. He had worked on a lake boat last summer. He said he had got sick of it, though, and quit.

What he said was, 'Yeah, fuckin' boats, I got sick of that.'

Language at the Turkey Barn was coarse and free, but this was one word never heard there. And Brian's use of it seemed not careless but flaunting, mixing insult and provocation. Perhaps it was his general style that made it so. He had amazing good looks: taffy hair, bright-blue eyes, ruddy skin, well-shaped body – the sort of good looks nobody disagrees about for a moment. But a single, relentless notion had got such a hold on him that he could not keep from turning all his assets into parody. His mouth was wet-looking and slightly open most of the time, his eyes were half shut, his expression a hopeful leer, his movements indolent, exaggerated, inviting. Perhaps if he had been put on a stage with a microphone and a guitar and let grunt and howl and wriggle and excite, he would have seemed a true celebrant. Lacking a stage, he was unconvincing. After a while he seemed just like somebody with a bad case of hiccups – his insistent sexuality was that monotonous and meaningless.

If he had toned down a bit, Marjorie and Lily would probably have enjoyed him. They could have kept up a game of telling him to shut his filthy mouth and keep his hands to himself. As it was, they said they were sick of him, and meant it. Once, Marjorie took up her gutting knife. 'Keep your distance,' she said. 'I mean from me and my sister and that kid.'

She did not tell him to keep his distance from Gladys, because Gladys wasn't there at the time and Marjorie would probably not have felt like protecting her anyway. But it was Gladys Brian particularly liked to bother. She would throw down her knife and go into the washroom and stay there ten minutes and come out with a stony face. She didn't say she was sick anymore and go home, the way she used to. Marjorie said Morgan was mad at Gladys for sponging and she couldn't get away with it any longer.

Gladys said to me, 'I can't stand that kind of thing. I can't stand people mentioning that kind of thing and that kind of – gestures. It makes me sick to my stomach.'

I believed her. She was terribly white. But why, in that case, did she not complain to Morgan? Perhaps relations between them were too uneasy, perhaps she could not bring herself to repeat or describe such things. Why did none of us complain – if not to Morgan, at least to Herb? I never thought of it. Brian seemed just something to put up with, like the freezing cold in the gutting shed and the smell of blood and waste. When Marjorie and Lily did threaten to complain, it was about Brian's laziness.

He was not a good gutter. He said his hands were too big. So Herb took him off gutting, told him he was to sweep and clean up, make packages of giblets, and help load the truck. This meant that he did not have to be in any one place or doing any one job at a given time, so much of the time he did nothing. He would start sweeping up, leave that and mop the tables, leave that and have a cigarette, lounge against the table bothering us until Herb called him to help load. Herb was very busy now and spent a lot of time making deliveries, so it was possible he did not know the extent of Brian's idleness.

'I don't know why Herb don't fire you,' Marjorie said. 'I guess the answer is he don't want you hanging around sponging on him, with no place to go.'

'I know where to go,' said Brian.

'Keep your sloppy mouth shut,' said Marjorie. 'I pity Herb. Getting saddled.'

On the last school day before Christmas we got out early in the afternoon. I went home and changed my clothes and came into work at about three o'clock. Nobody was working. Everybody was in the gutting shed, where Morgan Elliott was swinging a cleaver over the gutting table and yelling. I couldn't make out what the yelling was about, and thought someone must have made a terrible mistake in his work; perhaps it had been me. Then I saw Brian on the other side of the table, looking very sulky and mean, and standing well back. The sexual leer was not altogether gone from his face, but it was flattened out and mixed with a look of impotent bad temper and some fear. That's it, I thought; Brian is getting fired for being so sloppy and lazy. Even when I made out Morgan saying 'pervert' and 'filthy' and 'maniac', I still thought that was what was happening. Marjorie and Lily, and even brassy Irene, were standing around with downcast, rather pious looks, such as children get when somebody is suffering a terrible bawling out at school. Only old Henry seemed able to keep a cautious grin on his face. Gladys was not to be seen. Herb was standing closer to Morgan than anybody else. He was not interfering but was keeping an eye on the cleaver. Morgy was blubbering, though he didn't seem to be in any immediate danger.

Morgan was yelling at Brian to get out. 'And out of this town – I mean it – and don't you wait till tomorrow if you still want your arse in one piece! Out!' he shouted, and the cleaver swung dramatically towards the door. Brian started in that direction but, whether he meant to or not, he made a swaggering, taunting motion of the but-tocks. This made Morgan break into a roar and run after him, swinging the cleaver in a stagy way. Brian ran, and Morgan ran after him, and Irene screamed and grabbed her stomach. Morgan was too heavy to run any distance and probably could not have thrown the cleaver very far, either. Herb watched from the doorway. Soon Morgan came back and flung the cleaver down on the table.

'All back to work! No more gawking around here! You don't get paid for gawking! What are you getting under way at?' he said, with a hard look at Irene.

'Nothing,' Irene said meekly.

'If you're getting under way get out of here.'

'I'm not.'

'All right, then!'

We got to work. Herb took off his blood-smeared smock and put on his jacket and went off, probably to see that Brian got ready to go on the suppertime bus. He did not say a word. Morgan and his son went out to the yard, and Irene and Henry went back to the adjoining shed, where they did the plucking, working knee-deep in the feathers Brian was supposed to keep swept up.

'Where's Gladys?' I said softly.

'Recuperating,' said Marjorie. She, too, spoke in a quieter voice than usual, and 'recuperating' was not the sort of word she and Lily normally used. It was a word to be used about Gladys, with a mocking intent.

They didn't want to talk about what had happened, because they were afraid Morgan might come in and catch them at it and fire them. Good workers as they were, they were afraid of that. Besides, they hadn't seen anything. They must have been annoyed that they hadn't. All I ever found out was that Brian had either done something or shown something to Gladys as she came out of the washroom and she had started screaming and having hysterics.

Now she'll likely be laid up with another nervous breakdown, they said. And he'll be on his way out of town. And good riddance, they said, to both of them.

I have a picture of the Turkey Barn crew taken on Christmas Eve. It was taken with a flash camera that was someone's Christmas extravagance. I think it was Irene's. But Herb Abbott must have been the one who took the picture. He was the one who could be trusted to know or to learn immediately how to manage anything new, and flash cameras were fairly new at the time. The picture was taken about ten o'clock on Christmas Eve, after Herb and Morgy had come back from making the last delivery and we had washed off the gutting table and swept and mopped the cement floor. We had taken off our bloody smocks and heavy sweaters and gone into the little room called the lunchroom, where there was a table and a heater. We still wore our working clothes: overalls and shirts. The men wore caps and the women kerchiefs, tied in the wartime style. I am stout and cheerful and comradely in the picture, transformed into someone I don't ever remember being or pretending to be. I look years older than fourteen. Irene is the only one who has taken off her kerchief, freeing her long red hair. She peers out from it with a meek, sluttish, inviting look, which would match her reputation but is not like any look of hers I remember. Yes, it must have been her camera; she is posing for it, with that look, more deliberately than anyone else is. Marjorie and Lily are smiling, true to form, but their smiles are sour and reckless. With their hair hidden, and such figures as they have bundled up, they look like a couple of tough and jovial but testy workmen. Their kerchiefs look misplaced; caps would be better. Henry is in high spirits, glad to be part of the work force, grinning and looking twenty years younger than his age. Then Morgy, with his hangdog look, not trusting the occasion's bounty, and Morgan very flushed and boss-like and satisfied. He has just given each of us our bonus turkey. Each of these turkeys has a leg or a wing missing, or a malformation of some kind, so none of them are salable at the full price. But Morgan has been at pains to tell us that you often get the best meat off the gimpy ones, and he has shown us that he's taking one home himself.

We are all holding mugs or large, thick china cups, which contain not the usual tea but rye whiskey. Morgan and Henry have been drinking since suppertime. Marjorie and Lily say they only want a little, and only take it at all because it's Christmas Eve and they are dead on their feet. Irene says she's dead on her feet as well but that doesn't mean she only wants a little. Herb has poured quite generously not just for her but for Lily and Marjorie, too, and they do not object. He has measured mine and Morgy's out at the same time, very stingily, and poured in Coca-Cola. This is the first drink I have ever had, and as a result I will believe for years that rye-and-Coca-Cola is a standard sort of drink and will always ask for it, until I notice that few other people drink it and that it makes me sick. I didn't get sick that Christmas Eve, though; Herb had not given me enough. Except for an odd taste, and my own feeling of consequence, it was like drinking Coca-Cola.

I don't need Herb in the picture to remember what he looked like. That is, if he looked like himself, as he did all the time at the Turkey Barn and the few times I saw him on the street – as he did all the times in my life when I saw him except one.

The time he looked somewhat unlike himself was when Morgan was cursing out Brian and, later, when Brian had run off down the road. What was this different look? I've tried to remember, because I studied it hard at the time. It wasn't much different. His face looked softer and heavier then, and if you had to describe the expression on it you would have to say it was an expression of shame. But what would he be ashamed of? Ashamed of Brian, for the way he had behaved? Surely that would be late in the day; when had Brian ever behaved otherwise? Ashamed of Morgan, for carrying on so ferociously and theatrically? Or of himself, because he was famous for nipping fights and displays of this sort in the bud and hadn't been able to do it here? Would he be ashamed that he hadn't stood up for Brian? Would he have expected himself to do that, to stand up for Brian?

All this was what I wondered at the time. Later, when I knew more, at least about sex, I decided that Brian was Herb's lover, and that Gladys really was trying to get attention from Herb, and that that was why Brian had humiliated her – with or without Herb's connivance and consent. Isn't it true that people like Herb – dignified, secretive, honorable people – will often choose somebody like Brian, will waste their helpless love on some vicious, silly person who is not even evil, or a monster, but just some importunate nuisance? I decided that Herb, with all his gentleness and carefulness, was avenging himself on us all – not just on Gladys but on us all – with Brian, and that what he was feeling when I studied his face must have been a savage and gleeful scorn. But embarrassment as well – embarrassment for Brian and for himself and for Gladys, and to some degree for all of us. Shame for all of us – that is what I thought then.

Later still, I backed off from this explanation. I got to a stage of backing off from the things I couldn't really know. It's enough for me now just to think of Herb's face with that peculiar, stricken look; to think of Brian monkeying in the shade of Herb's dignity; to think of my own mystified concentration on Herb, my need to catch him out, if I could ever get the chance, and then move in and stay close to him. How attractive, how delectable, the prospect of intimacy is, with the very person who will never grant it. I can still feel the pull of a man like that, of his promising and refusing. I would still like to know things. Never mind facts. Never mind theories, either.

When I finished my drink I wanted to say something to Herb. I stood beside him and waited for a moment when he was not listening to or talking with anyone else and when the increasingly rowdy conversation of the others would cover what I had to say.

'I'm sorry your friend had to go away.'

'That's all right.'

Herb spoke kindly and with amusement, and so shut me off from any further right to look at or speak about his life. He knew what I was up to. He must have known it before, with lots of women. He knew how to deal with it.

Lily had a little more whiskey in her mug and told how she and her best girlfriend (dead now, of liver trouble) had dressed up as men one time and gone into the men's side of the beer parlor, the side where it said 'Men Only', because they wanted to see what it was like. They sat in a corner drinking beer and keeping their eyes and ears open, and nobody looked twice or thought a thing about them, but soon a problem arose.

'Where were we going to go? If we went around to the other side and anybody seen us going into the ladies', they would scream bloody murder. And if we went into the men's somebody'd be sure to notice we didn't do it the right way. Meanwhile the beer was going through us like a bugger!'

'What you don't do when you're young!' Marjorie said.

Several people gave me and Morgy advice. They told us to enjoy ourselves while we could. They told us to stay out of trouble. They said they had all been young once. Herb said we were a good crew and had done a good job but he didn't want to get in bad with any of the women's husbands by keeping them there too late. Marjorie and

Lily expressed indifference to their husbands, but Irene announced that she loved hers and that it was not true that he had been dragged back from Detroit to marry her, no matter what people said. Henry said it was a good life if you didn't weaken. Morgan said he wished us all the most sincere Merry Christmas.

When we came out of the Turkey Barn it was snowing. Lily said it was like a Christmas card, and so it was, with the snow whirling around the street lights in town and around the colored lights people had put up outside their doorways. Morgan was giving Henry and Irene a ride home in the truck, acknowledging age and pregnancy and Christmas. Morgy took a shortcut through the field, and Herb walked off by himself, head down and hands in his pockets, rolling slightly, as if he were on the deck of a lake boat. Marjorie and Lily linked arms with me as if we were old comrades.

'Let's sing,' Lily said. 'What'll we sing?'

' "We Three Kings"?' said Marjorie. ' "We Three Turkey Gutters"?'

' "I'm Dreaming of a White Christmas".'

'Why dream? You got it!'

So we sang.

Lewis Nordan
Sugar Among the Chickens

I had been fishing for an hour and still hadn't caught anything. I was fishing for chickens. Mama wouldn't let me walk to the town pond by myself. What else was I going to fish for?

I looked back over my shoulder through the torn-out screened door and tried to see Mama in there. I said, 'Mama.' I was using the voice that says you're being real good and not fishing for chickens.

Mama said, 'You better not be fishing for chickens, Sugar Mecklin, you going to get switched.' She's got this ability.

She was out in the kitchen, that was good anyway. I put a fresh kernel on my hook and scattered shelled corn on the slick dirt yard below the porch and dusted off my hands on my white blue jeans. A handful of old hens came bobbing and clucking up to the corn and poked at it with their heads and then raised their heads up and looked around, and then started poking at it again.

I dropped the baited hook in amongst them. I wished I could figure out some way to use a cork. The chickens bobbed and pecked and poked and scratched. I moved my baited hook into the middle of the chickens and eased it down onto the ground and waited. I still didn't get a bite.

My daddy didn't much care whether I fished for chickens or not. My daddy knew I never would catch one, never had, never would. It was my mama who was the problem. She said it would ruin your life if you fished for chickens.

I wasn't studying ruining my life right now. I was thinking about hooking and landing some poultry.

I wasn't using a handline, which is easy to hide if your mama comes up on you. I was using a cane pole and a bream hook, little bitty rascal of a hook. I liked a handline all right, I wasn't complaining.

Nothing better for fishing in real tight places, like up under your house on a hot day when the chickens are settled down in the cool dirt and have their neck feathers poked out like a straw hat and a little blue film of an eyelid dropped down over their eyes. A handline is fine for that. A cane pole is better from off your porch, though.

Or I guessed it was. I never had caught a chicken. I had had lots of bites, but I never had landed one, never really even set the hook in one. They're tricky, a chicken. I really wanted to catch one, too. I wanted the hook to snag in the beak, I wanted to feel the tug on the line. I wanted to haul it in, squawking and heavy and beating its wings and sliding on its back and flopping over to its breast and dragging along and the neck stretched out a foot and a half and the stupid old amazed eyes bright as Beau dollars.

I dreamed about it, asleep and awake. Sometimes I let myself believe the chicken I caught was not just any old chicken but maybe some special one, one of the Plymouth Rocks, some fat heavy bird, a Leghorn, or a blue Andalusian. And sometimes, as long as I was making believe, I thought I might catch an even finer specimen, the finest in the whole chicken yard. I thought I caught the red rooster itself.

The red rooster was a chicken as tall as me. It seemed like it, I swear, when I was ten. It was a chicken, I'm telling you, like no chicken you ever saw before. It could fly. There was no half-assed flying about it. It could fly long distance. Daddy said it could migrate if it had anywhere to go. It couldn't do that, but it could fly fifty times farther than any other chicken you ever saw. This was a chicken that one time killed a stray dog.

I dreamed about that rooster. The best dream was when I caught it not on a handline and not on a cane pole. I dreamed I caught it on a limber fine six-and-a-half-foot Zebco rod and spinning reel, like the ones in the Western Auto store in Arrow Catcher. That's the town I used to live right outside of when I was little, in the Delta. The line on that Zebco spool was almost invisible.

I watched the chickens. There was a fine old Plymouth Rock I would just love to catch. She dusted her feathers and took long steps like a kid wearing his daddy's hip boots. I moved the bait over closer to her and held my breath. She started poking around at the corn. She hit the bait once but didn't pick up the hook. My line was taut, so I felt the strike vibrate through the line and down the cane pole to my hands, which I noticed were sweating. I thought, if she hit it once, she just might . . . But she didn't. She stopped eating corn altogether and scratched herself with her foot like a dog.

I tried to listen for my mama. Mama couldn't be expected to stay in the kitchen forever. I needed to say something to her in my I-ain't-fishing-for-chickens voice, but I couldn't. The Plymouth Rock pecked the earth a few times, but not the bait. Then, all of a sudden, she shifted position a little and pecked right down on the corn with the hook in it, the bait. For the second time that day I felt a strike vibrate through my hands. But the chicken missed the hook again and I jerked the bait out of her mouth. She didn't know what happened to it. She looked like, What in the world?

I repositioned the bait, and the hen started pecking around it again. I had to say something to Mama. I held real still and tried to talk in a voice that maybe a chicken couldn't hear. In my head I invented a voice that seemed like it was going to be all throaty and hoarse and animal-like when it came out, but when it did come out, it didn't make any sound at all, not even a whisper, just a little bit of released breath and a wormy movement of my lips. I said, 'Mama, I ain't fishing for chickens.' Nobody heard it, not even me. The Plymouth Rock hit the bait a third time.

It wasn't possible to catch a chicken. I knew that. My daddy had convinced me. He said, 'A chicken is dumb, but not dumb enough.' So I knew it was impossible. But I also knew it had happened. I had the Plymouth Rock.

I jerked my pole skyward and set the hook hard in the chicken's beak.

The sound that rose up out of the chicken's throat was a sound that nobody who has never caught a chicken on a hook has ever heard. It sounded like chicken-all-the-way-back-to-the-beginning-of-chicken.

I was anchored to the porch, with the butt end of the pole dug into my groin for support. The heavy flopping squalling bird was hanging off the end of my line in midair. The sound didn't stop. The sound was like the fire siren in Arrow Catcher. As beautiful and as scary as that. It was like a signal. I thought it signaled danger and adventure and beauty.

I was screaming too, along with the chicken. I didn't even know I was screaming. I heaved on the heavy bird. The pole was bent double. I wanted to land the chicken. I wanted the Plymouth Rock on the porch with me.

I couldn't pick it up high enough. It was too heavy for me. It was up off the ground, all right, but I couldn't get it high enough to sling it onto the porch. The chicken was beating its wings and spinning in a wild circle. I held it there.

I heaved on the pole again. The bird swung up and around, but was still not high enough. It hit the side of the house and then swung back out into midair. Mama came out on the porch and stood behind me. I knew she was back there, because I heard the door slap shut. At first I didn't look back. I just stopped hauling on the chicken. I was still holding it up off the ground, though. I couldn't give it up yet, not all of it, even though I had stopped trying to land it.

Finally I did look back. The face of my mama, I thought, was the saddest face on this earth. It just had to be. I said, 'Hey, Mama,' real subdued, trying not to provoke her. I was still holding the chicken off the ground, and it hadn't stopped making its noise. I said, 'I been fishing for chickens.' No sense lying about it now.

I expected my mama to say 'I swan,' like she always said when she meant 'I swear.' What she really said surprised me. She said she was a big failure in life. She said she was such a big failure in life she didn't see why she didn't just go off and eat some poison.

I eased the chicken down onto the ground. It got loose and scooted off toward the garage with its feathers sticking out.

Mama cut a switch off a crape myrtle and switched me good on my bare legs and went back inside the house. She laid across her bed on the wedding-ring quilt my grandma Sugar gave her when she got married, with hers and Daddy's named sewed in a corner and a heart stitched around the names, and had herself a long hard cry. And so that part of it was over.

Some time passed. Some days and, I guess, some weeks. I watched my mama around the house. At night, after supper and after she had wiped off the table, she would do what she liked best. She would lay out on the table a new piece of cloth from Kamp's Low Price Store and pin to it a tissue-paper Simplicity pattern. She would weight the pattern down all around with pieces of silverware from the dark chest lined with green felt. The silver came from my mama's grandmama who lost her mind and threw away the family Bible and almost everything else and so left only the silverware, which she forgot to throw away. Mama would get the pattern all weighted down, and she would look around for a minute, in her sewing basket or in a kitchen drawer, and say, 'Has anybody seen my good scissors?' She would find the scissors and bring them to the table and cut through the paper and the cloth. She would poke through her sewing basket. I saw the faded pincushion and the cloth measuring tape and a metal thimble and about a jillion buttons and the pinking shears.

She would lay down a towel to keep from scratching the dining-room table and then heft the heavy old portable Kenmore onto it. She might have to thread the bobbin. She might lift the cloth to her nose and breathe its new-smell before she put it into the machine, under the needle, and on the shiny metal plate. She would touch the pedal with her foot.

Before any of this would happen, before supper even, my daddy would come home from work. I could hear the car pull into the drive and head around back of the house. He would get out of the car, and he would be wearing white overalls and a paper cap with the name of a paint store printed on it. He would smell like paint and turpentine and maybe a little whiskey.

Daddy would shoo the chickens back from the gate in the fence where the chickens flocked when they heard his car. He would open the gate and ease inside, real quick, before anybody could get out. I would watch him.

The chickens were gossipy and busy and fat and fine. Daddy would scatter shelled corn from a white metal dishpan, and pour out mash for those that needed it, and run well water into the troughs.

I always wished Mama would watch him do this. I thought that if she did she would stop thinking she was a big failure in life.

I went down the steps and into the chicken yard with him. He let me reach my hand into the fragrant dusty corn and pelt the old birds with it.

Then there was the part where the rooster attacks you. Every day I forgot it was going to happen, and then it would happen and I would think, Now why didn't I remember that?

It happened today, this particular day, I mean, a Tuesday and just before sunset. The rooster was on top of us. It hadn't been there before, and now it was all I could see, the red furious rooster. Its wings were spread out and its bones were creaking and clacking and its beak was wide open and its tongue was blazing black as blood. And the rooster's eye – it looked like it had only one eye, and the eye was not stupid and comical like the other chickens'. It seemed lidless and magical, like it could see into a person's heart and know all his secrets and read his future. And the feet – they were blue colored, but blue like you never saw before except in a wound. And the spurs.

And then it was over. Today, like other days, Daddy kicked the chicken in the breast with the toe of his work shoe and it flopped over on its back. It righted itself and stood up and started pecking at the corn on the ground. Daddy walked over to the rooster and petted its neck. The bird made a stretching motion with its head like a cat.

Then there was the next part. We watched the rooster eat. Without warning, as we knew it would, it stopped eating. It stood straight up and cocked its head so far that the comb flopped over. It looked like somebody who has just remembered something real important.

Then the rooster took off. Any other flying chickens you see are all hustle and puffing and heaving and commotion and getting ten feet maybe, no matter how hard they work at it. This chicken could fly like a wild bird, like a peacock maybe, or a wild turkey. There was nothing graceful about it, nothing pretty. It was just so amazing to watch. When the rooster flew, it looked like some fat bad child who has rung your doorbell and is running down the street away from your house, slow and obvious and ridiculous, but padding on anyway, uncatchable. It flew out and out, over the chicken-yard fence, over a little side yard where Mr Love kept a goat, over the trailer the midgets lived in, out farther like a kite, over a house, and finally into the branches of a line of hardwood trees across the railroad tracks.

We went inside the house then, and Daddy went into the bathroom and came out after a long time with his new smells of Fitch's shampoo and Wildroot and Aqua Velva and his wet combed hair. The whiskey smell was a little stronger, a little sweeter.

After supper, and after the sewing machine was turned off and put away, Mama said, 'Now all I have to do is hem it, and it'll be all done.' She was on the sofa, so she sat up straight and held the dress up to her front and pretended like she was modeling it. Daddy was moving out of the room. He was weaving a little when he walked, on his way to the kitchen.

I looked at Mama. She had a pleased look on her face that made me think she thought she looked pretty. She did look kind of pretty.

I picked up the package the pattern came in. There was a color picture of two women on it. I said, 'Where do these ladies live, Mama?'

She took the package out of my hand and looked at it with the same look on her face. She looked off somewhere away from my eyes and said, 'I think maybe these two ladies live in New York City. They live across the hall from one another in a penthouse apartment. I think they just met up downtown by accident.' She looked at me and smiled and handed the pattern package back to me.

I said, 'What are they talking about?'

Mama said, 'Hm.' She took the package from me again and looked at it, serious. She said, 'I think maybe, well, maybe the lady in the red dress is saying why don't we go somewhere real nice today. She's saying why don't they shop around a little and then maybe go to a picture show. They might even be talking about going to the opera, you don't know.'

I tried to think about the opera, men in turbans and women in white powdered wigs. The men carried sabers at their sides, and the women had Derringers in their purses. I said, 'I ain't studying no opera.'

Mama laid the package down and put the new dress aside too. She started poking through her sewing basket for something, but then stopped without finding it. She had lost the look she had before.

I said, 'Are you going to the opera?'

She said, 'No.'

I said, 'When you put that dress on, you know what?'

She didn't answer.

I said, 'You ain't going to look like neither one of those ladies.' I don't know why I said that.

Mama got up from where she was sitting. She said, 'Don't say *ain't*, Sugar. It will ruin your life.' She got up off the sofa and went into the bedroom and closed the door.

Daddy came back into the living-room. He was wobbly and ripe with whiskey. He said, 'What happened to Mama?'

I said, 'She's laying down.'

He eased back into his chair and started to watch *Gilligan's Island* on the television.

I went to my room. I sat on the bed and let my feet hang off. I had to do something. I felt like I was working a jigsaw puzzle with my family. I saw my mama and my daddy and the chickens and the midgets and Mr Love's goat and I thought I could never get it worked.

I started to fish for the rooster. Sometimes I fished with a handline, sometimes with a cane pole. The rooster never looked at my bait.

I fished every day, and every day I got older and the rooster didn't get caught. School started up again and I got new shoes. The leaves finally fell off the trees and I helped Mama rake them up in the afternoons. The rooster hated my bait. He couldn't stand to look at it.

I changed bait. I used raisins, I used jelly beans. I used a dog turd. You got to want to catch a chicken to bait a hook with dog turd. Chickens eat them all the time, no reason it wouldn't work. It didn't though.

I threw the cat in the chicken yard. I had ten hooks dangling off the cat, feet and tail and flea collar, everywhere you can put a hook on a cat. The rooster killed the cat, but it didn't take a hook. Too bad about the cat, but you're not going to catch a rooster without making a sacrifice or two.

After a while fishing for the rooster and keeping Mama from knowing about it became like a job; like an old habit you never would think about breaking. All that mattered was that I fish for him, that I never give up, no matter how hopeless, no matter how old or unhappy I got.

Something happened then that changed things. It was Saturday. I got on my bike and pedaled from my house to the picture show in Arrow Catcher. There was always a drawing at the matinee.

Mrs Meyers, the old ticket-taker-upper with the white hair and shaky hands and snuff breath – she would do the same thing every time. She would take your ticket out of your hand and tear it into halves and tell you what a fine young man you were growing up to be and to hold onto your ticket stub, you might win the drawing. I walked down the aisle and found me a seat up close to the front. I looked at the torn ticket in my hands, and the other seats filled up with people.

Mr Gibbs owned the picture show, called it the Strand Theater. The lights were all on bright and Mr Gibbs climbed up on the stage by a set of wooden steps around the side. He was huffing and sweating, waving his hands for everybody to be quiet. Like he said every Saturday, he said, 'Be quite, boys and gulls, be quite, please.' We laughed at him, and the underarms of his white shirt were soaked with sweat.

I watched Mr Gibbs crank the handle of a wire basket filled with ping-pong balls. Every ball had a number on it. Mr Gibbs would draw them out, one at a time, and put each one on a little cushioned platform with the number facing out to the audience, until he had four of them. He would draw them out slow and teasing and smiling.

It was something he loved to do, you could tell. He would call out each number in its turn, real loud and exaggerated. He would say, 'Fo-urrr,' or 'Nye-unn,' and he would hold up the white ball and show everyone he wasn't cheating, and then he would put the ball on the cushioned stand. You had to like Mr Gibbs.

Then it started happening. The first number he called out was the first number on my ticket stub. And then so was the second. It seemed impossible that the number in my ear was the same number as in my eye. It kept on being the same number, digit by digit, right down to the end. I had won the drawing.

I had never won anything before. One time I won a pink cake in a cakewalk. It tasted terrible and I hated it, but I ate all of it anyway, same night I won it. I had never won anything except that cake, so it was impressive enough to win the drawing.

But winning was nothing compared to the prize I was going to take home. I had won the Zebco rod and spinning reel from the Western Auto.

Mr Gibbs was standing up on that little stage like a sweaty fat angel. He was giving his heartfelt thanks to the Western Auto store, homeowned and homeoperated by Mr Sooey Leonard, and to all the other fine local merchants of Arrow Catcher who donated these fine prizes and made these drawings possible.

I went up on the stage. I climbed the same dusty wooden steps that Mr Gibbs had climbed. I showed Mr Gibbs my ticket stub. I was trembling. He shook my hand, and my hand was sweaty and slick against his manly palm and fingers. Mr Gibbs asked me if I didn't think every single other person in this fine audience ought to take his patronage to the Western Auto store and all the other fine local merchants of Arrow Catcher.

I said, 'Yessir,' and everybody laughed and clapped their hands.

Mr Gibbs said what was I going to do with my fine prize.

I said, 'Going fishing,' and everybody laughed again. Mr Gibbs said why didn't everybody give this fine young fisherman and all our fine local merchants of Arrow Catcher another round of applause, and so everybody did.

I don't know what was on the movie. I sat through it, and I watched it, with the fishing rod between my legs, but I didn't see it. I remember a huffing train and some wreckage, I remember an icy train platform and taxicabs and a baby growing up rich instead of poor. Barbara Stanwyck married John Lund, I remember that. Whatever was on the movie, one thing was all I was thinking about and that was that I was definitely going fishing, no doubt about it. The fish I was going to catch was as tall as me and had red feathers and was big enough and fine enough to ruin the life of every soul in Arrow Catcher, Mississippi.

I look back at the day I caught the rooster. I see the familiar yard, the fence of chicken wire. I smell the sweet fresh fragrance of grain and mash and lime and chickenshit and water from a deep well poured through troughs of corrugated metal. I smell creosote and the green pungent shucks of black walnuts under the tree. I see the trailer the midgets lived in and the goat next door. I see myself, a boy, holding the Zebco rod I won at the Strand Theater. The Zebco moves back, then whips forward.

The line leaps away from the reel, from the rod's tip. It leaps into Ss and figure eights. It floats like strands of a spider's web. At the end of the line I see the white fleck of sunlight that covers the hook: the bait, the kernel of corn. I watch it fly toward the rooster.

I look ahead of the corn, far down the chicken yard, and see the rooster. It seems to be on fire in the sunlight. For one second I lose my mind and believe that the rooster means something more than a rooster. I don't believe it long. I come to my senses and know that the rooster is a chicken, that's all. A very bad chicken. He is the same miserable wretched mean bad son-of-a-bitch that my daddy has called him every day of the rooster's life. I remember that the rooster is smarter than me, and faster and stronger and crazier. I remember that I am in the chicken yard with him and that he doesn't like me and that my daddy ain't home from work to protect me and my ass is in trouble, Jack.

I understand, at last, what the rooster is going to do. He is going to catch the bait in the air, like a dog catching a Frisbee. I can't believe what I am watching. The rooster has positioned itself, flat-footed, with its mouth open, its head cocked to one side. Until this moment I have not believed I would ever catch the rooster. I have meant to catch it, but the habit of fishing for it is all I have thought about for a long time. And now, in the presence of an emotion something like awe, I understand that the rooster is about to catch me.

It happens. The rooster, at the last moment, has to lurch a step forward, it has to duck its head, but it does so with perfect accuracy.

The bird might as well have been a large red-feathered frog plucking a fly from the air. He catches the baited hook in his mouth.

I do not move to set the hook. There is no point. The rooster has been fishing for me for three years, and now it has caught me. I have become old enough to catch. At eleven I am old enough to believe that doom will always surprise you, that doom is domestic and purrs like a cat.

The bird stands quiet with the bait in its mouth. The line droops to the ground from his chicken lips. I stand attached to him by the line. It is no help to remember that the rooster is a beast and without humor.

Then it does move. At first I thought the creature was growing taller. Nothing could have surprised me. I might have been growing smaller. Neither was true. I was watching what I had watched many times. I was watching the rooster take flight.

It left the ground. The hook was still in its mouth, attached to nothing. The rooster was holding the hook in its mouth like a peanut. More than ever the bird seemed on fire. It flew out and out, away from me. The nylon line trailed it in flight. The sun shone on the rooster and on the line and told me that I was in big trouble and had not yet figured out how.

It flew over the chicken-yard fence, over the goat, over the midgets. It gained altitude. I watched the line be stripped in coils from my open-faced reel. The bird flew and flew, high as the housetops, and then the treetops, out toward the railroad tracks. I was a child flying a living kite.

It took me a minute to see what the rooster was up to. I had never seen him do this before. Just when he was almost out of sight, out over the railroad tracks and ready, I thought, to light in the hardwood trees, the bird seemed to hang suspended. It seemed to have hung itself in midair and to have begun to swell out like a balloon. I was holding the fishing rod limp in my hand and studying the rooster's strange inflation. The rooster, above the treetops, ballooned larger and larger. It grew large enough that I could distinguish its particular features again, the stretched neck and popped-out eyes, the sturdy wings and red belly feathers. Nothing about the appearance of the rooster made sense.

And then everything did. I was not looking at the bird's tailfeathers, as I should have been. I was looking him in the face. He was not growing larger, he was coming closer. I looked at my reel and saw that the line was still. The rooster had turned around in flight and was coming back after me.

I looked at him. The rooster had cleared the goat and the midgets. It was big as a goose, big as a collie. Its feet were blue and as big as yard rakes. I dropped the fishing rod into the dirt. I turned to the gate and tried to open the latch. I could hear the rooster's bones creaking and clacking. I could hear the feathers thudding against the air. My hands were clubs, the gate would not come unlatched. I pounded at the gate.

I heard the rooster set its wings like a hawk about to land on a fence post. The rooster landed on my head. It didn't fall off. I thought it might, but it did not. It clung tight to my scalp by its fierce toenails. I clubbed at the gate with my useless hands. The bird stood on my head, and its wings kept up their motion and clatter. I could not appreciate the mauling I was receiving by the wings for the fire the feet had lit in my brain. I tried to climb the gate, but my feet had turned to stumps.

The chicken yard was in hysterics, the Plymouth Rocks and Leghorns and blue Andalusians. I clung to the gate with the rooster on my head. I imagined flames the shape of an angry chicken rising from my head.

I screamed, and still the rooster held on. It drubbed me with its wings. My eyes were blackened and swollen, my nose ran with blood. I didn't care, so long as someone put out the fire in my scalp.

I got the idea that it could be put out with water. I gave up at the gate and ran stumbling across the chicken yard. Layers and pullets and bantams, all the curious and hysterical, fanned away from me in droves. The rooster hung on.

I reached the hydrant hopeless. There was no hope of putting my head under the spigot while wearing the chicken. There was a garden hose in the old garage, but it was of no use. If I could not open the simple latch of the gate, there was no chance I could retrieve the garden hose from its wall hook and screw it to the spigot.

My mama was standing on the back porch watching. I longed for the days when I was young enough to be switched with crape myrtle. I saw her start to move toward me. She was moving toward me but I knew she would never reach me in time. Blood and chickenshit ran down the sides of my face and into my ears. The wings kept up the pounding, and the rooster's bones and ligaments kept up the creaking and clacking and clicking.

I had not noticed my daddy drive up but now I saw his car in the driveway. He left the car and was headed toward me. He also moved in slow motion.

I left the spigot. My motion and my parents' motion had become the same. They stood at the gate and pounded at it. Their hands were clubs too and the gate would not open for them. I motioned for them to stay where they were. They saw that I knew what I was doing. Something had changed in me. I was not running now. The rooster was still riding my head. I walked, purposeful, like a heavy bear through the chicken yard.

And yet my steps were not heavy. My life was not ruined. I could wear this chicken on my head forever. I could bear this pain forever. In a year no one would notice the chicken but myself. Then even I would not notice. My mama had believed that spending your life in the place of your birth, absorbing its small particulars into your blood, was ruination. I looked at my parents beside the gate. My daddy held my mama in his arms as they stood at the edge of the chicken yard and looked at me. My daddy had gotten the gate open now but again I held up my hand and stopped him. I knew now what I could give them. It was a picture of myself that I would live the rest of my life to prove true: they watched their son wear this living crowing rooster like a crown.

They were proud of me. I knew that they were. They were frightened also but pride was mainly what I saw in their faces as I kept them from helping me. They believed my life would not be ruined. They believed that a man who has worn a chicken on his head – worn it proudly, as I was beginning to do – would never be a fool to geography or marriage or alcohol.

I stood tall in the chicken yard. My parents looked at me from the gate and I felt their love and pride touch me. They believed that a man and his wife with such a son could not be ruined either, not yet, not forever. The rooster had stopped flapping its wings. It was heavy on me, but I straightened my back and did not slump. Now it balanced itself with more ease, it carried more of its own weight and was easier to hold. It stood on my head like an eagle on a mountain crag. I strode toward my parents and they toward me. The three of us, and the rooster, moved through the chicken yard in glory.

Edna O'Brien
My Mother's Mother

I loved my mother, yet I was glad when the time came to go to her mother's house each summer. It was a little house in the mountains and it commanded a fine view of the valley and the great lake below. From the front door, glimpsed through a pair of very old binoculars, one could see the entire Shannon Lake studded with various islands. On a summer's day this was a thrill. I would be put standing on a kitchen chair, while someone held the binoculars, and sometimes I marvelled though I could not see at all, as the lenses had not been focused properly. The sunshine made everything better, and though we were not down by the lake, we imagined dipping our feet in it, or seeing people in boats fishing and then stopping to have a picnic. We imagined lake water lapping.

I felt safer in that house. It was different from our house, not so imposing, a cottage really, with no indoor water and no water closet. We went for buckets of water to the well, a different well each summer. These were a source of miracle to me, these deep cold wells, sunk into the ground, in a kitchen garden, or a paddock, or even a long distance away, wells that had been divined since I was last there. There was always a tin scoop nearby so that one could fill the bucket to the very brim. Then of course the full bucket was an occasion of trepidation, because one was supposed not to spill. One often brought the bucket to the very threshold of the kitchen and then out of excitement or clumsiness some water would get splashed onto the concrete floor and there would be admonishments, but it was not like the admonishments in our own house, it was not calamitous.

My grandfather was old and thin and hoary when I first saw him. His skin was the colour of a clay pipe. After the market day he would come home in the pony and trap drunk, and then as soon as he stepped out of the trap he would stagger and fall into a drain or whatever. Then he would roar for help, and his grandson, who was in his twenties, would pick him up, or rather, drag him along the ground and through the house and up the stairs to his feather bed, where he moaned and groaned. The bedroom was above the kitchen, and in the night we would be below, around the fire, eating warm soda bread and drinking cocoa. There was nothing like it. The fresh bread would only be an hour out of the pot and cut in thick pieces and dolloped with butter and greengage jam. The greengage jam was a present from the postmistress, who gave it in return for the grazing of a bullock. She gave marmalade at a different time of year and a barmbrack at Hallowe'en. He moaned upstairs, but no one was frightened of him, not even his own wife, who chewed and chewed and said, 'Bad cess to them that give him the drink.' She meant the publicans. She was a minute woman with a minute face and her thin hair was pinned up tightly. Her little face, though old, was like a bud, and when she was young she had been beautiful. There was a photo of her to prove it.

Sitting with them at night I thought that maybe I would not go home at all. Maybe I would never again lie in bed next to my mother, the two of us shivering with expectancy and with terror. Maybe I would forsake my mother.

'Maybe you'll stay here,' my aunt said, as if she had guessed my thoughts.

'I couldn't do that,' I said, not knowing why I declined, because indeed the place had definite advantages. I stayed up as late as they did. I ate soda bread and jam to my heart's content, I rambled around the fields all day, admiring sally trees, elder bushes, and the fluttering flowers, I played 'shop' or I played teaching in the little dark plantation, and no one interfered or told me to stop doing it. The plantation was where I played secrets, and always I knew the grownups were within shouting distance, if a stranger or a tinker should surprise me there. It was pitch dark and full of young fir trees. The ground was a carpet of bronzed fallen fir needles. I used to kneel on them for punishment, after the playing.

Then when that ritual was done I went into the flower garden, which being full of begonias and lupins was a mass of bright brilliant colors. Each area had its own colour, as my aunt planned it that way. I can see them now, those bright reds, like nail varnish, and those yellows like the gauze of a summer dress and those pale blues like old people's eyes, with the bees and the wasps luxuriating in each petal, or each little bell, or each flute, and feel the warmth of the place, and the drone of the bees, and see again tea towels and gray flannelette drawers that were spread out on the hedge to dry. The sun garden, they called it. My aunt got the seeds and just sprinkled them around, causing marvellous blooms to spring up. They even had tulips, whereas at home we had only a diseased rambling rose on a silvered arch and two clumps of devil's pokers. Our garden was sad and windy, the wind had made holes and indentations in the hedges, and the dogs had made further holes where they slept and burrowed. Our house was larger, and there was better linoleum on the floor, there were brass rods on the stairs, and there was a flush lavatory, but it did not have the same cheeriness and it was imbued with doom.

Still, I knew that I would not stay in my grandmother's for ever. I knew it for certain when I got into bed and then desperately missed my mother, and missed the little whispering we did, and the chocolate we ate, and I missed the smell of our kind of bedclothes. Theirs were grey flannel, which tickled the skin, as did the loose feathers, and their pointed ends kept irking one. There was a gaudy red quilt that I thought would come to life and turn into a sinister Santa Claus. Except that they had told me that there was no Santa Claus. My aunt told me that, she insisted.

There was my aunt and her two sons, Donal and Joe, and my grandmother and grandfather. My aunt and Joe would tease me each night, say that there was no Santa Claus, until I got up and stamped the floor, and in contradicting them welled up with tears, and then at last, when I was on the point of breaking down, they would say that there was. Then one night they went too far. They said that my mother was not my real mother. My real mother, they said, was in Australia and I was adopted. I could not be told that word. I began to hit the wall and screech, and the more they insisted, the more obstreperous I became. My aunt went into the parlour in search of a box of snaps to find a photo of my real mother and came out triumphant at having found it. She showed me a woman in knicker bockers with a big floppy hat. I could have thrown it in the fire so violent was I. They watched for each new moment of panic and furious disbelief, and then they got the wind up when they saw I was getting out of control. I began to shake like the weather conductor on the chapel chimney and my teeth chattered, and before long I was just this shaking creature, unable to let out any sound, and seeing the room's contents swim away from me, I felt their alarm almost as I felt my own. My aunt took hold of my wrist to feel my pulse, and my grandmother held a spoonful of tonic to my lips, but I spilled it. It was called Parishes Food and was the colour of cooked beetroot. My eyes were haywire. My aunt put a big towel around me and sat me on her knee, and as the terror lessened, my tears began to flow and I cried so much that they thought I would choke because of the tears going back down the throat. They said I must never tell anyone and I must never tell my mother.

'She is my mother,' I said, and they said, 'Yes, darling,' but I knew that they were appalled at what had happened.

That night I fell out of bed twice, and my aunt had to put chairs next to it to keep me in. She slept in the same room, and often I used to hear her crying for her dead husband and begging to be reunited with him in heaven. She used to talk to him and say, 'Is that you, Michael, is that you?' I often heard her arms striking against the headboard, or heavy movements when she got up to relieve herself. In the daytime we used the fields, but at night we did not go out for fear of ghosts. There was a gutter in the back kitchen that served as a channel, and twice a week she put disinfectant in it. The crux in the daytime was finding a private place and not being found or spied on by anyone. It entailed much walking and then much hesitating so as not to be seen.

The morning after the fright, they pampered me, scrambled me an egg, and sprinkled nutmeg over it. Then along with that my aunt announced a surprise. Our workman had sent word by the mail-car man that he was coming to see me on Sunday and the postman had delivered the message. Oh, what a glut of happiness. Our workman was called Carnero and I loved him too. I loved his rotting teeth and his curly hair and his strong hands and his big stomach, which people referred to as his 'corporation'. He was nicknamed Carnero after a boxer. I knew that when he came he would have bars of chocolate, and maybe a letter or a silk hanky from my mother, and that he would lift me up in his arms and swing me around and say 'Sugarbush'. How many hours were there until Sunday, I asked.

Yet that day, which was Friday, did not pass without event. We had a visitor – a man. I will never know why but my grandfather called him Tim, whereas his real name was Pat, but my grandfather was not to be told that. Tim, it seems, had died and my grandfather was not to know, because if any of the locals died, it brought his own death to his mind and he dreaded death as strenuously as did all the others. Death was some weird journey that you made alone and unbefriended, once you had embarked on it. When my aunt's husband had died, in fact had been shot by the Black and Tans, my aunt had to conceal the death from her own parents, so irrational were they about the subject. She had to stay up at home the evening her husband's remains were brought to the chapel, and when the chapel bell rang out intermittently, as it does for a death, and they asked who it was, again and again, my poor aunt had to conceal her own grief, be silent about her own tragedy, and pretend that she did not know. Next day she went to the funeral on the excuse that it was some forester whom her husband knew. Her husband was supposed to be transferred to a barracks a long way off, and meanwhile she was going to live with her parents and bring her infant sons until her husband found accommodation. She invented a name for the district where her husband was supposed to be, it was in the North of Ireland, and she invented letters that she had received from him, and the news of the Troubles up there. Eventually, I expect, she told them, and I expect they collapsed and broke down. In fact, the man who brought these imaginary letters would have been Tim, since he had been the postman, and it was of his death my grandfather must not be told. So there in the porch, in a worn suit, was a man called Pat answering to the name of Tim, and the news that a Tim would have, such as how were his family and what crops had he put in and what cattle fairs had he been to. I thought that it was peculiar that he could answer for another, but I expect that everyone's life story was identical.

Sunday after Mass I was down by the little green gate skipping and waiting for Carnero. As often happens, the visitor arrives just when we look away. The cuckoo called, and though I knew I would not see her, I looked in a tree where there was a ravaged bird's nest, and at that moment heard Carnero's whistle. I ran down the road, and at once he hefted me up onto the crossbar of his bicycle.

'Oh, Carnero,' I cried. There was both joy and sadness in our reunion. He had brought me a bag of tinned sweets, and the most glamorous present – as we got off the bicycle near the little gate he put it on me. It was a toy watch – a most beautiful red, and each bit of the bracelet was the shape and colour of a raspberry. It had hands, and though they did not move, that did not matter. One could pull the bracelet part by its elastic thread and cause it to snap in or out. The hands were black and curved like an eyelash. He would not say where he had got it. I had only one craving, to stay down there by the gate with him and admire the watch and talk about home. I could not talk to him in front of them because a child was not supposed to talk or have any wants. He was puffing from having cycled uphill and began to open his tie, and taking it off, he said, 'This bloody thing.' I wondered who he had put it on for. He was in his Sunday suit and had a fishing feather in his hat.

'Oh, Carnero, turn the bike around and bring me home with you.'

Such were my unuttered and unutterable hopes. Later my grandfather teased me and said was it in his backside I saw Carnero's looks, and I said no, in every particle of him.

That night as we were saying the Rosary my grandfather let out a shout, slouched forward, knocking the wooden chair and hitting himself on the rungs of it, then falling on the cement floor. He died delirious. He died calling on his Maker. It was ghastly. Joe was out and only my grandmother and aunt were there to assist. They picked him up. His skin was purple, the exact colour of the iron tonic, and his eyes rolled so that they were seeing every bit of the room, from the ceiling, to the whitewashed wall, to the cement floor, to the settle bed, to the cans of milk, seeing and bulging. He writhed like an animal and then let out a most beseeching howl, and that was it. At that moment my aunt remembered I was there and told me to go into the parlour and wait. It was worse in there, pitch dark, and I in a place where I did not know my footing or my way around. I'd only been in there once, to fetch a teapot and a sugar tongs when Tim came. Had it been in our own house I would have known what to cling to, the back of a chair, the tassel of a blind, the girth of a plaster statue, but in there I held on to nothing and thought how the thing he dreaded had come to pass and now he was finding out those dire things that all his life his mind had shirked from.

'May he rest in peace, may the souls of the faithful departed rest in peace.'

It was that for two days, along with litanies and mourners smoking clay pipes, plates being passed around and glasses filled. My mother and father were there, among the mourners. I was praised for growing, as if it were something I myself had caused to happen. My mother looked older in black, and I wished she had worn a georgette scarf, something to give her a bit of brightness around the throat. She did not like when I said that, and sent me off to say the Confiteor and three Hail Marys. Her eyes were dry. She did not love her own father. Neither did I. Her sister and she would go down into the far room and discuss whether to bring out another bottle of whiskey or another porter cake, or whether it was time to offer the jelly. They were reluctant, the reason being that some provisions had to be held over for the next day, when the special mourners would come up after the funeral. Whereas that night half the parish was there. My grandfather was laid out upstairs in a brown habit. He had stubble on his chin and looked like a frosted plank lying there, grey-white and inanimate. As soon as they had paid their respects, the people hurried down to the kitchen and the parlour, for the eats and the chat. No one wanted to be with the dead man, not even his wife, who had gone a bit funny and was asking my aunt annoying questions about the food and the fire, and how many priests were going to serve at the High Mass.

'Leave that to us,' my mother would say, and then my grandmother would retell the world what a palace my mother's house was, and how it was the nicest house in the countryside, and my mother would say 'Shhhh,' as if she were being disgraced. My father said, 'Well, missy,' to me twice, and a strange man gave me sixpence. It was a very thin, worn sixpence and I thought it would disappear. I called him Father, out of reverence, because he looked like a priest, but he was in fact a boatman.

The funeral was on an island on the Shannon. Most of the people stayed on the quay, but we, the family, piled into two row-boats and followed the boat that carried the coffin. It was a jolty ride, with big waves coming in over us and our feet getting drenched. The island itself was full of cows. The sudden arrivals made them bawl and race about, and I thought it was quite improper to see that happening while the remains were being lowered and buried. It was totally desolate, and though my aunt sniffled a bit, and my grandmother let out ejaculations, there was no real grief, and that was the saddest thing.

Next day they burned his working clothes and threw his muddy boots on the manure heap. Then my aunt sewed black diamonds of cloth on her clothes, on my grandmother's, and on Joe's. She wrote a long letter to her son in England, and enclosed black diamonds of cloth for him to stitch onto his effects. He worked in Liverpool in a motorcar factory. Whenever they said Liverpool, I thought of a whole mound of bloodied liver, but then I would look down at my watch and be happy again and pretend to tell the time. The house was gloomy. I went off with Joe, who was mowing hay, and sat with him on the mowing machine and fell slightly in love. Indoors was worst, what with my grandmother sighing and recalling old times, such as when her husband tried to kill her with a carving knife, and then she would snivel and miss him and say, 'The poor old creature, he wasn't prepared . . .'

Out in the fields Joe fondled my knee and asked was I ticklish. He had a lovely long face and a beautiful whistle. He was probably about twenty-four, but he seemed old, especially because of a slouchy hat and because of a pair of trousers that were several times too big for him. When the mare passed water he nudged me and said, 'Want lemonade?' and when she broke wind he made disgraceful plopping sounds with his lips. He and I ate lunch on the headland and lolled for a bit. We had bread and butter, milk from a flask, and some ginger cake that was left over from the funeral. It had gone damp. He sang, 'You'll be lonely, little sweetheart, in the spring,' and smiled a lot at me, and I felt very privileged. I knew that all he would do was tickle my knees, and the backs of my knees, because at heart he was shy and not like some of the local men who would want to throw you to the ground and press themselves over you so that you would have to ask God for protection. When he lifted me onto the machine, he said that we would bring out a nice little cushion on the morrow so that I would have a soft seat. But on the morrow it rained and he went off to the sawmill to get shelving, and my aunt moaned about the hay getting wet and perhaps getting ruined and possibly there being no fodder for cattle next winter.

That day I got into dire disaster. I was out in the fields playing, talking, and enjoying the rainbows in the puddles, when all of a sudden I decided to run helter-skelter towards the house in case they were cross with me. Coming through a stile that led to the yard, I decided to do a big jump and landed head over heels in the manure heap. I fell so heavily onto it that every bit of clothing got wet and smeared. It was a very massive manure heap, and very squelchy. Each day the cow house was cleaned out and the contents shovelled there, and each week the straw and old nesting from the hen house were dumped there, and so was the pigs' bedding. So it was not like falling into a sack of hay. It was not dry and clean. It was a foul spot I fell into, and as soon as I waded out, I decided it was wise to undress.

The pleated skirt was ruined and so was my blouse and my navy cardigan. Damp had gone through to my bodice, and the smell was dreadful. I was trying to wash it off under an outside tap, using a fist of grass as a cloth, when my aunt came out and exclaimed, 'Jesus, Mary and Joseph, glory be to the great God today and tonight, but what have you done to yourself!' I was afraid to tell her that I fell, so I said I was doing washing and she said in the name of God what washing, and then she saw the ruin on the garments. She picked up the skirt and said why on earth had she let me wear it that day, and wasn't it the demon that came with me the day I arrived with my attaché case. I was still trying to wash and not answer this barrage of questions, all beginning with the word 'why'. As if I knew why! She got a rag and some pumice stone, plus a can of water, and stripped to the skin, I was washed and reprimanded. Then my clothes were put to soak in the can, all except for the skirt, which had to be brought in to dry, and then cleaned with a clothes brush. Mercifully my grandmother was not told.

My aunt forgave me two nights later when she was in the dairy churning and singing. I asked if I could turn the churn handle for a jiff. It was changing from liquid to solid and the handle was becoming stiff. I tried with all my might, but I was not strong enough.

'You will, when you're big,' she said, and sang to me. She sang 'Far Away in Australia' and then asked what I would like to do when I grew up. I said I would like to marry Carnero, and she laughed and said what a lovely thing it was to be young and carefree. She let me look into the churn to see the mound of yellow butter that had formed. There were drops of water all over its surface, it was like some big bulk that had bathed but had not dried off. She got two sets of wooden pats, and together we began to fashion the butter into dainty shapes. She was quicker at it than I. She made little round balls of butter with prickly surfaces, then she said wouldn't it be lovely if the curate came up for tea. He was a new curate and had rimless spectacles.

The next day she went to the town to sell the butter and I was left to mind the house along with my grandmother. My aunt had promised to bring back a shop cake, and said that, depending on the price, it would be either a sponge cake or an Oxford Lunch, which was a type of fruit cake wrapped in beautiful dun silverish paper. My grandmother donned a big straw hat with a chin strap and looked very distracted. She kept thinking that there was a car or a cart coming into the back yard and had me looking out windows on the alert. Then she got a flush and I had to conduct her into the plantation and sit on the bench next to her, and we were scarcely there when three huge fellows walked in and we knew at once that they were tinkers. The fear is indescribable. I knew that tinkers took one off in their cart, hid one under shawls, and did dire things to one. I knew that they beat their wives and children, got drunk, had fights among themselves, and spent many a night cooling off in the barracks. I jumped up as they came through the gate. My grandmother's mouth fell wide open with shock. One of them carried a shears and another had a weighing pan in his hand. They asked if we had any sheep's wool and we both said no, no sheep, only cattle. They had evil eyes and gamey looks. There was no knowing what they would do to us. Then they asked if we had any feathers for pillows or mattresses. She was so crazed with fear that she said yes and led the way to the house. As we walked along, I expected a strong hand to be clamped on my shoulder. They were dreadfully silent. Only one had spoken and he had a shocking accent, what my mother would call 'a gurrier's'. She sent me upstairs to get the two bags of feathers out of the wardrobe, and I knew that she stayed below so that they would not steal a cake or bread or crockery or any other things. She was agreeing on a price when I came down, or rather, requesting a price. The talking member said it was a barter job. We would get a lace cloth in return. She asked how big this cloth was, and he said very big, while his companion put his hand into the bag of feathers to make sure that there was not anything else in there, that we were not trying to fob them off with grass or sawdust or something. She asked where was the cloth. They laughed. They said it was down in the caravan, at the crossroads, ma'am. She knew then she was being cheated, but she tried to stand her ground. She grabbed one end of the bag and said, 'You'll not have these.'

'D'you think we're mugs?' one of them said, and gestured to the others to pick up the two bags, which they did. Then they looked at us as if they might mutilate us, and I prayed to St Jude and St Anthony to keep us from harm. Before going, they insisted on being given new milk. They drank in great slugs.

'Are you afraid of me?' one of the men said to her.

He was the tallest of the three and his shirt was open. I could see the hair on his chest, and he had a very funny look in his eyes as if he was not thinking, as if thinking was beyond him. His eyes had a thickness in them. For some reason he reminded me of meat.

'Why should I be afraid of you?' she said, and I was so proud of her I would have clapped, but for the tight shave we were in.

She blessed herself several times when they'd gone and decided that what we did had been the practical thing to do, and in fact our only recourse. But when my aunt came back and began an intensive cross-examination, the main contention was how they learned in the first place that there were feathers in the house. My aunt reasoned that they could not have known unless they had been told, they were not fortune-tellers. Each time I was asked, I would seal my lips, as I did not want to betray my grandmother. Each time she was asked, she described them in detail, the holes in their clothes, the safety pins instead of buttons, their villainous looks, and then she mentioned the child, me, and hinted about the things they might have done and was it not the blessing of God that we had got rid of them peaceably! My aunt's son joked about the lace cloth for weeks. He used to affect to admire it, by picking up one end of the black oilcloth on the table and saying, 'Is it Brussels lace or is it Carrickmackross?'

Sunday came and my mother was expected to visit. My aunt had washed me the night before in an aluminium pan. I had to sit in it, and was terrified lest my cousin should peep in. He was in the back kitchen shaving and whistling. It was a question of a 'Saturday splash for Sunday's dash.' My aunt poured a can of water over my head and down my back. It was scalding hot. Then she poured rainwater over me and by contrast it was freezing. She was not a thorough washer like my mother, but all the time she kept saying that I would be like a new pin.

My mother was not expected until the afternoon. We had washed up the dinner things and given the dogs the potato skins and milk when I started in earnest to look out for her. I went to the gate where I had waited for Carnero, and seeing no sign of her, I sauntered off down the road. I was at the crossroads when I realized how dangerous it was, as I was approaching the spot where the tinkers said their caravan was pitched. So it was back at full speed. The fuchsia was out and so were the elderberries. The fuchsia was like dangling earrings and the riper elderberries were in maroon smudges on the road. I waited in hiding, the better to surprise her. She never came. It was five, and then half past five, and then it was six. I would go back to the kitchen and lift the clock that was face down on the dresser, and then hurry out to my watch post. By seven it was certain that she would not come, although I still held out hope. They hated to see me sniffle, and even hated more when I refused a slice of cake. I could not bear to eat. Might she still come? They said there was no point in my being so spoiled. I was imprisoned at the kitchen table in front of this slice of seed cake. In my mind I lifted the gate hasp a thousand times and saw my mother pass by the kitchen window, as fleeting as a ghost; and by the time we all knelt down to say the Rosary, my imagination had run amuck. I conceived of the worst things, such as she had died, or that my father had killed her, or that she had met a man and eloped. All three were unbearable. In bed I sobbed and chewed on the blanket so as not to be heard, and between tears and with my aunt enjoining me to dry up, I hatched a plan.

On the morrow there was no word or no letter, so I decided to run away. I packed a little satchel with bread, my comb and, daftly, a spare pair of ankle socks. I told my aunt that I was going on a picnic and affected to be very happy by humming and doing little reels. It was a dry day and the dust rose in whirls under my feet. The dogs followed and I had immense trouble getting them to go back. There were no tinkers' caravans at the crossroads and because of that I was jubilant. I walked and then ran, and then I would have to slow down, and always when I slowed down, I looked back in case someone was following me. While I was running I felt I could elude them, but there was no eluding the loose stones and the bits of rock that were wedged into the dirt road. Twice I tripped. If, coming towards me, I saw two people together, I then felt safe, but if I saw one person it boded ill, as that one person could be mad, or drunk, or likely to accost. On three occasions I had to climb into a field and hide until that one ominous person went by. Fortunately, it was a quiet road, as not many souls lived in that region.

When I came off the dirt road on to the main road, I felt safer, and very soon a man came by in a pony and trap and offered me a lift. He looked a harmless enough person, in a frieze coat and a cloth cap. When I stepped into the trap I was surprised to find two hens clucking and agitating under a seat.

'Would you be one of the Linihans?' he asked, referring to my grandmother's family.

I said no and gave an assumed name. He plied me with questions. To get the most out of me, he even got the pony to slow down, so as to lengthen the journey. We dawdled. The seat of black leather was held down with black buttons. He had a tartan rug over him. He spread it out over us both. Quickly I edged out from under it, complaining about fleas and midges, neither of which there were. It was a desperately lonely road with only a house here and there, a graveyard, and sometimes an orchard. The apples looked tempting on the trees. To see each ripening apple was to see a miracle. He asked if I believed in ghosts and told me that he had seen the riderless horse on the moors.

'If you're a Minnogue,' he said, 'you should be getting out here,' and he pulled on the reins.

I had called myself a Minnogue because I knew a girl of that name who lived with her mother and was separated from her father. I would like to have been her.

'I'm passing your gate,' he said, and I was terrified that I would have to ask him up, as my mother dreaded strangers, even dreaded visitors, since these diversions usually gave my father the inclination to drink, and once he drank he was on a drinking bout that would last for weeks, and that was notorious. Therefore I had to conjure up another lie. It was that my parents were both staying with my grandmother and that I had been dispatched home to get a change of clothing for us all. He grumbled at not coming up to our house, but I jumped out of the trap and said we would ask him to a card party for sure, in December.

There was no one at home. The door was locked and the big key in its customary place under the pantry window. The kitchen bore signs of my mother having gone out in a hurry, as the dishes were on the table, and on the table, too, were her powder puff, a near-empty powder box, and a holder of papier-mâché in which her toiletries were kept. Had she gone to the city? My heart was wild with envy. Why had she gone without me? I called upstairs, and then hearing no reply, I went up with a mind that was buzzing with fear, rage, suspicion and envy. The beds were made. The rooms seemed vast and awesome compared with the little crammed rooms of my grandmother's. I heard someone in the kitchen and hurried down with renewed palpitations. It was my mother. She had been to the shop and got some chocolate. It was rationed because of its being wartime, but she used to coax the shopkeeper to give her some. He was a bachelor. He liked her. Maybe that was why she had put powder on.

'Who brought you home, my lady?' she said stiffly.

She hadn't come on Sunday. I blurted that out. She said did anyone ever hear such nonsense. She said did I not know that I was to stay there until the end of August till school began. She was even more irate when she heard that I had run away. What would they now be thinking but that I was in a bog hole or something. She said had I no consideration and how in heaven's name was she going to get word to them, an SOS.

'Where's my father?' I asked.

'Saving hay,' she said.

I gathered the cups off the table so as to make myself useful in her eyes. Seeing the state of my canvas shoes and the marks on the ankle socks, she asked had I come through a river or what. All I wanted to know was why she had not come on Sunday as promised. The bicycle got punctured, she said, and then asked did I think that with bunions, corns and welts she could walk six miles after doing a day's work. All I thought was that the homecoming was not nearly as tender as I hoped it would be, and there was no embrace and no reunion. She filled the kettle and I laid clean cups. I tried to be civil, to contain the pique and misery that was welling up in me. I told her how many trams of hay they had made in her mother's house, and she said it was a sight more than we had done. She hauled some scones from a colander in the cupboard and told me I had better eat. She did not heat them on the top of the oven, and that meant she was still vexed. I knew that before nightfall she would melt, but where is the use of a thing that comes too late?

I sat at the far end of the table watching the lines on her brow, watching the puckering, as she wrote a letter to my aunt explaining that I had come home. I would have to give it to the mail-car man the following morning and ask the postman to deliver it by hand. She said, God only knows what commotion there would be all that day and into the night looking for me. The ink in her pen gave out, and I held the near-empty ink bottle sideways while she refilled it.

'Go back to your place,' she said, and I went back to the far end of the table like someone glued to her post. I thought of fields around my grandmother's house and the various smooth stones that I had put on the windowsill, I thought of the sun garden, of the night my grandfather had died and my vigil in the cold parlour. I thought of many things. Sitting there, I wanted both to be in our house and to be back in my grandmother's missing my mother. It was as if I could taste my pain better away from her, the excruciating pain that told me how much I loved her. I thought how much I needed to be without her so that I could think of her, dwell on her, and fashion her into the perfect person that she clearly was not. I resolved that for certain I would grow up and one day go away. It was a sweet thought, and it was packed with punishment.

Ben Okri

A Bizarre Courtship

One morning, more golden than yellow, I went outside to our
housefront and saw that the beggars had gone. I scoured the street
and asked everyone I met. I went to Madame Koto's bar-front. I
searched for them along the edges of the forest, where they
scavenged for food and slept in unfinished houses, but I simply
couldn't find them.

Late in the afternoon when Dad returned from work, reeking of the
bags of fish he had been carrying on his head all day, I told him that
the beggars had gone.

'Gone?' he asked incredulously. 'How can they go? I'm going to
build them a school. I've even started asking about the cost of a plot
of land. They haven't really gone, have they?'

'They have,' I said.

Stinking of fish, his forehead glistening with iridescent scales, his
boots thick with mud, he bustled out into the street and went looking
for the beggars. He didn't even stop to change from his work clothes.
I hurried out with him. Great energies swirled around Dad. His spirit
was fiery. He walked with enormous strides, and I tried to keep up
with him as he erupted into a torrent of fantastical ideas and schemes.
He was going to build a unique school for beggars. He was going to
supervise the education of all poor and illiterate people. He said they
needed education the most.

'That is how the powerful people keep us down,' he maintained.
'They keep us illiterate and then they deceive us and treat us like
children.'

He swore that he was going to teach the beggars mathematics,
accountancy, law and history. He said I would teach them how to
read. He talked of turning all the ghettos into special secret service

universities where the most effective knowledge in the world would be made available.

We went up the street and got to the main road. Crowds of people all over the place were talking about politics. They talked about the forthcoming rally and the famous musicians who would be performing. And they also talked about those who had died in the political violence. We happened to notice a few beggars up the road and Dad went and talked to them as if they were old friends. I heard him asking one of them about Helen, a beautiful beggar girl with a bad eye. I heard him pleading with them to come back to our street and help with the building of the school. He was so fervent and earnest that he must have struck everyone as being quite mad. The beggars were frightened by him and they fled. Dad went after them, pleading, and they kept running: they must have thought that he was trying to steal what little money they had. Exasperated, Dad turned to me and said: 'What's wrong with them? Why are they afraid of me, eh?'

'They are not the same beggars.'

'Not the same beggars?'

'These are different beggars. They are not the ones from our street.'

Dad glared at them. Then he said: 'Let's go back.'

We pushed through the crowds, past bicyclists ringing their bells, cart-pullers groaning with their loads of *garri* and cement, past the tight throng of traders and market women. At the arena where the great rally was going to be staged carpenters were constructing a mighty dais with a zinc roof. Hundreds of artisans were working at the site, hammering away, sawing up wood, climbing up ladders, carrying thick planks, singing, shouting and arguing. Petty traders sat around selling soft drinks and ready-made food. Dad met some of his fellow load-carriers and engaged them in lengthy political disputations. And when we got back to our street we were astonished to find our beggars sitting round the broken vehicle, as if they had been there all along, and as if we had just re-entered their alien reality. Helen wasn't with them.

The beggars looked at us with dull eyes. They didn't move from their positions and their faces didn't light up at the sight of Dad. It was clear that they had reached a decision. Dad felt excluded from the closed circle of their resolution and he tried to regain their trust and inspire them with his lofty schemes. But they had heard his promises a thousand times and their faces registered no response. He joked, and laughed at his own jokes, but they remained sullen. He asked about Helen, but they made no reply. He became unaccountably desperate.

'Where has she gone? Has someone touched her? Did she run away? Has she deserted our cause?'

The beggars were silent. Dad stared at them for a long time, apparently confused. Then, muttering something, he hurried back to the house. I went after him. When I got to the room he was taking off his boots. He told me to polish them till they shone. He went and had a bath and washed the fish smells off him.

While he bathed, Mum returned from her day-long hawking of cheap wares. She seemed leaner, her eyes dulled by the yellow dust, her face darkened by the fiery marigold sunlight. After dropping her basin of provisions on the cupboard, she sat on the bed. She did not move. She did not speak. She stank of profound exhaustion.

When Dad came in from the bathroom he did not seem particularly happy to see Mum. In fact, he ignored her altogether. He sat on his chair and proceeded to anoint himself with coconut oil. He combed and parted his hair. Then he put on his safari suit, which used to be white but which had turned brownish with age. He applied cheap perfume to his face. Something odd had happened to Dad after his great dream: he had become more susceptible to invisible presences in the air. It was as if holes had opened up in his spirit through which wisps of malevolence could enter.

When he saw that his boots had not been cleaned or polished, he exploded into a short burst of rage. He chased me twice round the room with a thick belt in his hand. He caught me at the door, dragged me in and was about to lash me when Mum – in a deadly voice – said: 'If you touch my son, you will have to kill me.'

Dad lowered his belt and sat in his chair. He retreated into the barely contained whirlwind of his fury. He poured himself a generous quantity of *ogogoro*, lit a cigarette and, in between smoking, proceeded to decrust his boots. While he cleaned his boots his spirit boiled, and I watched as a strange demon in the form of a beautiful girl with green eyes entered him. The demon-girl moved into Dad's spirit and sat comfortably, and then I couldn't see it any more. As he cleaned his boots with fiery vigour, smoking his cigarette with a grim intensity, his spirit rising and swirling, Dad lashed us with accusations. Sweating through his suit, his temper seemed to burn around him. His forehead became an agitation of wrinkles. Mum sat very still, listening. While Dad was shouting at us an evil spirit went right through our room, on its way to the preparations for the great political rally. The evil spirit, passing through our spaces, made all of us edgy. It awakened deep irrational passions in Dad's brain. Fuming, he scraped the dried mud off his boots angrily. His face swelling, his chest heaving, his big muscles bristling, he accused us of betraying him, of not caring enough for his ideals. Mum, he said, only cared for herself. He complained that we had no respect for him, that we didn't even see the importance of carrying on his schemes while he recovered from his fight.

He harangued us as if we were failed members of a government cabinet. He was angry about the fact that we had not supervised the beggars, had not encouraged them, had not fed them, and had not looked after Helen the beggar girl, whom he said was a princess from a distant and devastated kingdom. He rounded on me because I had stopped spying at Madame Koto's bar. He rounded on Mum because she had not been keeping in touch with political developments and had done nothing to recruit women to his political party. And he turned on both of us for failing to keep alive his dream of a university for beggars and the poor.

Mum said: 'You spend all your time talking about this university for beggars, but what about us, eh? Are we not beggars? Don't you hear how cracked my voice is? From morning till night I walked this ungodly city, hawking my provisions, crying out, while you slept like a goat for seven days.'

Leaping to his feet, Dad vented his full fury at Mum. Blindly he hurled his boots at the cupboard. The cupboard door flew open, revealing the pots empty of food. Cockroaches were sent scampering everywhere. Stamping his feet, lashing the air with his big fists, he went quite beserk with shouting. He said Mum was entirely devoid of vision and spent all her energy counting her wretched profits, while he tried to improve the condition of the people.

'Improve our condition first,' Mum replied.

Dad was momentarily stunned at the boldness of Mum's interruption. She continued.

'Where will you get the money to build a school for mosquitoes, talk less of beggars, eh? Will you steal, eh? Do you think money falls out of dreams, eh?'

Dad stopped in the beginnings of an antagonistic gesture.

'But what about all the money I won?' he asked, staring at us in utter disbelief, his bewilderment tinged with rage.

We were silent. We had completely forgotten the huge amount of money due to Dad for winning the fight with the warrior from the land of Battling Ghosts. Worried about his injuries, awestruck by his fabulous sleep and distracted by his recuperations, we had not remembered that Sami, the betting-shop man, owed us what amounted to a sizeable fortune.

'WHAT ABOUT MY MONEY?' Dad cried again.

'We forgot,' I said.

Mum shot me a furious glance. Dad sat on his chair and kept staring at us alternately, as if we had committed acts of unbelievable criminality.

'Do you mean to tell me,' he said, pressing such menace into every word, 'that you people haven't YET collected my money, eh?'

We dug deeper into our silence. Mum started to fidget. Then Dad, jumping up, sending the three-legged chair flying from underneath him, truly unleased his mistral rage.

'You are not on my side,' he bellowed at Mum. 'You are clearly my enemy! You want me to fail! You want me to be destroyed by the world! You go around in dirty clothes and ugly shoes and a disgusting wig of a he-goat, when I have hundreds of pounds sitting just across the street! You starve me, you starve my son, you obviously feed yourself in secret and meanwhile you don't even bother to secure my investments! I carry loads that would break the neck of Hercules. I fight with giants and monsters and thugs. Yes, I fight and get beaten and manage to win – and I win only because of you two – and yet, through all this agony, you don't even bother to look after the fruits of my victory?'

Dad paused. Then he drew a deep breath and, thrusting his raw face at Mum, he shouted: 'GET OUT OF MY HOUSE, YOU USELESS WOMAN WITH YOUR STUPID WIG! GET OUT! Go and sell your stupid provisions from morning till night! YOU ENJOY SUFFERING – YOU ENJOY POVERTY! Fine! GO and enjoy your poverty somewhere else and DON'T COME BACK! I will not kill myself for an UNGRATEFUL WIFE!'

Mum bore his tirade in a dangerous and stiff-necked silence. When Dad had exhausted himself, Mum stood up. With the movements of one who was enacting a decision she had reached long ago, she began to bundle her possessions. She gathered her faded wrappers, her moth-eaten wig, her undergarments, her old blouses, her slippers, her cheap jewellery, her tin-can of money, and dumped them all into an ancient box. Having almost reached the end of her forbearance, she took Dad's words extremely seriously.

'Where are you going?' I asked.

She screamed at me, deafening me with the full volume of her life-long frustration. Dad stamped on his boots, downed a shot of *ogogoro*, and stormed out of the room. I followed him, but I kept a careful distance between us. The demon-girl was growing in him, becoming more luminous and ecstatic.

Outside, green moths were thickening in the air. No one seemed to notice. Dad was striding furiously to Sami's betting shop when he saw Helen. Her beauty was more hypnotic than ever. Her blind eye was darker, her good one more jewelled and she was sitting on the bonnet of the burnt political vehicle, surrounded by the moths.

As if magnetized by the force of her astonishing serenity, Dad changed direction and ran over to her. Her was about to speak when she turned her strange eyes to him and said: 'It's time for us to go.'

'Why?' Dad said.

'When the time is right we will be back,' she replied, turning away from him.

Dad pleaded with her to stay. The more he pleaded, the less interested she seemed. After a while she jumped down from the bonnet. The other beggars appeared mysteriously with rotting corn-cobs and mouldy bread in their hands. They gathered round Helen, awaiting her command. The moths had concentrated about them as if their poverty and their wretchedness were a unique kind of light. Without uttering another word Helen led the beggars up the road. The moths went with them, their clattering wings sounded oddly metallic.

Dad stood still for a long moment, watching the beggars leave. His face was disconsolate and it seemed his dreams were deserting him. The beggars had gone a short distance when Dad broke the trance of his abandonment and ran after them. The street watched us. The moths clicked in our faces. Thickly gathered around the beggars, they seemed a kind of shield. Was I the only one who saw the moths? Dad didn't seem to, for he had launched into an impassioned plea directed at the beggar girl. Staring deep into her gem-like eye, he begged her to give him one last chance to fulfil his promise. He blamed his neglect on his recuperation, on me and Mum; and swore that he was going to build a school for them as soon as he had collected his money from the betting-shop man.

'I will prove it to you,' he kept saying.

But the beggar girl, deaf to his entreaties, carried on walking. Glowing in a new delirium, Dad began to praise her beauty and her elegance, her face of a yellow moon, her limbs of a blue gazelle, her eyes of a sad and sacred antelope. He completely amazed me with his declaration of fearless love. In a burning voice, robust and insane, he said: 'I dream of you every day, my princess from a strange kingdom. Everyone else sees you as a beggar, but I know you belong to a golden throne. You are so beautiful that even these butterflies . . .'

'Moths,' I corrected.

Dad glared at me, tapped me on the head and proceeded with his bizarre, passionate courtship.

'. . . that even these butterflies cling to you as if you are honey. You have the head of a spaceship, your eyes are like those of the wonderful maidens of Atlantis, you belong to the angelic kingdoms beneath the sea. You are a moon-woman come to brighten the earth. Your skin looks like flowers from another planet. You are the mistress of beauty, princess of grace, queen of the road. Let the flowers of the earth see you and weep . . .'

Dad went on and on, pouring out a stream of contradictory praises. The beggars ate their mould-encrusted bread and laughed at Dad's ridiculous words. Helen remained indifferent. Unable to bear her indifference, his face twitching under the assault of the moths, Dad finally blocked her path, just before we got to Madame Koto's bar-front. He astounded me by saying: 'I want you to be my second wife. Stay and marry me. I will take care of your people.'

The beggar girl went on as if she hadn't heard anything. Then Dad – his spirit swirling in the new yellow delirium – boldly declared his intention to honour his promises. He said Helen should come with him to Sami's betting shop, and if all he was saying wasn't true, if he didn't have the money to build them a school, to feed and cater for them, then she was free to go. He made a solemn oath, loudly and with dramatic gestures.

For the first time Helen acknowledged his persistence. She stopped. Dad's face broke into a triumphant smile. Turning to the rest of the beggars, he told them to wait for him. Then he seized Helen's hand and set off with her towards Sami's shop. Pestered by the moths, she strode defiantly through the rumour-making stares of the street.

Just as we were going past our house, Mum emerged with her tattered wig on and her ancient box under her arm. Dad didn't notice her. She looked so unlike herself, so wretched and haggard, as if she were a tramp, or as if she were fleeing the compound in shame, that even I nearly didn't recognize her. She followed us a short way and then, loud enough for the whole street to hear, she shouted: 'So you want me to go, eh? So you are throwing me out because of that stinking beggar girl with a goat's eye, eh?'

Dad looked back, saw her through the eyes of the demon sitting comfortably inside him, made a dismissive irritated movement of his hand and carried on, dragging the unwilling but mesmerized beggar girl with him. The demon that had entered my father had moved in for good. The occupation was complete. I could see his spirit whirling with grand dreams of love. For as he went, oblivious to the terrible changes he was bringing into our lives, I realized how much Dad was brimming over with love, possessed by its secret madness, bursting with love for everything, a wild unholy indiscriminate love, a love so powerful that it made him feel like a god, so vast that he didn't know how to contain it or express it. The love in him had become a double demon and it propelled him towards chaos.

Mum began weeping bitterly, cursing all the years of her privation and suffering; cursing the day she set eyes on Dad in the village, during the most beautiful years of her life; swearing at Dad for having drained the life out of her in so profitless a marriage. And between them both I didn't know who to choose. Mum went off, wailing, in the direction of Madame Koto's fabulous bar. Dad marched on to Sami's place, unmindful of the destruction he was sowing behind him. I started after Mum, but she screamed at me, as if she perceived that I was in alliance with Dad. And it may have been because of the moths (which I alone saw as moths), because of Helen and her tattered yellow dress, her emerald eye; or because of Dad's polished boots and his bristling demonic love, or because I didn't really believe Mum would disappear from our lives, that I chose to go after Dad – for with his mad passion lay the greater magnetic adventure, the curiosity and the rage.

And so, watching Mum grow smaller in the distance, a slouching figure, wailing and renting her wig, I reluctantly stuck with Dad's story, and suffered the choice I made for many nights to come.

Catherine Petroski
Beautiful My Mane in the Wind

I am a horse, perhaps the last mustang.

This is my yard, this is my pasture. And I told her I hate her. My dam-mother. She does not understand horses. She doesn't even try. There are many things she doesn't notice about me.

Horses move their feet like this.

Horses throw their heads like this, when they are impatient, about to dash away to some shady tree. See how beautiful my mane in the wind.

Horses snort.

Horses whinny.

Horses hate her.

I am a girl horse. I am building a house under the loquat tree. It is taking me a long time.

My house is made of logs, logs that Daddy doesn't want. That is because our fireplace goes nowhere. It is just a little cave in the wall because this is Texas and it is mostly hot here. Our fireplace has a permanent fake log. I am six.

I will be six next month.

Anyway that is why I got the real logs when our weeping willow died and Mama pushed it over one Sunday afternoon. The bottom of the trunk was rotten and the tree just fell over and Mama laughed and the baby laughed and I didn't laugh. I hate her.

I hate also the baby who is a Botherboy.

Daddy cut the willow tree into pieces I could carry and gave them to me and now I am building a horsehouse under the loquat and waiting for a man horse to come along, which is the way it is supposed to happen.

I saw a picture of one and its name was Centaur.

Of a Sunday afternoon, in her stable

My room I also hate. Bother loves it best and squeals when he gets to its door, because he thinks it's nicer than his own room, nicer than the bigroom, nicer than anyplace at all. He likes best all the blocks and the toy people. I build temples and bridges sometimes but then he comes along. He throws blocks when he plays because he's just a baby. And a boy. And not a horse.

What I hate most about this room is picking up pieces of the lotto game when he throws it all over, picking up pieces of jigsaw puzzles that he has thrown all over. Picking up the spilled water, the blocks, the people. I hate his messes. I know that horses are not this messy. Mama says it is our fate to be left with the mess, but I don't think she likes it any more than I do.

She pays very little attention to me actually. She thinks I just read and I'm pretty sure she doesn't realize about the change. To a horse. She acts as though I'm still a girl. She doesn't observe closely.

Administering herself first aid

The fact is there is a fossil in my hoof.

At school we have a hill that is called Fossilhill because there are a lot of fossils to be found there. Actually the fossils are very easy to find. You just pick up a handful of dirt and you come up with fossils. The trick is to find big fossils. I can always find the biggest fossils of anybody, snails and funny sea snakes and shells of all kinds.

The boys run up and down Fossilhill and don't look where they're going. It's no wonder they don't find many fossils. They come and pull Horse's mane. They scuff through where Horse is digging with her hoof. They sometimes try to capture Horse, since she is perhaps the last mustang and of great value. But mostly they are silly, these boys. They don't make much sense, just a mess.

Today I was trotting on the side of the hill and found the biggest fossil I have ever found in my life, which in horse is I think twelve or maybe twenty-four years old. Then I found more and more fossils and other children came to the hill, even the girlygirls who never look for fossils because they always play games I don't know how to play. House and Shopping and Bad Baby. But they tried to find fossils today and asked me if this was a fossil or that, and they found many, many fossils. And we all had a good time. And when we had found all the fossils we had time to find, our teacher said, Put them in your pockets, children, and if you don't have pockets put them in your socks. And we did, and that's why there is a fossil in my hoof.

Girlygirls vs. Boyannoys vs. Horse

In my kindergarten there is a girl whose name is Larch. It is a funny name for a girl. It might not be such a funny name for a horse, but Larch isn't a horse because she is in fact the girl leader because she decides what games are going to be played and will let the boys tie her up. And the other girls too. When they tie people up they don't use real rope because our teacher wouldn't allow that. If they tie me up with their pretend rope it doesn't work. They think I just don't want to play, but the truth is I'm a horse and stronger than a girl and can break their girlygirl rope.

It's more fun being a horse. More fun than being a girl too, because they just play Housekeeping Area and none of them really knows yet how to read even though they pretend to. I can tell because they can't get the hard words. So they don't let me play with them. My mother says it's all right because they wish they could enjoy stories themselves and next year they will all read and everything will be all right.

The reading is the real problem between the horse and the girls, I guess. But sometimes they do let me play with them, if they need a victim or a hostage or an offering.

Herself among the others

Horses are I think lucky. They do not seem to have friends, such as people, you know, for they do not seem to need friends. They have enemies – the snakes, the potholes, the cougars, the fancy-booted cowboys who don't know the difference between a canter and a hand gallop. What friends they have are on a very practical basis. Other horses with the same problems.

The wind.

A talk with herself

If I tell her what I am she will not believe me.

If I tell the others what I am they may rope me and tell me to pull their wagon.

If I tell a boy what I am he will invade my loquat house, and maybe it will be good and maybe it will be bad.

If I tell Daddy what I am he will act interested for a minute and then drink some beer and start reading again.

And if I tell Bother he will not understand even the words but will grab my mane and pull it until he has pulled some of it out.

What does it matter? What does it all matter? I will whinny and run away.

Who could blame me? Horses should not be abused, ignored, or made fun of.

Discussing the weather or nothing at all

Just a little while ago, when I needed to go out to race a bit and throw my head in the wind, she stopped me, my dam-mother, and asked me who I thought I was. A girl? A horse? My name? I know what she's thinking. The others at school ask me the same question.

So I said, A girl, because I know that's what I'm supposed to think. One thing I know, not a girlygirl, which would be stupid playing games talking teasing being tied to the junglegym. I won't. Sometimes it's hard not telling her what I really think, what I know. That sometimes I'm a girl, sometimes I'm a horse. When there are girl-things to do, like read, which a horse never does, or go in the car to the stockshow or for ice cream or any of those things, I have to be a girl, but when there are hillsides of grass and forests with lowhanging boughs and secret stables in loquat trees, I am a horse.

Maybe someday there will be no changing back and forth and I will be stuck a horse. Which will be all right with me. Because horses think good easy things, smooth green and windy things, without large people or Bothers or other kids or school, and they have enough grass to trot in forever and wind to throw their manes high to the sky and cool sweet stream water to drink, and clover.

Sheila Schwartz
Out-of-the-Body Travel

My problems were simple: life and death, my mother and father. What *her* problems were I didn't know, didn't *want* to know.

It was 1968 that winter Clara arrived from the mental hospital and took my father's place in our household. A very poor substitute in my opinion, but, as my mother claimed, Clara had nowhere else to go, no one else who was willing to care for her – not her parents, not the hospital, where she had committed herself eight months earlier 'just for the weekend'. 'We can no longer be therapeutically helpful except on an outpatient basis,' the hospital people said. 'She's thirty years old,' her parents phoned in their long-distance wisdom. '*She* should be taking care of *us*.' She had no husband anymore, no friends that we knew of. For some reason *we* were responsible. 'We're all in the same boat now,' was how my mother put it.

I didn't want to be in the same boat as Clara. *Or* my mother. I didn't want to think about the way that felt – to lie there hour after hour beneath the quilts, wrapped in a brown bathrobe, sweating. I didn't want to think about her eyes fixed on the doors, the walls, on the ceiling, on nowhere.

I had already seen nowhere the day my father drove up to New York City for a Yankees' game, then called to say he wasn't coming home. Not right then, at least. Maybe not ever. Honestly – he really didn't know. He really couldn't say for sure. 'I've always had a false sense of security,' was the only reason he gave for this sudden defection – unless you counted out-of-the-body travel as reason.

'Out-of-the-body, and now, out-of-the-house,' my mother said. 'This is an explanation?'

But my father said, '*I* was the one. *I* was the one who almost died.'

He claimed to have had a 'transcendental' experience the spring before when he'd suffered a heart attack. As he was lying on the table in the emergency room he felt his spirit or his soul or whatever-you'd-call-it suddenly ripped away from his body – as if it were no heavier than a shadow. Then it was sucked through a long, dark tunnel quicker than an arrow, like a memo through a pneumatic tube. This wasn't the pleasant, near-death experience most people describe, the shimmering vista of fields and flowing rivers, the loved ones who have passed on sprouting like an enchanted forest to wave a wordless welcome: We missed you . . . We love you . . . 'I was frightened,' my father said. 'Absolutely *terrified*. There was nothing there. Not light. Not sound. Not water. There was nothing at all – nothing at the end of the tunnel. You understand?'

'*I* understand,' my mother said. 'I understand that your father hates us. I understand he believes *we* caused his heart attack. I understand how these things work. People think they can just throw you away when they get tired of you. They think they can drain every drop of your life's blood and never even say so much as "thank you". I understand your father thinks he's making up for lost time, that he's having a great whirlwind of fun.'

'What *is* he having?' I asked. And that invariably spurred on her lecture. I, too, had funny notions of right and wrong. I was getting just as bad as *he* was. I talked fresh to everyone all day long. I made a mess everywhere I went. I was always in trouble at school. I was ruining my chances for a college education, for the future.

I had to admit she was right about this. I hadn't been very cooperative, not since my father left, but what did she expect from me anyway? Of course I wasn't interested in the future. Each time I went to New York to visit my father, he told me the same story about his dying – the staring lights, the awful, chanting voices: Code! Run a CODE!

Somehow this chanting always led back to me. 'You're fifteen,' he told me. 'You're a beautiful, young girl. You're full of energy. Zest. Life! You should be having fun. Don't make the same mistake I did.'

I wasn't sure exactly what his mistake had been and he never exactly said, but I was convinced it had something to do with our curtains – the funereal, purple ones in the dining-room, the heavy, gold plush that fell in a gloomy cascade behind my mother's china orchestra. It was that orchestra which she dusted and rearranged daily, as if each night they performed a different symphony and had to be curried like horses after a long, hard race. It was the way she fussed over the furniture, polishing the wood, plumping the mattresses, patting, gently, the arms of the sofa. It was the way she punctuated each sentence with a sigh. 'Suzanne.' (Sigh.) 'Would you mind doing a little homework?' 'Suzanne.' (Sigh.) 'Would you mind explaining why you flunked this test?' 'Suzanne.' (BIG sigh.) 'If you keep behaving this way you're going to end up in the streets. You're going to end up just like your father.'

I didn't see what was so wrong with my father. He had his own apartment in the Village. Four new sets of tie-dyed sheets.

Maybe that was what drove me to misbehave, to cut off my nose to spite my face, as my mother described it. Maybe it was Clara's fault. Or maybe it was just 1968 and I thought I should feel the earth move the way everyone but my mother did. I owned a drawer full of literature on the subject, all forbidden, all cherished, especially a ravaged copy of the Kama Sutra my father's girlfriend, Donna, gave me after we all went to see *I Am Curious, Yellow* together. My father was embarrassed by that movie but Donna wasn't. 'Very honest,' she called it. She told me about her own sexual awakening, how she had been sprung, at an early age, from the 'bourgeois trap' of virginity. It had happened right there in my hometown of Philadelphia while she was visiting – a very groovy communal 'pad' near Rittenhouse Square.

It wasn't just the pad though. Or the guy. (Though he had studied Zen for many years and that certainly helped.) Or the drugs. It had been the combination of all these elements that had made it such a very beautiful experience for her – as if every one of her planets had suddenly snapped into perfect alignment.

While my father was out buying bagels, a Sunday *New York Times*, Donna gave me a fuller description of that 'slow, dark evening', the 'dark, murmuring room', the way this guy Geoffrey had unchained the oppressive links of society and her soul had opened just like that – had blossomed just like a flower.

I believed Donna. She wasn't that much older than I was. I wanted *my* soul to open like a flower, not shoot down a tunnel the way my father's had. Still, despite my efforts, the many afternoons I hung around the Square shivering in my miniskirt and jean jacket as I waited for interesting people to come along and guide me through the universe, nothing ever happened. The only thing that blossomed for me that winter was more misery. The very first Sunday in January when I arrived home from a ski vacation with my father and Donna, I found Clara there living in *my* room. Without my permission all of my belongings had been moved to the attic – books, posters, scented candles, even the stars I had pasted on my ceiling that glowed in the dark, pale blue. In their place Clara had filled the room with her despair. I saw this through the door my mother cracked open with her foot, only an inch, as if to keep Clara's grief from spilling out too quickly and drowning us.

Sad things. Sick things. There were rows of pill bottles on the dresser. Crumpled tissues in heaps, like withered roses from a forgotten prom. Dresses lay slumped on the wicker rocking chair, on my ruffled bed. Where I had painted the word 'LOVE' on the wall with magenta Dayglo, someone had draped a sheet.

'Why *my* room?' I asked my mother. 'Why do *I* have to be the one to sleep upstairs? It's *freezing*.'

'Skiing!' my mother exclaimed triumphantly, as if this were some kind of brilliant counterargument. 'What sort of vacation is that? Up the hill. Down the hill. *Up* the hill. *Down* the hill. Your father has a serious heart condition. Does he want to kill himself?' Before I could say a single word in his defense she answered her own question. '*Obviously.* Obviously he cares as little for his *own* welfare as he does for anyone else's.' Then she warned me to keep quiet; I was to resist the urge to tell her any more nonsense, such as what a terrific time we'd had, or how my father had confided, as we propped our legs before the ski lodge fire, that my mother was really very difficult to live with. 'I don't want to hear another word,' my mother scolded as if to illustrate. 'I want you to go right in there this minute and say hello to your cousin. Be nice to her. She's been waiting eagerly to see you.'

I doubted that my cousin had been eager to see anyone in the last twenty years, that she had even blinked during those decades. She was stationed in my bed like a zombie dedicated to the spell of the TV. It sat on the desk six inches from where she had collapsed against a mountain of pillows. The volume on the set was turned all the way down. The covers were bunched around her waist. She was wearing that brown bathrobe, twisted open so that one breast hung out, drooping to the side, and she was gazing intently at the screen, her lips moving, filling in the missing sound as if every catastrophe reported that evening were her own.

'Are you going to just stand there?' my mother demanded. She apologized to Clara. 'Please forgive my daughter. It seems like lately, unfortunately, she takes after her father. If you know what I mean.'

Clara didn't say a word. Apparently she didn't remember my father, nor his myriad misdemeanors.

'Clara,' my mother said. 'Clara, honey . . .' Though Clara lay there like a stone, my mother made me bend down and kiss her on the cheek. '*Tell* her,' my mother ordered. Clara's castoff breast glared up at me until finally I said, 'You're very welcome to use my room, Clara. I'm really glad you're here.'

Of course I hated Clara instantly. I hated how unhappy she was, how much the world upset her. Wind. Noise. A bright smile. The first three bars of 'Light My Fire'. The last three bars. Everything unnerved Clara. She cried when the window slammed. She cried if the knife scraped across the plate when you were cutting up her meat for her. She cried because the birds in the trees outside her window chirped too loudly, or because they *stopped* chirping when the sky clouded up. She asked my mother where they had gone. Who had chased them away?

The answer seemed to be *me*. At least that was what I made of Clara's refusal to speak to anyone but my mother, how, each morning when my mother made me perform a ritual kiss before I went to school, Clara pulled her head away. Her hand rose to the spot on her cheek where my lips had touched and rubbed at it over and over, as if I'd left a threatening message there in Braille.

I hated how my mother defended her for that ('Pay no attention – she's just a poor, frightened girl'), how often my mother defended her for just about anything. 'It's the medication,' she always said. 'She's not "koo-koo" as you so nicely put it!' But then she scurried through the house getting rid of lethal objects – the Clorox; the Lysol; her own prescription for a kinder existence, yellow, heart-shaped Valium. She even hid a pair of fingernail scissors that she'd swiped from my makeup tray then swaddled in a bolt of corduroy.

I hated all those implications of suicide, especially because my mother tried to speak of them in fables. As we prepared dinner together she recited from a menu of thwarted dreams. There was the accountant who worked in my father's office who hanged himself at tax time. There was Marilyn Monroe. There was her Uncle Isaac who had swallowed cyanide, many years back, when he read about the Jews in Europe. 'It happens,' my mother said, then added a last, liberal dash of gloom, 'People lose all hope.'

I couldn't stand that either – how many times I came home from school and misunderstood the eerie silence. I stepped gingerly across the living-room carpet as if it might be mined. A pool of blood would appear at any moment. And farther on, another pool of blood. A huddled form, arms outstretched. 'Mother?' I called. 'Mother? Mother!'

I hated most of all the way that felt, the moments that swelled between my question and her answer, the way I ran up the steps on trembling legs just to find her spooning applesauce into Clara's wobbly mouth, or folding up a newspaper she had just read aloud from start to finish as Clara grimly and deliberately slept.

I might have felt sorry for Clara if my mother hadn't decided to make such an issue of it. Each time I returned from New York her anger at me doubled as if I wore the days I had just spent with my father like a new mink coat, flaunting my good fortune. Before I even stepped inside the front door I'd already been condemned. I found a piece of my own flowered notepaper pinned to the mailbox, blazing a trail to her anger. 'Come upstairs *immediately*,' it warned. 'No dawdling.' I found my way to the glowering look my mother had prepared, to a lecture for all seasons. 'You've been getting away with murder the entire year,' she said when I came home wearing a T-shirt that Donna had designed. 'War kills', it declared beneath a GI's grinning face. 'Love heals', beneath two intertwined, naked figures. 'Is that some fool's idea of a work of art?' my mother marveled. 'Is that the great "learning experience" your father left us for?'

'I want you to understand that *other* people exist too,' she said after my next visit. She ambushed me as I was sneaking past Clara's bedroom hoping to tuck myself away in the attic before another strip search. 'Stop right there,' she commanded, and then she shook me down, my backpack and purse emptied right onto the steps without mercy, as if she were a border patrol looking for stolen contraband, or maybe my father's secret orders to defect.

Not finding these she chose innocent items to object to. She confiscated things like peace symbols, the stained glass, dangling earrings she called 'outlandish', and 'hypocritical'. She threw in the trash the magazines I borrowed from my father for the train ride, *Rolling Stone* and *Village Voice*, a *Playboy* Donna had bought him to counteract the blues after his latest visit to the doctor. ('What do doctors know?' Donna told him. 'They're just another front for the Pentagon. They tell them which chemicals to put in our water. That's what makes you feel so bad – those chemicals they make you swallow. That so-called "medicine" . . .')

'So *what?*' I protested after every seek-and-destroy mission was carried out. 'What's wrong with some different ideas? *I* haven't done anything.'

But my mother insisted I had. As she snatched a new piece of incriminating evidence, she interrogated me: 'Where were you all weekend? You were having such a wonderful time you couldn't phone me? Your father took you on another trip? Was that good-for-nothing Donna with you?'

When I answered yes to all her questions – '*Good* guess!' – she got furious. 'Where will it end?' she seethed. 'What will be the outcome?' She pressed the box of strawberry incense (a peace offering Donna had sent along) to her ear, as if maybe it held Donna's good-for-nothing philosophies. Maybe a ticking bomb.

That was where Clara came in. As punishment for everyone's sins my mother decided I had to spend time with her – an hour every day, longer if I felt like it. As atonement I had to sit by her bed and pretend to hold a conversation.

Fifteen minutes. Twenty minutes. Thirty-five minutes.

While Clara dozed I babbled into the thin air about clothes and boys and how institutionalized learning made me want to puke, how sometimes my mother made me want to puke.

When Clara didn't even stir, I made things up. I described the trouble I planned each day at school, the creative hours I spent in detention doodling obscenities on the bottom of my chair. SHIT. BARF. PISS. Nothing fazed Clara, certainly not the biology insurrection I told her I was going to lead on Monday. At a prearranged signal we would all throw our dissection pans right out the window, crayfish hurtling through space. Nor was she interested in the scenario I invented about the art supply closet, my interlude of cavorting there with four young aesthetes, the flurry of handprints that was left upon my skin.

'Red and green and blue,' I added to see if Clara might be listening.

'In some very touchy places.' But Clara just snored on peacefully, as if I had disappeared, into another dimension, perhaps, one set aside for silly young girls, for total ingrates. She didn't even ask about the prearranged signal.

When my hour was up my mother came to get me. 'Well!' she exclaimed, jolting Clara awake for a second. 'I hate to interrupt but Suzanne has some studying to do. Did you two ladies have a nice talk?'

'No we *didn't*,' I complained as soon as we got out into the hall. 'I'm not doing that *ever* again – she scares me! She's so out of it she doesn't even know where she is.'

'She certainly does,' my mother glared. 'She's in a place where people *love* her – do you understand what I'm saying?' I had to march back in there and spend another whole hour. I had to sit through Clara's moaning and sighing while I tried to read to her from some book my mother shoved at me on my way through the door: *Great Expectations*, or *Gone With the Wind*. Classics, but they both made Clara cry.

To console her, my mother suggested various, unpleasant strategies. Though the embarrassment alone would have killed a much heavier person than I, my mother made me sing lullabies to Clara recalled from my infant days. I had to tease Clara's hair into a 'becoming' bouffant, or sponge her face with a washcloth doused with witch hazel so strong it made me gag, though my mother swore this aroma was a sure bet. 'Very refreshing!'

Despite all these efforts, Clara held her ground. The one activity that seemed to give her any pleasure was her daily sojourn in the bathroom. As if it were a long-awaited voyage to Europe, she stuffed her overnight case with cosmetics and hand towels.

This packing required every ounce of her concentration. She wended her way across the carpet as carefully as if it were heaped with broken glass. Half a lifetime later, when she reached her destination, the vanity table, she paused and scanned the contents of the mirrored tray as if it were a puzzle to be deciphered, as if maybe the creams and bottles of lotion and the lipsticks all added up to something. Several minutes later, her arm, bewitched by a mysterious spell, rose slowly from her side and drifted forward. Her hand hovered above the tray, dazed, uncertain, until finally it dropped onto a nail file or a barrette or a compact filled with the bleakest of beige powders she spilled along the way back to her suitcase.

During this process she never noticed anyone, not me, standing in the doorway marveling, not my mother who tried, in her way, to be helpful: 'Would you like to take this with you?' (holding up a polka-dotted shower cap), 'What about this?' (a bar of scented soap), sometimes bringing offerings from her own room – ruby-colored bath oil beads ('My! Aren't these lovely?'), a pair of slippers encrusted with rhinestones, her voice aglow like Christmas lights. 'Oh, Clara. How would you like some of this perfume? Smell how nice!' But at these times Clara was oblivious even to my mother. We were ghostly detours that might lure her from her mission.

Neither of us knew the reason Clara spent so much time in the bathroom (unless, of course, somebody had the *gall* to propose out-of-the-body travel again as a reason). 'Can't you let up?' my mother asked me, but I said, 'Maybe she really hates it here – did you ever think of that? Maybe she doesn't give a hoot to be with people who "love her very much". Maybe she can't think of anything more *boring*.'

Only such 'smart-aleck' remarks could have torn my mother from the keyhole where she knelt, from her endless scrutiny of Clara. ('I don't want to deny her any pleasure, but I'd still like to be on the safe side . . .') 'What did you say?' my mother demanded. 'Did you dare say to me "boring"? Is that what you think makes the world go around?'

But I thought Clara had the right idea. Once the door clicked shut behind her we never heard a sound, not the gurgle of water, not the scraping of the sliding glass cabinet door, not even the clatter of a comb against the sink. It was as if she had escaped through the bathroom mirror into the backwards, soundless world where she longed to be.

I longed to be there too – especially since it came highly recommended by Donna. 'Turn on and tune out,' was her slogan. When she was in town I played hookey. In exchange for a dime of pot the girl who took roll in my homeroom agreed to mark me present whenever I wanted. On these mornings I hopped on the subway and rode downtown just in time for a 'perpetual party' that was happening in that pad near Rittenhouse Square, the magic scene of Donna's flowering. I joined Donna's friends who were draped, all day long, on the couches and easy chairs, who lolled on the floor wrapped in a sweet mist of marijuana, a humming lethargy of words and music and not caring.

The minute you walked in the front door it hit you, and it kept on hitting you the entire day if you wanted – all you had to do was take a few tokes and melt into the crowd. 'Perpetual high,' Donna said, 'equals perpetual freedom.' That was the 'square root' of her philosophy. 'It's OK to do anything here – except be uptight.' We could take off all our clothes and smear butter on our skin, if we liked that. We could sit in a closet for ten hours and stare at our knees. Not a critical word would be spoken. Only praise wafting from the four corners of the apartment, unlimited acceptance: 'That's OK, Suzanne. That was a really beautiful idea, Suzanne. You're a beautiful person, Suzanne.'

At home my mother said: 'Keep quiet.'
                                    'Don't argue.'
                                    'Watch it!'
                                    'Must you ruin everything you touch?'
Donna's friends were just the opposite – sweet and generous. We did everything as a family – drugs, meditation, analysis of our dreams – no one was excluded. We had rituals that made the day hold together in a kind and loving net, ready to catch us if our mood showed any signs of falling.

The first thing we did each morning was drink tea together, something mysteriously Eastern in a ceramic mug where the twigs and branches floated like a miniature logjam in the eddies of hot water. Bancha tea or ginseng – to cleanse the spirit. Often there were odd pastries, brown and chewy and flavorless. I was pleased to hear these were macrobiotic, the perfect balance of 'yin' and 'yang', the 'male component' and the 'female component' according to Geoffrey, who was still studying Zen at the university and knew the most about spiritual things.

After breakfast we did yoga. Sitar music buzzed like a hive of electric bees and we bowed down to it twisting our arms and legs to the contortions of the scales and breathing, 'deeply . . . deep-ly . . . DEEP . . . ly . . .' until objects began to waver, a shimmering haze crept around the outlines of the furniture and the curtains and people's faces, as if they were about to change form.

Sometimes we enhanced this effect by smoking dope beforehand. Sometimes we held back until after we had climbed the 'crystal-staircase-to-inner-peace', as Geoffrey identified it. 'So very fragile . . .' Then we passed around a joint or a pipe or a chunk of oily, black hash impaled on a tapestry needle. We sucked up the smoke through the end of a ballpoint pen. 'More precise even than a bong,' Geoffrey explained.

Getting high was my favorite time of day. I felt most at ease then as the smoke crept through my body, as if the sun were going down in my veins. I became a windowpane that warmth was pouring through. I could light up the whole room and make it glisten. I could touch the person next to me and his arm would glow.

I felt no such glow at home. If anything, Clara was more silent, my mother, even colder.

'Be more careful,' she warned when I tripped and dropped a load of schoolbooks as I ran past Clara's room.

'Turn that down!' she scolded when I crouched before the mumble of my radio.

'For crying out loud!' she exclaimed when I so much as coughed or sneezed or even shook my head 'No! No!' too vehemently.

All of my attempts to be helpful seemed to backfire, from the cheery, red polish I spilled in Clara's lap, to the burn mark I pressed into the blouse my mother bought for Clara as a Valentine's Day surprise. 'Who ever taught you to iron silk?' my mother cried. 'Are you *crazy*?'

That was the dimension I lived in. This was how it felt to be me, I told the people at Geoffrey's – as if I had shrunk to a pinpoint like the tiny dot on the TV screen once the power is turned off.

'This is what my mother does to me,' I told them. I described all the weird ideas she had lately, how she made lists, in a spiral notebook I wasn't using, of the many 'opportunities' she and my father had 'missed', the vacations they'd never taken, the plays they'd never seen, the exhibits, the operas. 'Daddy *hates* opera,' I reminded her, but it didn't seem to matter. 'He would have loved that new production of *Butterfly*,' she said mournfully. She made me sit next to her on the couch while she played me tragic arias. I had to nod my head as if entranced while Nellie Melba sputtered and trilled, trilled and sputtered from the hi-fi. 'Heavenly,' my mother pronounced this.

'Another tragedy,' my father affirmed. 'Your mother always loved them.'

And I agreed. On those nights she didn't sit in her chair and monitor Clara, she monitored me. I had to sleep with her in my parents' sagging double bed, curled up in a ball on my father's side as if I were a new recruit in training to betray her. I had to listen to her talking in her sleep: 'You liar . . . You murderer . . .' and wonder which one of us she meant. (Though, at dawn, she often gave me clues, unveiling them as if they were answers to a Zen koan, the kind that could live forever in a state of suspended animation: 'Your father doesn't miss anyone. Believe me – he cares only for himself. He doesn't care what we think of him. Or what we remember. If he had any compassion whatsoever . . .')

'What are you talking about?' I asked, still groggy from her restless nightmares, but she wouldn't repeat it. 'Far be it from me,' she said, 'to worry you for no reason.'

I thought maybe she was joking. But the next night was dead serious, often completely wordless. I had to endure her again, her smell, rank and sweating, as if she ran all night through her bad dreams, no doubt chasing my father. I was sure of this because, frequently, in the more troubled stages of her sleep, she flung her arm across my chest and clasped me so hard I couldn't breathe. When I complained about this the next day she stared at me, her eyes dark with bewilderment. 'What! I hugged you? My own daughter? Is that such a crime?'

But the next minute she was screaming at me again. I was clumsy. I was inconsiderate. I had absorbed my father's reckless spirit the way a sponge soaks up water. 'It's frightening,' she said, and for once we both agreed.

So did the people at Geoffrey's. 'Bad karma,' was their diagnosis. More pot, was their prescription. Keep smoking that weed, they advised. Around the clock. Around my mother's outbursts. 'Don't lose that buzz – whatever you do.'

They held joints to my lips and made me sip at them like precious water in the desert. They made me lie down in the middle of the floor and try to levitate my sorrow. They gave me little presents – a chunk of hash here, a bag of pot there, three hits of acid (as innocent-looking as pieces of white confetti) I was only to use in case of 'dire emergency'.

They gave me other presents too – words of wisdom from their favorite authors. They used to read aloud to me from 'Demian', phrases I was to repeat at home to build my confidence, to build an understanding of my condition, the HUMAN condition, the realities that were in conflict. As we lay side by side on Geoffrey's mattress (the whole group sometimes sprawled like a pile of pick-up sticks), he quoted his favorite passages. In a flourish of wafting smoke the words drifted past: 'Every man is more than just himself; he also represents the unique, very special, and always significant and remarkable point at which the world's phenomena intersect . . .'

I was usually too stoned at this point, actually, to appreciate the wisdom. I didn't quite see how it applied to my situation: I wasn't a man and I wasn't remarkable, no more than Donna whose parents divorced when she was only nine, whose older sister had run away and never come home again, whose mother was an alcoholic.

I was also too stoned to object to what went along with his words – another remedy, much more comforting – at least according to Geoffrey's theory. As the others floated off to meditate in separate bedrooms, Geoffrey grabbed my hand. 'Don't be afraid,' he whispered, and I whispered back, 'Afraid of *what*? Why should I be?' though I could feel the music from the stereo someone was blasting thudding through my body like a runaway heartbeat. The sound was turned up too high to say no; something was turned up too high, so that the walls threatened to cave in, the glass ornaments Geoffrey had propped on his windowsill somersaulted to their doom; it was impossible to tell where the music was coming from – from the speakers that were set up all over the house, or from the ceiling, or a violently yearning portion of my brain; it was impossible to remember how I'd gotten to Geoffrey's, to his bed, what room I was in, how long I'd been there, though even as I wondered I could feel his fingertips, brushing against me light as butterflies, hovering against my skin, his hands soothing my neck and arms, gliding onto my hip, very gently, on my thigh, my breast, and elsewhere, fluttering, fluttering. 'You're very sweet,' Geoffrey said. He leaned over and let his beard tickle my skin, poured words into my ear that drenched me in beautiful colors, just as Donna had promised. We smoked another joint and then he pressed me into the mattress, against the quilt his grandmother had sewn, many years ago, for *her* marriage bed, for marriage was *bodies*, not paper, patterns of past and present, though later he said, 'Hey, Babe – that was kind of interesting . . .' as if I had just told him a little-known fact about the weather, or described a new diet for enlightenment – brown rice mixed with cauliflower, Marxism mixed with Zen.

None of it made any sense – the way sex felt, why my mother hadn't found out yet the trouble I'd gotten into, the host of crimes I had committed – just like my father. When she did find out, I planned to blame it on the pot which, by then, I was smoking not only at Geoffrey's but everywhere, carrying supplies of it around the way a diabetic carries insulin. Whenever I had the opportunity I pulled a joint from the leather pouch Geoffrey had given me, and lit up – in the woods when I should have been at band practice, or in the girls' bathroom as I stood on the window ledge and waved the telltale fumes toward open air.

In the attic, on nights my mother set me free, I listened to her voice rising in a crescendo of useless comfort through the heating vent: 'It's not so bad,' she reassured the thin air, because, by then, Clara was snoring soundly. 'Things will get better if you just hang on a little while longer . . .' I lit a joint under the eaves and toasted her lies. 'You don't really believe that stuff,' I planned to tell her. 'Look how many pills *you* take.'

But she already seemed to know this, seemed to have caught whatever was bothering Clara. As if it were the proper show of sympathy, she began crying constantly. At the oddest moments – when she brought forsythia branches from the garden to decorate the dining-room table, or if the phone rang unexpectedly, she suddenly burst out: 'This is too much! I can't bear it!' I found her weeping in the kitchen when she was laying out the tablecloth and napkins.

'What's the matter?' I asked and, just like Clara, she wouldn't say a word, as adamant as if she'd taken a vow to confuse me. 'Nothing's the matter,' she finally replied, though the tears were still running down her cheeks. 'Everything's the matter. I'm sorry.' She took the cup of coffee she was holding and poured the contents into the sink. Then she stood there shaking her head at the grounds that seeped away into a dark and acrid ring on the white enamel. 'I just don't know what to do anymore.'

Neither did I. By then I thought that everything in the whole world was my fault – I couldn't see who else to blame. I was sure it was my complete lack of understanding (what Geoffrey called 'existing on a literal plane') that had caused the mess we were in – not just my mother's incessant weeping, but Clara's breakdown too, my father's desertion, the long, downward slide my mother said we were on (impossible given that she had already said many times we had hit 'rock bottom').

How many times can you hit? I wondered. Maybe I didn't understand that either. Not even the simplest things, such as why I hadn't felt the earth move, not even a fraction of an inch, not even with the inevitable practice of repetition, whenever I slept with Geoffrey. I couldn't understand why I continued to sleep with him in spite of this, in spite of the way I cried the first time, how I made Geoffrey turn away and sigh, 'Not *this* trip . . . *Please* not this bum trip . . .'

I couldn't understand why I didn't feel anything, though Donna said I probably just didn't notice. 'It's not necessarily an earthquake,' she elaborated. 'It's more like a landslide, a very slow landslide, sometimes moving slower than the naked eye can see. *Or* the naked body,' she added, but it still didn't make any sense.

Nor did it make any sense that she never told me she and my father were breaking up, that this was the last conversation Donna and I would ever have. From Geoffrey's she departed for points unknown. 'As a driven leaf,' Geoffrey commented – a much fuller analysis than the one my father gave me.

'What happened?' I asked him about two weeks later. Out of the blue, between sections of the Sunday paper, he casually announced that he and Donna were finished.

'Finished with what?' I asked. I stared around the room for new decor I hadn't noticed, curtains or bookshelves that had eluded my dizzy grasp, until it dawned on me it wasn't furnishings he meant. But I still couldn't grasp why they'd done it. 'Don't you love her anymore?' I demanded. 'I thought you LOVED her. Weren't you the one who said love was the only version of eternity?'

'That wasn't me,' my father shook his head, and I felt that swooping sensation that had rearranged my insides lately without any warning, making the room spin an indescribable number of RPMs. I truly couldn't remember whether he had said that or not. And if he hadn't said it, then who? Donna? Geoffrey? My mother? Surely not my mother – we all knew what she believed these days.

'Don't,' my father interrupted my chaos. His voice seemed to filter through a screen before it reached me. 'Be upset,' I heard. He put his arms around me and hugged, as if he could squeeze the disappointment out of me. 'Life is so much more complicated,' he reassured me, 'so much more difficult than a person can understand at your age, Suzanne.'

'I *do* understand,' I protested, but my father just smiled wistfully. For a 'treat' he took me upstairs to see a psychic reader, an old woman Donna had introduced him to, who wore a sleeveless house-dress though the living-room where we waited was so cold our breath steamed like clouds in a crystal ball.

At her order we sank into the lumpy sofa and she showed us pictures of people who were supposed to be dead, though 'magnet-ized', still attached to the living. They trailed behind them wispy as smoke. 'These are the departed,' she said, 'who still love us.' Then she told us to close our eyes, to imagine a great, white light. 'This is the future,' she intoned. 'All you have to do is *will* it.'

'What kind of a treat was that?' I asked my father after we had left our ten-dollar donation on her coffee table and retreated downstairs. 'Is something the matter? I mean *really* the matter?'

'I don't know,' was all my father would say. 'Don't worry, Suzanne – she just cheers me up sometimes.' I had to ride back through the racketing darkness of the train wondering what had gone wrong, why no one wanted to tell me anything. I had to lie there next to my mother that night, who cried that she had missed me terribly (her little girl, her precious daughter!), and wonder what had pro-voked this kindness, why it seemed to make the earth fall away, leaving me in a vast and empty space, so dizzy I wasn't sure which way was up which way was down.

I had to smoke four joints the next few mornings before I could get anywhere near that 'perfect buzz', before my head seemed to swell up like a giant helium balloon. I couldn't see any other solution though. At school, it made the hours stretch forever, the way the corridors stretched from one grim classroom to the next, though, in each, I sat completely dazed by the glare of the fluorescent lights as the teacher's voice pulsed secret messages I didn't remember copying, that appeared, days later, in my notebook: 'If two sides of a triangle are congruent . . .' 'In the early nineteenth century the doctrine of mani-fest destiny . . .' I watched as other students pantomimed interest in words that dissolved into syllables as soon as they struck air. What was the teacher saying? Why was everyone nodding? Why was *I* the only one who didn't understand?

I thought that acid might give me the answer – that was what Geoffrey claimed – it would bring me enlightenment. I believed him as much as I believed anyone at the time. What's more I had the perfect opportunity for a test run a few weeks later when I came downstairs one morning and found my mother hurling figures from her china orchestra onto the hardwood floor. 'My God!' she kept exclaiming, 'Oh, my God!' as if some cruel, outside force had taken control of her hands.

She had already destroyed most of her favorites when I asked her what on earth she was doing. They lay smashed on the shining wood my mother had just waxed and polished the day before, frozen in awful silence like a broken army on a terrible battlefield – arms and legs and torsos scattered everywhere. 'What's going on?' I asked again. 'Are you losing it?' But she didn't even get angry. Her only response was to kneel down and pick the pieces up one by one and hold them to the light – the cellist who had lost his cello, the conductor who had been beheaded. 'How *could* you?' she demanded, and I was afraid she had discovered everything – someone had called from school to say I was flunking out, or I'd been followed by narcs, or she had finally realized, while watching one of those endless documentaries she and Clara preferred, that the smell in the attic wasn't just that lousy incense Donna and I worshiped.

When no lecture erupted I imagined that maybe I was wrong, maybe this was a new form of therapy I hadn't heard of. It might have been that technique called 'Primal Scream' that Geoffrey had sworn was almost as good as sex itself, was used to enhance sensations, in cases such as mine especially, where feelings were blocked, buried under an avalanche of ice and snow, under many layers of repressive parenting.

If that's what she was doing it seemed to be working, because, in a few minutes, my mother put down the two halves of the flute she was holding and straightened herself up. She took a deep breath and informed me that the three of us, 'You and me and Cousin Clara,' were all going to take a trip to the seashore.

'What for?' I asked her as we packed up the car with picnic things – paper plates and egg salad sandwiches, a plaid blanket in case it got 'a little chilly'. This hardly seemed like a reprieve – three hours in the car with my mother and Clara, more hours doing who knew what? probably sitting on the freezing dunes in a sandstorm. Knowing my mother we would no doubt have to pretend to frolic in a landscape as cold and windswept as the moon.

That's when I took the acid, when my mother, once again, made it a moral issue not to answer me, as if answering meant she had joined the careless new social order my father and I now belonged to. 'Why do you have to ask so many questions?' my mother said, and her voice seemed unnaturally bright, like a banner shuddering in the wind. I couldn't believe the acid had worked *that* fast, but Geoffrey had refused to set a time frame. 'Some people take five minutes,' he said. 'Some people take hours. And every once in a while,' he sighed, 'you get stuff that's just placebo. You just *think* that you're getting off. That's life . . .'

'I only asked ONE question,' I said, just to see what my *own* voice would do.

Apparently it did nothing. My mother acted as if she hadn't heard me, as if my words just skittered away like seaweed blowing along the beach. She was more concerned with getting Clara into the car, leading her by the hand, slowly and carefully down the garden path. As if she were blind she kept prompting her, 'Come on, Clara – there's a little bump here. You can get over it. Just pick your feet up a bit. Watch out for that stone there. Be careful of this patch of ice. Suzanne didn't shovel very well.'

I might have protested, 'Yes, I *did*,' but I was still trying to decipher my mother's logic. I was concentrating very hard on noticing changes, the way it felt, for example, when my mother finally loaded Clara into the car and snapped the locks shut, as if we were all sealed in for a launch into outer space.

The way it felt as we sped along through the Pine Barrens, my mother's 'shortcut' that took us through the bleakest part of the forest, no forest really, just the burned skeletons of fir trees sticking up through the sand, sad reminders of other careless people, other hard times.

Was this enlightenment I was feeling? Was this hallucination?

As if to purposely confuse me, my mother called back over her shoulder to Clara, 'Isn't this lovely? This stark beauty . . .'

Of course there was nothing lovely about it, nothing lovely about going to the shore at all – forever the scene of some disaster for our family. I had broken my leg there one summer just by falling off my bike. My grandmother had died on the beach, in a deck chair, tucked away by the seawall, still squinting against the sun. My father always drank too much at the shore and ran around insulting people, especially my mother who fell into a deep depression she insisted was the fault of the ocean. ('I can't stand how it keeps repeating,' she used to moan.) This was also the same beach where my father had his heart attack during another off-season visit. There was no hospital on the island so we had to drive him forty miles to Tom's River where the nurse made him lie flat across the plastic chairs in the waiting room while she hunted up a physician.

Though my mother had sworn she would never set foot on sandy soil again, here we were barreling down the highway much faster than I'd ever seen my mother drive.

Seventy. Seventy-five. Eighty. Somewhere near the Green Top Market the speedometer actually nicked one hundred – I was pretty sure I didn't imagine that. 'My God!' I heard my mother exclaim once more. She slammed on the brakes for a second and the car fish-tailed. A spray of pebbles hissed across the shoulder into the ditch, but I couldn't tell if it was our velocity that had startled her or the sight of the market.

This was the spot where she started chattering about my father. She actually turned the car around half a mile down the highway and drove back. She told both Clara and me to get out of the car so we could see better, though there was nothing to see, just the weather-beaten stands that got painted a bilious green every summer so that the fruits and vegetables would look brighter, their glowing heaps would attract customers. That was what my mother said anyway. 'Sam and I always stopped here to buy produce. It was extremely fresh,' she told us. She ran her hand across the splintered wood as if it held an unspoken secret of their marriage, then herded us back into the car. 'I don't know if we should be doing this,' she said. 'I'm not sure it's wise.'

Not that this deterred her. Our ride to the shore was endless – even more so when we finally arrived. My mother seemed determined to give us a tour of her lost love. Her purpose in bringing us here was even worse than I'd suspected. She insisted on going over every inch of hallowed ground. 'This is the place!' she kept crying. She aimed each word as if it were an arrow shot straight to her own unsuspecting heart. Love. Love. Love. Love. Though there wasn't an ounce of love in sight, not even the faintest, glimmering aura. She kept stopping at inscrutable landmarks to trace the outlines of invisible happiness with her pointing finger. 'There! Over *there*,' I heard her say, as if it were a drifting spirit that she'd sighted, an elusive ghost that kept popping up to taunt her.

'Isn't it wonderful? What a life we had!' She made Clara and me crawl out of the car at every spot and wobble across the soggy ground, on a mysterious treasure hunt for artifacts of an abruptly halcyon past. We didn't know what we were looking for but we stared anyway as intently as searchlights in the midst of a foggy storm. We reached down for pebbles or twisted branches, for shining gum wrappers, bottle caps, as if maybe one of these had caused my mother's rapture, not the bent and twisted synapses of her ruined memory.

There didn't seem to be any other clues. Only these facades of ordinary objects my mother had the sudden and amazing power to see right through to a much deeper truth. 'He loved me,' she chanted to Clara. 'He really *was* crazy about me . . .'

'The material world is deceptive,' Geoffrey had once told me, as an excuse for turning away after sex. 'I *didn't* turn away.' Perhaps my mother knew this too; this was something else adults shared, truth was just a matter of willpower, of desire. As we rocketed along the asphalt, from shrine to shrine, she transformed ordinary reality. Even without acid my mother was capable of seeing what wasn't there. 'The beach is where Sam and I first met,' she told Clara as we stumbled up a mountainous sand dune. 'A big wave tumbled us into each other and we fell . . .'

'In love,' she added, several carefully timed minutes later when we were back in the car again blurring toward another gap in memory, as if she had rehearsed all night for this exact moment, had rehearsed her whole life to say it the exact second we were passing the spot where he'd proposed. It was a spot so indistinguishable she could only remember it by the mile market. 'Nineteen,' my mother alerted us. 'Coming up on your right.' She slowed down so we could honor it with our sighs, some tears, then sped toward other visions that appeared as quickly as she conjured them. We were passing the little gift shop where my father had bought her a string of seahorses . . . We were passing their favorite restaurant where they used to eat delicious lobster . . . We were passing the Seashell Inn where they had honeymooned in a room with a nautical theme, fishnets draped like delicate shawls along the walls, where shells and barnacles and starfish nested, where they didn't get out of bed for three days and three nights except for room service coming and going in a flurry of nectar and ambrosia . . .

'Some say life is a dream which never ends . . .' my mother announced later after we had swept the entire island for romantic inventions. I was hoping it was all just an interminable hallucination, that in fact I was at home safely burrowing through time, under the covers with my imagination. I hoped that I'd soon experience what Donna had described to me, the benign setting she beheld each time she tripped – the butterflies and rose gardens and rainbows all whirled together, that any moment I'd wake up and I wouldn't be tripping at all, would only be dreaming the dream which never ends . . .

But the next minute we were stopping once more. We were pulling up at the drugstore to buy hats and suntan lotion, we were leaping onto a tiny inboard boat my mother raved over as if it were a cruise ship, just like the one my father used to own! that he took us fishing in every Sunday afternoon in summertime, just trawling along through the absolute joy of sunshine, the open sea! the three of us, a perfect family without cares or disagreements, that was sure to make me seasick, this tiny garvey, as flimsy as the past my mother was reconstructing ('Such a glamorous life!') or fall apart as soon as it hit a wave. 'Isn't this exciting?' my mother asked. 'Suzanne – do you remember . . .?' as we staggered across the deck to our seats, nothing to grip for support except the gunwales that disintegrated beneath my touch, the paint shedding flakes like gritty snow, the air shedding smells so awful they made me retch, as if the boat had been entombed since last summer in brine and beer and fish scales, worse for my mother's rendition of it all: 'This is exactly the kind of outing that Sam would have loved. A fine day in the sun, a fine crew for company . . .' though there wasn't any sun, despite our sunglasses. The so-called crew consisted of three old men as scrawny as the burned up trees that lined the highway, all three of them exactly alike in horror except for the captain who had an additional blight, tattoos that swarmed across his face and arms, curling ropes that bound his wrists, a wriggling scythe on one cheek, a sheaf of arrows that rained across his forehead. Did my mother mistake him too? The way she was raving I thought she had. Or maybe she was just trying to encourage Clara. 'This will be a wonderful trip. Such a lovely guide. A terrific person . . . *You* are a terrific person,' she said to someone, as if she couldn't see clearly, the captain was so busy running back and forth, menacing us with fishing poles. 'Take one. Pick one. A light one if you don't know what you're doing. Take this plastic reel . . . it's easier . . .' as he hoisted up the bait traps from the murky water, and pulled in the anchor, and wrapped the line around and around in figure eights, maybe all of this just to refute my mother, to erase the sound of her voice, the lies that were apparent maybe even to him ('Our love was so strong . . . everlasting!'), who had never known my father, as he gunned the engine through her recitation and we chugged slowly out of the slip, the engines thrusting against the choppy sea, against my mother's delight with everything she saw. As far as she was concerned we were riding past the same sights we'd seen only a few minutes ago, that had loomed in our path for hours, years. As we plowed through the churning whitecaps of the bay, nothing discouraged my mother, though a furious wind kicked foam into our faces, biting and salty, my mother busily retold her strange backwards history to Clara, as if she had finally succumbed to *her* view, had entered Clara's world where everything was reversed – long became short, hate became love; my mother's voice looped, crazy as a gull in a hungry landscape: 'There's the Seaside Bar . . . There's the *Lucy Evelyn* – a famous ship that wrecked here a hundred years ago – they made a museum of it – Sam used to take us there – he adored stories of the ocean, the dangers . . .' as Clara sat there and nodded as if she believed every single word of it, the rippling of the waves, the billowing of the truth, and my insides began to lurch up and down with the boat as we slid up one hill of water and down another, smacking the bow each time we plummeted from the swell, as we headed towards the inlet, so that I had to grab the rail with both hands to keep from falling, so that the captain yelled at me, 'Don't do that! Sit down!' Or was that my mother forcing me backwards into my seat, 'Sit down! I have something to tell you . . .' forcing me to listen to her discoveries rushing like the tide: 'I always loved the shore this time of year – so stately, so romantic . . . You can see the boarding house where we rented the first summer after Suzanne was born. It had gingerbread trim all around the porch . . .' And on and on, describing scenes she had imagined – the clam bakes, the games of gin rummy, the miniature golf clubs swung high above our heads from sheer exuberance, 'Those were the days . . . We were blessed! . . . We were so lucky . . . Weren't we the happiest people we knew?' until I couldn't take another second of it. 'Shut up, Mother!' I heard myself yelling. 'Would you PLEASE just shut up? Daddy's gone – don't you get it? He *isn't* coming back – don't you understand anything?'

'You're right,' my mother said, I don't know how much time later. It might have been just a single minute, it might have been hours according to the way her voice went flat, as if I'd pressed a scorching iron to it, burnt it up like fragile silk. 'You're right,' she repeated, as if she weren't sure she'd actually said it the first time; she had never said this to me. 'I've been trying to tell you all morning . . . I didn't know how to tell you . . .' She put her hands on my shoulders so gently I felt my heart stop for a moment. She stroked my hair so fondly, I felt myself falling backwards into her arms.

That was the moment when I was finally convinced that the acid had kicked in. When I was small I used to dream of being electrocuted, of stumbling onto the subway tracks, onto the rail that hissed and sparked, then ignited a breathless fire up my spine. 'What *is* it?' I begged my mother as she pressed a loving kiss onto my cheek. I pretended for as long as I could that I didn't understand what she had to tell me, the whole afternoon, it seemed, as the waves or the water or the panic rose through my body, as the captain cut the engines and handed around the fishing poles, admonishing Clara to keep the rod upright, the tip pointed to the sky. 'You have to be able to see them bite,' he told her, and he made a demon face, working his jaws so that his whole face wriggled, his tattoos jumped and squirmed. Clara didn't seem to mind this. She let him bait her hook with a real live minnow; she let him stand behind her and hold her arm. She leaned back with him as if they were both going to throw a discus, then stepped forward just as unexpectedly and hurled the line toward the sea. She clapped when it hit the water. At least I thought she clapped. Maybe she couldn't hear the news my mother kept repeating, heard only the dip of the waves, the thundering fish on the end of her line, though my mother repeated it at least twenty times: 'He's gone . . . He's gone . . . He's gone . . .' as the captain trudged behind me: 'Is she sick? Is she going to pass out? . . . I have medical supplies in the hold . . .' And I said, 'No! . . . No! . . .' And then my mother again, 'He's gone . . . We've got to accept that . . .' And Clara's line went singing toward the horizon, a thin thread I thought might be holding her in place on the deck, might be holding all three of us from floating off into the ether, or jumping into the sea, from following my mother's words, 'I know it must seem like the end of the world . . .' that surged around me like waves. What happened? What happened?

Though of course I knew perfectly well what had happened, what couldn't be explained, not ever, no matter how many times my mother told me, 'I'm sorry. I wanted to spare you . . . I don't know what I was thinking . . . I wasn't thinking anything . . .' I could already see what would be there for years to come – what Geoffrey told me later, as consolation? were acid flashes – what a normal person couldn't possibly see or hear, what I had imagined for months was bothering Clara as she rolled back and forth beneath the covers at night in her starless room – moaning, trembling. I could see my mother when she washed up at night, drying her face with the towel, patting it softly upward as if it might break. Smoothing away the wrinkles. Tears. And my father, I could see him as clearly as if he were still up there in New York, mixing himself a gin and tonic, stirring it with a swizzle stick made of red plastic bent like a candy cane, lighting himself a cigarette, then squashing the cigarette out and going over to the window, pressing his forehead against the glass. I could see the two of them standing in the empty streets where they first met, completely empty, and the sand that blew across in patterns that wavered and swirled like snow. And the houses with their shades pulled down and their striped canvas chairs stowed away. The driftwood and the seashells knocking in the surf, though these were miles away. Years away. I could see the room where my parents had first made love when they were young, and conceived me – the bedraggled curtains and the fishing nets, the wallpaper festooned with red and blue anchors, the sandy footprints leading to the bed like clues in a murder mystery.

Linda Svendsen
Up Late

We were going for a moonlight swim. It was just us. She parked by
Trout Lake and said take off your pedal-pushers, panties will be OK.
Who will see? Her dress was over her head and gone. She wore girdle,
garters, a white bra with fat straps. She rolled the windows down,
turned the radio on, up, and the song said *you say potato and I say
potahto*. I kept my sneakers on; between us and water were rocks and
evergreen needles, and then in the lake, invisible nipping fish. My
mother took my hand. She said, 'Come on, small fry.'

That lake had no bottom. Every summer a boy fishing fell backward out of a canoe and it was curtains. None were found. I didn't
think about drowning: I was six, could kick and float, held Mum's
hand, would never die until God needed a new angel. We followed the
flashlight beam until the moon took over – down the little hill to
the dock. Then she remembered the emergency. She had parked on an
incline and the car might roll down the hill to sink in the lake. We
would have to sleep on the dock until sun-up or the lifeguard.
People – my father, who was dead – would wonder. She headed back
to the road.

I climbed the big water slide and sat up top. No breeze. Across the
lake were houses with sundecks, porch lights, wind chimes and pools,
and I could hear people living a late August life, and the ruckus of
grasshoppers rubbing themselves, and the radio host in our car say,
'Speak up, you're on the air.'

I was forbidden to slide in the dark, in the deep part. I stayed still
and sang 'Kookaburra', and when the door hadn't slammed, and I
didn't see her light, 'Policeman, policeman, do your duty, here comes
Adele, the bathing beauty, she can do the rumba, she can do the

splits,' etc., and then stuck in my mother's name, June, and then her middle name, Ruth.

I was the baby and Mum had taken me with her to the Elks Club. This was how she kept steak in our mouths, barrettes in my hair. I usually sat at the staff table with my coloring book and crayons and soft drink, guarding everybody's smokes. This time I had waited in the coat check. It was empty in hot weather. In the heat all the women were bare shoulders and napes and loud splashed cologne. A cocktail waitress named Cindy brought me a big glass of ice cubes with a pink straw and let me look at the photos in her wallet and read the backs. I wanted her for my sister.

When my mother touched the piano, the crowd shut up. They squeezed each other and slowed down. The men stood tall and swayed a little this way, a little that. Ladies closed their eyes and just didn't care. It was 'Que Sera, Sera'. Lights went off. I was lying on the cold linoleum under hundreds of thin wire coat hangers. This was where we were before the lake.

She walked back to the dock keeping the beam barely ahead of her next step. I saw a face in her knee. Without clothes on, my mother looked like somebody else and I didn't know who. She put towels down by the slide and raised her arms. I let myself into them. 'Ready, mermaid?' she said. Behind her the lake loomed like a trick. Light glinted off safety pins fastened below.

She clung to the rope ladder and lowered her body bit by bit. She said it burned. She was only waist-deep when I jumped. I liked getting things over with. I could hold my breath for seconds. My mother couldn't even swim. She hated getting her hair wet and losing her style. She wouldn't even duck her head underwater to see what was what. She found a warm spot and didn't budge.

When I asked, she spread her legs wide to let me swim between. The first time I couldn't find her. The lake was ink. Once I got the knack I couldn't get tired of this. I made it harder. If my hand brushed, if I bumped into, if the smooth rubber sole of my sneaker nicked, she would die. She would die before Christmas. I touched her. I changed the rule. She would die after I skipped grade two, before 1961, whenever I wanted. I kept touching. She stayed living. Her life stretched long, longer than mine. It was up to me. She was goosebumps. She was just a shadow I passed through to get to the other side.

She heard it first, of course. I was diving. I was beneath her. I was being pickled by the lake. I thought it was a speedboat – a fisherman trolling for breakfast with a bright hook. The motor was rude; it was a lawn mower chopping away at the water. Whether to stay under, I wasn't sure. If I came up, someone might see my no top, our hardly anything on. A little later, and I didn't hear it anymore.

After that I lost track: lost track of how long I'd skimmed bottom, of when she would be kaput, lost track of fun and was I good. I was more water than girl. I was on your mark, get set, go, keep going or else. The lake spilled up my nose. My mother was still my arch. This may have taken one sheer minute.

Her face wasn't like an ice cube, a crack, the flame of a match, or the moon. It didn't keep you looking. Sometimes the hook of her nose scared me and I could not hug her. I had to glance behind, around her waist, as if somebody surprising us had just walked in a door. Then she would turn around, turn back and say, 'What did you see?' and forget we were going to touch.

We were lying on towels on the dock and I was looking at her. She was looking up at the night. I shut off my flashlight and twinned her. I bent my knees, making my legs steep hills. I crossed myself. I tried to think about everything she could think of and this was too easy so I tried to look like I was thinking. I put her soft voice in mine and said *Look both ways* and *Did you have enough? There's more.*

'Who are you whispering to?' She rolled over. 'Do you have a secret friend?'

The stars were still out. Each star was part of a family picture, each family of light had a name. It all fit. People said stars told stories if you stared. I did this for a long time, different times, and I could not see a spoon spilling cough syrup or the dog lifting a hind leg or an arrow aimed at us. When I looked, each star was already gone. I was only seeing old light left behind. This was science. I stared at the space between two stars then shut my eyes to see which was darkest. It was darkest inside. I heard her go by, each plank making a new noise under her foot. 'Where are you going?' I said.

'I don't know.' She stopped by the ladder of the slide and grabbed the bars. 'I don't want to go home yet,' she said. She leaned back letting her arms do the work, hold her, and then climbed up. She looked down on me from the top of the slide. 'I think you took a nap,' she said.

I shook my head. I never slept, I was never not awake, I had never had a dream. In the middle of the night, if she woke thirsty, she was out of bed after me, after water ran cool and hit the glass bottom. When my father was sick, I sat big and close by his side and watched the life drip clear into him. He could not die if I was watching. We both knew it.

'I'm going to let go,' she said. 'I'm letting go.'

I slid the switch on the flashlight and buttered her in its cone. Her arms surrendered over her head. Her legs were crooked, straight when she slipped in. She was here, then gone. Her whoop, mouth wide open, was eaten by the lake. The splash – noisy, tall, a surprise, a lily shaking – made stars leap out of the lake and gleam where she had hung.

The night did not stop being hot. It kept getting warmer. Across the lake, the people in those houses were lying on top of beds listening to fans like big bugs. The trees were slack and bored, and the ones wearing leaves gave some up. They rode the water. When my mother tried to float, her face stayed above the water and the rest of her sank. She did not believe me when I told her. I had done breath bobs beside her. 'You're sinking,' I said and she said, 'I am not.'

I left. I could tell when she wanted to be alone. I leaned forward onto the lap of the water and kicked once. I didn't need her; I kept my chin down in the water and turned into a crocodile: all eyes, silence, might.

I looked up when the man walked out of the bush and onto the dock. He saw us and kept coming. He sat on the edge of the dock and undid his sandals. The moon lit us all. He looked older than her. He was seeing her in her brassiere. She saw him seeing and ran a hand through her hair, then hung onto a strand and twisted. He looked at me. Without blinking I looked back. He eased off a sandal, a black sock, and tucked the sock under the sandal straps, watching me. He did the same to the other foot. The socks weren't all black. There were stripes of lightning on the sides. He stood up and started taking off his shirt.

My mother glanced back where our car was parked like she had a kink in her neck or had to be somewhere by a certain time. The radio in our car gave the report. It would be the same again tomorrow and that was hot. Her face said she had lost something. I wondered where he had come from and when he would go. I wondered if he would be naked soon. 'Guess what I am,' I said to her. I spun in the lake. My sneakers slapped and raised mud. I tapped her. 'Guess.' 'Not now,' she said and tried to take my hand. 'Swizzlestick,' I said. 'In a drink.' He folded his shirt. I kept whirling. I refused to let go and be dizzy. I looked at the dock, her, the dark yards on the other side, the tongue of the slide, the dock, to keep my bearings. I wondered if he lived in a cave in the woods. 'Guess now. Guess what I am now,' I said. 'You're very loud,' she whispered. 'Do you want to wake up the fish?' He was pulling down his pants. I could see the shiny rim of swim trunks. 'I'm a swizzlestick in Orange Crush,' I said. I was exhausted. They were both tilting.

The man looked down on us. He was so strong, he looked like he could throw me high up in the air and catch me and keep doing it. He nodded at her, then me, and said, 'Ladies.' His hands made a prayer. He fixed upon a point and then sprang off the dock and flew over me. For a moment he made another kind of night, pale, closer to day. For a second I smelled his hair and under his arms and breath. He smiled back at me. I wasn't afraid. He entered the lake like a stone thrown sideways, skimming, and broke into a crawl. He swam without a splash, his stroke and kick caught no light. I watched until she clapped. 'Out,' she said. 'It's late. It's time to go.'

We got out and she wrapped me in a damp towel. I lost my balance and almost fell back in; she made me lie down and pulled me across and over her legs like a cape. Before Dad died, he could not hold me on his knees. I was too heavy. 'Keep your head down,' she said. 'Close these,' she said and kissed above my eyes. Her garter biting into my cheek would make a mark gone by morning.

I felt much better. When I asked who he was, in her story voice she said she didn't know. Maybe his wife read long books in bed and kept the light burning. Maybe he was on a team and had to practice to beat everybody. Maybe he was a man who could never fall asleep in August, or after midnight. Maybe he was king of the lake. She said he could have been anybody.

In my mother's arms, I looked for him. I couldn't tell if he was coming or going. He was a tear, a tiny rip in the white scarf tossed down by that moon. He could have been an angel.

Marly Swick
Heart

Mama was smoking a cigarette and talking on Cody's toy telephone when Aunt Lucette and Uncle Bob came for us. We had our suitcases packed. I'd packed Cody's for him because he was too little to know what he'd need. Cody and I sat out on the front stoop while Aunt Lucette and Uncle Bob went inside to see Mama. Cody dug a tunnel in the dirt with an old spoon and I twisted my birthstone ring this way and that to catch the sunlight and make it sparkle. It was an aquamarine and my daddy gave it to me right before he ran off with my teacher, Miss Baker. After a few minutes, Cody got bored and went inside. I could hear them all fighting in there. Uncle Bob was shouting at Mama and then the screen door banged open and he threw Cody's toy phone out into the yard where it landed in the tall grass with a little jingle. Then Aunt Lucette swished out carrying Cody and hurried me into the car. Cody sat in her lap in the front seat and I sat in the back seat with my suitcase. Cody let loose with his tears, like a cloudburst. Aunt Lucette reached over and beeped the horn until Uncle Bob marched out and slid in behind the wheel.

'She's C-R-A-Z-Y,' he said. 'Breaks my heart.'

He mopped the back of his neck with a handkerchief and started up the engine. I traced the letters on the side of my blue suitcase. I felt a little thrill. My daddy'd run off with my teacher and now my mama was crazy. I felt real special.

'She's skunk drunk,' Aunt Lucette said. 'She'd have to sober up to be crazy.'

'We can't just leave her.' Uncle Bob crossed his arms over the steering wheel and rested his head on them like he was about to take a nap. 'She's liable to burn the place down with one of them fancy cigarillos of hers.'

Ever since my daddy'd left, she'd been smoking these cigarettes that came in a flat box like crayons – pink and turquoise and purple. Sometimes she'd light one up and stand in front of the medicine chest mirror, watching herself smoke it down to a stub, and then she'd flush it down the toilet.

Uncle Bob shifted the car into reverse. 'Maybe we should call a doctor,' he said.

'She's heartsick and there's no medicine for that,' Aunt Lucette sighed, 'except time. We ought to know that.'

Uncle Bob nodded and squeezed her hand. 'Don't let's start,' he said. There were tears shining in his eyes. I figured he was thinking about Little Bob.

As we pulled out of our driveway onto the paved road, I turned around and looked back at our house. Mama was kneeling in the tall grass that hadn't been mowed since Daddy left, clutching Cody's pink plastic phone to her chest. She saw me looking at her and put the receiver to her mouth like she was trying to tell me something.

Once we were onto the highway, we stopped for gas at a Sinclair station. I pointed out the green dinosaur to Cody who was only half-crying now. Uncle Bob told the man to fill her up, then turned to us and said, 'Come on outta there. I wanna buy you kids a root beer.'

We climbed out of the car and followed him over to the soda machine. I held Cody while Aunt Lucette went to the ladies' room. Uncle Bob dropped some change into the machine and handed me a root beer.

'You kids,' he said, 'is going to come live with us. Your mama's sick.'

'How long for?' I asked, passing the root beer bottle to Cody.

'No telling,' he shrugged. 'Till your mama's her old self again.'

'You poor kids.' Aunt Lucette reached down and gave Cody and me a bear hug. 'It's gonna be all right.'

She took a pink Kleenex out of her skirt pocket and dabbed at her eyes. We climbed back in the car and I started whistling 'You Are My Sunshine, My Only Sunshine'. Daddy showed me how to whistle before he ran off and I'd been practicing up on some of the songs he used to like to whistle. Aunt Lucette swiveled her head around like Mama's old lazy Susan and looked at me like I was something real odd.

'Don't she beat all?' she asked Uncle Bob. 'Not one little bitty teardrop. You suppose that's normal?'

'I expect it's the shock,' Uncle Bob said.

I was whistling and watching the fields roll by. Some of them smelled real bad. I held my nose and breathed through my mouth. I saw a sign that said Welcome to Indiana.

'You know what, Cody?' I jiggled him on my lap.

'What?' He was half-asleep.

'We're in a new state.' I pointed over my shoulder. 'That back there's Kentucky.' I pointed over the front seat. 'And that up there's Indiana.'

'I wanna go home,' Cody whined.

'Look at my ring,' I said, holding it eye-level so it sparkled right in front of his face. 'See how pretty?'

He took his hands out of his mouth and tugged at my ring with his wet fingers.

Cody and I slept in the same bed at their house. At home we slept in the same room but in separate beds. We slept in Little Bob's room. In bed the first night I whispered to Cody about how Little Bob got run over by a bulldozer before Cody was even born. That made him remember his red dump truck my daddy gave him before he ran off, same day he gave me my ring. I'd set it out on the porch to take along, but at the last minute I forgot. Soon as he remembered it, I knew I wasn't going to get any sleep. Cody threw a fit and kept it up even when I lied and said we could go get it first thing in the morning.

The first week we stayed at home. I didn't go to school. Aunt Lucette was always asking me if I felt sad and telling me how it was good to cry.

'Cody cries enough for both of us,' I said. 'So does my mama. She cried for a solid week when my daddy ran off.'

I polished up my ring with the hem of the tablecloth.

'Well, life can be real sad sometimes,' Aunt Lucette said, her eyes filling with water. 'There's no shame in crying.' She looked at me like she was waiting for me to join in, but I just slid off my stool and went out the back door.

I liked sitting in the sun on the old aluminum milk box outside the back door. I'd sit out there with my eyes squeezed shut, pointing my face at the sun, whistling and rocking back and forth on the tin box. Sometimes, if no one bothered me, I could rock myself right into this trance. I felt like I just turned into pure sunlight.

The following Monday Aunt Lucette walked me to the school

down the road from their house. She dropped Cody off at the neighbor lady's and we could hear him wailing for most of two blocks. We found the principal's office and I shook the principal's hand and told her my name was Heart Patterson and I was in the fifth grade. Then I sat on a bench and waited in the hall while Aunt Lucette told her all about me.

My new teacher, Mrs Mitchell, was old and had a jelly belly. While she was writing spelling words on the board, I thought about how if I'd had Mrs Mitchell back home instead of Miss Baker, my daddy'd still be home and my mama wouldn't be crazy. He met Miss Baker when my mama was down with the flu and he went to a parents' conference by himself. They brought in a substitute after Miss Baker and Daddy left town, but my mama kept me home from school. She said all the kids would be talking and making fun.

After Daddy left, Mama sat around in her bathrobe all day, not even combing her hair. She cried and watched the TV and drank Daddy's liquor. But one morning she took a bath, set her hair on hot rollers, then put on a fancy dress and painted herself up. She walked out onto the front porch where I was painting my nails. To keep Cody happy, I'd paint the nails on my one hand and let him blow on them. Then I'd do the same with the other hand. I was just starting in on my toenails when Mama sat down on the glider, smelling of perfume.

'Heart,' she said, 'do you think I look as pretty as Miss Baker?' She patted at her hair. 'I want your honest opinion.'

I looked at her for a minute, squinting and tilting my head. 'No,' I said. 'But you smell real nice.'

She slammed the screen door and locked herself in the bathroom. When she came back out, she was wearing her old bathrobe and no makeup. She didn't talk to me for two days. She'd say, 'Cody, you tell your sister to bring me a beer,' or 'Cody, you tell that sister of yours she better run on down to the store and buy us some hamburger for supper.' Then Cody'd turn to me real serious and say, 'Buy hamburger.'

I was the one who found the note my daddy left. My mama was at the hairdresser down the road when I came back home from school and found it under the saltshaker on the kitchen table. He wrote:

Dear Coral,

I won't be home for supper tonight or ever again. I never meant to hurt you or the kids, but I just can't help it. Fourteen years is a long

time for two people like us to be married for. Maybe it's just too
long. I don't want that you should be the last to know I'm taking Jean
(Miss Baker) with me. She says Heart is a smart girl and she hopes
Heart won't hate her now. We both feel sick about this. The money in
the bank is yours and I'll send more on a regular basis. I got no
intention of letting you starve. It's nothing personal against you,
Coral. I never knew I was the type to do something like this.

I sat in the kitchen chair, shaking out little anthills of salt and
pushing them around the flowered tablecloth till Mama came home.
She set a bag of groceries down on the counter and took off her
kerchief.

'Hi, Sunshine, you have a nice day?' She put some half-and-half in
the refrigerator.

I shrugged.

Mama took some meat out of the bag. 'You want pork chops or
chicken for dinner?'

'I don't care.' I turned my ring backward so that you couldn't see
the stone and made a fist around it.

'You feel OK?' Mama studied me and rested her palm against my
forehead like a cool rag.

'I'm OK,' I said.

'Well, you look like you got a fever.' She began stacking some fruit
cocktail cans in the cupboard. 'How was school?' she asked. 'You like
my new haircut?'

'Looks real nice,' I said. 'We had a substitute 'cause Daddy ran off
with Miss Baker.'

Mama looked at me like she was going to haul off and smack me. I
handed her the note and ran outside. I started to skip rope as fast as
I could. My feet hardly touched the dirt. As I skipped rope, I sang
as loud as I could: 'A my name is Alice, my husband's name is Albert,
I come from Alabama, and I sell applejack.' Whenever I had to stop to
catch my breath, I could hear Mama inside cursing and crying up a
storm. Once, when I was on *Q*, she called me to the porch and asked
me had I ever seen my daddy with Miss Baker. I said no, and she went
back inside and I picked up where I left off.

Once a week in my new school, Mrs Mitchell would let me out of
class for an hour so I could go talk to the school psychologist. He told
me he traveled around from school to school, he was twenty-seven,

and I should call him Jack. His office was the prettiest room in the school. The walls were bright yellow, there was a hooked rug like Grandma Patterson used to make before she went blind, and there were framed posters on the walls. Jack liked for us, him and me, to sit on big pillows on the floor, but I liked the wood chair. The first time I went to his office we sat on the big pillows and he explained to me that a psychologist was like a special friend. He told me I should feel free to say whatever popped into my mind. He said everything I told him would be a secret. I said OK, but I didn't have anything to say to him really. I'd just sit on the wood chair and look around at the animal posters till it was time to go back to class. Some days Jack would move my chair over by the window where there was this sandbox on legs filled with toys – tiny plastic adults and babies and animals and furniture and cars. He was always trying to get me to play with the toys and make up stories, but I didn't want to. I thought how my mama would like all those little toys, but I didn't say it out loud. I figured Aunt Lucette and Uncle Bob wanted to find out if I was C-R-A-Z-Y like my mama. That's why I was there. He even had a toy telephone hidden in a box of junk in the corner. There was a tambourine and an Etch-A-Sketch on top, but I spied the receiver dangling down in the side of the box.

One night I had a dream our mama was lying in her bed with the house burning down around her. The firemen rescued her and took her to the hospital in an ambulance. When Cody and I visited her there, she was sitting all by herself in her yellow nightgown. The next morning at breakfast I asked Uncle Bob if Mama was in the hospital.

'Now where'd you go and get an idea like that?' he said. 'Your mama's at home like she always was. She's just resting up.'

'It's been a month,' I said. 'We gonna stay here forever?'

'Don't you like it here?' Aunt Lucette slid a pancake onto my plate. She looked like she was about to cry.

'I like it fine,' I said. 'I just like to know.'

'Maybe this Sunday we could call your mama and you and Cody could talk to her. I bet she'd like that,' Uncle Bob said.

Cody knocked over his milk and Aunt Lucette sponged it up.

'I don't want to talk to her,' I said. I felt cold inside like I'd swallowed an ice cube. I jumped up and ran outside. I sat on my milk box and rocked real fast. I did this whenever I felt like crying and it worked real well. I never cried. I thought about my dream. Jack wanted me to tell him my dreams. Every time he asked me about them I said I couldn't remember. Sometimes I'd tell them to Cody when I woke up in the morning. Cody was always whimpering in his sleep like a dog. I was always shaking him awake. 'Bad dream,' I'd say. 'Wake up.' Once he bit me in the shoulder during a bad dream – broke the skin. When I snapped on the light, he looked like one of those werewolves lying there sound asleep with my blood on his baby teeth.

We got two postcards from our daddy in the same week. One had a crocodile and the other was a map of Florida. He said he was missing us and hoping we were taking good care of our mama. He said he would send for us to visit him on holidays just as soon as they found them a permanent place. The postcards arrived in a white envelope with a letter from our mama, but Aunt Lucette wouldn't let me see the letter even though it had Cody's and my name on it. She folded it into squares and slipped it into her brassiere.

'I'll tell Jack if you don't give me that letter.' I looked her straight in the eye.

Aunt Lucette flushed and looked all flustered. 'Maybe I'll just discuss the matter with him myself,' she said. 'If he says to give it to you, then I will.'

'Hmmmph,' I snorted and stormed up to my room. I stared at the ceiling and suddenly hoped that Jack would tell her not to show me the letter. I'd seen this TV show where a crazy person sent a letter that was pasted-up words cut out of the newspaper. The words were all different sizes – some in tiny, thin print and some in fat black print. The envelope my mama sent had her fancy writing on it. Before my daddy ran off, my mama prided herself on her round, curlicued handwriting. I thought maybe my heart would stop beating if I opened up that envelope and saw those paste-up words.

While I was lying on the bed, Aunt Lucette knocked on the door. She put a plate of home-baked gingersnaps and a glass of milk on the bureau.

'I didn't mean to be mean to you, Heart honey,' she said. 'I'm just trying to do what's best.' Cody was dragging on her skirt and she reached down and brushed his yellow hair out of his eyes. 'I know you miss your mama, but that's not your mama talking in that letter.'

'Then who is it?' I reached over and took a cookie, still lying down.

Aunt Lucette was halfway out the door. 'It's the fury of hell,' she

Marly Swick

said. She put her hands over Cody's ears. 'You ever hear that expression "Hell hath no fury like a woman scorned"?'

'What's "scorned"?' I was sitting up now. I had the feeling Aunt Lucette was talking to herself and once she remembered I was there she'd hush up.

' "Scorned" is like when you get tired of something and throw it away,' she said. 'You understand?'

'You take it to the dump,' Cody piped up. Uncle Bob had bought him a new truck like the one we'd left at home.

'I understand,' I said. I sort of did.

Aunt Lucette walked over and took the empty plate from the bureau. 'You drink your milk up.' She started out the door again.

'Aunt Lucette?'

She turned around and smiled at me.

'You keep the letter,' I said. 'I don't want it.'

The next day I was sitting in Jack's office and he put the plastic dogs facing each other in the sand tray. 'What do you think the dogs are doing?' he said.

I studied them for a while. 'That dog there – the big one – is scorning that little dog,' I said.

Jack looked surprised. Usually I didn't answer him when he asked me questions.

'Why's he scorning him?'

'It's not a him – it's a her.' I pointed to the small white dog.

'Well, why's he scorning her?'

I shrugged.

'Those dogs remind you of anyone in particular?' He moved his chair closer to mine.

'No,' I said.

'Maybe this big dog's sort of like your daddy?' He accidentally bumped his chair against the table leg and knocked the dogs over in the sand.

'Maybe.' I picked up the white dog and set it on its four legs.

'Are you angry with your daddy?'

'No.' I moved my chair back a little.

'Then why'd you leave him lying there in the sand?' He pointed to the big black dog.

I just looked at him. 'My daddy's in Florida,' I said. I squeezed a

366

handful of sand, then let it sift out through my fingers. 'In Florida the sand is hotter than this. It's like walking on fire.'

'Actually it's not,' Jack said. 'It's white sand and it stays cool.'

A bell rang. I could hear the chairs scraping and everyone's loud footsteps racing downstairs to the cafeteria. In a minute it was all quiet again, like a storm had passed us by. Jack patted my hand and smiled.

'When I say Florida, what's the first word pops into your mind?' he asked.

'Sunglasses,' I said. I could see Daddy and Miss Baker driving in a convertible car wearing big sunglasses.

'What are you feeling right now, Heart?' His voice was soft and sneaky.

I looked out the window at the empty playground. One of the students had left his lunch sack by the jungle gym and some brown birds were pecking at it, pecking right through the paper.

'I'm hungry,' I said.

After supper Cody and I were watching TV on the floor in the den when Uncle Bob came in and said, 'There's someone on the phone wants to talk with you.'

I went into the kitchen and Aunt Lucette kissed me on the cheek as she handed me the receiver. 'Hello?' I said.

'Hello, Sunbeam, that you?'

'Daddy?' I put my hand over the receiver and whispered to Cody that it was our daddy.

'You get my postcards? I sent three so far,' he said.

'We got them. You still in Florida?'

Cody was yanking on the phone cord. I shooed him away.

'We're in Tallahassee. I just found out this minute you been staying with Uncle Bob. You seen your mama at all?'

'No,' I said. 'She's crazy.'

'That's no way to talk about your mama.' He didn't say anything for a minute. 'I know your mama. She'll snap out of it. You get your uncle to take you back home for a visit, you hear? Ain't nothing wrong with your mama that seeing you kids won't cure.'

Cody was climbing on the kitchen chair, trying to grab at the receiver. 'Cody wants to talk,' I said. 'He's talking real grownup now.'

'OK. You tell your Uncle Bob I said to take you home,' he said. 'You kids don't never forget your mama and I love you.'

'Here's Cody.' I sat Cody down on the chair and handed him the phone. Then I walked out into the living-room where Uncle Bob and Aunt Lucette were talking. They'd turned the volume down low. Aunt Lucette was twisting her Kleenex.

'Daddy says to tell you to take us home for a visit,' I said. Then I turned the volume on the TV back up loud and lay down on my pillow in front of the set.

Saturday morning we woke up early, while it was still dark out, and threw our pajamas and toothbrushes in our suitcases we'd packed the night before. I was making up our bed when Aunt Lucette came in to check on us.

'You got Cody's toothbrush in there?' She walked around to the other side of the bed and helped me with the quilt.

'Yes.'

'You excited?' she asked. 'You glad we're going?'

'Guess so,' I shrugged.

Aunt Lucette reached out and held my chin with her hand so I had to look right at her. 'It worries me, honey, the way you act like nothing bothers you. You don't cry, you don't laugh. Dr Jack says you're just "repressing" everything – you got all your feelings squashed way down inside you like a jack-in-the-box, and if you don't let them out bit by bit like a normal little girl, they're just going to pop out all at once some day.'

Uncle Bob walked up behind her, pressing a little wad of bloody Kleenex to his chin where he'd cut himself shaving. 'Everybody all set?' he asked, winking at Cody and me. 'Don't fill her head up with all that psychiatrist talk,' he said to Aunt Lucette. 'She got troubles enough already.'

Riding in the car I thought about what Aunt Lucette told me Jack told her. Cody and Aunt Lucette were snoozing. Uncle Bob was listening to the ball game on the radio. It was drizzling out and the car windows kept fogging up. I tried to picture my feelings all repressed together inside me – tears and laughs and frowns – trying to come out. I went limp and opened my mouth and closed my eyes and waited. I kept trying to coax them up, calling to them in my mind like you'd call a scared kitty. I pictured them flying up and out like a swarm of mad hornets. Then I pictured them floating up and out, nice and easy, like a row of bubbles. But nothing happened. I didn't feel a thing, except a little carsick. I wondered if Jack had actually said that about me. I figured Aunt Lucette must've got it all wrong.

I bunched my pillow up so I could lean my head against the window. I hadn't thought much about seeing Mama again. Uncle Bob said she was still sick, but he didn't want no one accusing him of keeping our mama from her kids. My birthday was next week. I was going to be eleven. This thought floated into my mind like a bubble that maybe this was my birthday surprise and when we drove up in front of our old house, Mama and Daddy would be standing out on the porch waving to us. Balloons would be tied to the porch railing, fluttering like butterflies in the wind, and inside there'd be a chocolate cake with pink marshmallow icing like I had last year, only with eleven candles instead of ten. Daddy'd be standing there with the camera while Mama lighted each candle with a match, trying not to burn her fingers. He'd be all ready to snap my picture as I blew out the candles and I wouldn't be able to think of anything to wish for.

Everyone was wide awake by the time we turned off the highway into Spottsville. Cody was standing on the seat looking out the window kind of puzzled. I think it was the first time in his life he was old enough to come back to a place he recognized. Aunt Lucette got her comb out of her purse and began yanking it through her hair. Then she handed it to me to do the same. When we turned down our street, we saw Farrah Hodge and Rusty Miller riding their bikes. They stared at us like they seen a ghost. Uncle Bob reached back and gave us two sticks of gum, the kind with sugar that Mama never let us chew. I put mine in my pocket. I didn't want to start off on the wrong foot with Mama.

Even from a distance, I could see there were no balloons. The grass still wasn't mowed and my daddy's red Chevy wasn't parked in the driveway. As we pulled up to the house, Uncle Bob cleared his throat and said, 'Remember what I said, now. Your mama's still feeling puny. Don't take anything personal.'

'Your mama loves you,' Aunt Lucette said. 'You just remember that.'

We got out of the car and headed up the steps behind Uncle Bob. Cody's dump truck was lying right where I left it on the porch all rusted up.

'It's broke,' he said like he was about to throw a fit.

'No it's not,' I said. 'That's just rust. Looks like a *real* dump truck now.'

He brightened up and began playing with his truck. He'd forgot all about Mama and he hadn't even seen her yet.

'Anybody home?' Uncle Bob shouted and knocked on the screen door.

Mama walked out of the bedroom buckling her belt. She had on her red party dress. She unlatched the screen door and we walked into the living-room. Her dress was half-unzipped in the back. Aunt Lucette walked over and zipped it up. Mama said hello to everyone and sat down in the rocker. We sat across from her on the sofa. No one said anything for a minute. Then Uncle Bob said, 'You're looking good, Coral.'

'Am I?' said.

'Real pretty,' Aunt Lucette said. 'Don't you think so, Heart?' Aunt Lucette jabbed me in the ribs.

'Real pretty,' I said. 'Prettier than Miss Baker.'

Uncle Bob coughed and lit a cigarette. Mama started to cry.

'You seen Frank?' she asked Uncle Bob.

'You know I haven't,' he said. 'I told you that on the phone.'

Mama got up and went to the kitchen. We heard the refrigerator door open. I saw Aunt Lucette looking around the living-room. It didn't look like Mama'd done much cleaning since we left. There were piles of dishes and magazines everywhere. I remembered how Mama used to yell at us for leaving a dirty glass or pair of socks in the living-room and how she was always wiping this or polishing that, smelling of pine or lemon. She walked back in with a six-pack of beer, which she set down on the floor next to her rocker. She peeled off three beers and handed one to each of us. Aunt Lucette reached over and grabbed mine away from me before I had a chance to open it.

'Really, Coral,' she said. 'Where's your mind at?'

Mama opened her beer and took a long sip. No one said anything. Outside on the porch we could hear Cody yelling, 'VVrrroomm, vroom! VVVrroommm, vroooooommm!'

'It's Heart's birthday next week, Coral,' Aunt Lucette said.

Mama didn't say anything. She took another sip of beer and spilled some down the front of her good dress. I got up and walked outside. Cody looked up from his truck.

'Mama's in there,' I said.

He steered his truck across the porch to the door. He could just barely reach the door handle now on tiptoe. I reached over and held the door open for him while he vroomm-vrooomed over to Mama's rocker. I saw Mama reach down. I thought she was going to pat his head, but she just moved her beer out of his way. 'Don't spill that,' she said.

I stood on the porch watching the rain drip off the roof. I heard Mama say, 'I saw Frank yesterday. He brought me some roses. He says he's tired of that woman.' I heard Uncle Bob say, 'You know you didn't see Frank, Coral. You know he's in Florida. You gotta snap yourself out of this. You ain't the only woman whose husband ever run off.' I heard Cody making his truck noises. The metal wheels made a real racket on the wood floor. Mama yelled at him to watch where he was going. Then I heard Aunt Lucette say, 'You've got to think of your children, Coral. The school psychologist says Heart is too withdrawn, she's like some walking zombie. He says she could end up real warped from all this.'

I never heard what Mama said 'cause I went out into the yard. I held my arms straight out in front of me and stared straight ahead like my eyeballs were frozen. I walked back and forth across the yard with my arms and legs stiff as boards like the zombies I'd seen on TV. The tall grass wet my kneesocks. I felt my hair frizzing in the rain. From inside I heard Uncle Bob shouting and Cody howling. I got in the car and curled up on the back seat with my head on the pillow. The rain sounded loud beating on the tin roof of the car. I remembered my stick of gum in my pocket and unwrapped it. I had just popped it in my mouth when the car door flew open and Uncle Bob dumped Cody in the back seat. Cody's pants were soaked with beer and he smelled like a brewery, which was what my mama used to tell my daddy when he came home late. Cody was crying and Aunt Lucette was crying, but she looked mad, too.

'What happened?' I said, my mouth full of gum.

'She hit me,' Cody said.

'Why?' I asked.

'She's crazy,' Uncle Bob said and threw the car into reverse.

Uncle Bob backed up so fast we ended up on the lawn and heard a soft crack.

'Hope that wasn't a glass bottle,' Aunt Lucette said.

'Jesus.' Uncle Bob pounded the steering wheel with his fist. 'Don't it never end?'

He got out and looked underneath the car. I noticed how my finger was turning green underneath my ring.

'Look at this.' Uncle Bob held Cody's toy telephone up to the window for us to see. It was squashed like a pink pancake. Just as he was about to toss it back into the weeds, I rolled down my window and reached out my arm.

'Give it to me,' I said.

Uncle Bob handed it to me. 'What you want with that old piece of junk?' He got back in the car.

'I just like it,' I said. 'It's all repressed.'

Uncle Bob shook his head and looked at Aunt Lucette. She reached over with her crumpled Kleenex and touched the little spot of dried blood from this morning still on his chin. Suddenly everyone seemed nice and calm, even Cody. Once we were out onto the paved road, I sat there staring at the telephone in my lap. It reminded me of those dead animals, skunks and squirrels, you see flattened on the highway. I picked up the receiver and tried to dial our home number on the mashed dial. 'Hello, Mama?' I said. 'This is Heart.'

Uncle Bob turned the radio down. It was so quiet I could hear her breathing on the other end.

'I know you're there, Mama,' I shouted. 'You hear me?'

Cody looked at me like he'd never seen me before in his life. 'Don't cry,' he said. He reached over and touched me on the arm. 'Don't cry.'

Aunt Lucette handed me her Kleenex. Cody put his ear up against the receiver and listened, real puzzled, like maybe there was something he didn't understand.

Amy Tan
Rules of the Game

I was six when my mother taught me the art of invisible strength. It was a strategy for winning arguments, respect from others, and eventually, though neither of us knew it at the time, chess games.

'Bite back your tongue,' scolded my mother when I cried loudly, yanking her hand toward the store that sold bags of salted plums. At home, she said, 'Wise guy, he not go against the wind. In Chinese we say, Come from South, blow with wind – poom! – North will follow. Strongest wind cannot be seen.'

The next week I bit back my tongue as we entered the store with the forbidden candies. When my mother finished her shopping, she quietly plucked a small bag of plums from the rack and put it on the counter with the rest of the items.

My mother imparted her daily truths so she could help my older brothers and me rise above our circumstances. We lived in San Francisco's Chinatown. Like most of the other Chinese children who played in the back alleys of restaurants and curio shops, I didn't think we were poor. My bowl was always full, three five-course meals every day, beginning with a soup full of mysterious things I didn't want to know the names of.

We lived on Waverly Place, in a warm, clean, two-bedroom flat that sat above a small Chinese bakery specializing in steamed pastries and dim sum. In the early morning, when the alley was still quiet, I could smell fragrant red beans as they were cooked down to a pasty sweetness. By daybreak, our flat was heavy with the odor of fried sesame balls and sweet curried chicken crescents. From my bed, I would listen as my father got ready for work, then locked the door behind him, one-two-three clicks.

At the end of our two-block alley was a small sandlot playground with swings and slides well-shined down the middle with use. The play area was bordered by wood-slat benches where old-country people sat cracking roasted watermelon seeds with their golden teeth and scattering the husks to an impatient gathering of gurgling pigeons. The best playground, however, was the dark alley itself. It was crammed with daily mysteries and adventures. My brothers and I would peer into the medicinal herb shop, watching old Li dole out onto a stiff sheet of white paper the right amount of insect shells, saffron-colored seeds and pungent leaves for his ailing customers. It was said that he once cured a woman dying of an ancestral curse that had eluded the best of American doctors. Next to the pharmacy was a printer who specialized in gold-embossed wedding invitations and festive red banners.

Farther down the street was Ping Yuen Fish Market. The front window displayed a tank crowded with doomed fish and turtles struggling to gain footing on the slimy green-tiled sides. A hand-written sign informed tourists, 'Within this store, is all for food, not for pet.' Inside, the butchers with their bloodstained white smocks deftly gutted the fish while customers cried out their orders and shouted, 'Give me your freshest,' to which the butchers always protested, 'All are freshest.' On less crowded market days, we would inspect the crates of live frogs and crabs which we were warned not to poke, boxes of dried cuttlefish, and row upon row of iced prawns, squid and slippery fish. The sanddabs made me shiver each time; their eyes lay on one flattened side and reminded me of my mother's story of a careless girl who ran into a crowded street and was crushed by a cab. 'Was smash flat,' reported my mother.

At the corner of the alley was Hong Sing's, a four-table café with a recessed stairwell in front that led to a door marked 'Tradesmen'. My brothers and I believed the bad people emerged from this door at night. Tourists never went to Hong Sing's, since the menu was printed only in Chinese. A Caucasian man with a big camera once posed me and my playmates in front of the restaurant. He had us move to the side of the picture window so the photo would capture the roasted duck with its head dangling from a juice-covered rope. After he took the picture, I told him he should go into Hong Sing's and eat dinner. When he smiled and asked me what they served, I shouted, 'Guts and duck's feet and octopus gizzards!' Then I ran off with my friends, shrieking with laughter as we scampered across the alley and hid in the entryway grotto of the China Gem Company, my heart pounding with hope that he would chase us.

My mother named me after the street that we lived on: Waverly Place Jong, my official name for important American documents. But my family called me Meimei, 'Little Sister'. I was the youngest, the only daughter. Each morning before school, my mother would twist and yank on my thick black hair until she had formed two tightly wound pigtails. One day, as she struggled to weave a hard-toothed comb through my disobedient hair, I had a sly thought.

I asked her, 'Ma, what is Chinese torture?' My mother shook her head. A bobby pin was wedged between her lips. She wetted her palm and smoothed the hair above my ear, then pushed the pin in so that it nicked sharply against my scalp.

'Who say this word?' she asked without a trace of knowing how wicked I was being. I shrugged my shoulders and said, 'Some boy in my class said Chinese people do Chinese torture.'

'Chinese people do many things,' she said simply. 'Chinese people do business, do medicine, do painting. Not lazy like American people. We do torture. Best torture.'

My older brother Vincent was the one who actually got the chess set. We had gone to the annual Christmas party held at the First Chinese Baptist Church at the end of the alley. The missionary ladies had put together a Santa bag of gifts donated by members of another church. None of the gifts had names on them. There were separate sacks for boys and girls of different ages.

One of the Chinese parishioners had donated a Santa Claus costume and a stiff paper beard with cotton balls glued to it. I think the only children who thought he was the real thing were too young to know that Santa Claus was not Chinese. When my turn came up, the Santa man asked me how old I was. I thought it was a trick question; I was seven according to the American formula and eight by the Chinese calendar. I said I was born on March 17, 1951. That seemed to satisfy him. He then solemnly asked if I had been a very, very good girl this year and did I believe in Jesus Christ and obey my parents. I knew the only answer to that. I nodded back with equal solemnity.

Having watched the other children opening their gifts, I already knew that the big gifts were not necessarily the nicest ones. One girl my age got a large coloring book of biblical characters, while a less greedy girl who selected a smaller box received a glass vial of lavender toilet water. The sound of the box was also important. A ten-year-old boy had chosen a box that jangled when he shook it. It was a tin globe of the world with a slit for inserting money. He must have thought it was full of dimes and nickels, because when he saw that it had just ten pennies, his face fell with such undisguised disappointment that his mother slapped the side of his head and led him out of the church hall, apologizing to the crowd for her son who had such bad manners he couldn't appreciate such a fine gift.

As I peered into the sack, I quickly fingered the remaining presents, testing their weight, imagining what they contained. I chose a heavy, compact one that was wrapped in shiny silver foil and a red satin ribbon. It was a twelve-pack of Life Savers and I spent the rest of the party arranging and rearranging the candy tubes in the order of my favorites. My brother Winston chose wisely as well. His present turned out to be a box of intricate plastic parts; the instructions on the box proclaimed that when they were properly assembled he would have an authentic miniature replica of a World War II submarine.

Vincent got the chess set, which would have been a very decent present to get at a church Christmas party, except it was obviously used and, as we discovered later, it was missing a black pawn and a white knight. My mother graciously thanked the unknown benefactor, saying, 'Too good. Cost too much.' At which point, an old lady with fine white, wispy hair nodded toward our family and said with a whistling whisper, 'Merry, merry Christmas.'

When we got home, my mother told Vincent to throw the chess set away. 'She not want it. We not want it,' she said, tossing her head stiffly to the side with a tight, proud smile. My brothers had deaf ears. They were already lining up the chess pieces and reading from the dog-eared instruction book.

I watched Vincent and Winston play during Christmas week. The chessboard seemed to hold elaborate secrets waiting to be untangled. The chessmen were more powerful than old Li's magic herbs that cured ancestral curses. And my brothers wore such serious faces that I was sure something was at stake that was greater than avoiding the tradesmen's door to Hong Sing's.

'Let me! Let me!' I begged between games when one brother or the other would sit back with a deep sigh of relief and victory, the other annoyed, unable to let go of the outcome. Vincent at first refused to let me play, but when I offered my Life Savers as replacements for the buttons that filled in for the missing pieces, he relented. He chose the flavors: wild cherry for the black pawn and peppermint for the white knight. Winner could eat both.

As our mother sprinkled flour and rolled out small doughy circles for the steamed dumplings that would be our dinner that night, Vincent explained the rules, pointing to each piece. 'You have sixteen pieces and so do I. One king and queen, two bishops, two knights, two castles and eight pawns. The pawns can only move forward one step, except on the first move. Then they can move two. But they can only take men by moving crossways like this, except in the beginning, when you can move ahead and take another pawn.

'Why?' I asked as I moved my pawn. 'Why can't they move more steps?'

'Because they're pawns,' he said.

'But why do they go crossways to take other men? Why aren't there any women and children?'

'Why is the sky blue? Why must you always ask stupid questions?' asked Vincent. 'This is a game. These are the rules. I didn't make them up. See. Here. In the book.' He jabbed a page with a pawn in his hand. 'Pawn. P-A-W-N. Pawn. Read it yourself.'

My mother patted the flour off her hands. 'Let me see book,' she said quietly. She scanned the pages quickly, not reading the foreign English symbols, seeming to search deliberately for nothing in particular.

'This American rules,' she concluded at last. 'Every time people come out from foreign country, must know rules. You not know, judge say, Too bad, go back. They not telling you why so you can use their way go forward. They say, Don't know why, you find out yourself. But they knowing all the time. Better you take it, find out why yourself.' She tossed her head back with a satisfied smile.

I found out about all the whys later. I read the rules and looked up all the big words in a dictionary. I borrowed books from the Chinatown library. I studied each chess piece, trying to absorb the power each contained.

I learned about opening moves and why it's important to control the center early on; the shortest distance between two points is straight down the middle. I learned about the middle game and why tactics between two adversaries are like clashing ideas; the one who plays better has the clearest plans for both attacking and getting out of traps. I learned why it is essential in the endgame to have foresight, a mathematical understanding of all possible moves, and patience; all weaknesses and advantages become evident to a strong adversary and are obscured to a tiring opponent. I discovered that for the whole game one must gather invisible strengths and see the endgame before the game begins.

I also found out why I should never reveal 'why' to others. A little knowledge withheld is a great advantage one should store for future use. That is the power of chess. It is a game of secrets in which one must show and never tell.

I loved the secrets I found within the sixty-four black and white squares. I carefully drew a handmade chessboard and pinned it to the wall next to my bed, where at night I would stare for hours at imaginary battles. Soon I no longer lost any games or Life Savers, but I lost my adversaries. Winston and Vincent decided they were more interested in roaming the streets after school in their Hopalong Cassidy cowboy hats.

On a cold spring afternoon, while walking home from school, I detoured through the playground at the end of our alley. I saw a group of old men, two seated across a folding table playing a game of chess, others smoking pipes, eating peanuts, and watching. I ran home and grabbed Vincent's chess set, which was bound in a cardboard box with rubber bands. I also carefully selected two prized rolls of Life Savers. I came back to the park and approached a man who was observing the game.

'Want to play?' I asked him. His face widened with surprise and he grinned as he looked at the box under my arm.

'Little sister, been a long time since I play with dolls,' he said, smiling benevolently. I quickly put the box down next to him on the bench and displayed my retort.

Lau Po, as he allowed me to call him, turned out to be a much better player than my brothers. I lost many games and many Life Savers. But over the weeks, with each diminishing roll of candies, I added new secrets. Lau Po gave me the names. The Double Attack from the East and West Shores. Throwing Stones on the Drowning Man. The Sudden Meeting of the Clan. The Surprise from the Sleeping Guard. The Humble Servant Who Kills the King. Sand in the Eyes of Advancing Forces. A Double Killing Without Blood.

There were also the fine points of chess etiquette. Keep captured men in neat rows, as well-tended prisoners. Never announce 'Check' with vanity, lest someone with an unseen sword slit your throat. Never hurl pieces into the sandbox after you have lost a game, because then you must find them again, by yourself, after apologizing to all around you. By the end of the summer, Lau Po had taught me all he knew, and I had become a better chess player.

A small weekend crowd of Chinese people and tourists would gather as I played and defeated my opponents one by one. My mother would join the crowds during these outdoor exhibition games. She sat proudly on the bench, telling my admirers with proper Chinese humility, 'Is luck.'

A man who watched me play in the park suggested that my mother allow me to play in local chess tournaments. My mother smiled graciously, an answer that meant nothing. I desperately wanted to go, but I bit back my tongue. I knew she would not let me play among strangers. So as we walked home I said in a small voice that I didn't want to play in the local tournament. They would have American rules. If I lost, I would bring shame on my family.

'Is shame you fall down nobody push you,' said my mother.

During my first tournament, my mother sat with me in the front row as I waited for my turn. I frequently bounced my legs to unstick them from the cold metal seat of the folding chair. When my name was called, I leapt up. My mother unwrapped something in her lap. It was her *chang*, a small tablet of red jade which held the sun's fire. 'Is luck,' she whispered and tucked it into my dress pocket. I turned to my opponent, a fifteen-year-old boy from Oakland. He looked at me, wrinkling his nose.

As I began to play, the boy disappeared, the color ran out of the room, and I saw only my white pieces and his black ones waiting on the other side. A light wind began blowing past my ears. It whispered secrets only I could hear.

'Blow from the South,' it murmured. 'The wind leaves no trail.' I saw a clear path, the traps to avoid. The crowd rustled. 'Shhh! Shhh!' said the corners of the room. The wind blew stronger. 'Throw sand from the East to distract him.' The knight came forward ready for the sacrifice. The wind hissed, louder and louder. 'Blow, blow, blow. He cannot see. He is blind now. Make him lean away from the wind so he is easier to knock down.'

'Check,' I said, as the wind roared with laughter. The wind died down to little puffs, my own breath.

My mother placed my first trophy next to a new plastic chess set that the neighborhood Tao society had given to me. As she wiped each piece with a soft cloth, she said, 'Next time win more, lose less.'

'Ma, it's not how many pieces you lose,' I said. 'Sometimes you need to lose pieces to get ahead.'

'Better to lose less, see if you really need.'

At the next tournament, I won again, but it was my mother who wore the triumphant grin.

'Lost eight piece this time. Last time was eleven. What I tell you? Better off lose less!' I was annoyed, but I couldn't say anything.

I attended more tournaments, each one farther away from home. I won all games, in all divisions. The Chinese bakery downstairs from our flat displayed my growing collection of trophies in its window, amidst the dust-covered cakes that were never picked up. The day after I won an important regional tournament, the window encased a fresh sheet cake with whipped-cream frosting and red script saying 'Congratulations, Waverly Jong, Chinatown Chess Champion.' Soon after that, a flower shop, headstone engraver and funeral parlor offered to sponsor me in national tournaments. That's when my mother decided I no longer had to do the dishes. Winston and Vincent had to do my chores.

'Why does she get to play and we do all the work,' complained Vincent.

'Is new American rules,' said my mother. 'Meimei play, squeeze all her brains out for win chess. You play, worth squeeze towel.'

By my ninth birthday, I was a national chess champion. I was still some 429 points away from grand-master status, but I was touted as the Great American Hope, a child prodigy and a girl to boot. They ran a photo of me in *Life* magazine next to a quote in which Bobby Fischer said, 'There will never be a woman grand master.' 'Your move, Bobby,' said the caption.

The day they took the magazine picture I wore neatly plaited braids clipped with plastic barrettes trimmed with rhinestones. I was playing in a large high school auditorium that echoed with phlegmy coughs and the squeaky rubber knobs of chair legs sliding across freshly waxed wooden floors. Seated across from me was an American man, about the same age as Lau Po, maybe fifty. I remember that his sweaty brow seemed to weep at my every move. He wore a dark, malodorous suit. One of his pockets was stuffed with a great white kerchief on which he wiped his palm before sweeping his hand over the chosen chess piece with great flourish.

In my crisp pink-and-white dress with scratchy lace at the neck, one of two my mother had sewn for these special occasions, I would clasp my hands under my chin, the delicate points of my elbows poised lightly on the table in the manner my mother had shown me for posing for the press. I would swing my patent leather shoes back and forth like an impatient child riding on a school bus. Then I would pause, suck in my lips, twirl my chosen piece in midair as if undecided, and then firmly plant it in its new threatening place, with a triumphant smile thrown back at my opponent for good measure.

I no longer played in the alley of Waverly Place. I never visited the playground where the pigeons and old men gathered. I went to school, then directly home to learn new chess secrets, cleverly concealed advantages, more escape routes.

But I found it difficult to concentrate at home. My mother had a habit of standing over me while I plotted out my games. I think she thought of herself as my protective ally. Her lips would be sealed tight, and after each move I made, a soft 'Hmmmmph' would escape from her nose.

'Ma, I can't practice when you stand there like that,' I said one day. She retreated to the kitchen and made loud noises with the pots and pans. When the crashing stopped, I could see out of the corner of my eye that she was standing in the doorway. 'Hmmmph!' Only this one came out of her tight throat.

My parents made many concessions to allow me to practice. One time I complained that the bedroom I shared was so noisy that I couldn't think. Thereafter, my brothers slept in a bed in the living-room facing the street. I said I couldn't finish my rice; my head didn't work right when my stomach was too full. I left the table with half-finished bowls and nobody complained. But there was one duty I couldn't avoid. I had to accompany my mother on Saturday market days when I had no tournament to play. My mother would proudly walk with me, visiting many shops, buying very little. 'This my daughter Wave-ly Jong,' she said to whoever looked her way.

One day after we left a shop I said under my breath, 'I wish you wouldn't do that, telling everybody I'm your daughter.' My mother stopped walking. Crowds of people with heavy bags pushed past us on the sidewalk, bumping into first one shoulder, then another.

'Aiii-ya. So shame be with mother?' She grasped my hand even tighter as she glared at me.

I looked down. 'It's not that, it's just so obvious. It's just so embarrassing.'

'Embarrass you be my daughter?' Her voice was cracking with anger.

'That's not what I meant. That's not what I said.'

'What you say?'

I knew it was a mistake to say anything more, but I heard my voice speaking, 'Why do you have to use me to show off? If you want to show off, then why don't you learn to play chess?'

My mother's eyes turned into dangerous black slits. She had no words for me, just sharp silence.

I felt the wind rushing around my hot ears. I jerked my hand out of my mother's tight grasp and spun around, knocking into an old woman. Her bag of groceries spilled to the ground.

'Aii-ya! Stupid girl!' my mother and the woman cried. Oranges and tin cans careened down the sidewalk. As my mother stooped to help the old woman pick up the escaping food, I took off.

I raced down the street, dashing between people, not looking back as my mother screamed shrilly, 'Meimei! Meimei!' I fled down an alley, past dark, curtained shops and merchants washing the grime off their windows. I sped into the sunlight, into a large street crowded with tourists examining trinkets and souvenirs. I ducked into another dark alley, down another street, up another alley. I ran until it hurt and I realized I had nowhere to go, that I was not running from anything. The alleys contained no escape routes.

My breath came out like angry smoke. It was cold. I sat down on an upturned plastic pail next to a stack of empty boxes, cupping my chin with my hands, thinking hard. I imagined my mother, first walking briskly down one street or another looking for me, then giving up and returning home to await my arrival. After two hours, I stood up on creaking legs and slowly walked home.

The alley was quiet and I could see the yellow lights shining from our flat like two tiger's eyes in the night. I climbed the sixteen steps to the door, advancing quietly up each so as not to make any warning sounds. I turned the knob; the door was locked. I heard a chair moving, quick steps, the locks turning – click! click! click! – and then the door opened.

'About time you got home,' said Vincent. 'Boy, are you in trouble.'

He slid back to the dinner table. On a platter were the remains of a large fish, its fleshy head still connected to bones swimming upstream in vain escape. Standing there waiting for my punishment, I heard my mother speak in a dry voice.

'We not concerning this girl. This girl not have concerning for us.'

Nobody looked at me. Bone chopsticks clinked against the inside of bowls being emptied into hungry mouths.

I walked into my room, closed the door, and lay down on my bed. The room was dark, the ceiling filled with shadows from the dinnertime lights of neighboring flats.

In my head, I saw a chessboard with sixty-four black and white squares. Opposite me was my opponent, two angry black slits. She wore a triumphant smile. 'Strongest wind cannot be seen,' she said.

Her black men advanced across the plane, slowly marching to each successive level as a single unit. My white pieces screamed as they scurried and fell off the board one by one. As her men drew closer to my edge, I felt myself growing light. I rose up into the air and flew out the window. Higher and higher, above the alley, over the tops of tiled roofs, where I was gathered up by the wind and pushed up toward the night sky until everything below me disappeared and I was alone.

I closed my eyes and pondered my next move.

Stephanie Vaughn
Dog Heaven

Every so often that dead dog dreams me up again. It's twenty-five years later. I'm walking along 42nd Street in Manhattan, the sounds of the city crashing beside me – horns, gearshifts, insults – somebody's chewing gum holding my foot to the pavement, when that dog wakes from his long sleep and imagines me.

I'm sweet again. I'm sweet-breathed and flat-limbed. Our family is stationed at Fort Niagara, and the dog swims his red heavy fur into the black Niagara River. Across the street from the officers' quarters, down the steep shady bank, the river, even this far downstream, has been clocked at nine miles per hour. The dog swims after the stick I have thrown.

'Are you crazy?' my grandmother says, even though she is not fond of dog hair in the house, the way it sneaks into the refrigerator every time you open the door. 'There's a current out there! It'll take that dog all the way to Toronto!'

'The dog knows where the backwater ends and the current begins,' I say, because it is true. He comes down to the river all the time with my father, my brother MacArthur, or me. You never have to yell the dog away from the place where the river water moves like a whip.

Sparky Smith and I had a game we played called knockout. It involved a certain way of breathing and standing up fast that caused the blood to leave the brain as if a plug had been jerked from the skull. You came to again just as soon as you were on the ground, the blood sloshing back, but it always seemed as if you had left the planet, had a vacation on Mars, and maybe stopped back at Fort Niagara half a lifetime later.

There weren't many kids my age on the post, because it was a small command. Most of its real work went on at the missile batteries flung like shale along the American-Canadian border. Sparky Smith and I hadn't been at Lewiston-Porter Central School long enough to get to know many people, so we entertained ourselves by meeting in a hollow of trees and shrubs at the far edge of the parade ground and telling each other seventh-grade sex jokes that usually had to do with keyholes and doorknobs, hot dogs and hot-dog buns, nuns, priests, schoolteachers, and people in blindfolds.

When we ran out of sex jokes, we went to knockout and took turns catching each other as we fell like a cut tree toward the ground. Whenever I knocked out, I came to on the grass with the dog barking, yelping, crouching, crying for help. 'Wake up! Wake up!' he seemed to say. 'Do you know your name? Do you know your name? My name is Duke! My name is Duke!' I'd wake to the sky with the urgent call of the dog in the air, and I'd think, Well, here I am, back in my life again.

Sparky Smith and I spent our school time smiling too much and running for office. We wore mittens instead of gloves, because everyone else did. We made our mothers buy us ugly knit caps with balls on top – caps that in our previous schools would have identified us as weird but were part of the winter uniform in upstate New York. We wobbled onto the ice of the post rink, practicing in secret, banged our knees, scraped the palms of our hands, so that we would be invited to skating parties by civilian children.

'You skate?' With each other we practiced the cool look.

'Oh, yeah. I mean, like, I do it some – I'm not a racer or anything.'

Every morning we boarded the Army-green bus – the slime-green, dead-swamp-algae-green bus – and rode it to the post gate, past the concrete island where the MPs stood in their bulletproof booth. Across from the gate, we got off at a street corner and waited with the other Army kids, the junior-high and high-school kids, for the real bus, the yellow one with the civilian kids on it. Just as we began to board, the civilian kids – there were only six of them but eighteen of us – would begin to sing the Artillery song with obscene variations one of them had invented. Instead of 'Over hill, over dale', they sang things like 'Over boob, over tit'. For a few weeks, we sat in silence watching the heavy oak trees of the town give way to apple orchards and potato farms, and we pretended not to hear. Then one day Sparky Smith began to sing the real Artillery song, the booming song with caissons rolling along in it, and we all joined in and took over the bus with our voices.

When we ran out of verses, one of the civilian kids, a football player in high school, yelled, 'Sparky is a *dog's* name. Here Sparky, Sparky, Sparky.' Sparky rose from his seat with a wounded look, then dropped to the aisle on his hands and knees and bit the football player in the calf. We all laughed, even the football player, and Sparky returned to his seat.

'That guy's just lucky I didn't pee on his leg,' Sparky said.

Somehow Sparky got himself elected homeroom president and me homeroom vice president in January. He liked to say, 'In actual percentages – I mean in actual per capita terms – we are doing much better than the civilian kids.' He kept track of how many athletes we had, how many band members, who among the older girls might become a cheerleader. Listening to him even then, I couldn't figure out how he got anyone to vote for us. When he was campaigning, he sounded dull and serious, and anyway he had a large head and looked funny in a knit cap. He put up a homemade sign in the lunchroom, went from table to table to find students from 7-B to shake hands with, and said to me repeatedly, as I walked along a step behind and nodded, 'Just don't tell them that you're leaving in March. Under no circumstances let them know that you will not be able to finish out your term.'

In January, therefore, I was elected homeroom vice president by people I still didn't know (nobody in 7-B rode our bus – that gave us an edge), and in March my family moved to Fort Sill, in Oklahoma. I surrendered my vice presidency to a civilian girl, and that was the end for all time of my career in public office.

Two days before we left Fort Niagara, we took the dog, Duke, to Charlie Battery, fourteen miles from the post, and left him with the mess sergeant. We were leaving him for only six weeks, until we could settle in Oklahoma and send for him. He had stayed at Charlie Battery before, when we visited our relatives in Ohio at Christmastime. He knew there were big meaty bones at Charlie Battery, and scraps of chicken, steak, turkey, slices of cheese, special big-dog bowls of ice cream. The mess at Charlie Battery was Dog Heaven, so he gave us a soft, forgiving look as we walked with him from the car to the back of the mess hall.

My mother said, as she always did at times like that, 'I wish he knew more English.' My father gave him a fierce manly scratch behind the ear. My brother and I scraped along behind with our pinched faces.

'Don't you worry,' the sergeant said. 'He'll be fine here. We like this dog, and he likes us. He'll run that fence perimeter all day long. He'll be his own early-warning defense system. Then we'll give this dog everything he ever dreamed of eating.' The sergeant looked quickly at my father to see if the lighthearted reference to the defense system had been all right. My father was in command of the missile batteries. In my father's presence, no one spoke lightly of the defense of the United States of America – of the missiles that would rise from the earth like a wind and knock out (knock out!) the Soviet planes flying over the North Pole with their nuclear bombs. But Duke was my father's dog, too, and I think that my father had the same wish we all had – to tell him that we were going to send for him, this was just going to be a wonderful dog vacation.

'Sergeant Mozley has the best mess within five hundred miles,' my father said to me and MacArthur.

We looked around. We had been there for Thanksgiving dinner when the grass was still green. Now, in late winter, it was a dreary place, a collection of rain-streaked metal buildings standing near huge dark mounds of earth. In summer, the mounds looked something like the large grassy mounds in southern Ohio, the famous Indian mounds, softly rounded and benignly mysterious. In March, they were black with old snow. Inside the mounds were the Nike missiles, I supposed, although I didn't know for sure where the missiles were. Perhaps they were hidden in the depressions behind the mounds.

Once during 'Fact Monday' in Homeroom 7-B, our teacher, Miss Bintz, had given a lecture on nuclear weapons. First she put a slide on the wall depicting an atom and its spinning electrons.

'Do you know what this is?' she said, and everyone in the room said, 'An atom,' in one voice, as if we were reciting a poem. We liked 'Fact Monday' sessions because we didn't have to do any work for them. We sat happily in the dim light of her slides through lectures called 'Nine Chapters in the Life of a Cheese' ('First the milk is warmed, then it is soured with rennet'), 'The Morning Star of English Poetry' ('As springtime suggests the beginning of new life, so Chaucer stands at the beginning of English poetry'), and 'Who's Who Among the Butterflies' ('The monarch – *Danaus plexipus* – is king'). Sparky liked to say that Miss Bintz was trying to make us into third-graders again, but I liked Miss Bintz. She had high cheekbones and a passionate voice. She believed, like the adults in my family, that a fact was something solid and useful, like a penknife you could put in your pocket in case of emergency.

That day's lecture was 'What Happens to the Atom When It Is Smashed'. Miss Bintz put on the wall a black-and-white slide of four women who had been horribly disfigured by the atomic blast at Hiroshima. The room was half darkened for the slide show. When she surprised us with the four faces of the women, you could feel the darkness grow, the silence in the bellies of the students.

'And do you know what this is?' Miss Bintz said. No one spoke. What answer could she have wanted from us, anyway? She clicked the slide machine through ten more pictures – close-ups of blistered hands, scarred heads, flattened buildings, burned trees, maimed and naked children staggering toward the camera as if the camera were food, a house, a mother, a father, a friendly dog.

'Do you know what this is?' Miss Bintz said again. Our desks were arranged around the edge of the room, creating an arena in the center. Miss Bintz entered that space and began to move along the front of our desks, looking to see who would answer her incomprehensible question.

'Do you know?' She stopped in front of my desk.

'No,' I said.

'Do you know?' She stopped next at Sparky's desk.

Sparky looked down and finally said, 'It's something horrible.'

'That's right,' she said. 'It's something very horrible. This is the effect of an atom smashing. This is the effect of nuclear power.' She turned to gesture at the slide but she had stepped in front of the projector, and the smear of children's faces fell across her back. 'Now let's think about how nuclear power got from the laboratory to the scientists to the people of Japan.' She had begun to pace again. 'Let's think about where all this devastation and wreckage actually comes from. You tell me,' she said to a large crouching boy named Donald Anderson. He was hunched over his desk, and his arms lay before him like tree limbs.

'I don't know,' Donald Anderson said.

'Of course you do,' Miss Bintz said. 'Where did all of this come from?'

None of us had realized yet that Miss Bintz's message was political.

I looked beyond Donald Anderson at the drawn window shades. Behind them were plate-glass windows, a view of stiff red-oak leaves, the smell of wood smoke in the air. Across the road from the school was an orchard, beyond that a pasture, another orchard, and then the town of Lewiston, standing on the Niagara River seven miles upstream from the long row of red-brick Colonial houses that were the officers' quarters at Fort Niagara. Duke was down the river, probably sniffing at the reedy edge, his head lifting when ducks flew low over the water. Once the dog had come back to our house with a live fish in his mouth, a carp. Nobody ever believed that story except those of us who saw it: me, my mother and father and brother, my grandmother.

Miss Bintz had clicked to a picture of a mushroom cloud and was now saying, 'And where did the bomb come from?' We were all tired of 'Fact Monday' by then. Miss Bintz walked back to where Sparky and I were sitting. 'You military children,' she said. 'You know where the bomb comes from. Why don't you tell us?' she said to me.

Maybe because I was tired, or bored, or frightened – I don't know – I said to Miss Bintz, looking her in the eye, 'The bomb comes from the mother bomb.'

Everyone laughed. We laughed because we needed to laugh, and because Miss Bintz had all the answers and all the questions and she was pointing them at us like guns.

'Stand up,' she said. She made me enter the arena in front of the desks, and then she clicked the machine back to the picture of the Japanese women. 'Look at this picture and make a joke,' she said. What came next was the lecture she had been aiming for all along. The bomb came from the United States of America. We in the United States were worried about whether another country might use the bomb, but in the whole history of the human species only one country had ever used the worst weapon ever invented. On she went, bombs and airplanes and bomb tests, and then she got to the missiles. They were right here, she said, not more than ten miles away. Didn't we all know that? 'You know that, don't you?' she said to me. If the missiles weren't hidden among our orchards, the planes from the Soviet Union would not have any reason to drop bombs on top of Lewiston-Porter Central School.

I had stopped listening by then and realized that the pencil I still held in my hand was drumming a song against my thigh. Over hill, over dale. I looked back at the wall again, where the mushroom cloud had reappeared, and my own silhouette stood wildly in the middle of it. I looked at Sparky and dropped the pencil on the floor, stooped down to get it, looked at Sparky once more, stood up, and knocked out.

Later, people told me that I didn't fall like lumber, I fell like something soft collapsing, a fan folding in on itself, a balloon rumpling to the floor. Sparky saw what I was up to and tried to get out from behind his desk to catch me, but it was Miss Bintz I fell against, and she went down, too. When I woke up, the lights were on, the mushroom cloud was a pale ghost against the wall, voices in the room sounded like insect wings, and I was back in my life again.

'I'm so sorry,' Miss Bintz said. 'I didn't know you were an epileptic.'

At Charlie Battery, it was drizzling as my parents stood and talked with the sergeant, rain running in dark tiny ravines along the slopes of the mounds.

MacArthur and I had M&Ms in our pockets, which we were allowed to give to the dog for his farewell. When we extended our hands, though, the dog lowered himself to the gravel and looked up at us from under his tender red eyebrows. He seemed to say that if he took the candy he knew we would go, but if he didn't perhaps we would stay here at the missile battery and eat scraps with him.

We rode back to the post in silence, through gray apple orchards, through small upstate towns, the fog rising out of the rain like a wish. MacArthur and I sat against opposite doors in the back seat, thinking of the loneliness of the dog.

We entered the kitchen, where my grandmother had already begun to clean the refrigerator. She looked at us, at our grim children's faces – the dog had been sent away a day earlier than was really neccessary – and she said, 'Well, god knows you can't clean the dog hair out of the house with the dog still in it.'

Whenever I think of an Army post, I think of a place the weather cannot touch for long. The precise rectangles of the parade grounds, the precisely pruned trees and shrubs, the living quarters, the administration building, the PX and commissary, the nondenominational church, the teen club, snack bar, the movie house, the skeet-and-trap field, the swimming pools, the runway, warehouses, the officers' club, the NCO club. Men marching, women marching, saluting, standing at attention, at ease. The bugle will trumpet reveille, mess call, assembly, retreat, taps through a hurricane, a tornado, flood, blizzard. Whenever I think of the clean squared look of a military post, I think that if one were blown down today in a fierce wind, it would be standing again tomorrow in time for reveille.

The night before our last full day at Fort Niagara, an arctic wind slipped across the lake and froze the rain where it fell, on streets, trees, power lines, rooftops. We awoke to a fabulation of ice, the sun shining like a weapon, light rocketing off every surface except the surfaces of the Army's clean streets and walks.

MacArthur and I stood on the dry, scraped walk in front of our house and watched a jeep pass by on the way to the gate. On the post, everything was operational, but in the civilian world beyond the gate power lines were down, hanging like daggers in the sun, roads were glazed with ice, cars were in ditches, highways were impassable. No yellow school buses were going to be on the roads that morning.

'This means we miss our very last day in school,' MacArthur said. 'No good-byes for us.'

We looked up at the high, bare branches of the hard maples, where drops of ice glimmered.

'I just want to shake your hand and say so long,' Sparky said. He had come out of his house to stand with us. 'I guess you know this means you'll miss the surprise party.'

'There was going to be a party?' I said

'Just cupcakes,' Sparky said. 'I sure wish you could stay the school year and keep your office.'

'Oh, who cares!' I said, suddenly irritated with Sparky, although he was my best friend. 'Jesus,' I said, sounding to myself like an adult – like Miss Bintz maybe, when she was off duty. 'Jesus,' I said again. 'What kind of office is home-goddamn-room vice president in a crummy country school?'

MacArthur said to Sparky, 'What kind of cupcakes were they having?'

I looked down at MacArthur and said, 'Do you know how totally ridiculous you look in that knit cap? I can't wait until we get out of this place.'

'Excuse me,' MacArthur said. 'Excuse me for wearing the hat you gave me for my birthday.'

It was then that the dog came back. We heard him calling out before we saw him, his huge woof-woof. 'My name is Duke! My

391

name is Duke! I'm your dog! I'm your dog!' Then we saw him streaking through the trees, through the park space of oaks and maples between our house and the post gate. Later the MPs would say that he stopped and wagged his tail at them before he passed through the gate, as if he understood that he should be stopping to show his I.D. card. He ran to us, bounding across the crusted, glass-slick snow – ran into the history of our family, all the stories we would tell about him after he was dead. Years and years later, whenever we came back together at the family dinner table, we would start the dog stories. He was the dog who caught the live fish with his mouth, the one who stole a pound of butter off the commissary loading dock and brought it to us in his soft bird dog's mouth without a tooth mark on the package. He was the dog who broke out of Charlie Battery the morning of an ice storm, traveled fourteen miles across the needled grasses and frozen pastures, through the prickly frozen mud of orchards, across backyard fences in small towns, and found the lost family.

The day was good again. When we looked back at the ice we saw a fairyland. The red-brick houses looked like ice castles. The ice-coated trees, with their million dreams of light, seemed to cast a spell over us.

'This is for you,' Sparky said, and handed me a gold-foiled box. Inside were chocolate candies and a note that said, 'I have enjoyed knowing you this year. I hope you have a good life.' Then it said, 'P.S. Remember this name. Someday I'm probably going to be famous.'

'Famous as what?' MacArthur said.

'I haven't decided yet,' Sparky said.

We had a party. We sat on the front steps of our quarters, Sparky, MacArthur, the dog and I, and we ate all the chocolates at eight o'clock in the morning. We sat shoulder to shoulder, the four of us, and looked across the street through the trees at the river, and we talked about what we might be doing a year from then. Finally, we finished the chocolates and stopped talking and allowed the brilliant light of that morning to enter us.

Miss Bintz is the one who sent me the news about Sparky four months later. BOY DROWNS IN SWIFT CURRENT. In the newspaper story, Sparky takes the bus to Niagara Falls with two friends from Lewiston-Porter. It's a searing July day, a hundred degrees in the city, so the boys climb down the gorge into the river and swim in a place where it's illegal to swim, two miles downstream from the Falls. The boys Sparky is tagging along with – they're both student-council members as well as football players, just the kind of boys Sparky himself wants to be – have sneaked down to this swimming place many times: a cove in the bank of the river, where the water is still and glassy on a hot July day, not like the water raging in the middle of the river. But the current is a wild invisible thing, unreliable, whipping out with a looping arm to pull you in. 'He was only three feet in front of me,' one of the boys said. 'He took one more stroke and then he was gone.'

We were living in civilian housing not far from the post. When we had the windows open, we could hear the bugle calls and the sound of the cannon firing retreat at sunset. A month after I got the newspaper clipping about Sparky, the dog died. He was killed, along with every other dog on our block, when a stranger drove down our street one evening and threw poisoned hamburger into our front yards.

All that week I had trouble getting to sleep at night. One night I was still awake when the recorded bugle sounded taps, the sound drifting across the Army fences and into our bedrooms. Day is done, gone the sun. It was the sound of my childhood in sleep. The bugler played it beautifully, mournfully, holding fast to the long, high notes. That night I listened to the cadence of it, to the yearning of it. I thought of the dog again, only this time I suddenly saw him rising like a missile into the air, the red glory of his fur flying, his nose pointed heavenward. I remembered the dog leaping high, prancing on his hind legs the day he came back from Charlie Battery, the dog rocking back and forth, from front legs to hind legs, dancing, sliding across the ice of the post rink later that day, as Sparky, MacArthur and I played crack-the-whip, holding tight to each other, our skates careening and singing. 'You're AWOL! You're AWOL!' we cried at the dog. 'No school!' the dog barked back. 'No school!' We skated across the darkening ice into the sunset, skated faster and faster, until we seemed to rise together into the cold, bright air. It was a good day, it was a good day, it was a good day.

Richard Yates
Oh, Joseph, I'm So Tired

When Franklin D. Roosevelt was President-elect there must have been sculptors all over America who wanted a chance to model his head from life, but my mother had connections. One of her closest friends and neighbors, in the Greenwich Village courtyard where we lived, was an amiable man named Howard Whitman who had recently lost his job as a reporter on the *New York Post*. And one of Howard's former colleagues from the *Post* was now employed in the press office of Roosevelt's New York headquarters. That would make it easy for her to get in – or, as she said, to get an entrée – and she was confident she could take it from there. She was confident about everything she did in those days, but it never quite disguised a terrible need for support and approval on every side.

She wasn't a very good sculptor. She had been working at it for only three years, since breaking up her marriage to my father, and there was still something stiff and amateurish about her pieces. Before the Roosevelt project her specialty had been 'garden figures' – a life-size little boy whose legs turned into the legs of a goat at the knees and another who knelt among ferns to play the pipes of Pan; little girls who trailed chains of daisies from their upraised arms or walked beside a spread-winged goose. These fanciful children, in plaster painted green to simulate weathered bronze, were arranged on home-made wooden pedestals to loom around her studio and to leave a cleared space in the middle for the modeling stand that held whatever she was working on in clay.

Her idea was that any number of rich people, all of them gracious and aristocratic, would soon discover her: they would want her sculpture to decorate their landscaped gardens, and they would want to make her their friend for life. In the meantime, a little nationwide publicity as the first woman sculptor to 'do' the President-elect certainly wouldn't hurt her career.

And, if nothing else, she had a good studio. It was, in fact, the best of all the studios she would have in the rest of her life. There were six or eight old houses facing our side of the courtyard, with their backs to Bedford Street, and ours was probably the showplace of the row because the front room on its ground floor was two stories high. You went down a broad set of brick steps to the tall front windows and the front door; then you were in the high, wide, light-flooded studio. It was big enough to serve as a living-room too, and so along with the green garden children it contained all the living-room furniture from the house we'd lived in with my father in the suburban town of Hastings-on-Hudson, where I was born. A second-floor balcony ran along the far end of the studio, with two small bedrooms and a tiny bathroom tucked away upstairs; beneath that, where the ground floor continued through to the Bedford Street side, lay the only part of the apartment that might let you know we didn't have much money. The ceiling was very low and it was always dark in there; the small windows looked out underneath an iron sidewalk grating, and the bottom of that street cavity was thick with strewn garbage. Our roach-infested kitchen was barely big enough for a stove and sink that were never clean, and for a brown wooden icebox with its dark, ever-melting block of ice; the rest of that area was our dining-room, and not even the amplitude of the old Hastings dining-room table could brighten it. But our Majestic radio was in there too, and that made it a cozy place for my sister Edith and me: we liked the children's programs that came on in the late afternoons.

We had just turned off the radio one day when we went out into the studio and found our mother discussing the Roosevelt project with Howard Whitman. It was the first we'd heard of it, and we must have interrupted her with too many questions because she said 'Edith? Billy? That's enough, now. I'll tell you all about this later. Run out in the garden and play.'

She always called the courtyard 'the garden', though nothing grew there except a few stunted city trees and a patch of grass that never had a chance to spread. Mostly it was bald earth, interrupted here and there by brick paving, lightly powdered with soot and scattered with the droppings of dogs and cats. It may have been six or eight houses long, but it was only two houses wide, which gave it a hemmed-in, cheerless look; it's only point of interest was a dilapidated marble fountain, not much bigger than a birdbath, which stood near our house. The original idea of the fountain was the water would drip evenly from around the rim of its upper tier and tinkle into its lower basin, but age had unsettled it; the water spilled in a single ropy stream from the only inch of the upper tier's rim that stayed clean. The lower basin was deep enough to soak your feet in on a hot day, but there wasn't much pleasure in that because the underwater part of the marble was coated with brown scum.

My sister and I found things to do in the courtyard every day, for all of the two years we lived there, but that was only because Edith was an imaginative child. She was eleven at the time of the Roosevelt project, and I was seven.

'Daddy?' she asked in our father's office uptown one afternoon. 'Have you heard Mommy's doing a head of President Roosevelt?'

'Oh?' He was rummaging in his desk, looking for something he'd said we might like.

'She's going to take his measurements and stuff here in New York,' Edith said, 'and then after the Inauguration, when the sculpture's done, she's going to take it to Washington and present it to him in the White House.' Edith often told one of our parents about the other's more virtuous activities; it was part of her long, hopeless effort to bring them back together. Many years later she told me she thought she had never recovered, and never would, from the shock of their breakup: she said Hastings-on-Hudson remained the happiest time of her life, and that made me envious because I could scarcely remember it at all.

'Well,' my father said. 'That's really something, isn't it.' Then he found what he'd been looking for in the desk and said, 'Here we go; what do you think of these?' They were two fragile perforated sheets of what looked like postage stamps, each stamp bearing the insignia of an electric light bulb in vivid white against a yellow background, and the words 'More light'.

My father's office was one of many small cubicles on the twenty-third floor of the General Electric building. He was an assistant regional sales manager in what was then called the Mazda Lamp Division – a modest job, but good enough to have allowed him to rent into a town like Hastings-on-Hudson in better times – and these 'More light' stamps were souvenirs of a recent sales convention. We told him the stamps were neat – and they were – but expressed some doubt as to what we might do with them.

'Oh, they're just for decoration,' he said. 'I thought you could paste them into your schoolbooks, or – you know – whatever you want. Ready to go?' And he carefully folded the sheets of stamps and put them in his inside pocket for safekeeping on the way home.

Between the subway exit and the courtyard, somewhere in the West Village, we always walked past a vacant lot where men stood huddled around weak fires built of broken cans of food held by coat-hanger wire over the flames. 'Don't stare,' my father had said the first time. 'All those men are out of work, and they're hungry.'

'Daddy?' Edith inquired. 'Do you think Roosevelt's good?'

'Sure I do.'

'Do you think all the Democrats are good?'

'Well, most of 'em, sure.'

Much later I would learn that my father had participated in local Democratic Party politics for years. He had served some of his political friends – men my mother described as dreadful little Irish people from Tammany Hall – by helping them to establish Mazda Lamp distributorships in various parts of the city. And he loved their social gatherings, at which he was always asked to sing.

'Well, of course, you're too young to remember Daddy's singing,' Edith said to me once after his death in 1942.

'No, I'm not; I remember.'

'But I mean really remember,' she said. 'He had the most beautiful tenor voice I've ever heard. Remember "Danny Boy"?'

'Sure.'

'Ah, God, that was something,' she said, closing her eyes. 'That was really – that was really something.'

When we got back to the courtyard that afternoon, and back into the studio, Edith and I watched our parents say hello to each other. We always watched that closely, hoping they might drift into conversation and sit down together and find things to laugh about, but they never did. And it was even less likely than usual that day because my mother had a guest – a woman named Sloane Cabot who was her best friend in the courtyard, and who greeted my father with a little rush of false, flirtatious enthusiasm.

'How've you been, Sloane?' he said. Then he turned back to his former wife and said, 'Helen? I hear you're planning to make a bust of Roosevelt.'

'Well, not a bust,' she said. 'A head. I think it'll be more effective if I cut it off at the neck.'

'Well, good. That's fine. Good luck with it. OK, then.' He gave his whole attention to Edith and me. 'OK. See you soon. How about a hug?'

And those hugs of his, the climax of his visitation rights, were unforgettable. One at a time we would be swept up and pressed hard into the smells of linen and whiskey and tobacco; the warm rasp of his jaw would graze one cheek and there would be a quick moist kiss near the ear; then he'd let us go.

He was almost all the way out of the courtyard, almost out in the street, when Edith and I went racing after him.

'Daddy! Daddy! You forgot the stamps!'

He stopped and turned around, and that was when we saw he was crying. He tried to hide it – he put his face nearly into his armpit as if that might help him search his inside pocket – but there is no way to disguise the awful bloat and pucker of a face in tears.

'Here,' he said. 'Here you go.' And he gave us the least convincing smile I had ever seen. It would be good to report that we stayed and talked to him – that we hugged him again – but we were too embarrassed for that. We took the stamps and ran home without looking back.

'Oh, aren't you excited, Helen?' Sloane Cabot was saying. 'To be meeting him, and talking to him and everything, in front of all those reporters?'

'Well, of course,' my mother said, 'but the important thing is to get the measurements right. I hope there won't be a lot of photographers and silly interruptions.'

Sloane Cabot was some years younger than my mother, and strikingly pretty in a style often portrayed in what I think are called Art Deco illustrations of that period: straight dark bangs, big eyes, and a big mouth. She too was a divorced mother, though her former husband had vanished long ago and was referred to only as 'that bastard' or 'that cowardly son of a bitch'. Her only child was a boy of Edith's age named John, whom Edith and I liked enormously.

The two women had met within days of our moving into the courtyard, and their friendship was sealed when my mother solved the problem of John's schooling. She knew a Hastings-on-Hudson family who would appreciate the money earned from taking in a boarder, so John went up there to live and go to school, and came home only on weekends. The arrangement cost more than Sloane could comfortably afford, but she managed to make ends meet and was forever grateful.

Sloane worked in the Wall Street district as a private secretary. She talked a lot about how she hated her job and her boss, but the good part was that her boss was often out of town for extended periods: that gave her time to use the office typewriter in pursuit of her life's ambition, which was to write scripts for the radio.

She once confided to my mother that she'd made up both of her names: 'Sloane' because it sounded masculine, the kind of name a woman alone might need for making her way in the world, and 'Cabot' because – well, because it had a touch of class. Was there anything wrong with that?

'Oh, Helen,' she said. 'This is going to be wonderful for you. If you get the publicity – if the papers pick it up, and the newsreels – you'll be one of the most interesting personalities in America.'

Five or six people were gathered in the studio on the day my mother came home from her first visit with the President-elect.

'Will somebody get me a drink?' she asked, looking around in mock helplessness. 'Then I'll tell you all about it.'

And with the drink in her hand, with her eyes as wide as a child's, she told us how a door had opened and two big men had brought him in.

'Big men,' she insisted. 'Young, strong men, holding him up under the arms, and you could see how they were straining. Then you saw this *foot* come out, with these awful metal braces on the shoe, and then the *other* foot. And he was sweating, and he was panting for breath, and his face was – I don't know – all bright and tense and horrible.' She shuddered.

'Well,' Howard Whitman said, looking uneasy, 'he can't help being crippled, Helen.'

'Howard,' she said impatiently, 'I'm only trying to tell you how *ugly* it was.' And that seemed to carry a certain weight. If she was an authority on beauty – on how a little boy might kneel among ferns to play the pipes of Pan, for example – then surely she had earned her credentials as an authority on ugliness.

'*Anyway*,' she went on, 'they got him into a chair, and he wiped most of the sweat off his face with a handkerchief – he was still out of breath – and after a while he started talking to some of the other men there. I couldn't follow that part of it. Then finally he turned to me with this smile of his. Honestly, I don't know if I can describe that smile. It isn't something you can see in the newsreels; you have to be there. His eyes don't change at all, but the corners of his mouth go up as if they're being pulled by puppet strings. It's a frightening smile. It makes you think: this could be a dangerous man. This could be an evil man. Well anyway, we started talking, and I spoke right up to him. I said, "I didn't vote for you, Mr President." I said, "I'm a good Republican and I voted for President Hoover." He said, "Why are you here, then?" or something like that, and I said, "Because you have a very interesting head." So he gave me the smile again and he said, "What's interesting about it?" And I said, "I like the bumps on it." '

By then she must have assumed that every reporter in the room was writing in his notebook, while the photographers got their flashbulbs ready; tomorrow's papers might easily read:

GAL SCULPTOR TWITS FDR
ABOUT 'BUMPS' ON HEAD

At the end of her preliminary chat with him she got down to business, which was to measure different parts of his head with her calipers. I knew how that felt: the cold, trembling points of those clay-encrusted calipers had tickled and poked me all over during the times I'd served as model for her fey little woodland boys.

But not a single flashbulb went off while she took and recorded the measurements, and nobody asked her any questions, after a few nervous words of thanks and good-bye she was out in the corridor again among all the hopeless, craning people who couldn't get in. It must have been a bad disappointment, and I imagine she tried to make up for it by planning the triumphant way she'd tell us about it when she got home.

'Helen?' Howard Whitman inquired, after most of the other visitors had gone. 'Why'd you tell him you didn't vote for him?'

'Well, because it's true. I *am* a good Republican; you know that.'

She was a storekeeper's daughter from a small town in Ohio; she had probably grown up hearing the phrase 'good Republican' as an index of respectability and clean clothes. And maybe she had come to relax her standards of respectability, maybe she didn't even care much about clean clothes anymore, but 'good Republican' was worth clinging to. It would be helpful when she met the customers for her garden figures, the people whose low, courteous voices would welcome her into their lives and who would almost certainly turn out to be Republicans too.

'I believe in the aristocracy!' she often cried, trying to make herself heard above the rumble of voices when her guests were discussing communism, and they seldom paid her any attention. They liked her well enough: she gave parties with plenty of liquor, and she was an agreeable hostess if only because of her touching eagerness to please; but in any talk of politics she was like a shrill, exasperating child. She believed in the aristocracy.

She believed in God, too, or at least in the ceremony of St Luke's Episcopal Church, which she attended once or twice a year. And she believed in Eric Nicholson, the handsome middle-aged Englishman who was her lover. He had something to do with the American end of a British chain of foundries: his company cast ornamental objects into bronze and lead. The cupolas of college and high-school buildings all over the East, the lead-casement windows for Tudor-style homes in places like Scarsdale and Bronxville – these were some of the things Eric Nicholson's firm had accomplished. He was always self-deprecating about his business, but ruddy and glowing with its success.

My mother had met him the year before, when she'd sought help in having one of her garden figures cast into bronze, to be 'placed on consignment' with some garden-sculpture gallery from which it would never be sold. Eric Nicholson had persuaded her that lead would be almost as nice as bronze and much cheaper; then he'd asked her out to dinner, and that evening changed our lives.

Mr Nicholson rarely spoke to my sister or me, and I think we were both frightened of him, but he overwhelmed us with gifts. At first they were mostly books – a volume of cartoons from *Punch*, a partial set of Dickens, a book called *England in Tudor Times* containing tissue-covered color plates that Edith liked. But in the summer of 1933, when our father arranged for us to spend two weeks with our mother at a small lake in New Jersey, Mr Nicholson's gifts became a cornucopia of sporting goods. He gave Edith a steel fishing rod with a reel so intricate that none of us could have figured it out even if we'd known how to fish, a wicker creel for carrying the fish she would never catch, and a sheathed hunting knife to be worn at her waist. He gave me a short axe whose head was encased in a leather holster and strapped to my cumbersome net with a handle that hung from an elastic shoulder strap, in case I should be called upon to wade in and help Edith land a tricky one. There was nothing to do in that New Jersey village except take walks, or what my mother called good hikes; and every day, as we plodded out through the insect-humming weeds in the sun, we wore our full regalia of useless equipment.

That same summer Mr Nicholson gave me a three-year subscription to *Field and Stream*, and I think that impenetrable magazine was the least appropriate of all his gifts because it kept coming in the mail for such a long, long time after everything else had changed for us: after we'd moved out of New York to Scarsdale, where Mr Nicholson had found a house with a low rent, and after he had abandoned my mother in that house – with no warning – to return to England and to the wife from whom he'd never really been divorced.

But all that came later; I want to go back to the time between Franklin D. Roosevelt's election and his Inauguration, when his head was slowly taking shape on my mother's modeling stand.

Her original plan had been to make it life-size, or larger than life-size, but Mr Nicholson urged her to scale it down for economy in the casting, and so she made it only six or seven inches high. He persuaded her too, for the second time since he'd known her, that lead would be almost as nice as bronze.

She had always said she didn't mind at all if Edith and I watched her work, but we had never much wanted to; now it was a little more interesting because we could watch her sift through many photographs of Roosevelt cut from newspapers until she found one that would help her execute a subtle plane of cheek or brow.

But most of our day was taken up with school. John Cabot might go to school in Hastings-on-Hudson, for which Edith would always yearn, but we had what even Edith admitted was the next best thing: we went to school in our bedroom.

During the previous year my mother had enrolled us in the public school down the street, but she'd begun to regret it when we came home with lice in our hair. Then one day Edith came home accused of having stolen a boy's coat, and that was too much. She withdrew us both, in defiance of the city truant officer, and pleaded with my father to help her meet the cost of a private school. He refused. The rent she paid and the bills she ran up were already taxing him far beyond the terms of the divorce agreement; he was in debt; surely she must realize he was lucky even to have a job. Would she ever learn to be reasonable?

It was Howard Whitman who broke the deadlock. He knew of an

inexpensive, fully accredited mail-order service called The Calvert School, intended mainly for the homes of children who were invalids. The Calvert School furnished weekly supplies of books and materials and study plans; all she would need was someone in the house to administer the program and to serve as a tutor. And someone like Bart Kampen would be ideal for the job.

'The skinny fellow?' she asked. 'The Jewish boy from Holland or wherever it is?'

'He's very well educated, Helen,' Howard told her. 'And he speaks fluent English, and he'd be very conscientious. And he could certainly use the money.'

We were delighted to learn that Bart Kampen would be our tutor. With the exception of Howard himself, Bart was probably our favorite among the adults around the courtyard. He was twenty-eight or so, young enough so that his ears could still turn red when he was teased by children; we had found that out in teasing him once or twice about such matters as that his socks didn't match. He was tall and very thin and seemed always to look startled except when he was comforted enough to smile. He was a violinist, a Dutch Jew who had emigrated the year before in the hope of joining a symphony orchestra, and eventually of launching a concert career. But the symphonies weren't hiring then, nor were lesser orchestras, so Bart had gone without work for a long time. He lived alone in a room on Seventh Avenue, not far from the courtyard, and people who liked him used to worry that he might not have enough to eat. He owned two suits, both cut in a way that must have been stylish in the Netherlands at the time: stiff, heavily padded shoulders and a nipped-in waist; they would probably have looked better on someone with a little more meat on his bones. In shirtsleeves, with the cuffs rolled back, his hairy wrists and forearms looked even more fragile than you might have expected, but his long hands were shapely and strong enough to suggest authority on the violin.

'I'll leave it entirely up to you, Bart,' my mother said when he asked if she had any instructions for our tutoring. 'I know you'll do wonders with them.'

A small table was moved into our bedroom, under the window, and three chairs placed around it. Bart sat in the middle so that he could divide his time equally between Edith and me. Big, clean, heavy brown envelopes arrived in the mail from The Calvert School once a week and when Bart slid their fascinating contents onto the table it was like settling down to begin a game.

Edith was in the fifth grade that year – her part of the table was given over to incomprehensible talk about English and History and Social Studies – and I was in the first. I spent my mornings asking Bart to help me puzzle out the very opening moves of an education.

'Take your time, Billy,' he would say. 'Don't get impatient with this. Once you have it you'll see how easy it is, and then you'll be ready for the next thing.'

At eleven each morning we would take a break. We'd go downstairs and out to the part of the courtyard that had a little grass. Bart would carefully lay his folded coat on the sidelines, turn back his shirt cuffs, and present himself as ready to give what he called airplane rides. Taking us one at a time, he would grasp one wrist and one ankle; then he'd whirl us off our feet and around and around, with himself as the pivot, until the courtyard and the buildings and the city and the world were lost in the dizzying blur of our flight.

After the airplane rides we would hurry down the steps into the studio, where we'd usually find that my mother had set out a tray bearing three tall glasses of cold Ovaltine, sometimes with cookies on the side and sometimes not. I once overheard her telling Sloane Cabot she thought the Ovaltine must be Bart's first nourishment of the day – and I think she was probably right, if only because of the way his hand would tremble in reaching for his glass. Sometimes she'd forget to prepare the tray and we'd crowd into the kitchen and fix it ourselves; I can never see a jar of Ovaltine on a grocery shelf without remembering those times. Then it was back upstairs to school again. And during that year, by coaxing and prodding and telling me not to get impatient, Bart Kampen taught me to read.

It was an excellent opportunity for showing off. I would pull books down from my mother's shelves – mostly books that were the gifts of Mr Nicholson – and try to impress her by reading mangled sentences aloud.

'That's wonderful, dear,' she would say. 'You've really learned to read, haven't you.'

Soon a white and yellow 'More light' stamp was affixed to every page of my Calvert First Grade Reader, proving I had mastered it, and others were accumulating at a slower rate in my arithmetic workbook. Still other stamps were fastened to the wall beside my place at the school table, arranged in a proud little white and yellow thumb-smudged column that rose as high as I could reach.

'You shouldn't have put your stamps on the wall,' Edith said.

'Why?'

'Well, because they'll be hard to take off.'

'Who's going to take them off?'

That small room of ours, with its double function of sleep and learning, stands more clearly in my memory than any other part of our home. Someone should probably have told my mother that a girl and boy of our ages ought to have separate rooms, but that never occurred to me until much later. Our cots were set foot-to-foot against the wall, leaving just enough space to pass alongside them to the school table, and we had some good conversations as we lay waiting for sleep at night. The one I remember best was the time Edith told me about the sound of the city.

'I don't mean just the loud noises,' she said, 'like the siren going by just now, or those car doors slamming, or all the laughing and shouting down the street; that's just close-up stuff. I'm talking about something else. Because you see there are millions and millions of people in New York – more people than you can possibly imagine, ever – and most of them are doing something that makes a sound. Maybe talking, or playing the radio, maybe closing doors, maybe putting their forks down on their plates if they're having dinner, or dropping their shoes if they're going to bed – and because there are so many of them, all those little sounds add up and come together in a kind of hum. But it's so faint – so very, very faint – that you can't hear it unless you listen very carefully for a long time.'

'Can you hear it?' I asked her.

'Sometimes. I listen every night, but I can only hear it sometimes. Other times I fall asleep. Let's be quiet now, and just listen. See if you can hear it, Billy.'

And I tried hard, closing my eyes as if that would help, opening my mouth to minimize the sound of my breathing, but in the end I had to tell her I'd failed. 'How about you?' I asked.

'Oh, I heard it,' she said. 'Just for a few seconds, but I heard it. You'll hear it too, if you keep trying. And it's worth waiting for. When you hear it, you're hearing the whole city of New York.'

The high point of our week was Friday afternoon, when John Cabot came home from Hastings. He exuded health and normality; he brought fresh suburban air into our bohemian lives. He even

405

transformed his mother's small apartment, while he was there, into an enviable place of rest between vigorous encounters with the world. He subscribed to both *Boy's Life* and *Open Road for Boys*, and these seemed to me to be wonderful things to have in your house, if only for the illustrations. John dressed in the same heroic way as the boys shown in those magazines, corduroy knickers with ribbed stockings pulled taut over his muscular calves. He talked a lot about the Hastings high-school football team, for which he planned to try out as soon as he was old enough, and about Hastings friends whose names and personalities grew almost as familiar to us as if they were friends of our own. He taught us invigorating new ways to speak, like saying 'What's the diff?' instead of 'What's the difference?' And he was better even than Edith at finding new things to do in the courtyard.

You could buy goldfish for ten or fifteen cents apiece in Woolworth's then, and one day we brought home three of them to keep in the fountain. We sprinkled the water with more Woolworth's granulated fish food than they could possibly need, and we named them after ourselves: 'John', 'Edith' and 'Billy.' For a week or two Edith and I would run to the fountain every morning, before Bart came for school, to make sure they were still alive and to see if they had enough food, and to watch them.

'Have you noticed how much bigger Billy's getting?' Edith asked me. 'He's huge. He's almost as big as John and Edith now. He'll probably be bigger than both of them.'

Then one weekend when John was home he called our attention to how quickly the fish could turn and move. 'They have better reflexes than humans,' he explained. 'When they see a shadow in the water, or anything that looks like danger, they get away faster than you can blink. Watch.' And he sank one hand into the water to make a grab for the fish named Edith, but she evaded him and fled. 'See that?' he asked. 'How's that for speed. Know something? I bet you could shoot an arrow in there, and they'd get away in time. Wait.' To prove his point he ran to his mother's apartment and came back with the handsome bow and arrow he had made at summer camp (going to camp every summer was another admirable thing about John); then he knelt at the rim of the fountain like the picture of an archer, his bow steady in one strong hand and the feathered end of the arrow tight against the bowstring in the other. He was taking aim at the fish named Billy. 'Now, the velocity of this arrow,' he said in a voice weakened by his effort, 'is probably more than a car going eighty miles an hour. It's probably more like an airplane, or maybe even more than that. OK; watch.'

The fish named Billy was suddenly floating dead on the surface, on his side, impaled a quarter of the way up the arrow with parts of his pink guts dribbled along the shaft.

I was too old to cry, but something had to be done about the shock and rage and grief that filled me as I ran from the fountain, heading blindly for home, and half-way there I came upon my mother. She stood looking very clean wearing a new coat and dress I'd never seen before and fastened to the arm of Mr Nicholson. They were either just going out or just coming in – I didn't care which – and Mr Nicholson frowned at me (he had told me more than once that boys of my age went to boarding school in England), but I didn't care about that either. I bent my head into her waist and didn't stop crying until long after I'd felt her hands stroking my back, until after she had assured me that goldfish didn't cost much and I'd have another one soon, and that John was sorry for the thoughtless thing he'd done. I had discovered, or rediscovered, that crying is a pleasure – that it can be a pleasure beyond all reckoning if your head is pressed in your mother's waist and her hands are on your back, and if she happens to be wearing clean clothes.

There were other pleasures. We had a good Christmas Eve in our house that year, or at least it was good at first. My father was there, which obliged Mr Nicholson to stay away, and it was nice to see how relaxed he was among my mother's friends. He was shy, but they seemed to like him. He got along especially well with Bart Kampen.

Howard Whitman's daughter Molly, a sweet-natured girl of about my age, had come in from Tarrytown to spend the holidays with him, and there were several other children whom we knew but rarely saw. John looked very mature that night in a dark coat and tie, plainly aware of his special responsibilities as the oldest boy.

After a while, with no plan, the party drifted back into the dining-room area and staged an impromptu vaudeville. Howard started it: he brought the tall stool from my mother's modeling stand and sat his daughter on it, facing the audience. He folded back the opening of a brown paper bag two or three times and fitted it onto her head; then he took off his suit coat and draped it around her backwards, up to the chin; he went behind her, crouched out of sight, and worked his hands through the coat-sleeves so that when they emerged they appeared to be hers. And the sight of a smiling little girl in a paper-bag hat, waving and gesturing with huge, expressive hands, was enough to make everyone laugh. The big hands wiped her eyes and stroked her chin and pushed her hair behind her ears; then they elaborately thumbed her nose at us.

Next came Sloane Cabot. She sat very straight on the stool with her heels hooked over the rungs in such a way as to show her good legs to their best advantage, but her first act didn't go over.

'Well,' she began, 'I was at work today – you know my office is on the fortieth floor – when I happened to glance up from my typewriter and saw this big old man sort of crouched on the ledge outside the window, with a white beard and a funny red suit. So I ran to the window and opened it and said, "Are you all right?" Well, it was Santa Claus, and he said, "Of course I'm all right; I'm used to high places. But listen, miss: can you direct me to number seventy-five Bedford Street?"'

There was more, but our embarrassed looks must have told her we knew we were being condescended to; as soon as she'd found a way to finish it she did so quickly. Then, after a thoughtful pause, she tried something else that turned out to be much better.

'Have you children ever heard the story of the first Christmas?' she asked. 'When Jesus was born?' And she began to tell it in the kind of hushed, dramatic voice she must have hoped might be used by the narrators of her more serious radio plays.

'...And there were still many miles to go before they reached Bethlehem,' she said, 'and it was a cold night. Now, Mary knew she would very soon have a baby. She even knew, because an angel had told her, that her baby might one day be the saviour of all mankind. But she was only a young girl' – here Sloane's eyes glistened, as if they might be filling with tears – 'and the traveling had exhausted her. She was bruised by the jolting gait of the donkey and she ached all over, and she thought they'd never, ever get there, and all she could say was, "Oh, Joseph, I'm so tired."'

The story went on through the rejection at the inn, and the birth in the stable, and the manger, and the animals, and the arrival of the three kings; when it was over we clapped a long time because Sloane had told it so well.

'Daddy?' Edith asked. 'Will you sing for us?'

'Oh, well, thanks, honey,' he said, 'but no; I really need a piano for that. Thanks anyway.'

The final performer of the evening was Bart Kampen, persuaded by popular demand to go home and get his violin. There was no surprise in discovering that he played like a professional, like something you might easily hear on the radio; the enjoyment came from watching how his thin face frowned over the chin rest, empty of all emotion except concern that the sound be right. We were proud of him.

Some time after my father left a good many other adults began to arrive, most of them strangers to me, looking as though they'd already been to several other parties that night. It was very late, or rather very early Christmas morning, when I looked into the kitchen and saw Sloane standing close to a bald man I didn't know. He held a trembling drink in one hand and slowly massaged her shoulder with the other; she seemed to be shrinking back against the old wooden icebox. Sloane had a way of smiling that allowed little wisps of cigarette smoke to escape from between her almost-closed lips while she looked you up and down, and she was doing that. Then the man put his drink on top of the icebox and took her in his arms, and I couldn't see her face anymore.

Another man, in a rumpled brown suit, lay unconscious on the dining-room floor. I walked around him and went into the studio, where a good-looking young woman stood weeping wretchedly and three men kept getting in each other's way as they tried to comfort her. Then I saw that one of the men was Bart, and I watched while he outlasted the other two and turned the girl away toward the door. He put his arm around her and she nestled her head in his shoulder; that was how they left the house.

Edith looked jaded in her wrinkled party dress. She was reclining in our old Hastings-on-Hudson easy chair with her head tipped back and her legs flung out over both the chair's arms, and John sat cross-legged on the floor near one of her dangling feet. They seemed to have been talking about something that didn't interest either of them much, and the talk petered out altogether when I sat on the floor to join them.

'Billy,' she said, 'do you realize what time it is?'

'What's the diff?' I said.

'You should've been in bed hours ago. Come on. Let's go up.'

'I don't feel like it.'

'Well,' she said, 'I'm going up, anyway,' and she got laboriously out of the chair and walked away into the crowd.

John turned to me and narrowed his eyes unpleasantly. 'Know

something?' he said. 'When she was in the chair that way I could see everything.'

'Huh?'

'I could see everything. I could see the crack, and the hair. She's beginning to get hair.'

I had observed these features of my sister many times – in the bathtub, or when she was changing her clothes – and hadn't found them especially remarkable; even so, I understood at once how remarkable they must have been for him. If only he had smiled in a bashful way we might have laughed together like a couple of regular fellows out of *Open Road for Boys*, but his face was still set in that disdainful look.

'I kept looking and looking,' he said, 'and I had to keep her talking so she wouldn't catch on, but I was doing fine until you had to come over and ruin it.'

Was I supposed to apologize? That didn't seem right, but nothing else seemed right either. All I did was look at the floor.

When I finally got to bed there was scarcely time for trying to hear the elusive sound of the city – I had found that a good way to keep from thinking of anything else – when my mother came blundering in. She'd had too much to drink and wanted to lie down, but instead of going to her own room she got into bed with me. 'Oh,' she said. 'Oh, my boy. Oh, my boy.' It was a narrow cot and there was no way to make room for her; then suddenly she retched, bolted to her feet, and ran for the bathroom, where I heard her vomiting. And when I moved over into the part of the bed she had occupied my face recoiled quickly, but not quite in time, from the slick mouthful of puke she had left on her side of the pillow.

For a month or so that winter we didn't see much of Sloane because she said she was 'working on something big. Something really big'. When it was finished she brought it to the studio, looking tired but prettier than ever, and shyly asked if she could read it aloud.

'Wonderful,' my mother said. 'What's it about?'

'That's the best part. It's about us. All of us. Listen.'

Bart had gone for the day and Edith was out in the courtyard by herself – she often played by herself – so there was nobody for an audience but my mother and me. We sat on the sofa and Sloane arranged herself on the tall stool, just as she'd done for telling the Bethlehem story.

'There is an enchanted courtyard in Greenwich Village,' she read.

'It's only a narrow patch of brick and green among the irregular shapes of very old houses, but what makes it enchanted is that the people who live in it, or near it, have come to form an enchanted circle of friends.

'None of them have enough money and some are quite poor, but they believe in the future; they believe in each other, and in themselves.

'There is Howard, once a top reporter on a metropolitan daily newspaper. Everyone knows Howard will soon scale the journalistic heights again, and in the meantime he serves as the wise and humorous sage of the courtyard.

'There is Bart, a young violinist clearly destined for virtuosity on the concert stage, who just for the present must graciously accept all lunch and dinner invitations in order to survive.

'And there is Helen, a sculptor whose charming work will someday grace the finest gardens in America, and whose studio is the favorite gathering place for members of the circle.'

There was more like that, introducing other characters, and toward the end she got around to the children. She described my sister as 'a lanky, dreamy tomboy', which was odd – I had never thught of Edith that way – and she called me 'a sad-eyed, seven-year-old philosopher', which was wholly baffling. When the introduction was over she paused a few seconds for dramatic effect and then went into the opening episode of the series, or what I suppose would be called the 'pilot'.

I couldn't follow the story very well – it seemed to be mostly an excuse for bringing each character up to the microphone for a few lines apiece – and before long I was listening only to see if there would be any lines for the character based on me. And there were, in a way. She announced my name – 'Billy' – but then instead of speaking she put her mouth through a terrible series of contortions, accompanied by funny little bursts of sound, and by the time the words came out I didn't care what they were. It was true that I stuttered badly – I wouldn't get over it for five or six more years – but I hadn't expected anyone to put it on the radio.

'Oh, Sloane, that's marvelous,' my mother said when the reading was over. 'That's really exciting.'

And Sloane was carefully stacking her typed pages in the way she'd probably been taught to do in secretarial school, blushing and smiling with pride. 'Well,' she said, 'it probably needs work, but I do think it's got a lot of potential.'

'It's perfect,' my mother said. 'Just the way it is.'

Sloane mailed the script to a radio producer and he mailed it back with a letter typed by some radio secretary, explaining that her material had too limited an appeal to be commercial. The radio public was not yet ready, he said, for a story of Greenwich Village life.

Then it was March. The new President promised that the only thing we had to fear was fear itself, and soon after that his head came packed in wood and excelsior from Mr Nicholson's foundry.

It was a fairly good likeness. She had caught the famous lift of the chin – it might not have looked like him at all if she hadn't – and everyone told her it was fine. What nobody said was that her original plan had been right, and Mr Nicholson shouldn't have interfered: it was too small. It didn't look heroic. If you could have hollowed it out and put a slot in the top, it might have made a serviceable bank for loose change.

The foundry had burnished the lead until it shone almost silver in the highlights, and they'd mounted it on a sturdy little base of heavy black plastic. They had sent back three copies: one for the White House presentation, one to keep for exhibition purposes, and an extra one. But the extra one soon toppled to the floor and was badly damaged – the nose mashed almost into the chin – and my mother might have burst into tears if Howard Whitman hadn't made everyone laugh by saying it was now a good portrait of Vice President Garner.

Charlie Hines, Howard's old friend from the *Post* who was now a minor member of the White House staff, made an appointment for my mother with the President late on a weekday morning. She arranged for Sloane to spend the night with Edith and me; then she took an evening train down to Washington, carrying the sculpture in a cardboard box, and stayed at one of the less expensive Washington hotels. In the morning she met Charlie Hines in some crowded White House anteroom, where I guess they disposed of the cardboard box, and he took her to the waiting room outside the Oval Office. He sat with her as she held the naked head in her lap, and when their turn came he escorted her in to the President's desk for the presentation. It didn't take long. There were no reporters and no photographers.

Afterwards Charlie Hines took her out to lunch, probably because he'd promised Howard Whitman to do so. I imagine it wasn't a first-class restaurant, more likely some bustling, no-nonsense place favored by the working press, and I imagine they had trouble making conversation until they settled on Howard, and on what a shame it was that he was still out of work.

'No, but do you know Howard's friend Bart Kampen?' Charlie asked. 'The young Dutchman? The violinist?'

'Yes, certainly,' she said. 'I know Bart.'

'Well, Jesus, there's *one* story with a happy ending, right? Have you heard about that? Last time I saw Bart he said, "Charlie, the Depression's over for me," and he told me he'd found some rich, dumb, crazy woman who's paying him to tutor her kids.'

I can picture how she looked riding the long, slow train back to New York that afternoon. She must have sat staring straight ahead or out the dirty window, seeing nothing, her eyes round and her face held in a soft shape of hurt. Her adventure with Franklin D. Roosevelt had come to nothing. There would be no photographs or interviews or feature articles, no thrilling moments of newsreel coverage; strangers would never know of how she'd come from a small Ohio town, or how she'd nurtured her talent through the brave, difficult, one-woman journey that had brought her to the attention of the world. It wasn't fair.

All she had to look forward to now was her romance with Eric Nicholson, and I think she may have known even then that it was faltering – his final desertion came the next fall.

She was forty-one, an age when even romantics must admit that youth is gone, and she had nothing to show for the years but a studio crowded with green plaster statues that nobody would buy. She believed in the aristocracy, but there was no reason to suppose the aristocracy would ever believe in her.

And every time she thought of what Charlie Hines had said about Bart Kampen – oh, how hateful; oh, how hateful – the humiliation came back in wave on wave, in merciless rhythm to the clatter of the train.

She made a brave show of her homecoming, though nobody was there to greet her but Sloane and Edith and me. Sloane had fed us, and she said, 'There's a plate for you in the oven, Helen,' but my mother said she'd rather just have a drink instead. She was then at the onset of a long battle with alcohol that she would ultimately lose; it might have seemed bracing that night to decide on a drink instead of dinner. Then she told us 'all about' her trip to Washington, managing to make it sound like a success. She talked of how thrilling it was to be actually inside the White House; she repeated whatever small, courteous thing it was that President Roosevelt had said to her on receiving the head. And she brought back souvenirs: a handful of note-size White House stationery for Edith, and a well-used briar pipe for me. She explained that she'd seen a very distinguished-looking man smoking the pipe in the waiting room outside the Oval Office; when his name was called he had knocked it out quickly into an ashtray and left it there as he hurried inside. She had waited until she was sure no one was looking; then she'd taken the pipe from the ashtray and put it in her purse. 'Because I knew he must have been somebody important,' she said. 'He could easily have been a member of the Cabinet, or something like that. Anyway, I thought you'd have a lot of fun with it.' But I didn't. It was too heavy to hold in my teeth and it tasted terrible when I sucked on it; besides, I kept wondering what the man must have thought when he came out of the President's office and found it gone.

Sloane went home after a while, and my mother sat drinking alone at the dining-room table. I think she hoped Howard Whitman or some of her other friends might drop in, but nobody did. It was almost our bedtime when she looked up and said, 'Edith? Run out in the garden and see if you can find Bart.'

He had recently bought a pair of bright tan shoes with crêpe soles. I saw those shoes trip rapidly down the dark brick steps beyond the windows – he seemed scarcely to touch each step in his buoyancy – and then I saw him come smiling into the studio, with Edith closing the door behind him. 'Helen!' he said. 'You're back!'

She acknowledged that she was back. Then she got up from the table and slowly advanced on him, and Edith and I began to realize we were in for something bad.

'Bart,' she said, 'I had lunch with Charlie Hines in Washington today.'

'Oh?'

'And we had a very interesting talk. He seems to know you very well.'

'Oh, not really; we've met a few times at Howard's, but we're not really – '

'And he said you'd told him the Depression was over for you because you'd found some rich, dumb, crazy woman who was paying you to tutor her kids. Don't interrupt me.'

But Bart clearly had no intention of interrupting her. He was backing away from her in his soundless shoes, retreating past one stiff green garden child after another. His face looked startled and pink.

'I'm not a rich woman, Bart,' she said, bearing down on him. 'And I'm not dumb. And I'm not crazy. And I can recognize ingratitude and disloyalty and sheer, rotten viciousness and *lies* when they're thrown in my face.'

My sister and I were halfway up the stairs jostling each other in our need to hide before the worst part came. The worst part of these things always came at the end, after she'd lost all control and gone on shouting anyway.

'I want you to get out of my house, Bart,' she said. 'And I don't ever want to see you again. And I want to tell you something. All my life I've hated people who say, "Some of my best friends are Jews." Because *none* of my friends are Jews, or ever will be. Do you understand me? *None* of my friends are Jews, or ever will be.'

The studio was quiet after that. Without speaking, avoiding each other's eyes, Edith and I got into our pajamas and into bed. But it wasn't more than a few minutes before the house began to ring with our mother's raging voice all over again, as if Bart had somehow been brought back and made to take his punishment twice.

'. . . And I said, "*None* of my friends are Jews, or ever will be . . ." '

She was on the telephone, giving Sloane Cabot the highlights of the scene, and it was clear that Sloane would take her side and comfort her. Sloane might know how the Virgin Mary felt on the way to Bethelehem, but she also knew how to play my stutter for laughs. In a case like this she would quickly see where her allegiance lay, and it wouldn't cost her much to drop Bart Kampen from her enchanted circle.

When the telephone call came to an end at last there was silence downstairs until we heard her working with the ice pick in the icebox: she was making herself another drink.

There would be no more school in our room. We would probably never see Bart again – or if we ever did, he would probably not want to see us. But our mother was ours; we were hers; and we lived with that knowledge as we lay listening for the faint, faint sound of millions.